WHITEWASH

...about an NSA contractor

a novel by
Robert Landori

One Printers Way
Altona, MB R0G 0B0,
Canada

www.friesenpress.com

ISBN
978-1-03-910466-2 (Hardcover)
978-1-03-910465-5 (Paperback)
978-1-03-910467-9 (eBook)

1. FICTION, THRILLERS, CRIME

Distributed to the trade by The Ingram Book Company

This book is dedicated to Susan, my life partner, without whose patient presence and extraordinary depth of love it would never have happened.

CAST OF MAIN CHARACTERS

Tom Karas, a.k.a Alejandro Samos
--------------------------A Hungarian-Canadian-Panamanian

Alan McIsaacs ----------------------- A US diplomatic courier

Disda --------------------------------Karas's Cuban girlfriend

Greg DiMauro, a.k.a Roberto Mauro------------------ A pilot

Mike DeAngelis----------------------------- DiMauro's cousin

Maria-Isabel Echenique ----------Samos's Mexican girlfriend

Jack Longhurst ---------------------A US Treasury bureaucrat

Ilona Keszthelyi -------------- A Hungarian-Mexican refugee

Alfred Hauptmann -----------------------------A Swiss banker

Jose (Jozsi) Vargas----------------------------------- A guitarist

Richard Grabowski ---------Assistant Deputy Director, NSA

BOOK ONE

CHAPTER 1

A military hospital, somewhere in the US 1969

His mouth was full of glass and he was having difficulty breathing. Someone, presumably the good doctor, was sitting on his face. He tried to move his arms, but they did not respond.

His face hurt, but it wasn't too bad—a dull, itching kind of pain, but bearable. Disda came out into the courtyard, but this time she could hear him screaming at her and she said that he needn't worry because everything was going to be all right. McIsaacs was going to look after things and he knew what to do.

He tried his eyes, but they refused to open and he panicked. Maybe he was blind? McIsaacs's voice said not to worry about his eyes. They were OK, but it was important that he not leave the room because if he left he would never find his way back.

Then there was this truck. It had a very loud motor that hurt his ears quite a bit, especially as the truck seemed to be inside his head. He pitched forward and hit his head against the steering wheel and that hurt a lot because it wasn't really a wheel but the edge of a razor that cut his face wide open and that pain was unbearable.

He screamed out loud, but nobody, not Disda, not even McIsaacs, heard him. A wasp stung him on his arm and that was a good thing because the sting made him sleepy. In fact, Dr. Wasp came back quite often and kept stinging him to the point that he started to look forward to the stings because they made the terrible pain in his head go away.

Then he had the feeling that his parents came into the room and Disda was with them. His eyes were still sealed, so how did he know his mother looked much younger than when he had seen her last? She kissed him, but Disda wouldn't and his parents went away.

He fell mercifully asleep and when he awoke he was finally able to open one eye. He was in a hospital bed and McIsaacs, his Control officer, was bending over him, offering a glass of water with a straw. The straw had spiral stripes like a barber pole and control guided it between his peeling lips.

"Welcome back among the living, sport," he said.

Then Dr. Wasp buzzed in and gave him an injection in the arm and Tom fell asleep again.

*

The next time he awoke he was propped up in bed and it was Dr. Wasp leaning over him, assisted by a nurse with pale blue eyes.

"I'm Dr. Ostiguay. If you understand what I'm saying please nod your head."

Tom did and sharp pain slashed through his left cheek. He tried to bring his hands to his face, but his arms wouldn't budge.

"Tom, you survived a helicopter crash a couple of weeks ago," the doctor continued. "You suffered severe burns on your face and some broken bones."

The doctor consulted a chart. "Your right clavicle, your right radius and ulna, your left scaphoid are fractured, and we had to wire your right orbital and cheek. We had to put a rod in your right femur, but it all went very well."

Tom absorbed all this information as his eyes sought out the nurse's.

"Your bones are on the mend and we are in the process of healing your face, but, to do this, we need for you not to touch your face, so your arms are tied to the side of your bed." The doctor looked at Tom questioningly. "Please speak to me."

Tom moved his lips. "I'm trying," he mumbled and began to panic. The doctor sensed this. "Don't worry. You're out of danger and you'll regain use of your limbs and both your eyes. For now, breathe. Rest." The doctor summoned the wasp and Tom fell asleep.

CHAPTER 2

Georgetown, DC. Easter 1970

The eerie quiet in the reading room of the medical clinic was calming after the Easter bustle, and Tom welcomed it. He needed tranquility; he had major decisions to make.

Tom's last ten months had been spent at a clandestine CIA facility on Reservoir Road opposite the Duke Ellington School of the Arts. The Georgetown MedStar Center for the Wounded catered to "patients" requiring "facial adjustment" through plastic surgery before entering the agency's personnel protection program.

A month after his helicopter crash, McIsaacs, the only visitor to see him regularly after the event, arrived bearing very bad news. It was unlike his control to hesitate when delivering bad news so Tom was immediately on edge. Control had a strained look on his face as he quietly informed Tom that his elderly parents had been killed in an automobile accident on their way home from their weekend cottage in the Laurentians Hills north of Montreal. Shade descended from that unholy reserve at the top of Tom's consciousness. He did not speak, but let control swing there, the horrible news hanging from his liver-colored lips like a final blasphemy. Tom was not permitted to travel to the funeral, which led to a period of severe depression. It had never occurred to him that they might die any day, so soon and in such an arbitrary manner. There would be no time for engineering some sort of a reconciliation. It was the finality of the loss that pinned him to the sick bed. No second chances.

As a little boy in Budapest, before the war, he had been very close to his mother, maybe a little "in love" with her. When he was home from school, he'd sit at her side for hours, watching as she painted or sculpted, marvelling with a gradual understanding of what she was in the process of creating. A thin, angular woman with a constantly sad, but haughty expression on her face, delicately chiselled features, and an aristocratic nose framed by graceful eyebrows, she would reward him with a smile and explain what she was about. He would fall into a vague state of awe, watching the speckles of dust illuminated by a shaft of sunshine dance around her head as she worked. It had seemed to him that the sun was always shining on his mother and that she was always smiling whenever he was next to her. Her smile and the sun conspired to light up the living room where she kept her easel and paints.

He had far fewer moments of intimacy with his father—in fact, almost none. An autocratic and demanding man—himself an only child whose father had died when he was in his early teens—he did not know how to befriend Tom because he had no role model to help him. He was not a tall person, barely five feet eight inches, blonde with pale green eyes that flickered grey when he was angry, which was often, as he was short-tempered. Like many men of moderate height, he continually sought affirmation of his own worldview. Tom was possessed of well-above-average intelligence and his father thought naively that by pressing him to be "always first at everything," he would draw Tom enthusiastically to his studies. He did not realize that Tom idolized him and desperately craved time with him not as his disciple, but as his loving father.

When he was ten, the war came and split up his family. For a full year, Tom did not know where his parents were or even if they were alive. Immediately after the Germans had invaded Hungary in 1944, his grandmother sent Tom as a boarder to a school run by the French Marist brothers. He was reunited with his parents only about a year later.

CHAPTER 3

Budapest, Hungary, 1944

The shades slowly lift as Tom lies in his bed, mourning the present and ruminating on the past. The dusty curtains draw back, the audience squirms into the creaking, comforting cuddle of the theatre seats, and observes. . . .

His mother was in the bathroom when Tom heard the knocking on the door. Forgetting what he had been told, and without thinking, Tom opened it and recognized the man instantly.

A boy's world is small, familiar, every sidewalk crack, every errant kitten, every sweet odor, every corner bully is noted, catalogued, revised, and recalled. Tom's four-square-city-block world was memorized down to the dust motes and this man, this funny man with the huge built-up shoe on his left foot, had been noted. His demeanour had been noted as well, that of a furtive man of medium height with a pronounced limp, a man who was ruled by his resentment, contempt and envy, a man used to being the object of cruel, practical jokes by schoolboys and scorn, ridicule from his contemporaries.

The man had been seen at the corner bakery, notebook in hand, chatting, writing things down. He had been seen at the schoolyard, the teachers calling the students away when they shouted obscenities and epithets at the limping cripple as he skulked by in his dark coat. And Tom had noted this man lingering, hovering in the shadows, under the awnings, and now, he was here.

"Are you alone little boy?" the man asked.

Tom's eyes went irresistibly to the funny left shoe and its massive, built up sole.

"No sir," respectfully.

The man sighed, drawing Tom's eyes up to his.

"Who else is here?"

"My mother..."

"Where is she?"

"In the bathroom," apprehensively.

"Go get her." The man stayed by the door.

Cold quiet gripping his insides, Tom retreated to the bedroom and knocked on the bathroom door, guilt now nudging aside the fear with sharp, persistent elbows.

"Mom, there's a man to see you."

"Who is it?"

"I don't know him."

His mother opened the door smartly, the panic plain in her eyes. The man with the limp and funny shoe was in the bedroom by then.

"Mrs. Karas?"

"No – I'm Miss Lenzner..."

"Come on Mrs. Karas," the man sighed. "Don't give me a hard time. I have your wedding picture here." The man held out a photograph for her to see.

The boy watched, frozen, as the man, handcuffs in hand, advanced on his mother.

"We know all about your cover story. Very creative. Poor Miss Lenzner with her illegitimate kid, bombed out during an air raid in June. Not very original and certainly unconvincing."

"Who are you?"

He flashed an identity card into his terrified mother's face.

"Detective Sergeant Práger from the Ministry of the Interior. Now get your things, we're leaving."

His mother backed away, retreating toward the bathroom, discretely but desperately signaling for her son to take off, to leave her, to get away. Tom looked up at her face, a splinter of time, a chard that would embed itself in his soul forever. It said, "Run! Survive."

Práger grabbed his mother by the arm and was putting on the handcuffs when the boy, sensing that it was now or never, crept out of the room, snatched his mother's bag from the hall table and fled; running, slipping, stumbling down the stairs and into the street, putting distance between himself and the human being he loved most in the whole wide world, leaving her alone, terrified, abandoned to God knows what horrible fate.

Tom had no idea what to do. In the street, as always, people were jostling each other in the afternoon sun, rushing to get home after work, too busy to notice a forlorn little boy. Tiring quickly, he slowed down, first to a trot, then to a walk... but *where to? Surely not to his friend Mike's house; his parents were closet fascists and they'd throw him out. To the janitor of the building where they used to live? That wouldn't be fair, he had already helped them more than he should have. To his beloved teacher's house? He didn't know where the man lived.*

Where to then? Where to...?

He found himself in a park he knew well. Sitting on a bench, he gingerly opened his mother's bag. Her scented handkerchief, the big fountain pen that always leaked, her lipstick and wallet were items he knew well. Much too well. He almost broke down and cried, but that would not do. Little boys, alone, crying on a bench in the park might attract attention: attention from the gatekeeper, from the police, from the Prágers of his world.

There was a wallet in the bag with money in it: nearly two hundred pengős folded into the wallet, a small fortune. And there were the papers, the hated papers. He knew about them because his mother had sat him down, on two successive afternoons, and told him about them. She told him the truth about their situation. The truth about what was going on in their world. She told him without emotions, without drama. She spoke to him quietly, simply, gently, but as an adult talking to a person who could understand. And when she had told him what he needed to know about the papers, she quizzed him.

And then she quizzed him again. And again. And once more. And he never faulted or got stuck. The hated papers said he wasn't Tom Karas but Robert Lenzner, father unknown, the bastard son of a common prostitute, Elizabeth Lenzner. His mother. His mother, a whore? What was a whore? The word carried its own schoolyard , but the technicalities were still vague. How could he ever pretend to that.

And what about his father? He wasn't unknown; he was a respectable Jewish businessman, a wealthy factory owner, picked up by the Gestapo the day after the Germans had invaded and now serving in a labor battalion on the Russian front. The Nazis did not like Jews. They wanted to kill them all: young, old, men, women. Tom did not understand why. Their world has changed so suddenly, just a few weeks ago, on March 19, a Sunday. The date, indelible. All he knew was that he and his mother had to flee and hide to survive.

What to do with her bag? Little boys didn't carry bags. What to do with the papers? They were bad; he knew that they proved his mother had broken the law. But he couldn't carry the papers in his hand, he needed the bag. It was a nice bag, made of shiny brown leather. Smooth. But anyone who'd see him with a bag would think he had stolen it. They'd stop him and look inside and they would find the papers, the awful papers.

He took the money out of the wallet and put it in his trouser pocket. It made a big bulge. Then he took out the photos of himself and his mother together, smiling, in happier days, and of himself alone, and one of his mother, looking beautiful with pearls around her neck. He threw the bag into the bushes as far as he could.

He felt better, smarter.

But what if someone found the bag and turned it over to the police? They'd find the papers and use them against his mother. No, he mustn't let that happen; he had to retrieve the bag. But you weren't allowed to go into the bushes, you had to stay on the path. Keep off the grass, or the gatekeeper will spank you.

He looked around, frightened and disorientated, but feeling a growing defiance. No one was watching. He scooted into the bushes, extracted the papers from the bag and threw it further into the undergrowth. Then he hid, afraid someone would see him come out with the papers clutched in his trembling hands.

He was exhausted, so he sat down to rest a bit with his back against a tree.

He must have fallen asleep for a while because, when he came to, it was dusk and chilly. He peeked around the tree: nobody around. He crawled out onto the path and suddenly, it came to him. He started to run. Idiot! Why hadn't he thought of her before. Ohmi's house. She'd take him in! Good old Ohmi: his mother's mother. Sure, there was a funny smell about her and she was shrunken and shriveled because she was very old and she walked with a cane, but she was kind and gave him licorice when he visited her, which was not very often because young people tired her, or so his mother had told him when he had asked if they could go and see her and she had said 'no'.

Ohmi's house was near the ghetto and his mother had told him, with dread in her eyes, that he was never to go into the ghetto. But, Ohmi – he began to cry! No. He was never to go into the ghetto, ever. His mother… His mother – Oh my God – his mother! She needed help and he had forgotten. The papers; they had to be destroyed. Then he'd go to Ohmi and they would get help.

He went into the urinal by the gate. It smelled strongly of excrement. The stink in the stall was worse, even with the door broken. But he managed somehow to shred the papers and to flush them down the filthy bowl. On his way out he momentarily panicked when a drunk, intent on relieving himself, stumbled noisily into the urinal. He made a grab for the boy, hoping to molest him, but Tom eluded his fumbling grasp and slipped past him into the evening chill.

Near Ohmi's place, less than three blocks away from the ghetto entrance, he spotted a gang of four boys: Brownshirts, young Nazis. They were there, all day, every day, like jackals, wetting their pants at the thought of the fun they might have harassing an old Jew, or even better, a young one. Tom crossed the deserted street to avoid having to confront them, but it was too late; they had spotted him and immediately surrounded him.

"Are you a Jew?" their leader asked. He was older than Tom, maybe fourteen, and taller by a head.

"No I'm not," Tom answered wearily.

"Where are you going?"

"To my Ohmi's."

The smallest of the four – about the same age as Tom – then piped up. "I don't believe him. I think he is a filthy, lying Kike. Look, he's been crying..."

The gang leader turned on Tom. "Prove it... prove that you're not Jewish."

"But . . . bu . . . I have no papers."

"Never mind the papers—let's see your dick."

Tom shrank back, but the boy behind him grabbed him. Tom tried to shrug him off, but the Brownshirt was strong and Tom couldn't break his grip. The other boys were on him in a second like a pack of dogs and wrestled their fiercely struggling victim to the ground. One of them straddled his chest, another pinned his arms, and the third knelt on his legs while their leader tore at Tom's shorts viciously.

The material ripped, exposing the little boy's underwear and allowing his money to tumble out.

"What have we got here?" the leader shouted gleefully. "Not only a Jew, but a rich Jew." He grabbed at the money.

"I'm not Jewish. Give me back my money," Tom hissed, fighting to free himself.

"Sure, you're not," his tormentor said mockingly and, ripping off his victim's underpants, grabbed his uncut penis.

Tom had never been circumcised because, by the time he was born, his parents had converted to Catholicism. "I'll be damned," the gang leader yelled out, disappointed. "The little bugger was telling the truth. He's no kike."

Whereupon the boy straddling his chest got off and Tom could breathe again.

"Give me back my money," he screamed.

"Not so fast, my little friend," the goon riposted. "We have expenses. Look, you made us dirty our uniforms. You must pay for the cleaning."

The raw, unbridled injustice of it all was too much and something engaged inside Tom that had never existed before. A metallic coldness seized him and by way of an answer, Tom spat in the older boy's face. The little Nazi, furious and frustrated at having been caught out, hit Tom hard in the face, breaking his nose.

The searing pain was the trigger. He kicked free by knocking the boy kneeling on his shins sideways. He kicked again, this time catching the gang leader solidly in the chest. Then, somersaulting backward in an instinctive move to double over and lessen his pain, he inadvertently kneed the assailant pinning his arms in the head with a satisfying "crack!"

Some passers-by, attracted by Tom's cries for help, approached to investigate. The Brownshirts, now wounded and unnerved, fled, leaving their victim, his tattered clothes, and some of his money behind. Almost blinded by his rapidly swelling eyes and nose, and dripping blood all over himself, the little boy somehow managed to struggle into his torn trousers.

Aided by a kindly lady, he groped about for his money and, having collected what he could find, resumed his way to his Ohmi's place, his body trembling from the adrenaline rush, the metal leaving his thoughts.

"Little boy," the woman shouted after him, but he didn't stop. "Little boy!" She ran to catch up with him. "This is yours, too, I think," she said and thrust a photograph into his grimy hand. "Looks like your Mama."

She was right. Through his swollen, bloodshot, tearful eyes Tom could just make out that the picture was that of his mother, his beautiful mother, with pearls around her neck. . . .

Tom was barely noticed as he went up the stairs leading to Ohmi's apartment. When Ohmi opened the door for him, he made a superhuman effort to sound coherent while recounting what had befallen him. The woman, ashen-faced, thrust Tom into the housekeeper's arms and rushed out.

The little boy collapsed.

The young have amazing recuperative powers, so it took Tom only four days to get over the most serious effects of the physical *damage caused by the beating. During two of these he ran a high fever and slipped in and out of delirium, constantly begging for help for his mother, alternating between screams and moans, pleas and threats. On the third day, the fever broke and he was able to sit up and swallow some broth: solids were too painful. But, although the doctor had set his nose the day after it had been broken, the swelling and the huge, ugly black circles under the eyes remained very much in evidence. The carefree, inno-cent good looks of a pleasant ten-year-old had been replaced by the caricatured mask of a bruised child in torment: gaunt face, swollen nose and lips, sunken, hollow, haunted eyes reflecting fierce pain everywhere— inside and out.*

Detective Práger showed up on the fifth day, and insisted on speaking with Tom there and then, his Ohmi's pleas to give the boy a chance to recover ignored. Limping heavily and pushing the old woman aside, Práger barged into the bedroom where Tom had just awakened from his afternoon nap, weak and deeply distressed. Frightened by the sight of Práger, he rolled out of bed, poised to fight the cripple.

"Not so fast my little friend." Práger blocked the way. "You got away from me once, but not this time. Believe me, you have my full attention."

Tom stood mute, tense, his fists clenched, his face suddenly luminous with the fever.

"What did you do with the papers?"

"Papers?"

Práger sighed, edgy.

"The ones in your mother's bag—the bag you stole."

"I didn't steal it, I took it. It was my mother's."

"So you did take it!"

Tom realized that he had been trapped, and felt a fool.

"Do you always take your mother's purse without asking for her permission?"

"She didn't mind, ask her!" The boy was defiant. If only he could stop his teeth from chattering—it was the fever, not fear— the detective must not know that he was afraid.

"I can't ask her."

"Why?"

"Because she is no longer with us."

Práger's words had a shattering effect. Tom's mind raced out of control and his tongue followed.

"You killed my mother. . . . You killed her . . . my mother!" he screamed. Ohmi came to the door. "Ohmi, they have killed Mummy. Oh, Ohmi, it's too late to help. . . . It's all my fault . . . . it's all my fault."

Out of control, the boy leaped at Práger, raving, spitting, and screaming, to tear viciously at the thick, unemotional face, the hands, the musty, moldy clothes of the surprised policeman. A shirt button popped, a pocket tore.

Reacting instinctively, Práger slapped the boy's face—not a hard blow, but sharp, and the excruciating pain from his broken nose nearly cost the child his consciousness. Through a searing, red fog of almost unbearable ache, he barely managed to make sense of what Práger was saying.

"Your mother isn't dead, you little shit, so stop sniveling," said Práger, as he pawed ineffectively at his torn shirt. "What I said was that she is no longer with us at the Ministry of the Interior."

"Where is she?" The boy's voice was barely audible.

"She is being processed, in a holding camp for deportation." Práger looked away, evading the boy's searching eyes.

"When will I see her again?"

"If you want to see her, tell me what you did with her papers."

Despite his cursed infirmity and his generally slovenly personal habits, Práger had a tidy mind. The file on Eva Karas had to be complete before it could be closed, and the hard evidence was missing. With the papers in the dossier he would be rid of yet another case and his stats would improve. He needed a win—the only reason they kept him in his job, although a cripple, was that he was a member of the Arrow Cross Party. His Nazi overlords were very big on statistics!

He looked across at Tom. Cowering, the boy had moved to the furthest wall, trying to shrink into the corner, futilely seeking assistance from Ohmi standing in the doorway.

"I don't know where the papers are," he whispered.

"What do you mean you don't know? I saw you take them, you little liar. Tell me, or I'll hit you again!"

Trapped and only semi-conscious, the boy stared back at Práger with narrowed eyes and such hate that the man recoiled involuntarily, the faces of a thousand mocking street kids filling his eyes.

"The papers are gone, Mister Práger. I flushed them down the public toilets in Petőfi park," Tom said in a firm voice and then promptly fainted.

It took Tom a full month before he could sleep through the night without repeatedly awakening to nightmares. In that month, his Ohmi pulled the last strings available to her as a former "Grande Dame," and was able to obtain a "Schutz-pass" *from Raul Wallenberg, the Swedish consul, who was desperately trying to save Hungarian Jewry single-handedly. This document allowed Tom's mother to move from the holding camp, located near the Austro-Hungarian border, to the 'csillagos ház,' an extension of the main ghetto, a building with its gate festooned with a Star of David, in which his Ohmi lived.*

Tom waited out the interminable days until his mother returned, but at the first sight of his exhausted mother's wan face, what should have been a joyous occasion became, for Tom, permanently tainted. His mother had looked forward with all her heart to holding her only child in her arms again, hugging him, kissing him, praising him for having been a brave boy, but, perversely, Tom could not cooperate. In the weeks apart, something had changed irrevocably. As is the case with spoiled only children, his anxiety and distress had fermented into reproach. Even as he loved her, he blamed her. There would be no more cuddling and kissing.

At the homecoming, Tom holed up in the attic and refused to come down to greet his mother. Ohmi advised her daughter not to force things, but this was the poor advice of a doting grandmother. Had Tom's mother forced open the attic door and taken the boy, struggling and kicking, into her arms, and brushed aside his infantile bitterness, perhaps Tom's life would have been different, or, at least, less Manichean. But she did not force herself on her son as she was swallowed by guilt and in the thrall of the princeling.

And so, traumatized at the age of ten, Tom had learned three dreadful things that his mother had inadvertently taught him: you had to lie to stay alive, you could trust no one, and, above all, you must not allow yourself to love anyone, because it hurt too much.

In the attic redoubt, the day before his mother's return, Tom had taken a solemn oath: never again would he ever love anyone, especially not his mother. To love was to be weak, to be vulnerable, to be exposed and open to betrayal.

*

Tom was crushed by the enormous guilt he felt about having missed the chance to say goodbye to his parents. He had wanted to scream, to cry, to shake his fist at cruel Fate, which had robbed him of this opportunity. He tried to force himself to cry as one might force a finger down the throat to provoke vomiting, but his eyes remained dry. He was too unwell to travel and, therefore, not permitted to attend his parents' funeral, which he discovered later, had been attended by their many Montreal friends, the ex-pat Hungarian crowd, none of whom understood or condoned his apparently unexplained, pitiless absence.

This broke his heart.

As a nurse fussed with changing his sheets and adjusting his IV drip, Tom mused out loud, but was careful to murmur in Hungarian.

"I guess we've gotten to the end of the Karas family line," he muttered. "So much for my mother's high hopes for our people. She persuaded the family to risk everything and leave Hungary for America, land of opportunity. A grave in Montreal's Mount Royal Cemetery with four people in it:

father, mother, and two grandmothers who had emigrated with us."

Tom addressed all this at the nurse, who smiled back, though she had no clue what he was saying. Tom chuckled. The gravesite could accommodate sixteen; there was plenty of room left for him.

"I wonder where my two grandfathers are buried," he muttered in the language of the Magyars. "And the rest of my ancestors. Probably scattered all over the Austro-Hungarian monarchy."

Of course, these thoughts affected his recovery. He had cheated a bit. He had been able to pry up the bandages and catch glimpses of his face reflected in his butter knife, the side of his lighter, a drinking glass, but nothing prepared him for the full horror of his terribly disfigured face. Even the surgeons, dispassionate and accustomed to the devastation of fire on the skin, hesitated and revealed nervousness that alerted Tom to the extent of his new reality. They did not allow Tom to keep the small, improvised mirrors. For the first time in his adult life, Tom felt helpless, vulnerable, and totally alone in the world. Alive, yes, but without a purpose.

As the days went by, Tom's thoughts drifted toward suicide, but not quite yet. He had to be careful not to alert anyone, lest they took prophylactic measures. The pain drugs were muddling his thoughts already. Wiser to keep a clear head. A nurse was finishing changing the bed linen. He often spoke to her in his few words of Tagalog, but now he drew her attention, this time, speaking in English.

"I need a ream of really good-quality, acid free, 25 percent cotton laid, lined, writing paper, 110 pound, and a half-dozen Biro ballpoint pens." The nurse dutifully noted his request and, by the next morning, they were on the bedside table. He started to write with a swift, crisp, and impressively legible hand.

McIsaacs, Tom's NSA control officer from the first days, was a hulk of a man. Six-foot-two, fit and muscular, a football player at Notre Dame and ex-marine, he had been recruited by the NSA immediately after leaving the military. They had liked his intelligence and good humor and, of course, his devotion to duty and desire to continue serving his country. As befitted his position—initially diplomatic courier —he attempted to remain politically neutral, though in his heart, he was right of center, a position with which Tom, a left-of-center intellectual, had difficulty dealing at times.

Despite all the rumors to the contrary, McIsaacs did have a soul and felt responsible for what had happened to his erstwhile *protégé* and wanted Tom near his home in Georgetown so he could keep an eye on him. With his parents dead, Tom had no one to speak for him, to protect his interests. He had Tom transferred to the MedStar facility near Washington, where McIsaacs knew the medical director. McIsaacs got daily calls from the nursing staff treating Tom and weekly briefings from the head surgeon in charge of the facial reconstruction.

When he was made aware of Tom's incessant writing, McIsaacs was puzzled, but unconcerned. A man, any man, had the right to deal with pain in his own way. He did have the presence of mind to ask Tom's favorite Filipino nurse what Tom was so intent on putting to paper but the woman explained that she could not read it. Tom was writing in a language she did not know.

"Faxing," said the nurse as an afterthought.

"Pardon me?

"He does a lot of faxing. Early in the morning, before the day shift comes in. There's a machine at the nurses' station and he just stands there in his robe and slippers and he faxes. Lots of papers."

"Do you know where he is faxing to?"

The nurse shook her head and McIsaacs made a mental note to check the fax machine log. Faxing.

McIsaacs had to gird himself every time he visited Tom after a facial operation. Keeping a positive outlook and hiding his own reservations about Tom's return to "normalcy" was an emotional challenge. So he always entered Tom's room with a grim smile, as though a drill sergeant facing a recalcitrant inductee. They had established a routine of banal banter, followed by a mutual toast from a mickey of plum brandy smuggled in for the purpose and then, always, a lingering handshake over the bed-sheets as the two men, remembering *les 400 coups* of the past, eyed each other with respect and some kind of affection.

After the eighth extraordinarily painful procedure to reattach nerves, Tom challenged McIsaacs with a troubling question.

"The surgeons tell me that for my face to be restored, even to the level of appearing unremarkable, I will have to undergo another series of operations, while my skin and tissues are still plastic. Very painful operation, over the next nine months."

McIsaacs looked at Tom steadily, but his sharp glances had already taken in the subtle changes in Tom's room. The box of Biro pens had been replaced by a solitary one, the pile of lined pages, covered with Tom's fine script, had grown and was now the thickness of a small town phone book.

"What do you think? Should I?"

McIsaacs sat down heavily on the edge of the bed. He wanted to be close to Tom for this little chat.

"What do you mean?"

"Look, I'm all alone in the world now. I've been thinking."

"Really?"

"I've inherited about a million and a half dollars from my parents, what with their condo and their investments. I have another half million in my bank, so call the total two million bucks."

McIsaacs thought he knew where this was going and had already prepared a series of what he thought were fresh, life-affirming answers for his sullen friend. He was just waiting for Tom to draw a breath. Instead, Tom pulled off the covers and pivoted his feet over the side of the bed. McIsaacs moved quickly to place Tom's slippers beneath his feet, feeling like the younger man's *aide-de-camp*.

"If I had died in the line of duty, that would have given my estate another ten million dollars from my life insurance, correct?

Control nodded.

"So, theoretically, the executor of my estate could take the twelve million and set up a foundation in memory of my mother. Something for arts education. You know, she was a very talented artist, and versatile painter-etcher-sculptor. She was rather well-known."

McIsaacs found himself with an odd facial rictus of his own, something between a wry smile and a grim frown.

"And what would this hypothetical foundation do with the money?" McIsaacs had miscalculated gravely. He had not realized the depth of Tom's desperation, but he also knew that these kinds of extravagant gestures were common among those committed to public service, a desire that the service go on even after the public servant is gone. He kept his stone, grim smile.

Tom waddled back and forth, gesticulating, speculating.

"I've given it some thought, boss. It could enable poor Montreal children, orphans, the physically and intellectually challenged, to attend university and study fine arts."

"If you want to help orphans, why not do some volunteer work? Wouldn't that be more meaningful?"

Tom turned suddenly, lifting off the elastic bandages that covered half his face.

"With this face?"

McIsaacs rose, planting his feet firmly.

"I'm not taking this crazy shit! Get that self-pitying head out of your liberal ass, Tom! After the plastic surgeons have finished with you, you'll look like Mel Gibson."

Tom grinned, but the smile hurt him so much he moaned. McIsaacs apologized, "Tom, I'm so sorry."

Tom waved him off.

"Why are you apologizing? You're right. It *is* crazy. Who said I was rational?"

Tom sat down on the edge of his bed, looking up at his mentor.

"My face cannot be reconstructed without very painful surgery and I am no longer motivated to put up with the pain. I detest all of it, boss. The pills, the doctors who have to grit their teeth every time they take off my bandages, the nurses whom I used to seduce, but who look at me now with naked pity."

Tom slowly pulled his legs onto the bed, sighing as he lay back.

"I'd like to disappear quietly in a way that would at least generate some money that may do a little good. You understand, don't you? Al?"

Deeply concerned, McIsaacs reflected on the last few moments.

"This isn't about your face, is it?"

Tom smiled slightly, avoiding the pain threshold. "It's never about what it's about. You taught me that."

So, what was all this really about? thought McIsaacs. He didn't have to wait long.

"I never thought of myself as an arrogant man, but I am. I was proud of the way I looked, proud of my body and happy to keep myself in shape. And let's be frank—I liked my life, my work, my pastimes. I liked the women in my life, seducing them, living with them when that was possible, knowing them, and even leaving them. When all else in the world failed me, I had myself. Now, I don't."

McIsaacs wandered over to the side table and put his beefy, well-manicured fingers on the stack of Tom's manuscript.

"And this?"

Tom was completely open, guileless.

"It should be obvious. This, accident has given me a chance to reflect on the past. Trying to get it down on paper. I have had a very colorful life, you know? Lots of adventures, lots of interesting people."

The older man picked up the manuscript, trying to read, frowning.

"Hungarian?"

"It comes to me easiest. Like breathing. It's a Finno-Ugric language, you know. Difficult for outsiders. Related distantly to Finnish and a few other obscure Uralic languages."

"It will need to be translated."

"Or simply archived?"

McIsaacs had a subtle mind and Tom's underlying message was suddenly coming into sharp focus. He hefted the manuscript.

"Still, if it's the only copy . . ."

Tom smiled. He had never made a secret of his early morning fax sessions to a small but highly regarded Montreal law firm. Quite the opposite, actually. He knew it was only a matter of time before his control became aware of it.

"Oh, there might be a copy somewhere."

Message received. All was clear. He made motions indicating that his time was up, but thought one last try was worth it.

"Tom, you're a young man, not even forty. The best years of your life are ahead of you."

Tom shook his head. "Not with *my* face. I'd really like your help, Al."

McIsaacs became very worried. He knew his man. Tom was serious. He decided to temporize. "OK, let me think about what you said and see what I can come up with."

Tom got up painfully and hobbled to the door, holding it open. "Maybe by the end of the month?"

CHAPTER 4

Washington, DC, mid-1971

McIsaac's interest in Tom's welfare was that of a friend, but it was not entirely altruistic.

Though blown, the Canadian was still an "asset" with unusually high qualifications, a man in whom the NSA had invested a considerable amount of money. Losing him to death by suicide would certainly not look good on McIsaacs's performance sheet and might even cause the powers that be to delay his promotion from deputy assistant director of plans for Latin America to assistant director.

This was not an outcome that McIsaacs wanted. He was approaching fifty and it was essential for him to reach the rank of assistant director before his next birthday to have a chance at grabbing the brass ring he coveted—directorship of plans, policy, and programs, NSA. Although he was working in a section so obscure that fewer than a dozen people knew about its existence, climbing its senior executive ladder was an extremely competitive exercise. He was not going to let a disfigured, misguided field agent with delusions of benevolent grandeur blot his copybook!

No, blotting his copybook was out of the question. He had to do something about Tom's thinly veiled and ominous threat, not only for his asset's sake, but also for his own, especially given Tom's propensity to keep his promises, however onerous.

Thinking strategically and now pressed for time, McIsaacs took a calculated risk and turned to his boss, Richard Grabowski, for help.

"I have a delicate situation, Richard," he told the Assistant Director, "and I think my pay-grade is too low to enable me to do it justice."

Richard Grabowski and McIsaacs enjoyed an unusually close working relationship. The Pole was known as the "idea guy," and the Irishman the "executor" of the Byzantine schemes they had cooked up during their decade-long partnership. A career civil servant, Grabowski was a master at agency politics and, consequently, was envied and respected by his colleagues, most of whom begrudged his success at climbing the promotion ladder. Resentment, however, would get you nowhere with him. Crossing Grabowski was not healthy for one's career within the NSA.

"I'm listening." Grabowski could guess what was coming. A verbal pitch for another inspired but eccentric idea that McIsaacs was going to ask him to sell up the chain of command to the director, their überboss.

"Tom Karas."

Grabowski looked up from fiddling with his new Motorola flipphone. McIsaacs had his full attention.

"Helicopter crash and burn. . . . How is he?"

"He's in pain. . . . His face . . ."

McIsaacs grimaced and gestured vaguely around his own face, allowing his voice to trail off. Grabowski's imagination filled in the picture.

Grabowski searched his memory, narrowing his eyes.

"That was a very odd event, wasn't it?"

"The crash? We looked into it. Still looking, actually."

Grabowski focused suddenly. "Really? Why?"

"Like you said, odd event. Anyway, unfortunately for us, our crafty, thirty-six-year-old asset and one of our long-term contract players has developed some funny ideas."

"Oh? What's so funny and why aren't we laughing?"

"He has endured eight preliminary procedures, all very painful, and with no real improvement to his face."

"So, he's depressed."

McIsaacs got up to pace. Grabowski's eyes followed him, waiting for the pitch.

"Then, a couple of months ago, his parents died in a car accident up in Montreal and he now finds himself alone in the world."

"Shit," hissed Grabowski. "Fucking bad luck. He's got no one?"

McIsaacs shook his head and assumed his bargaining stance.

"To finish reconstructing his face will take a minimum of two years, cost a fortune, and be maddeningly painful. And there's no guarantee that he'll look presentable at the end of it."

Grabowski relaxed inwardly but kept the edge in his voice. There would be no crazy pitch, just a banal bureaucratic decision to make. He reached into a drawer and took out a bottle of Jameson and two tumblers, then poured a couple of fingers for each of them. McIsaacs leaned in to take his.

"What's the problem, Al? Buy out his contract, cut him loose, and wish him a good life."

McIsaacs chuckled ironically and mentally adjusted the hand he was about to play.

"That's just it. He doesn't want a good life. He wants to die, and in a way that will allow him to collect on his agency life insurance policy and leave the money to charity."

Grabowski was gobsmacked. The fucking chutzpah!

"Well, that's definitely not going to happen, is it?"

McIsaacs pretended to be constrained.

"He's smart, he's thought this through. And he's written a book."

Grabowski's stomach churned around the little ball of whisky in his gut.

"What kind of book? We'll have it suppressed under national security guidelines. We'll crush it."

McIsaacs sighed and sat down heavily, draining his tumbler.

"Don't forget, he's Canadian and we won't be able to block it. Knowing Tom, he's already made plans for a posthumous publication."

Grabowski rubbed his forehead as though trying to squeeze out the menacing implications of McIsaacs's revelations.

"What can he reveal?"

"Tom was part of the team that helped us in the Guzenko deal, which, as you know, was illegal in Canada. He was in Havana, running our operation in Cuba for a while, then in Santo Domingo and Bogota, followed by Venezuela."

Grabowski cut him off. "I get it, I get it! So, it's another God damn tell-all? Have you seen it, this book? Has he threatened to publish?"

It was McIsaacs's turn to pre-empt his boss.

"No. Tom's too artful for that kind of threat. And, yes, I've seen it. A manuscript, in Hungarian. I picked up the trail he meant me to follow, right to a small but powerful Montreal law firm. He faxed them a copy."

"Jesus! How bad can he make us look?"

"Bad."

Grabowski nodded, his mind going through the options, the exits, and potential solutions. "Do you have any ideas?"

McIsaacs leaned in, rubbing his hands in front of him.

"I've come up with something that may convince him to go on living and endure the pain for another eighteen months. My plan is to give him everything he wants. He'll get a face back, his "death," so that he can cash in that insurance policy and, maybe, in return, he'll help us with a problem we have been struggling with since the last strategic planning conference. But before I talk to him, I wanted to be sure that you would approve of my idea."

"Al, I don't like negotiating with a gun to my head."

As though to underline his point, Grabowski snatched the bottle of scotch off his desk and stashed it in a drawer. He then hit his phone and called for coffee before leaning back in his chair, his game face firmly in place. "I'm listening. Go on, enthrall me with your latest bullshit fantasy."

McIsaacs shook his head. "You got me wrong, Richard. My idea is very simple and straightforward. I want us to invent a problem that feels real, a challenge that will engage Tom totally for the next two years until he gets past this suicidal moment. There was something that came up in the strategic planning conference, remember?"

Grabowski sat back and started to reflect.

"There were a lot of issues that came up—domestic surveillance legislation, the continued infiltration and attacks on our web systems, backdoors . . ."

"And PEPs."

Grabowski's mouth worked wordlessly until he was able to spit out the disagreeable acronym. "Politically exposed people? C'mon, Al, you're losing it."

"No, listen to me. I want to challenge Tom to start working on the solution to PEPs. The agency is anxious to have a solution *now* for when the situation *does* arise, and we all know, it will. The opposition never stopped their PEP program, but we did, to our constant regret. Our problem has always been that we have no idea which end of the beast to grab."

"And Tom does?"

"About two years ago, he wrote an uncanny, predictive memo on the subject, outlining a plan of action. He presented it at the summer strategic planning conference. I sent it on up, but nothing came of it."

"I remember," said Grabowski, warming up to the idea. "I remember it well. It went to the director but at the time, PEPs were seen as a Cold War strategy, easily defeated, no longer relevant because the targets no longer had any shame. Catch some government minister screwing a honeypot, it's a mark of pride!"

"Tom has extraordinary talents. That's why he was such an exceptional field operative. His field experience is singular and he has a CPA designation. We can make something of this, I know it, I feel it."

"How much time do we have?" Grabowski's mind was ticking over like a clock. On the one hand, this was exactly the type of problem he liked to tackle: forecasting future dangers and shaping appropriate responses. On the other hand, his section could not handle another suicide. There had been a couple over his tenure and there had been shadows cast, even though it was accepted that a certain number were to be expected, given the stress of the job.

"He indicated that he wanted an answer by the end of the month."

The Assistant Director looked at his agenda. "Come back on Friday." He got up and shook McIsaacs's hand. "By the way, your asset is multilingual, no?"

"English, Spanish, French, German, Hungarian, all five almost like a native, Italian, Portuguese, and Greek so-so."

"Impressive."

*

McIsaacs was surprised when Tom suggested eating at the clinic's cafeteria, but not because of the food. It was definitely not a deluxe eatery, but served remarkably wholesome, home-cooking-tasting fare. The Agency made a special effort to make its loyal "members" as comfortable and contented as feasible while they were adjusting to the circumstances of their new lives. What surprised him was Tom's apparent nonchalance as to how the other diners might react to his face.

As Tom cut his authentic *Wienerschnitzel-à-la-Holstein* into bite-sized pieces, McIsaacs moved his slices of *foie-de-veau* around on his plate, absentmindedly trying to make them look like the boot of Italy.

"I met with Grabowski last Friday and told him about your situation," McIsaacs said and watched Tom's fork stop midway toward his scarred mouth.

"What the hell for?" The Canadian had a shrunken look, face sallow, eyes lustreless. "I'm of no interest to him."

Time for McIsaacs to play rope-a-dope.

"I told you, Al. I'm on my way out."

McIsaacs took a deep breath. "Actually, he agrees with you."

The big man pretended renewed interest in his veal liver while Tom absorbed this information.

"He thinks you have made a rational decision."

Tom had prepared himself for a long, drawn-out, and exhausting fight, but faced with an apparent and speedy capitulation, he melted, the tension coming off his shoulders with sweet relief. He reached for his G&T, his hand a bit shaky. McIsaacs, felt rather than saw Tom's defences drop.

He looked up from his plate, eyed Tom's chin, and folded a corner of his linen napkin.

"Got some of that egg on you." Tom's Control gently wiped the errant yolk off his chin like a father might do for a son and, suddenly, Tom found himself facing a wall of squishy emotions. His own father would never have done such a thing. Tom ventured to use his voice.

"So, we're good. I mean, my plan?"

Rope-a-dope. . . . McIsaacs gestured with his fork, as though it was obvious.

"Huh? Well, yeah. I mean, we still gotta work things out, right? Things need to be arranged carefully. It needs to be bulletproof. But, in principle . . ."

He purposefully never completed his phrase, counting on Tom's emotional state to carry him through. It did.

"Al, you have no idea what this means to me. I . . . I . . ."

McIsaacs waved him off, wouldn't stand for it.

"Forget it, Tom. I wasn't going to let you dangle. Not after what we've been through." He lowered his head and voice and kept his lips together, muttering, "If all my problems were as easy . . ."

Rope-a-dopey-dope-dope. . . . Tom flicked at the bait.

"Why, what's up?"

"Nothing, nothing," he said in a dismissive tone.

Now it was Tom's turn to act.

"No, c'mon, I'm sitting here. We're OK. What's up?"

McIsaacs dropped his cutlery, rubbing his palms together, smiling wryly.

"Well, it was because we were talking about you that it came up." He leaned forward, huddling against possible interlopers. "Remember that paper you gave at the SPC about two years ago?"

"Which one? The Middle-Asian containment doctrine?"

"No, not MAC-D. The other one, on PEPs."

Tom sighed and leaned back in his chair. "Politically Exposed People. As I recall, no one was interested."

"That was then. Things have changed and so has Grabowski. He told me a couple of things that were quite interesting. They were kind of forward-looking, like, you know, which way the Agency should be heading during the next five years so as to maintain the US's world leadership position."

"Maintain world leadership? Fucking arrogant!"

"Maybe, but PEPs have become part of his thinking. A major challenge, sure, but worthy of implementing if one wants to keep the Other Side in check."

Tom sighed again, his appetite quite lost, devoured by frustration.

"The 'Other Side?' Al, there is no 'Other Side.' We won the Cold War, remember? The time for a program based on PEPs is over. In the past, the only thing we had to offer compromised targets was democracy. The West no longer holds the monopoly. Democracy is spreading like the plague."

"I'm surprised at you. That's short-sighted. Grabowski doesn't see it that way. He's looking at the east, at the Brezhnev Troika and the fucking oligarchs and satellite strongmen in their fucking Adidas tracksuits and he sees the shameless wholesale rape of their economies and the people's desire for law and order. This will drive politics back toward a new kind of totalitarianism, based on what?"

Tom was in his thrall.

"The middle classes are already begging for a return to order. It won't take much to undermine what we achieved. A strongman, someone who knows how to play on fears, insecurities, someone to remind them of how great they once were. In ten or twenty years, a renewed Russia, financed by oligarchs and guided by a jealous leader, could become an existential threat to the USA."

"Grabowski's position is that the old levers and wrenches won't work in a world without shame. Fornication, consorting with the lowest criminals is commonplace."

Tom nodded his head. "That, I did not anticipate."

"How could you? You hate mass culture. You never watch TV."

The two men chuckled and sat back, but McIsaacs's senses were focused like lasers on Tom.

"So, how would an updated program based on PEPs succeed?" Tom mused out loud.

Now it was time for McIsaacs to eat and stay silent. Tom had the bait in his mouth and was rolling it around like a *somelier*.

McIsaacs waited, watching Tom's eyes as his asset's brain, now onto something other than righteous self-pity, took up the puzzle.

"How would an agency develop a network of controllable PEPs, solid enough to direct policies worldwide, when public shame and scandal were no longer weapons?"

McIsaacs downed his Jameson in one go. He made a move to wrap things up, removing some files from his briefcase, making a show of looking for something. A file marked "PEPs" was now sitting on the table. Tom noticed without reacting as McIsaacs snatched it up and held it out.

"Grabowski has some ideas, not very strong though."

"Hmmm . . ."

"You?"

Tom reached out, almost before he knew what he was doing, and touched the file with his fingertips. Intelligence is forbidden fruit, and highly addictive.

"While we're working out the details on your thing, you know. Something to occupy your mind."

"My mind."

Tom's fingers closed on the edge of the file.

The applied psychology had been correct. Tom Karas, too conceited by far to tolerate a challenge to his above-average intellect, real or imagined, began work on developing a reliable, long-term, PEP program for the NSA: how to influence politically exposed persons effectively, but secretly, to promote, or at least defend, unpopular policies in their native lands that were advantageous for the US.

Two quick months later, Tom signalled that he was ready to pitch to both McIsaacs and Grabowski *at the same time*, something that had never been done before, an idea for their special consideration. Thereupon, on his end, Grabowski added two young analysts from each intelligence sector to form a peanut gallery of about twenty individuals. They would listen, take notes, but offer no comments till after Tom had left the boardroom.

Tom had asked for a whiteboard and when he arrived at the secure conference room, he took a long minute to scan the peanut gallery, even though the lighting had been set so that he could not see their faces. It was a bit unnerving for all. A man, his face bandaged like a veteran of the Somme, scanning a row of faceless intelligence agents while Grabowski and McIsaacs squirmed.

Grabowski hated dramatics. "So? Are you done? Can we get on with it.?

Tom turned his scarred face fully toward his control.

"Of course."

Tom walked stiffly over to the white board and drew: "$."

He turned to the peanut gallery.

"Huh?" No response.

Tom continued slowly and methodically with his beautiful hand script;

"€."

"£."

"₱."

"ريال

"₹."

"Ƒ."

"₰."

"¥."

The peanut gallery murmured while Grabowski turned in his chair to give McIsaacs the "What's up?" shrug.

Tom placed the whiteboard marker down and faced his interlocutors, holding their attention for a long thirty seconds before speaking.

"When there is no shame left in the world, there is still money."

Tom turned toward Grabowski, his head down, his voice soft and modulated.

"For the past two months, I've been looking into banking regulations, domestic and foreign, as they pertain to national security, tax law, bank charters, and legislation governing the transfer of currencies between countries and legal entities. I even took a close look at the foreign banking laws of the countries whose currency symbols you see on the board, and quite a few more. I did all of this because I am a CPA and I hate people who talk through their hats addressing issues about which they know nothing."

Tom turned to the peanut gallery, his arms open wide.

"So, as Alfie once said, 'What's it all about?'"

Pennies started to drop one by one as the murmurs multiplied.

"We have been playing a shit game of country-store checkers while the other side has been playing 'Go.' And it stops now."

The murmurs were interrupted by one lone female voice saying almost inaudibly, "Fuck, yeah!"

Grabowski reacted, frowning as Tom gathered energy from the assembled.

"This nation is the richest on the planet and our financial and intelligence resources are almost unlimited. And what do we do with them?"

Tom waited for an answer and it came again from the peanut gallery: a quiet "Not much."

Tom whirled on his heels, pointing in the direction of the voice and thundering through his pain-addled lips, "Not much!"

Tom approached Grabowski, invading the neutral zone of the man's personal space. "Since the collapse of the Soviet Bloc, the Other Side has deposited an estimated $5 trillion in assets in American banks, and what do we do with it? Not much!"

McIsaacs was getting into it and leaned across the conference room table, rubbing his palms together. He ventured a leading question.

"And what do you want to do with those assets, Tom?"

Tom took a moment to gather his thoughts. When he spoke, it was with the firm voice of a true zealot.

"We cannot use that money. Under our own banking legislation, we can't touch it, it's too late." Tom paused to catch his breath and gather his thoughts. "Al, what I want to do is set up an organism that will attract that dark money into bank accounts over which *we* will have indirect control, even though we will *not* have ownership."

"The Swiss do that now. What's new about that?"

"No. They're neutral, they do not tell the owners of the money deposited with them how to act *politically*. I want to set up an organization that will host companies whose owners will listen to us about how to act politically, in return for money and favors that we will arrange for them.

"How? Where?"

Tom went back to the whiteboard and wrote down two possible locations.

"Either in Panama or in the Cayman Islands. Both have just begun to pass legislation to facilitate so-called *offshore banking*, with far looser restrictions than Switzerland, or, for that matter, Bermuda or Hong Kong or Lichtenstein or Beirut."

Grabowski was now all ears. "And what will you do to attract politically exposed people of interest to us?"

Tom referred to a map of the world that hung near the whiteboard.

"As we all know, the world is divided into ten areas of financial influence: North America, Central and Latin America and the Caribbean, Western Europe, the ex-Soviet Bloc, Africa, the Middle East, the Far East, China, India-Pakistan, and Australasia. All of these areas are potentially rich in politically exposed people whom we can seduce."

Tom placed a finger on the map.

"I suggest we start a trial project focusing primarily on Central and Latin America and the Caribbean. We would welcome PEPs with dark money from everywhere, of course, but in these two areas we would encourage our embassies' commercial attachés to recommend a 'friend' in, say, Panama, as a remarkably successful money manager."

Tom turned back to his bosses, wavering from the effort.

"I want these people to deposit their dark money into funds and accounts over which we will have some control. I want them to profit from the little tips and influence we can exert and then I want to bend them to our will by threatening the only thing left in the world they really, truly love: money and connections!"

Despite Grabowski's stern warning to the contrary, the murmuring in the peanut gallery swelled in appreciation of the subtlety of Tom's proposal. The applause started as they rose, one by one, out of their seats and out of the shadows.

McIsaacs turned to find Grabowski smiling grimly, but with newly hardened steel in his eyes.

*

Nine months later, Operation Not Much was in full swing. Grabowski had to pull every one of his impressive political levers to get the special judicial permission to implement the scheme.

Eighteen months after Tom's presentation and nine extremely painful operations on his face, McIsaac's team arranged a fake lethal heart attack for Tom Karas during one of his "surgical interventions." Tom had then been whisked away from the Georgetown facility to Panama City, Panama. Once there, Tom Karas was reborn as Alejandro Samos, born in Colon in 1944, educated stateside, a graduate of the University of Southern Florida, with a verifiable CV indicating work at Price Waterhouse while studying for his CPA.

In Montreal, McIsaacs's team published an understated and close-enough-to- the-truth obituary for Tom Karas, son of Richard and Eva-Maria Karas, deceased. This was followed by a proper internment notice, the ashes of the deceased to be placed alongside those of his parents in the family grave. A few months later, Tom's lawyer let it be known that he had wound up his late client's substantial estate and that, in accordance with the deceased's wishes, an $8-million bequest to McGill University had established the Eva-Maria Karas Memorial Scholarship Fund for needy fine arts students.

The balance of the estate, some $5 million, was left to an obscure US charity called The Veterans' PTSD Recovery Program, administered by the US Veterans Affairs. In fact, the $5-million bequest (one half of the proceeds from Tom's life insurance policy, as per contract with the NSA) was a sham. The money was washed through the labyrinthine bureaucracy of the VA and funnelled to the NSA, which then turned it over to Tom, now Alejandro Samos, CPA, with instructions to establish a *boutique* "offshore" company management service operation in Panama designed to cater to high-profile PEPs—in other words, politicians of influence worldwide.

The Tom Karas file at the NSA was destroyed, and an *Alejandro Samos* file was created at the National Resettlement Operations Centre. For operational support, Alejandro Samos, CPA, had a new control, a dour New Englander named Prewitt, a seasoned denizen of Foggy Bottom, better known as the US State Department.

CHAPTER 5

Montreal, Canada, 1955 (1)

In the '50s, Purvis Hall housed McGill University's School of Commerce and Faculty of Management. The former mansion was named after Arthur Purvis, president and managing director of Imperial Chemical Industries Ltd., who bought it from tobacco magnate Sir Mortimer B. Davis, one of Canada's richest and most influential Jewish citizens. Purvis had bequeathed the property to the university in the early forties. Needless to say, members of the student body immediately nick-named it Perverts' Hall, a sophomoric insult to the man who had been the head of the British Supply Council in charge of British purchases in North America during WWII.

Originally an elegant villa and adjacent coach house situated on Pine Avenue, opposite the Allan Memorial Institute of Psychiatry, it is part of the Royal Victoria Hospital complex, itself an impressive collection of buildings consisting of three pavilions: the Main, a huge all-stone replica of the Edinburg's Royal Infirmary with the modern-looking medical wing; the Women's Pavilion up the hill at the end of University Street overlooking the McGill University Sports Stadium, and the Allan Memorial Institute of Psychiatry, opposite Perverts' Hall..

Between the Main and the Allan Memorial there are two more buildings nestled into the hillside: the elegant nurses' residence, accommodating the 500 unmarried nurses who care for the hospital's patients, and the Ross Memorial Pavilion, for those wealthy enough to pay for luxurious private rooms with breathtaking views of the city below. The Ross had been built for the hospital with a donation from James Leveson Ross, the incredibly wealthy Montreal financier. Legend has it that, once the building was completed, Ross moved into the top floor as a "patient" and stayed there for the rest of his life, using the place as his private hotel with the nurses and housekeeping staff running errands for him as if they were his domestic servants.

For Tom Karas, the location of Perverts' Hall was of great help. On Mondays, Wednesdays, and Fridays, he could dash down after morning lectures, 200 yards to the Royal Vic, wolf down an abbreviated lunch, and still get to work on time. During the winter months, the "dashing" was more like dangerously slithering, sliding, and lurching on a sidewalk covered with snow and ice on which the city would sprinkle an ineffective mixture of salt and sand. Maintaining balance with feet clad in bulky, army-surface flying boots, purchased from a second-hand store, a student affectation, was no mean feat either.

Tom's title was assistant controller of the hospital, responsible for the accounting records of forty-eight special funds—an impressive title for a position that came with little authority. In fact, his job had been created specifically for him by a kindly vice president of operations to help him finance his university education. Tom was very grateful to the VP, not only for the financial help, but also for teaching him the skills he needed to deal with people without rubbing them the wrong way. Tom was acutely conscious of the unearned haughtiness he had inherited from his mother that gave people the impression that he was arrogant. Tom *was* arrogant, but he disliked arrogance in others and was determined to hide this character trait.

Friday was a busy day for Tom, who had to submit a detailed report of what moneys had been contributed to the various funds during the week. He had also to attend to the "payroll," but that was a breeze. The only employee to be looked after was a solitary technician of the Behaviour Lab. Oddly, none of the other funds had employees.

Odd, but so what? The job was an easy, part-time sinecure, three times a week from one in the afternoon until nine at night, which meant he was free to carry a full load of lectures at McGill. As he grew into adulthood, Tom's relationship with his parents had remained respectful and polite, but aloof, even as he continued to live under their roof. The money he earned came in very handy because it meant less dependence on them. Tom was discreet and never bothered his busy boss with unimportant questions and was reasonably sure that his sinecure job would last until graduation.

As he dutifully entered his figures in his accounting reports, the goings-on at the lab did nag at him: why were the services of a full-time photographer who often worked overtime and at night required? What was he doing? The Behaviour Lab occupied two spacious rooms next to the psychiatric ward, so for no other reason except his dislike of any mystery, Tom began to fantasize. Perhaps this Leonard Rosenberg, the night owl lab photographer, was using the lab for pin-up photography or shooting porno films at night to supplement his income?

There was something else odd about the lab: the cash flow. All the other funds that he administered received money in dribs and drabs, seasonal donations from individuals, corporations, institutions. Not the Behaviour Lab. It received a lump sum at the end of each month in the form of a bank transfer in US funds drawn on the Bank of Virginia by the world-famous physician who headed the hospital's psychiatric unit. Like clockwork.

Six months into his job, Tom acted on his aroused curiosity. As he handed over the biweekly paycheck to the mysterious Leo Rosenberg, with whom he had developed a nodding acquaintance, he invited the technician to join him for the evening meal at the hospital cafeteria.

The twenty-eight-year-old Rosenberg—tall, thin, and somewhat bent, with a mop of jet-black, curly hair and a matching, fierce-looking beard and a pair of owlish, thick-rimmed bifocals—seemed curiously eager to accept.

It was well past eight o'clock on a Friday night and nary another soul in sight. "So, what's with the phony British accent?"

Rosenberg had his mouth full of shepherd's pie, which he splattered as he spoke. They were in the large and almost empty, clinically clean but boringly decorated, cafeteria on the third floor of the medical wing.

"Went to school in England." Tom pushed his barely eaten meal aside and took a sip of his insipid coffee.

Rosenberg was puzzled. "But you're Hungarian."

Tom hesitated. "It's a long story. My family left after the war in 1949, when the Communists took over. They chased us out because we were part of the bourgeoisie, the middle class. We left everything behind. I went to live with my Swiss grandmother for a while, then they sent me to England and from there to Canada."

"You living with your parents?"

"Yeah, but it's not a peaceful scene. My father and I don't get along."

One hell of an understatement, to put it mildly, Tom thought to himself. Ever since Tom had turned fifteen he and his father had been engaged in a desperate battle of wills. Karas Senior had never been warm and even after the war, when everything had been lost, he seemed oblivious to the pathetic irony of his stolid "always first at everything" credo. Something had happened during his time under the Nazi thumb. He had hardened in a way that was inaccessible, and now it seemed the only way he could validate himself as a father was to stand in opposition to his son's ambitions.

Tom had hoped to continue his studies at Cambridge with a view of eventually becoming a lawyer—or, worse (in his father's eyes), an actor. The old man wanted the family to immigrate to Canada, and, being an absolute despot, had not deemed it necessary to consult Tom about *his* desires with regard to *his* future.

Whenever Tom challenged him they did not discuss, they fought, and as the fights became more and more frequent, he gradually withdrew from family life until "home" had become nothing more than, "bed and breakfast."

Rosenberg picked at his teeth. "Ah, that explains it, the part-time work while you're studying."

Tom nodded. "I shouldn't complain. I get free board and lodgings at home and I can limit my interaction with my father. The rest I have to earn. I won a scholarship at McGill so I don't have to worry about tuition fees. What about you, Leo?"

Rosenberg laughed. "Well, I'm certainly no university scholar. My grandparents were Polish Jews who fled Przytyk pogroms in the late twenties. I was born and brought up in Montreal, went to school here, and became a technician after finishing LaSalle College, a trade school."

"What kind of technician?"

"Oh, mainly photographic and mechanical. I'm good at figuring out how things work and fixing them when they break down. I also have an eye for photography."

"So, what kind of work do you do in the lab? Repair machinery?"

"Well, we've got lots of photographic equipment and a number of recording devices, tape recorders—as well as the ECT machines."

"ECT?"

"Electroconvulsive therapy."

Tom took a moment to digest this.

"For people suffering from depression. To snap them out of it?"

Tom felt as though Rosenberg had been monitoring his reaction.

"Something like that." Rosenberg got up, stretched, and yawned. "Enough of this shit, I'm tired." Rosenberg turned on his heels and left without saying good night, leaving Tom alone with the disagreeable feeling that he had just been dismissed.

CHAPTER 6

Montreal, Canada, 1955

The Leo Rosenberg who came to pick up his paycheque the following Friday was a completely different person. He apologized for his bad manners at the cafeteria, ascribing his behavior to fatigue, and presented Tom with a ticket to the Saturday afternoon football game of the Montreal Alouettes.

Tom loved to watch Canadian football. Despite his early Hungarian sports formation, he found it more exciting than soccer and, because of the wider, longer field, twelve rather than eleven men on each team, and only three downs rather than four, he also preferred it to American football. The game was faster.

Tom accepted the invitation without hesitation.

The game was being played in early October, Indian summer weather, at McGill's Percival Molson Memorial Stadium, named after Captain Percival Molson, a McGill graduate killed in 1917. Kickoff was scheduled for two in the early afternoon, which meant that the sun would still be shining when the game ended. Ideal football weather. The autumn air would be crisp, but not cold. The stadium was relatively small with room for no more than 20,000 people, and that made for coziness—spectators were almost close enough to the play to hear the players chatter in the huddles. The fall sunshine, the intimacy, and the fierce loyalty of the crowd validated McGill's reputation as the Ivy League's northern cousin.

Tom met Rosenberg at their seats and was intrigued to find that the technician had brought along another invitee. Allan McIsaacs was an American who was just as enthusiastic about the game as he was. During the after-game impromptu dinner of steaks at Moishes on St. Laurent Boulevard, McIsaacs revealed an encyclopedic knowledge of both the Canadian and the American game, regaling them with a seemingly endless flow of anecdotes about famous footballers he had met.

"I went to Notre Dame and tried out for the Fighting Irish, but, although I was fast, I wasn't fast enough, so I never made it to the NFL," he said, laughing as he downed his beer. Boston-born, McIsaacs's English had an Irish lilt to it. A big, muscular man, over six feet tall, he had a full head of reddish hair and pale blue eyes that were difficult to read. Tom had the impression that those roving eyes were constantly analyzing what was happening around them, alert to everything. Tom was impressed by Al's invariably well-tailored suits, shirts, and ties. His casual football games wardrobe, featuring an endless number of sweaters, made his two companions look like bums.

Tom sympathized with Al and his short-lived athletic career. A bit of an athlete himself, Tom had been an outstanding high-school soccer goalie, but, at five-foot-ten, not tall enough to turn pro.

"What did you do after you graduated from Notre Dame?"

"Who said I graduated?" The Irishman, on his sixth beer, dissolved into boisterous laughter. His guffaw was open, sincere, heartfelt.

"Did you?"

"No. I enlisted in the marines in forty-four because I wanted to serve my country. They sent me overseas to the Pacific Theatre and I stayed there until the war ended. Went back to school under the GI bill and obtained a BS in chemistry at Columbia."

"BS?" Tom was lost.

"Bachelor of science. You call it BSc in Canada."

Tom motioned to Leo with his scotch glass.

"How do you guys know each other?"

"Cocktail party at the US Embassy in Ottawa. We started talking football, which led to going to games together and we became friends."

Tom sensed that this was not the truth. He could not imagine Leo Rosenberg rubbing shoulders with the diplomatic anointed at any embassy.

"Do you live here?"

"No, in Washington, but I come here quite often. I'm a diplomatic courier."

*

From then on, Tom and Rosenberg began attending weekend home games of the Alouettes together, with McIsaacs joining them every time he was in town. This annoyed Pamela Blair, Tom's casual girlfriend, because, on each such occasion, Tom would have dinner with Leo and McIsaacs rather than with her.

Pamela was born in Greenock, Scotland. Her father had been a remittance man seconded to Canada by his Scottish engineering firm. But unlike so many of his countrymen who never acclimatized to the Canadian way of life, Mr. Blair liked Canada, and especially Montreal. Pamela never lost her lilting burr, and couldn't shed her robust, rounded form, but, in all other aspects, she was a modern North American girl and she needed to feel that the man in her life, to whom she had surrendered the pink, was attentive and at her beck and call. This, Tom could never be, but Pamela was still naïve enough to believe that if she just persisted, and handled the carrot and the stick wisely, he would change. It still grilled her when Tom went off with Rosenberg and that Yank.

On Canadian Thanksgiving weekend, the Alouettes were scheduled to play at home on the Saturday. McIsaacs wrangled a three-day trip to Montreal and Rosenberg then proposed that, on Sunday, weather permitting, he drive the Trio (as they had begun to call themselves) to *La Cocotte Rouge,* a small restaurant in the Laurentians owned by a chef who had earned an honorable mention in the *Guide Michelin,* the *gourmet's* bible.

"It'll take us a little over an hour, even in traffic, but it is picturesque and worth the effort," said Rosenberg and McIsaacs didn't need much convincing. His was a solidly American palette, but his frequent visits to Montreal and exposure to ex-pat European cuisine via Tom and Leo were broadening his tastes. So, on Sunday morning, they squeezed into the technician's small Austin A40 Somerset sedan and headed for Morin Heights, a village fewer than fifty miles north of Montreal.

Situated at the head of *Lac Bouchette*, *La Cocotte Rouge* was a two-story inn with the strictly French bourgeois dining room on the ground floor. The dining room faced the lake, thereby offering its patrons a splendid view of a long, oval reflecting surface of water along the shores of which a few pretty cottages could be seen poking through the surrounding forest. It was mid-October and the sap had already risen, warmly tinting the leaves of the maple trees so abundant in the region.

The weather was mild. "Thank heaven for this late summer," Rosenberg murmured as they took their places on the terrace, cognac glasses in hand, after a five-course meal of a spectacular crown of lamb stuffed with wild rice and tarragon, late-season asparagus, and Duchess potatoes, washed down with two bottles of Chianti Rufino Riserva Ducale. McIsaacs even allowed them to order the roast rare. "Look at that view!" Rosenberg gestured toward the lake with his balloon glass. "Truly amazing."

The sun was setting early and its rays illuminated the leaves of the trees from behind, making them look transparent.

Their red and yellow color contrasted dramatically with the vivid blue of the cloudless autumn sky. With the water mirror-like, the reflection of the houses and the trees on the lake looked as if they were elements of a painting by Alfred Sisley or Claude Monet.

No breeze, no rustling of leaves, just peace and quiet. After a while, McIsaacs turned to Tom, interrupting their reverie.

"So, just how Hungarian are you?"

Tom was so taken aback he almost spit out his Remy Martin.

"I mean, you don't strike me as your typical, cozy little *coffee klatch* Magyar."

For a moment, Tom was lost for words, but he recovered his aplomb.

"Well, I suppose I'm not, really. Typical, I mean. Can't say the *paprikash* is hanging from my chin."

The other two thought this image hysterical and Tom waited for their laughter to subside, smiling indulgently.

"You have to remember, I was a boy when we left Budapest. I have no fond memories, just the sense of being hounded out by faceless, angry shapes. I suppose I'm one of those who have never cared to look back."

McIsaacs took a long pull on his cognac.

"Do you still have family there?"

"I suppose so, but I don't know for sure. My mother writes them occasionally, but to family? Friends? I don't know and I don't ask. We are not a family with ties."

It appeared as though McIsaacs was weighing something in his mind, but he continued quietly. "I am hearing rumors about unrest brewing . . ."

"Meaning?"

"There are serious signs of trouble in Budapest. It seems the people are certainly not in love with their Soviet masters." McIsaacs shifted his gaze from the lake and, as he did so, their eyes met, the American's expressionless, cold blue eyes boring into Tom's, seeking . . . what, exactly? Those eyes, so damp with jovial mirth just seconds ago, seemed to be measuring something deep within Tom's emotional core.

Confused, Tom shuddered and looked away.

When the time came to leave, he was surprised to find that Rosenberg had paid the entire bill.

CHAPTER 7

Montreal, Canada, 1956

Hungary's 1956 Revolution broke out a week after the trio's visit to Morin Heights.

"What I don't understand is how the bloody hell did McIsaacs know that something would happen in Hungary?"

Pamela was getting impatient with Tom's infatuation with his American friend and his 'insider' status. They had just spent the last hour making hard, fierce love and yet Tom couldn't get his mind off McIsaacs and on to her.

"You *did* say he was working for the US State Department, didn't you?" Pamela made her voice sound measured, disinterested. She did not like the American and Tom knew this, so she made sure she did not offend her boyfriend by being critical.

Tom bristled. "He's just a courier."

It was Saturday evening and getting dark outside their rented room at the Gabriel Motel on the Upper Lachine Road. Since Tom and Pamela were living with their respective parents, sex was not possible at either of their homes.

Pamela had come out of the shower and was carefully putting herself back together. She was a true Scottish girl, with soft lips and yielding hips, but it was Tom who had sensed and then cultivated her well-developed libido far beyond what she would have considered possible before meeting him. Pamela considered herself to be Tom's main squeeze though *he* never thought of her in those terms, because he did not believe in "main squeezes." Letting down her thick auburn hair, she lay back, snuggling in the crook of Tom's neck. "Couriers travel and hear things," she whispered in his ear. Having just made love, Pamela was sated and assumed Tom was, as well.

She chose her words carefully. "You know, I don't really understand the relationship between those two—Rosenberg and your Irishman. They're thick as thieves. Does Leo need McIsaacs in some way, or vice versa?" She left the question up in the air for a while, then added "What does Rosenberg do at the lab, anyway?"

Tom gathered the many strands of his thoughts and tried them on for Pamela.

"He modifies cassettes so they become endless tapes that can keep repeating the same message for hours at a time. It's a kind of training, you know, like learning while you sleep? The hope is that if the tape contains a positive message, the listener will eventually respond to it." Tom turned on his side, nuzzling his lips between Pamela's freckled breasts.

Pamela's curiosity was piqued.

"How would Rosenberg use the tapes?"

Somewhat older, but emotionally way more mature than Tom, she was instinctively suspicious of her boyfriend's two close companions. In her mind, the Trio did not fit any usual pattern. A worldly Irish-American hanging around a Canadian Jew of Polish origin, seven years younger, who had a Hungarian-born friend, was all a bit too much. In her world, like stayed with like—she thought herself very daring indeed to be sleeping with a European while dear old daddy brought home one pasty-faced Scottish boy after another for her approval.

Pamela suspected that McIsaacs was the twenty-eight-year-old Rosenberg's gay lover and they were both trying to corrupt Tom, as well. She couldn't blame them. She had fallen hard for Tom's lean, well-proportioned body, his handsome face with that haughty, elegant air, his thick, wavy dark hair, and pair of grey-green eyes that were to die for. . . . If she squinted, she could see why any man of that persuasion might try.

No. In her opinion, football and Rosenberg were not a sufficient attraction for McIsaacs to be charging up to Montreal from Washington every six weeks. And didn't the courier always stay at Rosenberg's place when he was in town, never in a hotel? Certainly a government courier had a travel budget?

It was obvious to Tom that Pamela didn't like the American, but he ascribed this to a form of jealousy. He assumed she didn't care for him because he encroached on the already limited time they could spend together.

He had to change the mood because the clock was ticking and they did not have much time left. He thought a little confidential information might humor her. "Rosenberg puts football helmets with earphones embedded in them on patients' heads and plays the tapes to them, off and on, for eighty-six days while the patients slip in and out of insulin-induced comas," he explained. "It's called 'psychic driving' and it attempts to wipe clean the patients' bad memories and implant new ones on a 'clean slate.'"

Pamela sat up suddenly, not amused.

"And the photography?"

"Well, he showed me a few shots. While the patients are in coma, after shock treatment, they are 'cocooned' in sheets to make them feel as if they are back in the womb. The nurses lay them down like spokes of a wheel around a ladder. Rosenberg climbs the ladder and takes photos of their facial expressions from the top."

Pamela shook her head. "How cruel and unfair," she said, "to rob a person of his memories. I wish you hadn't told me."

Tom placed his hand fully on Pamela's vagina. The woman's cool, incredulous look made him pull it away as though it were on fire.

CHAPTER 8

Montreal, Canada, 1956

It was so romantic—*le P'tit Train du Nord.* It ran between Montreal and the Laurentian ski hills north of the city.

Tom met Pamela at Central Station on Saturday morning. Skis and poles on their shoulders, they were off on an overnight ski adventure, both having told white lies about it to their respective parents. The train was packed since there was no *autoroute* yet, but they were not worried. They had reservations to sleep at La Petite France, a restaurant-boarding house in Saint-Sauveur.

The first error they made was to ski first and then check in at their hostel rather than the other way round. By the time they got to La Petite France at six, the opportunistic owner, a plump French lady from Nantes, had given away their reservation. To compensate, she offered them free dinner with a bottle of wine and a promise that when the restaurant closed at nine, she'd put four tables together, top them with a sheet of plywood, and crown the contraption with a mattress.

Knowing full well that there wouldn't be a free bed in the neighborhood that late at night, they accepted. Luckily, the space could be divided into two by a concertina-type sliding door so they managed to organize some privacy for themselves, but acrobatic love-making with its accompanying sighs and groans, to which they had been coyly looking forward all day, was definitely not on.

The second error was not to have checked Pamela's ski bindings before leaving Montreal. One of her straps tore just after lunch on Sunday so they had to call it quits as far as skiing went. They took the early train home, fed up and irritated. Oblivious to Pamela's frustration, Tom committed a third gaffe by suggesting that they check in to a motel for a couple of hours before going to their respective homes.

Pamela's jaw dropped and her pale, lovely face turned red with anger.

"I cannot believe you. No way, Tom. It's three o'clock. My parents expect me home by six!" she hissed at him while they waited for the streetcar to take them to NDG, the sleepy, middle-class neighborhood where they both lived.

"You make me feel like all I am to you is a fast fuck. You have no respect for me as a person. I'm just a piece of ass."

He knew better than to contradict her, but he was also aware that the combination of her pretty, flushed, WASP face, and the dirty accusations coming out of her mouth, garnished with that Scottish burr, aroused him terribly.

Before going to sleep that night he spent time examining his feelings for Pamela and concluded that she was essentially right: he liked her, but did not love her, nor did he have plans to make her a permanent fixture in his future life. Pamela was a convenience, someone to go to a movie or a dance or a party with, and to go to bed with when the urge to do so overtook both of them at the same time, which prior to this weekend, had been often, but not enough.

And then, as he closed his eyes and his waking self paused on the threshold of the hour between the dog and the wolf, another thought came to him in the form of the promise that a hurt, bitter, and spoiled nine-year-old boy had made to his future self. Never again would he ever love anyone. To love was to be weak, to be vulnerable, to be exposed and open to betrayal.

CHAPTER 9

Montreal/Toronto

Predictably, McIsaacs resurfaced a week before the annual Canadian football classic, the Grey Cup. He had scored three wonderful seats to the game and, how about Rosenberg driving down to Toronto with Tom for the weekend? "We could all stay at the suite the consulate maintains for VIP visitors at the King Edward. I am allowed to use it when available."

"And is it?"

"Of course, shmuck! Otherwise, I would not have called."

"And the tickets?" Tom knew they were criminally expensive.

"My treat."

"Come off it, Al. They must have cost a fortune."

McIsaacs chuckled. "They didn't, actually. They were a gift from the consul. He had a slew of them to give away to friends."

So they drove to Toronto.

The game, between the Edmonton Eskimos and the Montreal Alouettes, was played at Varsity Stadium, a field that still holds the record for the number of times any stadium has hosted the Canadian professional football championship for the Grey Cup. The Eskimos' ground game was too much for the Alouettes and they lost. The Trio was mortified and, after the game, made the rounds of a number of bars around town to drown their sorrow. The result: more than somewhat inebriated, they finally hit the sack well after midnight.

Their hangovers on Sunday were world class, so severe that it took them until three in the afternoon to recover. Rosenberg had an aunt he had promised to visit, so McIsaacs and Tom, left to their own devices, decided to giddily raise their pinkies and take in the delights of the hotel's famous afternoon English high tea service.

In the fifties, Toronto was Canada's second-most-important city, but far less "fun" than Montreal, a cosmopolitan, bilingual city that held the number-one position culturally by a very healthy margin. Sunday drinking was frowned upon in Toronto and alcoholic beverages were only available with meals.

The King Edward Hotel was granted its name by King Edward VII, the year it was opened, 1903. On the two top floors of its tower was the Crystal Ballroom, the most fashionable venue in the city until the late 1950s. Notable dignitaries and luminaries housed in the hotel have included Mark Twain, Rudolph Valentino, Louis Armstrong, and Ernest Hemingway, who had lived in the hotel for quite a period.

Rivaling the ballroom's fame for elegance was the lobby.

After they were seated on velvet-covered armchairs under the painting of King Edward himself in full royal regalia, they were handed elaborate menus: cranberry scones with clotted cream and strawberry jam, dainty finger sandwiches— salmon, chicken, egg or shrimp salad—plum compote, and assorted pastries. The serving staff took note of their order and withdrew.

Tom took a deep breath and decided to beard the lion in its den by asking his companion, ten years his senior and far more self-confident, the question he had asked Pamela in bed a few weeks earlier.

"How come you knew in advance that there would be a revolution in Hungary?"

The American gave Tom a bright smile as though he had been anticipating the question. "In my line, you hear all kinds of information, some based on fact, some pure speculation. We have our sources. The art of staying ahead in our game and to surviving in my environment, is to know who to believe." His pale blue roving eyes surveyed Tom's face with care. "Why do you care about what happened in Hungary? I thought you were somewhat hostile, considering how they chased you and your family out—communists and fascists alike."

McIsaacs had touched a raw nerve. Tom hesitated as cold, uncontrollable rage from a dark, hidden place suddenly welled up within him. His voice was measured, but rose in intensity. "Hostile?" he scoffed. "I despise and loathe them!" He was almost shouting, his eyes flashing, his face flushed.

Their conversation was interrupted by the arrival of their high tea, which the wait staff arranged on the small table between them. When they withdrew, McIsaacs helped himself to tea and *petit fours,* giving Tom a moment to collect himself. Tom didn't make a move to eat anything. McIsaacs lowered his own voice as he addressed his companion dispassionately. "You're angry with the bastards. Why don't you do something about it?" he asked quietly.

This exasperated Tom even more. "Because, my smug American friend, I don't know how."

McIsaacs held Tom's eyes with his own and enunciated his words carefully. "And if I showed you how, what would you do?"

Epiphany. The Lincoln penny dropped

The answers to the annoying questions about Rosenberg and McIsaacs that had been bothering Tom for months were suddenly resolved with such force and clarity that it almost stilled his tongue. He started to reply, stopped, and started once more.

"So, that's what all this is about," he muttered and calmed down immediately. Tom felt McIsaacs waiting for an answer, but decided to challenge his host.

"Leo's operation at the Behaviour Lab. . . . I've read Condon's *The Manchurian Candidate*. Amusing as speculative fiction, but I'm guessing you and Leo aren't dealing in make-believe."

McIsaacs appeared to be enjoying Tom's analysis as he helped himself to finger sandwiches. He leaned back in his club chair as Tom continued.

"I must have been blind. I've seen the monthly cheques come in to Dr. Cameron's account through the Bank of Virginia. My guess is CIA," he said and looked McIsaacs squarely in the eyes. "You're no State Department courier. You are a recruiter and Leo is your spotter."

McIsaacs merely smiled and called for the bill. "Now that we understand each other, let's go upstairs and get down to business."

CHAPTER 10

Montreal, 1957

The six months that followed his conversation with McIsaacs were stressful. While finishing his master's thesis in economics and working almost full time at the hospital, he had also had to create a plausible "legend" for his boss, his parents, and Pamela, to explain why he would be absent from Montreal for a whole month during the Easter holidays.

His parents had been the easiest. They were planning an Easter cruise in the Caribbean and were relieved to hear that they would not have to be concerned about their son in their absence. Things had been even easier with his boss. Tom was due two weeks' vacation time and, when he asked for two more, he was granted them "no questions asked," but without pay.

With Pamela, a credible story seemed more appropriate. He invented a trip to Argentina where he was enrolled in tango classes at a school that offered not only tuition, but also a trip to Buenos Aires at Easter.

"Great! We finally get to travel together," she said, eyeing him steadily.

Tom squirmed as she maneuvered outside his prepared playbook.

"Well, I've been teamed up already, with an Argentinian partner. You see, that's their method . . . the school. They team you up. So . . ."

Pamela nodded to herself as she gathered her cigarettes, lighter, purse. She slipped on her shoes slowly as Tom watched, marveling once more at how her form moved him. She straightened out her skirt.

"What fucking arrogance," was her first, quiet salvo and it hit directly, mercilessly. "You know, Tom, deep down, I believe you're a decent person. You've got good values. But you're deeply wounded emotionally."

Pamela's steady, green-flecked hazel eyes searched Tom's face for any signs of acknowledgment, but the shutters had come down at her first words.

"I was ready to love you. I may have already been a little in love with you, but you are on your own path, alone. You've decided that you can't have anyone in your life. . . ."

Love no one.

"Be careful, Tom. Keep going down that path and pretty soon you won't be able to reverse it. Even if you want to later on, for someone like me."

She was gone and Tom felt a strange, metallic divide in his chest, as though he was being pried apart, but it only lasted a moment. McIsaacs had talked about the many such sacrifices he would have to make if he wanted to serve his new masters well. He searched his emotions and felt a forced, macho pride about the indifference with which he had treated Pamela.

At the same time, he realized that, as time passed, his manner of denying his feelings would slowly change his core values. The cruel and inevitable process of his humanity atrophying had begun.

"Strictly speaking, you will not be working for the CIA," McIsaacs had explained during their meeting in the suite after their high tea at the King Edward.

"You'll be hired as an outside contractor by the NSA. If you don't wash out in basic, you'll start getting assignments."

"Basic training?"

"Yeah. Everyone gets some basic training at the Farm. It's the CIA's classified training facility at Camp Peary in Virginia, which is also used by the NSA. We have designed a course especially for you. Four weeks, starting the week before Easter."

"Do I report to you?" With McIsaacs still involved, Tom felt more at ease and the American knew it.

"Yes, I will act as your Control for now. Good?"

"Good."

"As for compensation, you'll get a generous monthly stipend, deposited offshore, so tax-free, and, as a sign-up bonus, a prepaid health and life insurance policy worth ten million that will remain in force as long as you live."

Tom accepted, inwardly giddy with excitement, and went to war.

*

The NSA is a huge and complex organization. At its head are the Director, Deputy Director and Executive Director, who run a number of Directorates, one of which is the Directorate of Plans. 'Plans' contains a sub-directorate, Division AX, dedicated to running "wet" operatives—contractors that are not employees and, as such, do not need to be US citizens. These independents are free to carry out "dirty tricks" world-wide as required, without their actions blowing up in the faces of the various directorates. These suppliers are engaged by contract and directed by so-called Group Controllers.

Division AX was so secret that only the Director, the Deputy Director and the Assistant Deputy Director knew about it. This was to become Tom's world, if he didn't wash out of basic and, once committed, there was no way Tom would allow that to happen.

The basic training may have been designed by McIsaacs and other "experts" at the agency to be difficult and provoke a washout, but in Tom's case, they missed by a disturbingly wide margin. Although they had hours of taped interviews and volumes of written questionnaires, plus all the clandestine research done on him stretching back to his schoolboy years at the *sziv altalanos iskola,* they simply did not understand the one compelling formative event in Tom's life: wartime deprivation.

To say that Tom took to the physical and psychological stresses of basic training like a *bec-fin* to *foie gras* would be a gross understatement. The physical training was overseen by nameless Army Rangers—tall, imposing men with few words, narrowed eyed, and buzz-cuts. Their regard toward the thin, medium-height, reserved Canadian in their midst was clearly biased, but in a quiet, menacing manner. Tom was indifferent, because at the first 04h00 reveille, his concerns for physical comfort or due consideration had been safely stowed away. The Rangers did not know it, but they were training a wiry Budapest street kid, wits sharpened to avoid conflict with forces greater than his, senses alert and desires suppressed.

War and post-war deprivation had given Tom two minds about comfort. He appreciated physical well-being as well as the next man, but his had been a childhood of countless dark nights with no heat, fighting lice and bedbugs, trying to sleep on an empty stomach while the night was rent with the sounds of approaching Soviet artillery. These discomforts grew callouses on his sensitivities. Tom liked and enjoyed good food, but had been content with bacon rinds, vegetable peelings, and whatever dubious foodstuffs could be scrounged or ripped from the soil. Fatigue was a familiar friend and ally, making Tom less reactive, more cautious and wary.

All the recruits at basic wore the same drab, anonymous gray fatigues and third-hand army boots. Tom knew how to make ill-fitting footwear tolerable with molded paper and tissues scrounged from the latrine. During the first week, stress was applied by sleep deficit, limited calories, and intense physical conditioning. After the third day, Tom was always at or near the head of the column. By the end of the week, his young body, responding quickly to the stress, put him at the head of all activity. By the second week, after the usual luxurious cold shower, Tom caught sight of his body in the mirror and had to stop and appreciate the muscles, tendons, and veins in his legs, now standing out in relief, and the multiple lateral ripples down his stomach. His face had narrowed and his eyes were becoming "Ranger-like," so much so that the trainers started to warm up to him, giving him a forbidden nickname: Hollywood.

The early morning cross-country marathons were difficult at first and Tom hated to find himself in the back of the mute, gasping pack, *always first at everything* . . . but at the end of the first week, he found himself in the middle of the pack. By the third week, he was at the head, running smoothly with the Rangers, and by the fourth week, he ran ahead, leaving Rangers and the other trainees, running now as a coherent group, far behind. At the end of the run, he held out his hand to one of the Rangers, who ignored him, but made a point to congratulate every other candidate. Tom was puzzled, but unconcerned.

The physiological training was a breeze. As an undergraduate, Tom had been dared to take the Mensa exam by a brainy girl he was seeing. She was quite competitive and was certain she would score higher. The bet was her maidenhead against a trip to New York, on Tom. He was only into the third question when he understood that success in the exam was learning to think and seeing each question in a certain manner. It reminded him of the kind of thought that went into playing Scrabble or contract bridge, games he excelled at, but that also bored him.

The NSA exams were of a similar design and he aced each one with times that were impressive. As for Mensa, he declined to join, even though he scored higher than the girl. He found members to be notably odd—intelligent, but rude, socially inept, awkward, and lacking elegance, with enormous gaps in their culture. As for the girl, ever the gentleman, he took her to New York and claimed his prize after taking her to see *Oklahoma* on Broadway, feeding her a mile-high pastrami sandwich at the Carnegie Deli, and sneaking her Lindy's cheesecake dessert into their hotel room at the Edison. In the morning, he let her beat him at the New York Times crossword, Mensa-style.

If he could have, Tom would have remained with his Ranger buddies and their "thousand yard stares" for the rest of his life. But in due course, after his fourth week, McIsaacs came to collect him, walking right past Tom without recognizing his recruit. As a parting gift, some of the Rangers gave him a tiny notebook with minute pencil sketches of their faces, their first names and dog tag numbers. It had been slipped into his duffle bag without his knowledge and he only discovered it later. The gesture brought emotions to the surface that he quickly, forcefully repressed. But he kept that notebook among his most precious possessions.

*

It was normal that things changed between Tom and McIsaacs. They now observed a certain formality, which Tom regretted but understood implicitly. Occasionally, after a difficult assignment or when they had a few drinks under their belts, the old ease and camaraderie would surface, but usually they were Control and asset, and behaved as such.

There were no drinks being served in the secure conference room at Camp Peary where they met, just files with the results of Tom's basic training. McIsaacs made a show of perusing Tom's exams.

"You did good, sport." McIsaacs was all smiles. He waved a bunch of papers at Tom, still dressed in his grey army fatigues and boots. "We designed your course for you to fail. Somehow, you managed to pass and even to distinguish yourself in four areas."

"Really."

McIsaacs looked up and took Tom in fully for the first time and found the changes startling. His asset was relaxed, suntanned, in top form, and more sure of himself. It was clear that the four weeks he had spent with like-minded, ambitious, and focused men and the physical training he had been required to complete had done him good. McIsaacs made a mental note not to allow Tom to shy away from physically challenging assignments.

"You have an exceptionally good memory, you are in the top percentile at pure and applied mathematics, and you are rated as a level 4 linguist. You are also, apparently, a crack shot—a born sniper."

As his tension released, Tom burst out laughing. "Sounds like the perfect agent: a bookkeeper who can do your taxes, remember account numbers, and lie in four languages while shooting himself invariably in his own foot!" Tom could not stop himself from sounding sarcastic and cocky.

"Not so fast, sport." His Control's voice was suddenly not so friendly as he held another set of reports between his finger and thumb, like they were soiled with dog shit.

"You also have a tendency toward anger, and your examiners found you aloof and lacking in empathy. This makes it difficult for you to interact with others and to lead them successfully. In other words, you are neither collegiate nor a good leader. You are a loner and possibly a misfit."

. . . always first at everything . . .

"But then, we already knew all of that," said McIsaacs, looking up at his new charge. "And that is precisely why I have decided to give you a chance, because the work we do requires men who are dedicated, callous loners."

"Gee, thanks, I guess."

"There is no such thing as a perfect agent, Tom." His control smiled wistfully. "Always keep in mind that I know how difficult and painful it can be to be a loner."

He opened the manila envelope in his hand, extracted a glossy photograph, and handed it to Tom.

"This is your first assignment."

The picture was of a somewhat rotund, middle-aged man with a full head of graying hair, eyes sparkling with intelligence behind rimless bifocals, and an engaging smile. The man's European origins were slightly hidden behind his wind-burned prairie complexion, but those bifocals were the giveaway.

"The man you're looking at is Ray Moore, born in 1920 and christened Radovan Mogilyenski in Manitoba, Canada. His family emigrated from the Ukraine immediately after the First World War and settled in the prairies on a farm that Radovan's father worked into the ground for a dozen years."

Tom scanned the other photos in the file: grainy, black and sepia-tinted pictures of a prairie sod house and a large family with kids barefoot and in rags. The archetype complete.

"The father struggled to make ends meet, but in the end, he failed during the Great Depression and committed suicide when Radovan was ten, leaving his family penniless. Radovan's mother changed the family name to Moore and, with the help of the local priest, obtained a boarding scholarship for her son Ray, an unusually bright kid, at the Jesuit-run Saint Boniface College in a suburb of Winnipeg."

Moore's photo revealed a weal on his right jaw that caught Tom's attention. "What's with the dueling scar?"

"Knife wound inflicted by a jealous flamenco dancer during a bar brawl in Barcelona."

"This guy?"

"After graduating with honors, Moore was broke, but now fluent in French, several Slavic languages, and, of course English. He rode the rails to Montreal and got a job at *The Montreal Star* as a copy-boy. After a year, he was moved up to copy editor and, a year later, talked his editor into sending him to Spain, where the civil war was just starting."

"This guy? Now I'm impressed."

"Ray was embedded in the Abraham Lincoln Brigade, and reported on the war till Madrid fell to the Nationalists in 1939."

"Fascinating."

"When the war ended, he didn't want to come home and got a job with Radio-Canada as its Moscow correspondent."

"I'm guessing one of those Slavic languages was Russian?"

"Presumably."

"So, what has the hero of Madrid done to deserve our attention?"

"Patience!" McIsaacs's voice was edgy. "While in Moscow, Moore met, fell in love with, and married Ekaterina Yegorova, a senior editor-librarian at *Mezhdunarodnaya Kniga*," McIsaacs said, stumbling over the pronunciation as he dropped a photograph of Ekaterina in front of Tom.

"Let's call it 'MK,' for short. Ekaterina came back with him when he returned from Moscow in 1945."

Tom's pronunciation was better, "Mezhdunarodnaya Kniga?"

"Literally translated, it means 'international book,' but it's also the name of the Soviet government's book publishing and import-export agency.

"Once he got back to Montreal, Moore expected his contract with Radio-Canada would be renewed, but the Mounties cast a shadow over him for some minor wartime fumbles and he was let go. He found it difficult to get a suitable job, so he decided to go into the rare book business by using his wife's connections at MK."

"So?"

"So nothing. His business is viable, he supports his wife, pays his taxes, and makes a modest living. They have no children."

McIsaacs stopped talking and fished another photo out of the envelope, a picture of a comfortable-looking home with an oversized garage attached to it.

"This is where Moore and his wife live and from where they conduct their business. The building and the garage contain a huge inventory of books accumulated over a dozen years—over 7,000 volumes, we estimate."

The American got up and began to pace, uncharacteristically nervous.

"Here is the thing. Officially, we are not allowed to operate in Canada, so we use cooperative Canadian citizens like you to do our work for us. This is not illegal or improper. However, if we ask you to do something that is not legal, such as, for example, burglarize a house, we cannot protect you from the consequences."

Tom was taken aback. "I thought you were operating hand in hand with the RCMP's Security and Intelligence Division."

"In fact, we are, but they only extend protection to our people in cases where they have been informed about the details of an operation in advance."

"So what's the problem?"

"The Mounties leak like a sieve. They are lousy with double agents and just plain big mouths. I don't dare brief them officially about what I'm going to ask you to do because it is bound to leak back to the Russians."

"And what is the illegal thing you want me to do?"

McIsaacs sat down again, his meaty hands flat on the conference table.

"The Moores' bookkeeper is pregnant and will be quitting her job in about four months. I will create an opportunity for you to apply for her job and you are to do your very best to get it."

"That's not illegal."

"Initially, it won't be, but it might become so later on. Do you understand me fully?"

Tom nodded, but he was thinking rapidly, analytically.

"Why are the Moores so important for us?"

"Because, we believe that Ray Moore is one of the pay-masters of the Soviets' North American spy network."

That's when the consequences of his decision to accept McIsaacs's offer became concrete and real for Tom. This was a real assignment with a defined goal, involving a real menace. There was nothing theoretical, nothing speculative about Ray Moore. Tom's life suddenly materialized before him and he grasped in a moment what enormous conse-quences working for the NSA might have on his well-being, his career, his life, and his right to pursue his own happiness.

McIsaacs continued. "Until you get that job with the Moores, you are to keep your job at the hospital and your friendship with Leo, but do not tell him what you are doing for us. Remember this: as soon as you appear on Moore's horizon, he'll start checking up on you in depth, so do not call me."

"How will we communicate?"

"Through Leo, but only if and when absolutely necessary. In such an event, tell Leo and I'll arrange a meeting with you through him."

The American's last remarks left Tom with the slightly nauseating feeling of being suddenly in the deep end of the pool and a bit too far from the edge. He was being asked to take much, maybe too much, on pure faith. He had no copy of the employment contract he had signed with the NSA; he had no copy of the health and life insurance policy that the NSA had arranged for him; access to his offshore bank account was tricky, and he could not easily verify if his stipend was being paid regularly.

And now McIsaacs, his only direct link to his employer, AX, a tiny part of the huge NSA quagmire of bureaucracy, was beginning to distance itself from him. What would happen if McIsaacs died or was relieved of his duties? Rosenberg would have been directed to deny everything.

"What happens if one morning, after a night on the tiles, you leave the comfort of your warm DC bed and your latest playmate, stumble into the bathroom, have a heart attack, and fall so hard that you crack your head wide open?"

The corners of McIsaacs's mouth fought in vain to prevent the wry smile from creasing his face. "Well, if that happens, I hope you'll say nice things about me at my funeral."

Tom gestured to the space around them.

"Al, for all intents and purposes, I don't exist here. You are my only contact. Even the Army Rangers didn't know my name. I feel vulnerable, Al, and frankly, I don't like it." Tom said. "If you suddenly disappear, for whatever reason, I could find myself swinging helplessly in the wind."

McIsaac allowed himself a grim, confirming smile.

"Good. You're so fucking trusting, *Canadian*, I thought the moment would never come." Another rueful smile. "You've begun to trust no-one, not even your control."

McIsaacs produced a small, velvet jewelry box from his pocket and handed it to Tom, who snapped it open and extracted what looked like an ordinary military dog-tag on a chain, seemingly made of silver. The engraving on one side said *From Pamela with Love, 1956.* The other featured Tom's astrological sign, a set of scales.

McIsaacs picked up the dog-tag. "The dog-tag and chain are of an especially hard steel alloy that is made to look like silver. There's even a legit jeweller's marque, but it isn't silver, so no hocking. Don't wear it all the time. just keep it within reach, always."

His Control then handed Tom a piece of paper with a telephone number on it. "Memorize and destroy. If you have a problem, and I mean *real* problem, call the number from anywhere in the world. A male voice will answer and say, '*This is the major,*' whereupon you are to say, '*My name is Barbara.*' He will then ask, '*Alias?*' Your answer is '*Frosty the Snowman.*' He will then say, '*Go ahead, the line is secure.*' You will tell him what your problem is. If he does not say the bit about the line being secure, hang up."

"Hang up?"

"Call back a few minutes later and see if the major completes the dialogue. If not, head for the hills because we're up the proverbial creek—all of us."

Tom was having trouble digesting this.

"You can't be serious."

"As a heart attack. Look, you'll be given several protocols in case of problems, but, remember always, as a last resort, head for the nearest US embassy or consulate, ask for the military attaché and hand him your dog-tag. Your personal NSA file number is encoded in it."

CHAPTER 11

Montreal, 1958

James McGill, a Scottish immigrant from Glasgow and graduate of that city's university, became one of Canada's richest men through participating in a variety of business ventures, including the fur trade. In 1777, McGill settled in Montreal with his wife, the widow Marie-Charlotte Trottier Desrivières, and her two sons, François-Amable and Thomas-Hippolyte, joining the previously adopted Charlotte Porteous, an orphan of his late business partner, John Porteous, as a blended and happy family. McGill's household also included five slaves: Marie Louise, property of McGill's wife, Sarah Cavilho, a Black woman, Jacques, a Black man, and two Indigenous children, one named Marie and one whose name has been lost to history, both of them dying at around the age of ten.

In January 1811, at age sixty-seven, James McGill made his will. Having been active for years in public life, he knew exactly how important education was for the still emerging nation that would become Canada.

McGill shed his mortal coil in December of 1813. He left £10,000 and his Burnside estate of some forty-six acres at the foot of Mount Royal toward the endowment of a college or a university. One of his stipulations was that the university, or at least one of the associated colleges, bear his name. The bequest became operative when the Royal Institution for the Advancement of Learning, the agency of the Quebec provincial government responsible for schools, granted a charter to the bequest in 1821, but it was not till 1829 that teaching began in what is now the aptly named McGill University.

On an autumn morning, about a month after his last meeting with McIsaacs, Tom got off the 24 bus that runs along Sherbrooke Street at the Roddick Gates, and crossed the road into the McGill University campus. Every Tuesday and Thursday, he headed across the games field to the entrance of the Redpath Library, an impressive Romanesque building to which a modern-looking annex had recently been built, thereby totally destroying the original structure's look of elegant majesty.

It was a few minutes past ten. The subject of his visit was already in her usual seat at the long reading table. In her late fifties, Ekaterina Moore was a plain, round woman with silvery gray hair that she braided daily, Russian-peasant-style, and wound around her head like a crown. It made her look faintly proletarian and willfully unstylish. Steel-rimmed reading glasses hung by a thick, sweat-stained strap around her neck. There were deep creases around her slightly almond-shaped, dull hazel eyes, and her aura and energy were those of a much older woman. Her face was heart shaped, with high, ruddy cheekbones that spoke of a Tartar heritage. She smoked almost incessantly and her wake was tainted by the heavy funk of her Turkish cigarettes. Tom thought that she had either suffered a lot or suffered fools greatly.

Taking his usual carrel, not too near to or too far from the Russian, Tom smiled inwardly, recalling his meeting with McIsaacs when they were joined by a bland, emotionless NSA asset with a pile of file folders, whom his control introduced as a forensic accountant named "Chef."

Tom was adamant. "I'm not up to this—unveiling a Russian spymaster of Moore's calibre is far beyond my capabilities. You've got the wrong recruit!"

Chef cleared his throat, glanced at McIsaacs, gathered his files, and made motions to leave the conference room. McIsaacs brusquely waved him back into his seat, but the man remained on the edge of his chair.

"Don't be so modest, Tom. You're raw, but, we know you have potential."

"But what is the brief, exactly?"

McIsaacs knew that he had to steady his asset, build him u,p and engage him intellectually. He motioned to Chef, who spoke in an unmodulated monotone.

"We've been watching Moore for some time. We've analyzed his bank accounts and tax returns, even took a peek at his safety deposit boxes, but we still can't figure out where the money comes from to do his pay-mastering.

Tom squirmed. "What makes you think I can?"

"Here's the bet," said McIsaacs. "None of our agents has your education and experience in finance and accounting. I've seen your test scores. I know that once you become familiar with his operation, you'll figure it all out."

"All the analysis has been done by field agents," added Chef. "They wouldn't know a GAAP from a hole-in-the-wall. Moore's GL has never been parsed by a guy like you."

The American had then locked his pale blue eyes on Tom. "The beauty of it is, you will not have to be a secret NSA 'agent' at all. You just have to be what you are: an accountant. A bookkeeper. I'm counting on you. Don't let me down." He had seemed to be almost begging.

Tom took the compliment and noted the stress in McIsaacs's voice.

"How many people does he employ?"

McIsaacs motioned to dismiss Chef, who gathered his files and left the room without a word.

"That, my insightful friend, is the problem. His wife does the correspondence and research for him. A male clerk handles the heavy lifting and classification of the books on the shelves, and his bookkeeper looks after his banking and finances. He, himself, does the buying and selling. That's it. We have not been able to penetrate his setup.

"Ekaterina visits the Redpath Library every Tuesday and Thursday morning. She has a reserved carrel for her research on rare books. We have arranged a nearby carrel for you.

Pretend to be working on your PhD thesis in economics. Find a way to get to know her."

"And persuade her to hire me in the spring to replace her present accountant."

McIsaacs smiled. "You see? Quick study."

*

Breaking the ice with someone as guarded and antisocial as Ekaterina Moore turned out to be a hard task. Tom's easy-going manner with women was something he rarely thought about. It was part of his nature and, as such, effortless, which in turn made it effective. Tom also had to admit to himself that Mrs. Moore was not anyone's typical idea of a warm, affable person. She wore clothing that looked like it still came from the Soviet Women's Culture Worker's Collective: terylene suits thick as an armadillo's hide, mated rudely with sensible leather shoes deformed by bunions and hammer toes. Her jewelry was spare, plastic, and ugly. What little make-up she wore was garish and ineptly applied. She favored colors that only emphasized her foreignness, though she appeared to like richly colored polyester scarves. Her small, blunt hands were like a man's, ravaged by constant nail-biting, the skin raw from neglect.

Tom decided on a purely "civil" approach. After nodding to her every time he had entered the library during the autumn months, she had finally favored him with a pained smirk. Two weeks later, he managed to be near the door when she exited the reading room, greasy brown-bag lunch in hand, as usual, precisely at noon. He held the door open for her and said casually, "Lunch time." He held up his own bag.

She stared blankly and exited with Tom a few steps behind her. The terrace where they often ate their separate lunches was crowded, with only a small table for two available. Tom motioned to it, asking, "Do you mind sharing?"

"No," Ekaterina replied, leading the way. It was toward the end of October, but a pleasantly late summer wave made it warm enough to eat outdoors without discomfort. They exchanged very few words as Tom buried his nose in a standard text on economics. This prompted several bland questions from the Russian, who appeared satisfied with Tom's answers.

During the weeks leading up to Christmas, they ate together sporadically, Tom sticking to coffee and cheese bagels while Ekaterina gulped down dripping sardine sandwiches. Tom was careful not to appear pushy, but made sure she gradually became aware of his actual academic and work qualifications as well as his ambitions as construed by himself and McIsaacs. Sitting close to her, Tom became aware of her scent, a sad wan mixture of rose water, nicotine, and herring.

"I talked to my husband about you," she said to him through the first puff of her usual post-lunch, filter-less Balcan-Sobranie. They were snugly inside the Redpath cafeteria, their first shared lunch in the New Year. "He would like to meet you. Would you like to come to dinner one day next week?"

Tom did not have to act surprised, it was an authentic reaction to a plan that, if he was honest with himself, he though had a slim chance of success.

"Oh? What did you tell him about me?"

Ekaterina flicked her ashes with her beleaguered fingers in a manner that was messy and clumsy, and which Tom found so repellent that it only increased his usual distaste toward smokers. He imagined that Jimmy Hoffa dropped his ashes that way.

"That you are a neat, ambitious, courteous, and eager young man with an education in accounting, who needs a job," she smiled, her eyes crinkling into porcine slits. "I told him you had the scent of the Magyar about you, but he didn't mind."

Tom laughed heartily, the better to hide the tension that had been building in his chest. Ekaterina left her cigarette burning in the ashtray and rose, straightening in vain her deeply wrinkled suit. She held out a business card.

"Shall we say Friday, at 08h00?"

Tom accepted the card and then, for reasons he could not explain, he took her hand in his, turned it slightly and bending low, tried to kiss the air above it. Entranced, the lumpy woman allowed it.

The brownstone house on Jeanne-Mance, just north of Sherbrooke Street, was deceptively small and plain from the outside, but once past the spacious, ornately tiled vestibule, revealed itself to be three floors of richly wood-panelled style and coziness. The ground-floor dining room opened up via leaded-glass pocket doors to the salon, which was decorated with an odd mix of massive Edwardian furniture and several modern pieces. There were several extraordinarily ornate Russian icons mounted on the walls as well as two eighteenth-century Bokhara rugs. The room was heated by a hard coal fireplace.

Ray Moore's file photo did not do him justice. He was just under six feet tall and his rotundness hid a good layer of muscle, the shoulders being broad and sturdy. Tom had trouble keeping his eyes off Moore's facial scar and forced himself to observe his subject's hands, which were large, with wide, strong fingers tapering down finely. Moore was dressed in a light tweed suit and cream-colored vest, plain Oxford cloth white shirt, dark knit tie, and oxblood red brogues, which were comfortably worn.

Moore, Ekaterina, and Tom had settled in the salon after a meal of avocado filled with Matane shrimp, Holsteiner schnitzel, mashed potatoes, salad, and a killer apple pie with chocolate ice cream. Too much food, but, then, Moore was a big eater. The older man poured cognac as he warmed up to his subject.

"We have a turnover of about three-quarters of a million dollars and our profit margin is in the 15 percent range." Moore emptied his espresso cup and reached for his Upmann No. 2 cigar. Ekaterina reached for a Balcan-Sobrainie from a small Japanese lacquered box and Moore offered his Ronson.

"That means you have close to $100,000 to cover your expenses and your living costs." Tom knew he was being probed, tested. "Sounds a bit tight."

"I understand what you're driving at. You're wondering if I can afford to hire you."

"Well, can you?" Tom said, trying to lighten the question. McIsaacs had instructed Tom to play very hard to get.

"Katie told you I need someone to organize my paperwork and do my bookkeeping, so you know where we're at. As I understand it, you are just starting out and don't quite know where you want to end up."

"Not exactly. I know where, but not how or when." Tom chuckled and sipped his espresso.

"Precisely. My bookkeeper is pregnant and will be leaving. So why not come to work for us in the spring, for two days a week, and only after you've finished your thesis?"

"That very generous of you, but I currently do work at the hospital."

"Keep your job at the hospital. Between that and what we'll pay, you'll earn enough to have some options as you launch your career. Maybe you want to move away from your parents and start your own *life*?"

Tom did not have to pretend some embarrassment at having his adult nose shoved into his current, cushy living arrangements.

"Is this your idea, or your wife's?"

Ekaterina smiled and raised her cognac glass ever so shyly toward Tom.

"My wife's."

"Well, then I have no other choice but to accept."

Moore suggested a figure and they bargained a bit, but in the end they all toasted another round to Tom who would come to work for the Moore Book Company starting in early March.

CHAPTER 12

New York City, 1959

In mid-November, nine months into working for Moore, Tom requested a meeting with his control. It had taken him that long, but he had figured things out.

They met in the American's room at the Wyndham in New York. Tom took one look and decided that he didn't like the place. It was too big and gaudy for his taste and he found the food in its restaurant third-rate. For the price McIsaacs was paying, they would have been far better off at the Park Lane with its elegant eatery and Bohemian bar, not to mention the view onto Central Park.

McIsaacs had been adamant and found Tom's objections precious. "This place has better security for us," he said. "It's big and has multiple entrances. It's easy to avoid someone we might know. Nothing to tie us together, if we're careful about how we go."

To Tom's dismay, his Control had ordered club sandwiches and beer for lunch. The food had been delivered before he had gotten there, so the toast was now cold and limp and the beer warm. McIsaacs was apologetic, but in a hurry. He also seemed hungry as he waved Tom into the room.

"I have another meeting late this afternoon so let's eat and talk," he said by way of a greeting. "I know we haven't seen much of each other during the last six months, but you'll have to forgive me. We're stretched thin in my shop man-power-wise and I have to prioritize."

Tom looked around the room, pulling up a chair to the room service table.

"No problem," he said, assuming a slightly mocking, plaintiff voice. "I get it. I'm no longer the new golden boy, just another small cog in a big machine, barely important enough to merit a short 'must-show-the-flag' meeting."

McIsaacs laughed and some of the tension went out of him and the room. His shoulders dropped a little.

"OK, OK, cry me a river," he kidded and sipped his beer

Tom could have felt slighted, but he did not. He understood instinctively that showing some empathy to his hard-pressed control would bank him some brownie points for future use. He made a show of looking at his watch; it showed a few minutes past one pm.

"Give me two hours. I'll be out of your hair by three."

"I can do better. You can stay till four." McIsaacs bit into his sandwich. Tom cracked open his beer and settled back into an armchair.

"Moore's business operates on a very tight budget and he's always just short of money. The margins in the book trade are slim as it is. And he has this highly specialized niche in which he has no real competition. But still, he has an active overdraft that sometimes touches four figures. However, while doing his books, I've gained their trust and I managed to go back several years and discovered an odd but very regular pattern. Regularly, almost predictably, he is able to wipe out his overdraft and it starts all over again."

"How?"

Tom took a breath. "He gets these little bonuses from his Russian supplier."

McIsaacs looked up from his plate, a soggy quarter of limp club sandwich flopped over his broad knuckles.

"Meaning?"

Tom shook his head as though in wonder.

"It is dead simple and brilliant at the same time. He obviously did his research and found a tiny loophole in the rules governing customs and excise taxes. His arrangement with Mezhdunarodnaya Kniga operates on a *barter* basis."

"Barter? What the fuck?"

"His loophole is based on the fact that no actual money trades hands between the Moore Book Company and the Russians. Every second month, Moore sends the Russians bulk shipments of 10,000 pages of English text. It's mostly novels, textbooks, scientific studies, and pamphlets. In return, the Russians send him back 10,000 pages of similar stuff, but in Russian and German."

"Ten thousand pages? I don't get it. You mean books?"

"Yes, often, but it is brokered through as '10,000 pages.' That's how he fills out the customs broker form. 'Gross amount: 10,000 English text pages.' Not books."

"But why?" McIsaacs was puzzled and getting annoyed.

"It's a simple way to avoid any duties. That's the loophole! There is literally no duties on 'text pages.' It is rated as scrap paper. And since no actual money changes hands, just one bulk paper shipment for another, there are no duties to pay."

Tom got up out of his chair.

"Moore receives the bulk pages and then reconstitutes them back into books, novels, textbooks, and scientific journals, and then sells this bulk material at a profit of about 15 percent, which is barely enough to cover his total expenses."

McIsaacs stepped in. "Certainly not enough to support the agents he is running in here. So, what gives? Why are we here, Tom?"

"It's what I discovered." Tom paused for effect, "Every now and then, the Russians slip a very rare book or some desirable print into the bulk bundle. And those are items he can sell at a considerably higher profit."

It was clear by his expression that McIsaacs was skeptical. "So, run it for me."

"Here's an extreme example: Moore sends Moscow a thousand Mickey Spillane, 'Mark Hammer' thriller *pages*, deconstructed hard covers, which cost about fifteen dollars in total. Moscow sends back a thousand pages of illuminated manuscripts of Russian Orthodox liturgy. Moore reconstitutes this material, translates some of it, and goes on a selling trip to peddle the Russian volumes to rare-book dealers across Canada and the US, such as H. P. Kraus or Bernard Quaritch or Louis Caron, for thousands of dollars, and then asks me to deposit the money in his bank to cover his overdraft."

McIsaacs was getting impatient. "OK, so it is a bit weird. He figured out a way to game the customs and duties on rare books. But what's suspicious about all this? Sounds like clever little business. But the Russians, they can't publish Mickey Spillane, what about copyright".

"The Russians, the entire Soviet Bloc, are not signatories to the Bern Convention. They ignore copyright claims and print anything they like!" Tom's voice had gone up a pitch and he realized he was moving too fast and off track. He felt momentarily embarrassed, but quickly recovered, slowing himself down.

"Sorry, Al. I'm a bit excited and I haven't run it for you correctly, didn't give you the whole process," said Tom, calming himself and gathering his thoughts.

"About two months ago, Moore went out on the road with a couple of these rare books. When he returned, he gave me cash and invoices representing about $5,000 to enter into the books and deposit against his overdraft. Later on that day, Moore and Ekaterina were in his office, invoices and receipts and cash spread out on the bureau. I was only able to catch a glance but, there were thousands."

Tom knew he had McIsaacs's attention and sat down, then leaned across the lunch table.

"He's collecting cash for those rare books, reporting part of it so that it looks kosher and he can then use the balance for whatever he wants. On that trip, I estimate that he sold for over $10,000, cash."

McIsaacs shook his head. He wasn't buying it.

"But Tom, how do you know? How do you know he got $10,000?"

"Well, I don't," Tom said. "But, I am putting it together."

"Oh, jeez, Tom" said McIsaacs. "What am I supposed to do with this?"

"No, listen, hear me out," Tom pleaded. "I do the principal books and business ledgers and, after nine months, everything balances to the penny."

"Big deal," moaned McIsaacs, rubbing his eyes.

"Al, you're not listening! I said, everything balances to the penny!"

"So, he's careful with his petty cash?"

"It's a mathematical impossibility, Al. Even a small business like Moore's has some losses, here and there. And Moore is terrible with his petty cash, a disaster! Missing taxi receipts, regular errors in his broker's fee, tips to doormen noted on matchbook covers. But, on the books, there's nothing. The books are impeccable."

"So?"

"So, the only way this can be achieved is to spot the losses, the imbalances, and cancel them with money that isn't accounted for. Money that doesn't exist."

"Proof?" said McIsaacs.

"I suspected that there was a second set of books and I was right. It makes sense, Al. The Russians are not stupid. They know the value of the material they send Moore. They need to know what he gets for it, and the stipends he disburses to their agents has to jibe. Ekaterina keeps the other set of books, in Russian, using special codes that I think I have figured out. When Moore comes back from his trips, the two of them sit in the office and they talk low, in Russian, as she counts the money. He will then ask me how much the current overdraft is and, after a while, she will give me an envelope and deposit slip for exactly the overdraft amount. The balance of the money is put into the safe."

Tom could almost hear the wheels inside McIsaacs's head turning. "What about documentation and such? There must be a paper trail?"

"From one end to the other, nothing that is worth bothering with. Like I said, there is no cash involved, Moscow does not send out invoices in dollars. It only keeps track of the number of *pages*."

The big American got up to pace the room as Tom continued.

"The rare book dealers are a bunch of secretive, extremely closemouthed creatures and they deal in cash. Moore Book Company only invoices for what we deposit in the bank. Our invoices for these specials do not feature details, only code numbers. That's why Ekaterina does that accounting. She's also the one who researches what books should be ordered from Moscow and then sold and for how much."

'Jesus." McIsaacs's brain suddenly went into overdrive. "Do you have access to this information?"

"That's just it, I do not. She keeps it locked up in a safe they have in the basement."

"How often do such special shipments take place?"

"Like I said, on average, every eight weeks."

"Do you ever see the rare books and their titles when they arrive?"

"No. The packages are opened at night and the rare books are hidden until Moore gets ready to go on the road with them. I was told that they did this to make sure they cannot be found by burglars."

"Are they kept in the safe, as well?"

The question surprised Tom. "Come on, Al. Think about it! There are close to 10,000 books on three floors, and in a large, converted garage. Once an item is hidden among them it cannot be found quickly by anyone who doesn't know where to look."

He could see that McIsaacs was impressed, though grudgingly. Tom also sensed that although there was time left in their meeting, his Control appeared preoccupied and eager to see him off.

"Have you got all this down in a case memo?"

"Almost. I was waiting for this meeting before completing it, in case . . ."

McIsaacs scratched his head, thinking.

"Remove all the speculation, or, at least, as much as possible. Stick to the cold facts and the numbers and get it to me before you leave."

Tom reached for his coat.

"There is another little thing, but I don't know what it means, exactly."

McIsaacs raised his head and his pale blue eyes sought out Tom's.

"Moore is very interested in what is going on in Cuba right now. He thinks there are opportunities for locating rare books."

McIsaacs's low voice revealed his full attention.

"Why?"

"The wealthy and middle classes are leaving, in a hurry. Book collections are heavy, bulky, hard to move at the last minute. Moore has the idea that many personal collections will be left behind and that Castro's people will be looking to sell them for cash."

The American didn't need the tableaux to be completed, he could fill in the missing pieces in living color, all by himself.

"Cash," he mused. "Our economics section predicts Fidel and Raoul are running out of cash, even as we stand here. So?"

"Moore mentioned something about me doing a little run down to Havana, to check out the book scene, follow up on contacts that he has."

McIsaacs sat down in a cozy chair and reached for his beer, smiling like he had just grabbed Fidel himself by the beard.

CHAPTER 13

Montreal, 1960

The technician McIsaacs assigned to crack Ekaterina Moore's safe was a dour New Englander called Bowcher from Burlington in upper Vermont. Tall, awkward, and angular with elongated fingers and bad breath caused by rotting teeth from chain-smoking, he exuded doom and gloom. Tom, who had gone to fetch him at the Bleury bus terminal, spotted the man easily, based on McIsaacs's description.

"Bowcher?" said Tom, extending his hand and unconsciously leaning away from the stink coming out of the tall man's mouth.

"Karas?" replied the technician, shaking Tom's hand and responding to the unstated question in his greeting. "It was originally 'Boucher.' Kanuk for 'butcher.'"

The two men exited the bus terminal and grabbed a cab from the line in front. Bowcher never lost hold of the leather grip he was carrying. Ten minutes later, they slipped through the entrance of the Sheraton Mount Royal and headed, separately, to the elevators.

McIsaacs's suite at the Montreal Sheraton was large, cozy, a bit like the man himself. Tom immediately noticed the mickeys of gin, rye, and vodka arrayed on the bathroom vanity and the little bottles of mixers. His American friend had learned not to order drinks from any hotel he stayed in, but to stock his suites with fifths. It was safe to use the mixers from the room fridge. They were innocuous on the hotel bill. McIsaacs liked to stay in large hotels, especially those that had gourmet restaurants. The Sheraton certainly qualified; its *coq au vin* and *ile flottante* were famous, as was its wine cellar.

"The safe we're talking about was manufactured by the Herring, Hall, Marvin Safe Company in Cleveland, Ohio, and imported into Canada about fifty years ago." The toothpick in Bowcher's mouth travelled from the right corner to the left.

"Has the safe been opened recently?"

"Daily," answered Tom, fascinated by the man's ability to manipulate the toothpick.

"What's the model number?"

"I don't know, but I can tell you this: it has three active door-locking bolts, all on one side and an iron interior 'safe' deposit box with a nice oak inner drawer and four more drawers to the side."

Bowcher's toothpick was in motion again, this time from left to right. "I know the model. Piece of cake."

"No operation is a piece of cake," snapped McIsaacs, his mood hardening in the moment. "An infinite number of things can go wrong, so listen up."

He spread out a map of Montreal on the table and placed a meaty finger on Lafontaine Park, with *Plateau Hall* circled in red. Conscious of Bowcher's halitosis, Tom kept some distance, but he could see McIsaacs getting the full benefit of it and he giggled internally.

"The concert the Moores are attending tomorrow night starts at eight sharp and is scheduled to last an hour and a half. There is no intermission so we can be reasonably sure they will not leave the concert hall before nine thirty."

McIsaacs subtly moved downwind of Bowcher, catching Tom's eye, but remaining deadpan.

"They always walk and since it will take them at least twenty minutes to get back home, the two of you will have a comfortable seventy-five minutes inside the house to open the safe, photograph everything that's inside, lock up, and leave."

McIsaacs handed Tom a Minox camera and several film cartridges. Bowcher's eyes traced the trajectory from Jeanne-Mance Street to the concert hall.

"I assume I have to gain access through the front door? What kind of lock and alarm system will I have to deal with?" The safe-cracker sounded pensive.

Tom shook his head. "No. Come in through the rear entrance to avoid being seen from the street." He handed Bowcher a piece of paper. "Here's the code you need to use to disarm the alarm. The keypad is to the right of the door on the wall as you come in."

"And the lock on the door?"

"There are two, both Yale."

Bowcher was about to say "piece of cake" again, but caught himself in time. He almost swallowed his toothpick.

McIsaacs gave him a sour look. "You'll have a Motorola and I'll drop you off at a street corner two blocks from the target at seven-forty-five. Tom will be there, too. You have the address?" Bowcher nodded, the toothpick firmly in place again between his lips.

"We'll have someone watch the house to make sure the Moores leave for the concert as planned. We'll also have someone at the concert-end to make sure they take their seats. When I hear that all's in order I'll give you the 'go-ahead' signal via the walkie-talkie and you'll proceed with the operation." He refolded the map and gave it to the safe-cracker. "Any questions?"

There were none.

McIsaacs took Bowcher to dinner at the restaurant down-stairs, allowing Tom to beg off with a knowing glance. Dinner with Bowcher could only be a stomach-churning adventure.

They got lucky the following day. Moore asked Tom to prepare up-to-date financial statements for a meeting he was having with his bank manager the next day. Tom seized the opportunity. "Actually, I can give you a complete fresh set as at the end of last month if you let me stay and work late. I'll need until ten," he volunteered.

"Sure, but . . ." Moore was puzzled.

Tom explained. "You're going to the concert at eight, right? You may not get back before ten or later."

"Oh! OK, no sweat. You know the code for the alarm, so lock up if you get finished before we get back. After you set the alarm, pull the door closed behind you when you leave and it will lock automatically."

"Where should I leave the statements? It's my day off tomorrow."

"Leave them on your desk. I'll look them over in the morning and call you if I have questions."

*

The operation started off smoothly.

Tom let Bowcher into the house through the back door at eight sharp. The man was in front of the safe by five past the hour, his stomach gurgling and burping repeatedly.

"You missed a hell of a meal last night. I ate like a pig. Couldn't resist having two servings of Floating Island," he confessed as he manipulated the levers, the toothpick firmly planted in the left corner of his mouth, trembling at each rotten belch. "We're almost done," he announced, and ten minutes later, he jerked the safe's door open.

Tom was methodical and swift. He used two goose-necked desk lamps to illuminate his desktop and placed each of the safe items between them. He was very familiar with the Minox and he used the beaded carrying chain to measure the distance and the pocket meter to set the aperture. It took Tom just over forty minutes to photograph everything while Bowcher paced, watching the windows, burping, belching, and now farting, incessantly. Tom wanted nothing more than to see the back of this man and inwardly cursed McIsaacs for choosing him for this job. Bowcher relocked the safe at a quarter past nine, slightly doubled over and farting wetly, clearly in some discomfort.

"Look, I gotta use the can."

Tom pointed down the hallway.

"Make sure you clean up after yourself, flush everything down and make sure it stays flushed. Light a match!"

Tom went back to work on the accounts. A few minutes later, he heard the toilet flush once, then again, and then a third time. The technician emerged and Tom could see, even at a distance, that his face was wet and pale, almost green. Bowcher paused in the corridor, patting his face with a handkerchief. He hefted his leather grip and caught Tom's eye before making for the rear of the building. Tom lost sight of him when the man took the few steps down that led to the back door.

A scant moment later, a loud thud made Tom jump up and run to investigate. He found the safe-cracker lying on his back in the open rear doorway, his body stock still across the threshold, his eyes wide open, his mouth cracked wide in an obscenely exaggerated death grin and his right hand clutching his jacket above his heart.

Tom felt for a pulse and found none. Bowcher had dropped dead from a massive heart attack. Tom checked his watch. It was twenty-two minutes past nine and he figured he had maybe twenty minutes to resolve the situation. He totaled up the possible charges: aiding and abetting forcible entry and robbery and, perhaps, murder . . . his first priority was getting rid of the body. If the Moores got home early, the entire operation would be blown and he would certainly go to jail. He also knew that if he was arrested he could not turn to McIsaacs and company for help. The rules had been made crystal clear. If he ever got caught, they would deny having had anything to do with him, ever.

Controlling his mounting panic, Tom killed the lights, picked up the walkie-talkie Bowcher had dropped, and called his control. McIsaacs listened carefully and simply said, "Cool down, Tom." He was at the house within seven minutes and Tom helped him roll the body into a canvas drop cloth. His driver backed into the driveway and Tom helped McIsaacs stuff the dead safe-cracker into the trunk, but the drop cloth got caught on the trunk lid and it pulled off the dead man's face. Again, Tom found himself staring into that horrible death *rictus*, a death-distorted grin of rotting teeth and seeping green bile.

"Tom," said McIsaacs softly as he covered the safe-cracker's face but the younger man did not answer. "Tom!"

Tom snapped to and found McIsaacs's hands on his shoulders. Instantly, the cold dread left him and his face grew warm.

"Complete the mission."

Tom handed McIsaacs the Minox camera and the exposed film cartridges. As his Control drove off, Tom went back into the house, locked the back door, and returned to his desk to await the Moores' return. He felt incredibly calm and, against his will, his memory went backward over the last half hour in detail, the specter of that grinning corpse lingering like an overlay, illuminating memories far more horrifying than the specter of having to do time in a Canadian prison in peacetime.

Budapest, January 1945.

Wartime deprivation.

Bitter, bitter cold. No food. Utter desperation. What to do? Steal wood, take it home to burn. Starve to death, but at least warm.

No. Forage for wood and food or give up and die in the street.

A ten-year-old Tom climbs into the ruins of a house and is picking at bits of a parquet floor when a Russian soldier spots him. He unslings his Kalashnikov and points it at Tom. "Idji suda—come here."

Tom obeys and is led to a truck. It is a field kitchen. The Russian sergeant in charge speaks German, a language in which Tom is fluent. He tells Tom he'll give him a bowl of hot bean soup and a piece of bread if he comes to work for him. Tom wolfs down the food and is led around the corner where he joins a group of boys aged between ten and thirteen, just like him.

"Robotny, robotny—work, work," says the Russian guarding them, pointing at the frozen cadaver of a German soldier lying in the street. The boys understand. They fan out and begin dragging the cadavers—German soldiers, Russian soldiers, Hungarian soldiers, civilians—toward the nearest intersection. They pile the bodies high.

The Russians douse the pyre generously with gasoline and light it, the flames fanned hot by the crossing wind. Spurred by the mounting heat, the frozen cadavers come to life, their faces, stretched taught by death and the cold, grimace as their jaws work wordlessly. They thaw out and begin to wave, wink, kick, and twist—all for a bowl of hot bean soup and a piece of bread.

CHAPTER 14

Montreal—end of 1960

For six months, Tom could almost begin to believe that working for the Moores was his life. He had successfully compartmentalized the Bowcher affair and wondered if McIsaacs would ever call again. There has been no word on his work, no feedback about his spy craft. Radio silencio.

And then, as the holiday spirit descended on the charming city, the call came. They met at the Holiday Inn on Cote de Liesse road, near Dorval airport. No in-house restaurant, but there was an excellent, quiet steakhouse across the street. Tom understood that this was a touch base, not a social call.

McIsaacs wasted no time getting to the point.

"I suppose you want to know?"

Tom shrugged with professional nonchalance, but couldn't keep the anticipatory smile off his face. McIsaacs spun his thick glass tumbler of scotch around so that the clear ice cubes tinkled.

"Thanks to the financial information and your photos of Ekaterina's records, we were able to ascertain that, last year, Moore 'suppressed' about $150,000 that he then distributed among the five agents he was bankrolling in the US. We've identified the individuals involved."

He paused while Tom took it all in.

"We do not need to do anything rash, but we *will* slowly neutralize them during the rest of this calendar year. Maybe turn one or two of them around. There will be no way to trace any action back to you." His Control held out his hand. "Well done, my friend."

Tom allowed himself a deep breath and shook the American's hand warmly.

"What, about the Moores? To tell the truth, I have grown somewhat fond of them."

McIsaacs laughed, drained his glass, and signaled to the bartender to keep them coming.

"Well, they have broken no Canadian laws except, perhaps, failure to report income. We can't tell the Horsemen what really happened, can we? Not without blowing your cover and dropping you into deep doodoo." The American sighed. "I guess we'll just leave Moore alone. By the end of the year he will have figured out that his network is being rolled up so he'll keep his head down and stay in Canada where he is safe from prosecution."

"With his network gone, he won't be able to make a living, unless he is asked to service other agents."

McIsaacs shrugged and gave Tom one of his special looks. "My heart bleeds. . . . I think you should start to distance yourself from Moore. Tell him you need to move on, to further your career."

"I don't think I should do that."

"Why not?"

Tom began to laugh. "Remember Moore's thoughts about Cuba?"

"Oh, yes," replied McIsaacs, bending closer.

"Moore asked me to go to Cuba for him. He finally wants to start trading with the Castro regime. The embargo does not apply to Canadian persons or companies as long as the goods being traded did not originate in the good old US of A. And, frankly, I've got some business plans of my own."

McIsaacs raised his glass. "Bring me back a box of Monty's, will you?"

CHAPTER 15

Havana, Cuba, September 1968

Tom is blinded by the darkness, locked in solitary, arrested, accused of spying. There is a diesel generator in the prison yard outside his cell and it runs during a power outage. When it turns over he is rendered deaf, as well. All he can hear is the low roar of its motor, all other sounds are drowned, even his shouts for it to stop.

Being this way drives him crazy, makes him feel helpless, totally defenceless, desperate.

But they don't seem to *know*. At least, not yet. During his interrogation sessions they have not asked about his recent trips around Latin America. They are interested only in what he has been up to in Cuba, whom he met and where, what they had to say. Questions easily answered because truthful answers to them are harmless.

His cell is comfortable as cells go, and clean. They force him to sweep it daily with a broom they throw through the slot in the steel door. Three paces by seven, with a steel door at one end and three slits high in the wall at the other. Substitutes for windows that let in some light, air, and noise.

For sleep there's a hinged, horizontal slab of wood held against the wall by chains, no mattress, just a worn blanket. He uses his shoes, suede crepe-soled Hushpuppies as pillows.

It is the generator that is driving him crazy. Tom is not only practically blind in the dark, but slowly going deaf, as well. The low, throbbing, vibrations wash over him in thick, smothering waves and he cannot hear a thing.

He wears orange overalls night and day over his single pair of underwear. He sleeps on his stomach to avoid wracking backache caused by the wooden cot, his arms under his chest, folded, and hands around his shoes. He awakens often to the pain caused when his arms fall asleep.

He stinks.

His jailers give him a bar of soap to wash himself and his clothes. It takes ages for them to dry in the dampness of his concrete cell. He can feel the humid chill of the tiled floor under his feet right up through his sockless shoes. The entire cubicle is cold, especially during the night.

The roar continues. The first hurricane of the season is upon them. Power lines must be down.

He's freezing to death on a tropical island. Tom awakens from a dream of the fluttering of mechanical wings. Confused, he peers over the edge of his sleeping platform, convinced that he is no longer alone. An odd whirring sound followed by a high-pitched "peep" draws his attention underneath. Huddled against the wall, a water-logged tree swallow, a juvenile.

"How did you sleep?"

"Wet."

"How come?"

"The wind drove the rain into my cell, but I didn't mind."

"Why not?"

"It drove a small bird into my cell."

"Through the ventilating slits?"

"Yes."

"Where is it now?"

"In my cell."

"Do you want to keep it?"

Tom doesn't answer

"Tell me about your trip to Nicaragua."

A bombshell of a question! The first inquiry into his regional activities. The real fun has begun.

He fabricates a story about exporting fertilizer. He glances at their faces to see if they are buying what he is selling, but these young Communist functionaries have not had the time or the experience to know if they are really being played or not. A few years ago, most of them were either radical students or working-class underdogs. They are acting as though they know, but they do not know. They are trying to save face and their machismo, and failing at both. Tom has a slight edge: the ten-year-old boy living inside him who survived the hardscrabble existence in post-war Budapest

They return him to his cell. The bird lies on the tiles, his head crushed. A pointlessly cruel and perfectly hamfisted, totalitarian message. Tom is furious and then somewhat relieved that his jailers are even more ignorant than he initially assumed.

Three weeks of silence. The guards don't talk because they do not know what to say, what questions to ask. They just open the steel door four times a day for a few seconds, three times for food and once for the disinfectant liquid they splash into the drain basin beneath the waterspout that doubles as shower and toilet flush. The guards wear slippers so they can't be heard walking up and down the corridors.

Attempts at communicating by voice or tapping are forbidden. Absolute silence, except reveille, at seven, when Jackson in cell number one loudly curses the guard who is trying to wake him up by rattling a broom handle in his spy-hole.

Three weeks of silence punctuated by fear, fueled by his sometimes too vivid imagination, is long. He replays the past months, the trips, the meetings, and the moments with Disda, trying to understand how all of that ended him up here.

Tom knows he must play for time, give the Canadian government time to work on Fidel Castro to let him go. His arrest is now, probably, an inconvenient embarrassment for the Cubans, considering that they could not follow up on their suspicions with hard facts.

Prime Minister Pierre Trudeau is a great friend of Fidel, and Fidel is in love with Margaret, the prime minister's young, pretty, smart and ever-so-charming wife. The trio,

Castro and the Trudeaus, spent four hours deep-sea fishing for blue marlin together during the last state visit. The protocol called for half an hour's fishing. It stretched into four hours! Must mean something, no?

The other question that carousels in Tom's mind like a bad pop song you can't get out of your head is: does anyone give a damn about Tom Karas? His parents, obviously, but the Canadians? Al and the Americans? Only Disda. And now she, because of him, is totally compromised and in the slammer like he is. They had been arrested together.

Bullshit! After three weeks, Tom was trying hard, and failing with each passing day, to avoid accepting the notion that maybe Disda was the reason he was in the stinking, chilly cell and not the other way around. Al had warned him to keep his head down and his cock in his pants, but Tom Karas was never one to ignore the Fates. He should not have ignored Fidel's younger brother, Raúl. And Raúl could not ignore how this Canadian "businessman" Tom Karas had seduced Disda, one of the revolution's great heroines, and perverted her to his ways.

And so the weeks go by and every time they fetch him to visit the barber he panics, fearing he is being taken to the execution yard. That wild imagination. It is a strictly bush-league ploy, but that is where the Cubans are in their counter-intelligence education. They know that uncertainty is Tom's weakness, so they schedule the visit at irregular intervals, hoping that the momentary fear will weaken his resolve.

But he chides himself for his vulnerability and resists, giving them nothing.

There is a checkerboard scratched into the wood of the upper bunk. He uses chewed bread to form little balls and thin tablets with which to play, even in the dark. The guards catch him playing and erase the board with a wood plane.

Finally, a day after his last visit to the barber, the cell-door brusquely opens and his interrogator appears. "Get your things," he orders. "You're being deported."

He grabs his checker pieces and follows the man to a room where he finds his suitcase and, on a table, all his belongings laid out neatly. "Get dressed."

He obeys wordlessly, regretting having to put his clean clothes over his unwashed body. He finds his clean under-wear and manages to toss his stained pair into a corner.

They drive him to the airport where, in the VIP Lounge, Bata, the third secretary of the Canadian Embassy, is waiting for him. There is no warm welcome from Bata, he's all business. "The Brits and Australians fly a diplomatic flight shuttle between Nassau and Havana every Wednesday. We've arranged for you to be on today's flight."

Tom mumbles his thanks, collapses into an armchair, and looks around. They're not alone. A number of men from MININT—the Ministry of the Interior, the state security apparatus, wearing *verde y olivo* uniforms—are milling about, pretending that they're examining the pictures on the walls and the periodicals strewn about the room while constantly flicking their eyes his way. One of them walks over to him and Tom prepares himself to be the brunt of another cruel mind trick until he recognizes, with a shock, that he's one of Disda's friends, with whom they had frequently dined in the past. "Telmo," he blurts out. "Oh, my God. You're one of them!"

"Yes, and you are too, now."

"How can you say that? I don't work for MININT."

Telmo's smile is deprecating, pitying. "That's not what I mean, Tomás. I mean you have now experienced what it is to be locked up, helplessly waiting to be executed."

"Have you?"

"Under Batista's regime, yes. Except that, unlike you, I was often tortured." Telmo holds out his fingers. They are deformed, most of his nails are missing. Tom sighs, patting the man's shoulder. He looks around, slowly scanning the room and when he speaks he does not look at Telmo.

"How close did I get?"

"Close."

"Why didn't they finish me? It's not like they needed any evidence."

Telmo snorts, a wry smile creasing his handsome revolutionary face.

"Ask your girlfriend Disda."

Bata intervenes. "Mr. Karas, it's time to go." He hands Tom ham sandwiches in a paper bag. "There is no food service on the plane and, from the looks of you, you must be very hungry."

"Yes, I am." Tom, suddenly overwhelmed by suppressed emotions, fights back tears as he shakes Bata's hand. "Thank you for everything," he whispers and heads for the plane.

CHAPTER 16

Havana, Cuba

Ray Moore had followed up on his suggestions and Tom Karas first got to Havana in mid-1960, about a year and a half after Fidel Castro had come to power. Moore had arranged for a ticket on Pan Am to Havana via Miami, but when Tom arrived there he had found that Pan Am had suspended all flights to Cuba and that he had to fly BWIA to reach his destination.

After the airplane rolled to a stop in front of the terminal at the former Rancho Boyeros Airport in the outskirts of Havana, now renamed Aeropuerto Internacional Jose Marti, they opened the doors and Tom found himself overwhelmed by a pleasantly rich, sweet scent that he could not initially identify. The memory of that perfume, his first whiff of fresh vanilla it turned out to be, would haunt him for the rest of his life.

The airport terminal may once have been charming, and even after eighteen months of destruction and neglect, it was still comfortably at the head of the class of Third World aerodromes. There were not many "gringo" travelers coming off the plane and Tom tried to meld into the background as much as possible. He was dressed in very plain beiges and browns, sensible desert shoes, no jewelry, nothing flash. He approached the counter of the teenaged immigration officer and presented his passport. He noticed the boy would not meet his eyes so Tom gave him a supplicant profile to peruse. When the lad spoke, it was almost too fast for Tom to grasp and so he decided to play up the gringo aspect.

"¿Cual es el propósito de tu visita?"

"Sorry, I do not speak Spanish."

The boy officer hesitated for a second and then, with a spark of pride, came alive.

"WadisthepurposeofyourvisittoCubaseñor?"

Tom was so taken aback by the linguistic acrobatics that he almost laughed, but he managed to keep his mirth hidden.

"Business? Tourism?"

The young officer appeared to be checking Tom's passport with close scrutiny, perhaps eager to find a bribe.

"Señor, indique el motivo principal de su visita a Cuba hoy."

Tom cocked his ear with a smile and the boy sighed, repeating.

"SeñorwhatistheprincipalreasonforyourvisittoCubatoday?"

"Tourism. Principally. But, I am also looking for business opportunities between Canada and Cuba."

The young man reacted as though Tom's Canadian passport had been insufficient. He looked Tom directly in the eye, his handsome face suddenly all smiles.

"Canada? Ah, Canada! Montreal?"

His passport received the dubious pleasures of several hearty stamps and smudges as well as a few initials and he was directed to the waiting taxi rank.

"¡Bienvenido a Cuba, territorio libre de America!"

Tom had read all the recent press reports on post-revolutionary Cuba, as well as the dossiers prepared for him by his Control at the Agency. He had thought he was prepared, but he was not. Instead of a reborn, functioning, socialist society, Tom found a fledgling dictatorship, in thrall of the "Bearded One" and his charismatic Argentinian goon, "Ché," still finding its legs and trying desperately to cleanse itself of the lingering after-effects of centuries of corruption and failed attempts at democratic autonomy. The streets and parks were alive with hundreds of thousands of young people, still high on what a handful of committed rebels had achieved and blithely ignoring the efforts of their own parents to flee the country with whatever they could. Tom was prepared for the low level of abilities and intelligence in those to whom the reins of power had been ceded. He had seen the same in post-war Hungary and Europe, where the Communists had made it an obsession to liquidate anyone with a modicum of intelligence and experience. Those left behind to pick up the pieces were often not of the highest caliber. He amused himself remembering Marx's adage that history repeats, first as a tragedy, and then this time, it would appear, as a Latin farce.

During the ride to his hotel, he tried to engage his driver by talking with him about Jose Marti, the famous Cuban-born poet, considered a national hero and an important figure in Latin American literature. "He was also politically active and perceived to be an important revolutionary philosopher and political theorist," the driver said in English, surprised that a Canadian, who had never been in Cuba before, would know about the man. Tom tried to switch the conversation back into Spanish, but found that he needed practice before being able to maintain meaningful conversation in that language. Cubans, he learned, not only spoke very rapidly, but also had a tendency to swallow their s's.

In the Cuban capital, echoes of revolutionary fervor were still in evidence everywhere. The walls had been blitzed with the most childish, naïve slogans and pictograms.

Tom had a reservation at the Havana Hilton, now called Hotel Havana Libre, a spanking new, twenty-five-story building opened with great fanfare less than a year before Fidel Castro came to power. In fact, Castro used the hotel, situated kitty-corner to the well-known Coppelia ice cream parlor, as his headquarters for a while during the early days of his rule. At the time of the regime change, the Havana Hilton was Latin America's tallest and largest hotel. It boasted a Trader Vic's restaurant as well as a casino, supper club, pool and rooftop bar.

As Tom entered the lobby, the Latin farce was apparent. It appeared that most of the staff had stayed on, but not the direction and management class, the "bourgeoisie." They had fled and already the hotel was shabby, dusty, and dull, and smelled of the kitchen. Only three elevators worked out of six. The staff were sullen, taciturn, and suspicious.

This was the error that Fidel and Raúl had committed and that so many other revolutionary regimes had made and would continue to make through history. Middle-class management was held in low esteem compared to the working classes, those who actually toil and sweat for their daily crust. So it was no concern of the revolution that managers, directors, and owners of companies were fleeing in hordes as long as the real workers remained. After all, the workers knew their respective businesses even better than their bosses, no? The regime did not understand that the so-called "real workers" had not been formed to manage. They had no organizational skills outside their work titles, no wider vision of how things are run, and no sense of service and no motivation since all industries and sectors had been nationalized. On his way up to his room on the seventeenth floor, Tom gave his Spanish another try, but the bellboy driving the elevator immediately switched to English.

The next day, Tom went for an exploratory stroll and found the casino, the supper club, and Trader Vic's closed. The hotel's cafeteria had been divided into two: the so-called inner section was reserved for *estrangeros*—foreigners. You had to show your passport to get in. All were equal, but some were more equal than others. A year and half in and this primarily agrarian society was already running short of some food items. Bacon, ham, and eggs were becoming scarce in the capital. What ended up on Tom's breakfast plate was barely edible, but the morning coffee was good. As Tom got up to leave, he noticed the staff alert and hovering, but pretending nonchalance. He stopped at the door to look back and his stomach gave a little turn as he watched the waiter drop his uneaten breakfast into plastic bags that were then covered by napkins to be secreted away. Not yet the bowl of hot bean soup and stale bread, but that was certainly coming.

One of Moore's contacts, a librarian by the name of Cañisares, was operating out of the Bacardi building in downtown Havana that the revolutionaries had "borrowed temporarily." Tom called on him and found that Señor Cañisares was now a buyer of pharmaceuticals and had ceased to have anything to do with buying or selling books. Cañisares insisted that they not stay in his office, but take their conversation outside.

They went for coffee at a street-level stand where Cañisares continuously scanned the people within earshot while explaining that the revolutionary government intended to centralize the purchase of all material from outside Cuba through a company called ECUBIM: *Empresa Cubana de Importaciones.*

Tom was amused by his host's restlessness. "You expecting someone?"

Cañisares sighed then allowed himself a little smile.

"At any moment." He drained his espresso. "I am tolerated. We are of the 'tolerated' classes, but it will not last. I know my country. The people, her needs, and the needs of the revolution. But I don't kid myself. I'm not Black enough and even if I were, my family were strictly upper class. We are useful to the regime until we are not. In the time left here, I just need to salt away enough for the rest of my life."

Tom thanked him and headed for the Canadian embassy in the Vedado district to register, just in case. His conversation with Cañisares brought home, once again, how totalitarian governments worked.

Tom spent the next ten days bumming around the city, visiting the sights that also included restaurants, bars, and nightclubs. He made it a point to use as many cabs as possible during his meanderings because experience had taught him that taxi drivers were major sources of information all over the world. Since he spoke Spanish fluently (eight years of studying Latin in Jesuit high school had made it easy for him to pick up the language at McGill), he had no difficulty communicating with them, especially since many of them spoke some English. His problem was not to *speak* the language, but to *understand* the rapid-fire responses to his questions.

As an initial expedition, his visit was a modest success. He managed to go down Moore's list of contacts and found that the majority of them were either cooling their heels in Miami or, like Cañisares, no longer in the book business. As for rare books? A few small shops remained open under threat of nationalization. Anything rare had either been "donated" to the nation or had simply vanished into countless down-market houses and apartments, where they were kept as a potentially valuable items for exchange. What was much more important was the confidence that had grown within Tom that he could move in this society-in-flux, that he could "deal," and seize the opportunities as they surfaced. Cuba had begun to feel familiar.

"Stay away from Cuba for a couple of months," McIsaacs ordered Tom upon his return to Montreal. "Shit is happening, purges, re-education camps, forced resettlement. Let the chaos settle some more, then we'll see what we'll do."

The CIA safe house was near the Forum in Montreal. "Our political analysts in Cuba section feel that Fidel will turn to the middle class and ask them to intervene and help the *Castristas* develop a democratic way of governing."

"That's pure bullshit." Tom was adamant. "I was just there! The middle class are leaving in droves for Miami. The country is crawling with Chinese, Russians, North Vietnamese. Fidel is trying them all on for size, seeing which one fits. Besides, Fidel's best buddy and comrade-in-arms, Ché Guevara, is an ardent Communist. Those two are joined at the hip."

McIsaacs shrugged. "I might agree, but the Cuban Section has spoken. Ours is not to reason why."

Tom's next trip to Cuba was booked for October so he had ample time to settle old business in Montreal. He stayed close to home for a few weeks to satisfy his mother and placate his father, who was puzzled by his son's interest in what he considered a "failed state."

"There are good opportunities for business, Father."

"I would think that someone with your education and experience would be able to find profitable opportunities right here? What about your boss, Moore?"

Indeed, what about Moore?

Tom had invited the Moores to meet him at Le Paris, an authentic, family-style bistro on St. Catherine Street run by a French family who knew their onions. When the Moores appeared in the doorway, Tom noticed their reduced state immediately.

"So, nothing?" Moore asked plaintively.

"I think your notion was a good one, but we were just a few months too late. Every single one of your contacts was either no longer in the country or had moved on to more lucrative businesses."

Ekaterina shrugged her rounded shoulders and attacked her *rognons de veau sauce moutarde* with gusto. Moore himself was more tentative, picking restlessly at his *pavée de saumon, sauce beurre blanc.*

"And how have you been?"

Moore squirmed a little. "Things have turned against us lately. Our American clients do not seem interested in what we have to sell. I hope this will not be a disappointment to you, but I'm afraid we will not be able to make use of your services."

Tom felt a twinge of regret, but also triumph. *You little Commie weasel*, he thought.

"But, how will you . . . ?"

Moore waved off his concern with a little smile. "It's just a little drop. We'll be back soon and I do hope we can call on you?"

Tom paid the bill and led them out onto the sidewalk into a lively crowd of citizens enjoying the soft air of an Indian summer evening. He tried to hail them a cab, but, again,

Moore waved it off. Tom watched the couple as they made their way down the street, arm in arm, fading into pointless penury. Better than a bullet in the back of their head. Years later he heard that Moore and Ekaterina had scraped together enough money to make their way back to Russia where they disappeared up someone's blacklist.

A week before he was to return to Cuba he spotted Pamela at an art gallery *vernissage* at Sir George Williams College. Tom was trailing his latest convenient, winsome blond and could see that Pamela was being well attended to by a square-jawed block of a beast. The engagement ring, though garnished with a minuscule diamond of poor quality, was hard to miss as Pamela kept her hand at her neck, stroking her pale skin in an attempt to appear bored. He was about to walk over to congratulate her, but she stopped him in his tracks with a cold, hard stare and an almost imperceptible shake of her head. Chastened, Tom made small talk with his date until Pamela and the Beast left. His blond was a perceptive creature.

"Someone you know?"

"Knew."

With the last dangling strings of his past either cut or tied up in a bow, Tom, like a good soldier, obeyed his control and went back to Havana in October. His first stop: the Canadian Embassy.

It was now very obvious that the revolution had started to affect the lives of ordinary people in many negative ways, which the regime tried to cover up by flooding the landscape with ridiculous posters and billboard slogans and graffiti. The food supply chain had broken down and was exacerbated by Kennedy's executive order placing a trade embargo on the island nation. Women from respectable families were fucking for food and Tom made a sport of spotting them. Divorced people were forced to continue to sleep in the same bed due to a serious housing shortage. Members of the middle class, now referred to as *gusanos,* worms, were continuing to flee in large numbers, leaving their belongings behind.

"In descending order of importance, the Cuban economy's five pillars are tourism, sugar, tobacco, cattle and nickel," said the Canadian Embassy's third secretary and commercial attaché, Chuck Bata, who had invited Tom for dinner at the Gato Tuerto, a popular eatery in Havana's Vedado district, where, according to well-informed sources, the food was still edible.

"Tourism is tanking as are all the service industries because of the unrest here, world sugar prices are plummeting, rumors about a coming agrarian reform are causing important landowners to curtail sowing, which will impact tobacco growing and cattle breeding."

"So what will happen?"

"The US government doesn't like Castro and has imposed this fucking trade embargo in retaliation for the nationalization of US-owned businesses. The American are chasing Castro into the open arms of the Soviets." Bata mopped up what remained on his plate of *arroz con pollo* and gulped down his beer.

"Really. So what should a businessman do? Quit and go home?"

"No. There are opportunities for smart intermediaries like you, especially if they are Canadian citizens." The attaché ordered coffee, brandy, and cigars. "Don't cast a wide net like the others do. Specialize."

Tom nodded. He was finally getting somewhere. "For example?"

"Why don't you go and see my friend Arasosa at Cubatransport? It's a division of ECUBIM." Bata lit his cigar, a Romeo & Julietta. "You'll find him on the third floor of the Bacardi building downtown. Do you know where it is?"

Tom nodded. That's where he had met Cañisares, Moore's contact, during his first visit. "What does this guy Arasosa do?"

"Buys tires."

Tom knew the routine by now. He met Arasosa at the Bacardi building office, but as soon as they started to talk business, he was invited out for coffee. Arasosa was a fast-talking, deeply tanned, bald Cuban of Middle-Eastern and Chinese extraction. Thin and wiry, he gave the impression of being in constant movement, even when at ease.

"You've seen the carts they use to transport the cut stalks of the sugar cane from the field to the *central,* where the sugar cooking—melting the sugar out of the stalks—takes place?"

"Yeah, sure. They use those carts for everything. Tobacco, fruit . . ."

"The tires for the carts are manufactured exclusively in the US and, now, because of the *maldito* embargo, are unavailable for Castro's Cuba."

Tom took out his notebook. "Just give me the specs and I'll source them in Canada."

Arasosa smiled indulgently, shaking his head slowly. "You will not make a penny, my friend. Those are very special tires. Made for the airplane industry. You think any of our farmers have that kind of money?"

Tom looked up from his notebook, his pen hovering uselessly.

"So?"

Arasosa slowly drew out his cigar case, and offered Tom a brandless panatella.

"The Douglas Aircraft company built these airplanes during WWII. Maybe you have heard of them? DC2? DC4?"

"Yeah, sure."

"They roll on these special tires, 11.25x28 inches. Some are Goodyear. Some are Goodrich. Eleven-and-a-quarter by twenty-eight inches. Aircraft landings are very hard on tires. By law, they have to be discarded after a specified number of landings, even if they are still good. They are piled up in dumps all over the world."

Arasosa got up to return to his office. "I'll buy all you can send me."

Tom set up a Montreal receiving and shipping office and asked his control for a list of the location of every aircraft landing strip, runway, and depot in the American theatre of WWII, Korea and the current debacle in Vietnam. Using this list, Tom began to scour the world and found that the landing gear of all DC2 and DC4 aircraft were fitted with the same size caliber tires: 11.25x28 inches.

Contacted by phone and cable, the dump owners were only too glad to get rid of their piles of tires for almost nothing. Tom used this new business venture as an excuse to travel the world. He toured dumps from Alaska to the Philippines to Guam to Sicily to Texas and bought up as many used tires as he could for eventual shipment to Cuba. This activity gave him the perfect cover for his frequent legitimate returns to Havana, which Control appreciated.

To diversify, he also began to sell special, hard-to-find, non-US-made tires: for the Havana police's Harley Davidson motorcycles (the tires had to have suction cups on their walls so as not to skid while cornering sharply) and for the Cuban *nomenklatura*'s vehicles—the Castro brothers' and their ministers' forty-eight-odd Oldsmobiles.

Within two years, Tom Karas was the Tire Prince of Cuba.

CHAPTER 17

Havana, Cuba, December 1968

There was a short walk across the scorching tarmac to the waiting BWIA Metroliner. Tom was weak with fatigue and mental stress and stumbled awkwardly when he reached the mobile stairs. He would have fallen had the British Embassy's third secretary accompanying him not offered a kind, steadying hand. "Easy, old chap," he said. "There's no rush. The plane will not take off without us." His gentle attempt at humor fell on Tom's deaf ears. He was in shock, almost totally out of it.

It was only after the co-pilot announced that they were out of Cuban airspace that Tom relaxed. He wolfed down his sandwiches and napped for half an hour without uttering a word. In Nassau, his diplomatic guide dropped him off at the Royal Victoria Hotel, where he checked in using his American Express card. He was still amazed that the Cubans had not confiscated it, and all his other cards, but he chalked it up to another of their maddening idiosyncrasies. A note from Control in the coded guise of a "Welcome to Nassau" card eased his mind and reminded him that a debrief was expected.

Once settled in his room he called his parents. His mother began to sob when she heard his voice. This surprised him because neither of his parents were given to displaying overt emotion, at least not toward him. Of course, he knew why. He had made it clear time and again that he wanted to have as little to do with them as possible, convinced as he was, that love of any kind was unforgivable weakness. Tom knew that they tacitly agreed, as least in theory, and so he was puzzled when from time to time, in situations such as the current one, their agreement broke down and their emotions bubbled to the surface.

He spent a half-hour speaking first to his mother to calm her down then to his father, who began to remonstrate about having probably pushed "the confines of the envelope," as he put it, too far.

"Dad, I'm tired," he interjected after a while. "Let's talk about all this after I get home."

"And when will that be?"

"In a day or two. I'll let you know tomorrow night," he replied and hung up, proud of having stuck to his principles regarding "love."

But, oh, how the Fates mock the pretensions of Magyar schoolboys with skinned knees, runny noses, and faces twisted by tears and fatuous notions of betrayal. Never fall in love. Except once, with Disda. And he was duly punished for it. Disda, as well.

Disda. He could have put her off, as he had done with all the others, through his callous disregard, his habitual indifference. Instead, he let her follow him down that rank, banal, sickly sweet rabbit hole with the crude hand-painted sign above it, proclaiming, "Romance." He should have resisted and kept his distance, but he couldn't because he was also smitten. Laid out, emptied of all resistance, like a rube at a carnie midway. The unbearable ache of guilt twisted round his heart.

"Disda, where are you now," he mumbled. "Did they lock you up like me? Are you being tortured? Will you and your children be shunned by the regime forever? How will you live? Suspected. Observed. Uninvited to the glorious revolution." The guilt wound tighter and tighter around that malnourished lump in his chest.

He stripped off his clothes and took the first warm shower in over two months, feeling the salt of his sweat pass over his lips, luxuriating in the warm spray and marveling about having gotten out of a terrifyingly dangerous situation almost sane and sound. Then, like a coin flipping through the air on the point of a lousy bet, his emotions flipped from self-congratulation back to intense blame.

It had taken six years of his back and forth between Montreal and Havana before that tossed coin had finally landed against his bet. Now, in this deluxe, five-star confessional, Tom, the perfect accountant, could not stop his own internal, immoral audit. He had used Disda shamelessly as his alibi while he helped people hiding in the Caves of Bellamar to escape from Fidel's clutches via cigarette boat; he provided an anti-Castro group with shoulder-born Hudson sprayers and herbicides with which to destroy acres and acres of tobacco plants in Pinar del Rio Province; he had befriended the manager of the Posada Monumento Nacional, a hot pillow establishment, who let him watch—*inter alia*—the antics of a sadistic female major serving in the Soviet Army's rocket division who enjoyed beating up her Hungarian male lover, and, after, bragging about top-secret details of her job; and finally, his *chef d'oeuvre*, the rigging of explosives at the Santa Clara "Imput" Soviet Truck Hub that destroyed dozens of vehicles, seriously setting back Russian efforts to complete the rocket-launching facilities at San Cristóbal.

He had done these things and more during the nights Disda covered for him by pretending that he was with her, asleep at her side, in her Edificio Lopez Cerrano apartment.

Tom braced himself against the shower stall as he felt the floor being to sway. "What, oh, what have I done to you, my beloved?" he kept repeating while his knees gave out and he sank slowly to the tiled basin, the tears finally coming, ragged and convulsive. The tears of a person unaccustomed to crying. Disda must have kept her mouth shut, he thought, and began to shake as it slowly dawned on him how close he had come to losing his life.

CHAPTER 18

Havana, Cuba. 1964

Adisdania Flores, Duque de Estrada, AKA "Disda."
Tom had met Disda in 1964, the year he started to diversify out of the tire business because competition from Japan and the UK was beginning to squeeze his margins. He was navigating two revenue streams in Cuba: tire salesman and clandestine intelligence agent for the NSA.

In Montreal, his modest used tire import/export and fulfillment operation had sprouted quills and was now home to several partners in a fast-growing accountancy concern in which he played the role of rainmaker. Fun for a young, footloose clerk, but also a life of acute tectonic pressure from all quarters.

His partners in the budding concern were a combination of fellow graduates from McGill and a couple of independents who were tired of facing another day of working alone in dingy, brown offices. Tom also had the insight to sniff around Sir George Williams University computer science faculty, where he dislodged a couple of keen, young, budding computer engineers and tasked them with developing accounting, management, and payroll systems to offer clients in need of such services. The firm invested in one of the first IBM terminals in Montreal and Tom negotiated computing time with several universities.

The concern soon found its footing with the senior and junior partners finding their individual roles without too much friction. His main ally, the man on whom he relied most heavily, was Harley Hampton, an alumnus from the McGill CA program and a solid numbers man. But it was Tom who established the tone, the attitude, and the character of the firm. He was the rainmaker by default. It is a given that most CAs, even very successful ones, lack culture. They spent so much of their youth with their noses to the grindstone that they forgot about art, theater, music, the culinary arts and popular culture. Most can't even dress themselves properly. Any firm that deals on a one-to-one basis with clients needs a key person with culture and polish, a person who could speak with sophisticated clients in the same idiom. And that was Tom.

Tom found the office space in a chic, beautifully restored, turn-of-the-century building in Old Montreal. Tom supervised the interior design, chose the Canadian artwork that hung on the walls, picked the color swatches for the carpets, and hired the support staff. Tom taught the younger partners how to dress and groom themselves, coached them how to order correctly in fine restaurants, what wine to suggest and which fork to use. He made some of them change their look, change their manner of speaking, their posture and leisure activities. He poured much of himself into the concern and was gratified when it started to gain traction in Montreal's burgeoning, competitive business world.

At the time, Tom still lived alone. His apartment was close to his parents' home in Montreal, though he seldom saw them more than once a month. He had no siblings, no close extended family and no more, "main squeezes," having convinced himself that he had no time for lengthy liaisons. His disapproval of love, and the weakness it bred, was fixed in his mind more than ever. He had the convictions of an arrogant and unseasoned youth that his position was righteous. Strings of hasty one-night stands provided only fleeting moments of intimacy and allowed him to validate his wager that love was weakness, even if he stacked the odds in his favor.

No close friends. Well, there was Leo Rosenberg, but his relationship with Tom had become somewhat strained and ambiguous. His control had made it clear that Leo was to know nothing of Tom's activities. And yet it was also clear from the way McIsaacs referred to Leo that the technician, who had moved on from the laboratory, was still employed in some manner by the agency.

Whenever Tom was back in Montreal, Leo uncannily turned up. They would meet, seemingly by chance, serendipitously, in a bar or café, at a party or concert. Sure, these could easily be brushed off as the foreseeable intersection of their social orbits, but Tom always had the feeling that serendipity had an organizing mentation. They still booked time together occasionally, and although Leo never asked him anything specific about his work, he seemed to have an idea. Leo had a way of looking into Tom's eyes that made the accountant want to open up. Of course he resisted the impulse. Still, it was almost as though Leo knew everything that Tom was up to, without knowing anything.

Tom was unaware of the constant stress under which he was laboring until it started to affect him. Deep sleep was eluding him and, consequently, he was often tired during the day and not as sharp as he should have been. He often felt shaky on his pins and slightly out of phase with the world around him. He kept such feelings to himself, having no one in whom to confide.

In any case, he reasoned, how could he resolve his official and *sub-rosa* activities with an intimate life with anyone? So, no close friends, only acquaintances, of which there were many, far too many, without true, human contact, which is the way Tom wanted it. The Fates look down with unbridled mirth at such arrogance and descend, in a relentless gyre, on the unsuspecting and contemptuous, carrying with them that which brings those, such as Tom, to their knees. And so, as a rejoinder to his arrogant certainties, the universe devised a divine ordeal and placed Disda on Tom's path toward foolish misanthropy.

Tom had no way of knowing his true destiny as he sipped his pre-lunch mojito on the patio of his hotel's swimming pool. Despite the deprivations of the post-revolutionary period, Cuba was again coming to life, financed by its burgeoning relationship with the Soviet Bloc and other countries in the Communist sphere. They were all here now, lounging around the pool, the potato-white, sunburnt, bloated *nomenklatura,* the more austere Vietnamese, and the chubby, fussy Chinese.

The local girls had been quick to adapt to the new reality; after all, one cannot live on revolutionary doctrine alone. It was the rare foreigner who did not have a Cuban girl on his arm. Some of these couples appeared to be genuinely attached, and in fact, the number of international families was growing.

Tom didn't know whether to snort in derision or moon with envy. He laughed out loud when he was caught by the realization that he had created a life for himself in which, in the midst of unbelievable social *sang und klang,* of *va-et-vient,* he was living a solitary, emotionally arid life, devoid of intimate human companionship. The question which nagged at him, having finally achieved his island-like status: was he happy? Or was happiness, like love, an emotion for the weak and needy?

Tom loved no-one, trusted no-one, except, perhaps, McIsaacs. And even that was a maybe. Happy? What did that even mean? Who the fuck was happy?

After lunch on the patio at the Havana Libre, he left the hotel, turned right and right again, then headed for the Malecón along Calle 23, Twenty-third Street, called *La Rampa* in popular parlance. He eschewed the uniform of short-sleeved shirt and chinos favored by most of the foreign commercial travellers who peddled their wares in Havana, opting instead for super lightweight, 6.5-ounce tropical worsted wool suits with Brooks Brothers, 4.5-ounce Pima cotton shirts, and old-school silk ties to match. He had dressed in order to show respect toward the person he was scheduled to meet. Clara Leyva was the head of MAQUIMPORT, the agency responsible for purchasing spare parts for the myriad machines that kept the country functioning and he needed to make a good impression.

A late afternoon breeze was blowing landward and he was glad of it. It would keep him cool while he walked downhill for two blocks to reach the *Comercio Exterior* building.

As usual, the elevator was not working. Elevators: the first casualties of revolutions. This meant a climb of some forty stairs to the second floor and a guarantee that he'd be glistening with sweat by the time he got to his destination. Though Tom was fit and slim, the humid air drew the sweat out of every gringo—but, curiously, not the Cubans.

The receptionist, an incongruously obese, middle-aged woman with badly dyed blond hair piled in a beehive and sweat-dissolved eyeliner coursing down her cheeks, made him wait for a couple of minutes before acknowledging his presence with a curt, unfriendly "Si?"

Ah, the continuing revenge of the Cuban underclass. Prior to the revolution, a woman like this receptionist would have been fortunate to have found employment in the service industries or, if she had skilled hands, would be a *despalilladora* in a tobacco factory. Now, she had a cushy government job where the most trying part of her day was conquering the forty steps from the lobby to her desk.

He swallowed hard to control his temper and forced a smile. "I have an appointment with *Compañera* Clara Leyva at four."

"She's not here."

"Pardon me, *señorita*, but my appointment was made through the Canadian Embassy. *Señor* Bata's secretary made it."

This got the secretary's attention.

"You a friend of *Señor* Bata?"

Tom took a deep breath. "I'm his cousin, actually," he lied shamelessly.

Impressed, the receptionist reached for the phone. "Let me see what I can do. Sit down, please." She indicated the armchairs around a low table opposite.

Tom chose a chair with its back facing half away from the receptionist, indicating that he was unhappy about his welcome. A copy of *Gramma*, the Cuban Communist Party's official daily, was lying on the table. He picked it up and, with a resigned sigh, immersed himself in the verbatim transcript of the three-hour speech that Fidel, *Lider Massimo* of the nation, had delivered the night before on *la Plaza de la Revolución* to 250,000 true believers.

Much sooner than he expected, a voice came from directly behind him.

"*Señor* Karas?"

Caught off guard, he jumped to his feet, spun around, and was struck dumb.

Adisdania Flores, Duque de Estrada.

Tom could not see the affirmative smirk on the receptionist's face as she logged Tom's reaction. She also had her running tally of the men struck mute at the first sight of Adisdania Flores, Duque de Estrada, AKA, "Disda."

Coup de foudre—clobbered by lightning!

There are perhaps hundreds of thousands, maybe millions, of men and women who would have been unmoved by Adisdania Flores. They would have found her pleasant enough, even pretty, if pressed to describe her, but they would not have seen the devastating *Kali* that confronted Tom at that moment. Millions would not have felt the mighty blow, like to the solar plexus, of primordial heat and lust and desire that shot through Tom.

And yet, what was she? A woman, statuesque in her perfect heels. Beautiful, impossibly beauty that worked its way behind Tom's eyes, blitzing his optic nerve. Sparkling, emerald-hazel eyes, narrowed with humor, were looking him over openly. Her nose, finely wrought, perfect above a full, carnal mouth in a gorgeous, perfectly symmetrical oval face, surrounded by blond hair caught up in a ponytail behind.

She was wearing a long-sleeved white silk blouse that showed off her form to advantage. A wide black belt above a green, knee-length skirt, matching her eyes in color, completed her outfit. In a country where taste and design had been displaced by penury and brutality, she was an exotic.

Her lushly curved body belonged to her in the manner of a person so confident of their physical allure, it was no longer a concern.

"*Señora* Leyva?" he stammered.

The woman burst out laughing, and extended her hand. Tom took it and noticed it was slender, dry, and smooth, yet the handshake was supple and strong.

"Oh, no, *Señor* Karas, you could not confuse us. My name is Disda and I´m her assistant. She is the head of MAQUIMPORT and quite a bit older than me. She was called away urgently at the very last moment and cannot meet with you today."

Disda made a point of looking down and Tom realized to his embarrassment that he was still holding her hand. Seeing the disappointed look on his face, she added, "Please sit down and let me at least offer you a cup of coffee."

He recovered his wits. "I accept as long as you keep me company while I drink it."

Ignoring the receptionist, they drank their tepid espressos looked each other over with mounting tension and chatted. They did not hear the Fates laughing as Tom fell totally and passionately in love, never suspecting that their meeting marked the beginning of a physically and emotionally intense relationship that would end tragically just four years later.

As the work day faded into evening, Tom and Disda took their chat out of the office building and into the street. Disda directed them to an acceptably good restaurant off the Malecón that party cadres frequented and, in the tradition of so many great romances, the two spent the evening and the night pulling back the curtains of their lives and revealing the secrets behind.

Idealism had been the overriding dynamic of Disda's life, just as cynicism had been Tom's. Neither life had been easy and both had paid dearly for their beliefs. The difference was that cynicism gives permission to negate Forster's admonition to "only connect," so Tom could convince himself that his flight from human connection was justified. Idealism decrees that "Everything is connected!" Disda had paid dearly for the idealism that had led her to join Fidel's revolutionary movement.

From the restaurant, the lovers walked down the Malecón, not arm in arm like the other refugees from austerity, but close, their eyes fixed on each other, as though to indelibly imprint their forms, faces, and expressions on each other, to be branded by longing. Disda was fortunate. Her teenage years in the mountain and forests serving *El Lider Maximo* guaranteed her a job and certain privileges, one of which was an airy, tenth-floor apartment in the art-deco López Serrano building. But Disda was not ready. She needed to be sure, at least a bit more certain, that the trim, handsome gringo with the wry smile and devastating sense of humor, was for real. She recognized his emptiness, almost from the first handshake, but that did not concern her much. Many of her lovers had been pretty on the outside, but cold and aloof and guarded, wounded to the core, like her. The animal attraction was there, but was there more to this Tom Karas? Was there enough?

She took Tom by the hand and they headed for the port, where they joined a small group of Cubans as they boarded an old, tiny diesel ferry headed for Regla, a working-class neighborhood at the base of the port. They pressed close together and watched the dull, hazy glow of Havana's few lights grow dimmer. There was no moon so, how to explain the azure light in Disda's eyes? The faceted reflections on her full lips? They moved even closer as the sea breeze chilled them and Tom put his arm around her shoulders, aroused by the heat and perfume coming off her body as she nuzzled his neck, finding his scent delicious.

Tom walked her to her apartment building, the formerly luxurious, art-deco designed Serrano, fully expecting to be asked in for a nightcap and more. Disda stopped at the front door, a hand on his chest as she arched her back and stretched her lips up to his.

"I would invite you in, but I have a little family drama going on in my flat."

Tom was amused. "A littler *drama* was what I was hoping for."

Disda laughed and kissed him again. "No, you don't understand. It's my younger sister, Graziella and her husband. They were all set to emigrate to Canada, Toronto. There is a company there that offered Gustavo a job, a really good job as a controller for a big grocery chain, but they withdrew the offer."

"Really, why?"

Disda sighed in frustration. "They don't know. The company would not say, they just withdrew the offer and so his work visa is no longer valid. They've been up in my flat for a week, bawling their eyes out. I'm going crazy."

"He's a comptroller, by profession?"

"He has a degree in accounting and an MBA from U of T. That was the Toronto connection."

Tom nodded, thinking aloud. "One of my clients, Central Food Distribution, was looking for a comptroller. They just opened offices in Toronto."

Disda shrugged. Tom leaned down and swept Disda into his arms for a long smooch. She moaned with pleasure as their lips slipped and molded against each other. When they broke, Disda wiped her mouth and licked her lips.

"Don't worry, I'll throw them out soon."

It was Tom's turn to laugh. "Let me see what I can do."

Disda turned to slip through the front door of the apartment. Tom called out after her.

"When can I see you again?"

Disda looked back over her shoulder, her smile wry and sexy. *"En cualquier momento, guapo."*

The next day, Tom called his firm and had his assistant, Joe Kovàcs, call Karl Van der Voort at CFD to find out if they had filled that comptroller position. They hadn't and were desperate.

*

The crush bar at *La Floridita* was thick with sun-burnt tourists, local hookers, and Hemingway fans, seeking the thirst-quenching daiquiris made famous by the legendary red waist-coated barmen. Disda thought the club would be amusing for Tom, who elbowed his way to the bar to place their order.

"Gustavo was second in his graduating class, he speaks four languages, Spanish, English, French, and German. He's tall and very easy-going, but a genius when it comes to numbers."

Tom took a deep gulp of the ice-cold daiquiri, feeling it chill his stomach and causing a little brain freeze. "You can stop the hard sell. My client saw Gustavo's CV and fell in love. They are submitting the paperwork for his visa."

Disda's mouth fell open with a squeal of surprise and total delight. Pushing aside his raised glass, she threw herself into his arms, pasted her supple form against his, and glued her mouth to his lips. An encouraging roar went up all around them from the tipsy crowd. Disda put her lips right next to Tom's ear and murmured, "You're a good man, Tomás. *Tengo muchas ganas para conocerte mas intimamente . . .*"

The following Saturday, Disda joined Tom poolside at the Nacional for drinks and giggles with some casual friends. It was a calm, sultry evening that melted into a dark, moonless night. As they dined at the rooftop restaurant, Disda leaned over at one point to whisper, "I threw them out."

By the time they left the hotel, they were both slightly smashed and walking on air, their hands all over each other's body, their mouths seeking each other's every few steps. Their mutual denial had fiercely stoked their lust and they barely made it to the Serrano.

As usual, two out of the three elevators were no longer working. Disda had a two-bedroom flat on the tenth floor and had furnished it with a mix of what had been lost to the revolution and what little had been gained. For all Tom cared, it could have been an oyster shell. His restraint up to this moment had been admirable, as had hers, but now, facing each other across two feet of humid, empty space, all bets were on the table. Disda had no shame, no hesitation as she took Tom's face between her strong hands and pressed her mouth to his. Quietly humbled, the shadowy Fates stepped away from this spin on the karmic wheel and left the mortals to wanton acts that they, themselves, could only dimly recall, but never again perform.

They were both young, in their prime, and so that night, there was no end to the moment as both of them were too eager to surrender and be consumed. Their passion never waned, their desire to know every pore, every bend and fold remained unsated. No beginning, no end, endlessly fulfilling and then, finally drained for the moment and passed on to blessed, winged Oblivion.

In the instant of embraces, Tom suddenly and overwhelmingly realized all that he had gotten wrong in his life, and what little he had gotten right. Suddenly, the sad, regretful faces of all the women he had managed to avoid, to string along but keep at bay, he now understood very differently. That which he took for disappointment, anger, or betrayal, he now understood as pity toward a callous young man who wouldn't come across for love. He had always thought that the road to transcendent Eros was through detachment, but now, in Disda's wet embrace, every liaison, every sexual encounter of the past, was revealed as ridiculous.

Later, at some unknown time, some gathering of minutes, Disda awoke, startled struggling in his arms and buried her face, wet with tears, into his chest. Tom was unequipped by life and experience to deal with such an admixture of emotions. Sensing his unease, Disda pulled away and looked him square in the eye.

"There are things you need to know."

She rose from her bed, her body still damp and toned and so frankly sexual that he held his breath. She wrapped herself in a throw and placed a cheroot between her lips, lighting it and allowing the smoke to float up into her nostrils, and then deep inside her lungs. She curled up on a wide bench under the open window that looked out onto the ocean. She could see the night fishers in their inflated truck tire inner tubes, jigging for whatever would bite.

"You need to let me speak, OK? You need to let me speak and you can't say anything. And then you will know what you need to know."

Tom settled back in the bed, his eyes on her even as her eyes were somewhere else. She drew another deep puff of her cheroot and folded back the years. . . .

"My father was a teacher of Fidel's in Santiago. Although he sympathized with the revolutionary students at the university, he did not take part in the revolutionary struggle. My mother, Josefina, was strictly bourgeoise, very Catholic. As soon as I hit puberty, she started to groom me for some ideal match she had in her mind.

"My father was different. He wasn't as violent as Fidel and that gang. He was an intellectual, a poet, thoughtful and so relaxed and at ease with everyone, from any class. He was more truly of the country than Fidel and he loved the country people. He didn't care for the high-society life my mother had planned for me. He was more likely to throw me onto the back of a horse and let me ride without a saddle. I adored him. He was sympathetic to the cause, but not a man of action. He preferred to contribute through his role as a professor at the university."

"After Batista's coup, things got very bad. My father was opposed on democratic principles, but my mother liked the general. She would say things to me like, 'He is not like your father with his soft words.' She thought Batista was a strong man who brought order and she had this idea fixed in her mind that Fidel and Raúl and the others were just pampered, spoiled middle-class bullies who had not been spanked enough as children."

"So, there was conflict between my parents, and between myself and my mother. I always sided with my father, even when I thought he was wrong or naive. The tension got worse when my father brought home Roberto, one of his star students. Roberto was ten years older than me and deep into the movement. I was strongly attracted to him, even though I was just a teenager. My mother noticed and didn't like how my affection for Roberto might screw up her high society plans for me."

"Roberto was one of those involved in the attack on the Moncada Barracks in '53. After the amnesty, Fidel and Raúl fled to Mexico. Roberto remained in Santiago, planning for their return and the revolution. I suppose he could have aligned himself with less radical forces and I think that maybe he wanted to, but Fidel had a way of bringing him back in.

"Around that time, my parents split. Josefina wanted to live the high life in Batista's Havana and my father wanted his quiet university life. We had a horrible screaming fight. Josefina told me that if I didn't come to Havana, I would be dead to her. I was fifteen and wanted to stay with my father. Josefina tore out her hair and screamed that she would never forgive me, that I was a stain on her life. I learned later that she had openly flirted with the regime and had caught Batista's eye; my mother was possibly mad, but also a great beauty.

"When Fidel returned with Raúl and Ché in 1956, I joined Roberto to link up with the Fidelistas and we ended up hiding in the Sierra Maestra. By that time, I was sixteen and thought myself fully grown, and not just physically. Ideologically, I had already rejected Josefina's world, as had many of my schoolmates. To be cool at that time meant having revolutionary sympathies. We were so easily led, but Batista's regime had alienated us."

"I stayed with my Roberto and Fidel, learning guerrilla techniques, going on missions to pass information to the other revolutionary groups that were attacking Batista, and growing up. I was now seventeen. Roberto was a simple, sweet man, ten years older than I was and, I don't know how, but we fell in love. There was this idea going around, which no one discussed openly, that the women in the mountains could be good revolutionary fighters, but could also be of comfort to the men who would give up their lives to the cause. No one dissuaded us of this notion. We were a little stupid."

"There was no question of marriage. That did not happen in the mountains. We just sort of claimed each other. By the end of March 1958, I was pregnant. My father hid his disapproval. To reveal his true feelings would have been considered retrograde and patriarchal. Still, we were all living in a society ruled by machismo, so there were words exchanged and not very kind ones. I felt this pressure, a need to justify our value to the cause. So, when Fidel asked me and Roberto to sneak into Havana at the end of December to coordinate with rebel cells who were already taking action, a few days before Batista fled the country, I jumped at the opportunity."

"I was nine months pregnant and we thought this was the perfect ruse. Who would suspect us? Unfortunately, we were betrayed and arrested at a road block and taken to the Via Viento prison complex. You could smell the fear and chaos in the city. The military and police were in a blind panic.

"There was this monster, Ventura, Batista's police chief, and he wanted to know our contacts in the city. His henchmen took Roberto to another room for interrogation, but he would not cooperate. I could hear Roberto's screams as they pulled out the fingernails of his left hand. I grew blind with anger and struck out at the policeman guarding me. He tried to hit me and we struggled viciously. The effort caused my water to break. The guards lost their nerve and rushed me to the prison hospital.

"I tried to hold back the labor but it was no use. I never felt anything as powerful as that and it shattered me. So foolish and naïve! I had trusted Fidel. I would never have thought he would have put us in such obvious danger. I was torn up inside; part of me wanted to hold my baby girl and part of me was crying for Roberto."

"They posted a guard at the door, but allowed a doctor to examine me and my baby. He was a Castro sympathizer and he told me that I had to run because Roberto and I were scheduled for execution on New Year's Day. I begged him for some help, but he told me he had no money for me. He said that when he left, he would draw the guard away from the door. He would not lock it and I had to seize this opportunity."

"I don't know where I found the strength to get out of bed. My light coat was hanging in the wardrobe and my shoes were there, as well. I swaddled my baby tightly, as I had seen comrade mothers do in the mountains, and sneaked out of the hospital. I could not go to any of our safe houses. If Roberto and I had been betrayed there was a good chance that all of them had been compromised already. I had the idea of making my way to Josefina's house. She was with the regime and above suspicion."

"OK, so, I had not seen Josefina for two years. She was no longer in my life, but over the years, my father would press me to send the odd present, the occasional card. Once, I had the chance to make a long-distance call to her. It did not go well."

Disda paused to light another cheroot and sip from a tumbler of wine.

"She's my mother, I thought, and she is bound to help me. I don't know. I guess I was trying to convince myself. I was in such terrible pain, I wasn't thinking clearly. I had no money, I was very hungry, and I hurt all over. The baby was crying and had begun to shiver. I knew of Josefina's new house on Calle 28 because of our informants.

"As I made my way to her house, I tried to catch the eye of someone, anyone, who might help me. The weather wasn't too bad for December so there were a lot of people in the streets, but there was also a strange tension in the air and the crowds around the *cafeteros* were more skittish than usual. Whenever a police jeep cruised by, the people fell silent and watched apprehensively. Fidel had left the mountains and was on a winning streak. Rumor had it that Batista's days were numbered, but with the *casquitos* around, nobody was celebrating just yet."

"I could now see the house on Calle 28, near Avenida 3. Spanish Colonial, somber, dignified in the late afternoon sun, but not even the faded and patchy, peeling paint could entirely stop it from exuding middle-class pretentiousness. Josefina had paid cash for the house after a particularly successful turn at the nearby Hilton's gaming tables. True to her character, she took this as some kind of divine providence and had given up gambling forever. She turned the house into a proper, respectable rooming house."

"I barely made it up the few steps leading to the front door. I was dizzy with fatigue and the loss of blood, but I gathered my courage and rang the bell."

"Mother, it's me and I'm desperate," I said to her when she came to the door.

"She did not raise her voice. She just looked at me and I could see immediately that I had made a big mistake. She was quietly furious at me for endangering her existence. And it all came out—how I had been trouble ever since I was born, how I was just like my father, who filled my head with crazy ideas about revolution and human rights. Human rights! She guessed I was in serious trouble and told me that she would not have me . . . and that was all there was to it!"

"I begged her, I told her that the Batistianos had caught me and Roberto, how my baby, her grandchild, was born in the prison hospital. I pleaded with her, told her I had no money, that I hadn't eaten for two days and hadn't slept much either. I had lost contact with my comrades, and had nowhere to go, so I had to come to her. I was practically on my knees and asked her for a little money and some rest, that's all—just for the night, or for a few hours, at least. I was sobbing, and held out my baby, but Josefina just stood there, unmoved, her face a mask and her eyes dark and sunken into her face."

"She tried to close the door but I wouldn't let her and she struggled not to shout for fear of drawing attention. She wanted nothing to do with me, or my Roberto and his Fidelista friends. She spoke so coldly, as if reciting a catechism of all my past sins against her: 'You never cared about what happens to anyone and now you are doing the same to an innocent life. You play at revolution, you disturb the peace and you create trouble. Go away, I don't want to see

you again!' She pushed me out and slammed the door shut
in my face.

"I crawled down the stairs and turned toward the hotel
near the corner, but I knew I would never make it. I got to
the newspaper kiosk by the intersection, but my legs just
wouldn't carry me any further. I pressed my baby to my
breast and curled up on the sidewalk and closed my eyes,
waiting for the worst.

"The baby screamed.

"Then, a miracle! The owner of the newspaper stand, the
kiosk on the corner, appeared, hovering above me. I knew
him and he helped me. Would you believe it? My own
mother wouldn't, but that man from whom I would steal
candy did. His wife helped me pick myself up off the pave-
ment. They gave me something to eat and they looked after
the baby while I slept in the nearby basement room that they
called their home.

"My next memory is waking to an odd sound. It was like
a choir in some great cathedral, like a song, echoing, repeating over and over, 'Viva Fidel! Viva Fidel!' And the ground
itself, the city, was vibrating, shaking, as hundreds of thousands of feet were dancing and jumping. I left the basement
and emerged into another world, such a beautiful world of
people who swept me up, who hugged me and my baby.
Fidel had entered the city and the people were delirious with
joy. I wanted to join them, but I had to find Roberto.

"I met people whom I knew from the mountains and
told them and we went to the police station and found my
Roberto. Ventura, the chief of police, had given him a very

rough time. They had him beat up badly, repeatedly. He was barely able to stand, to hold his daughter in his hands, but he was so ashamed, he could not look us in the eyes. Ventura had broken him, they had beaten him terribly and they had pulled out all the nails of his left hand and he wept as he told us that he had given up names. We didn't care and we told him that it did not matter. Nothing mattered! It was over. We heard that cadres had tracked down Ventura and we all knew that Batista had left the night before with his cronies to Miami."

Disda poured herself another tumbler of wine and lit another of her dark brown cheroots.

"In the beginning, I thought he would be all right. Fidel himself had arranged for an apartment for me and the baby and I took Roberto home from the hospital and he seemed to recover quickly. After a few weeks he was well enough to work part-time at the newspaper, *Granma*, I'm sure you know it? Everything was going well, but then Roberto began to get terrible headaches and he had to quit."

"I got a job as the manager of El Encanto, the finest department store in Havana, and Roberto stayed home with the baby."

Tears began to well up in Disda's eyes. She did not allow her emotions to carry her away, but even more frightening, kept recounting her story as her face began to shine with her flowing tears.

"I should never have done that, never! But I wanted to be a loyal cadre, I wanted to assume my position in the new world, to contribute. Everyone around me, all the young

people, we were so devoted to the cause, to Fidel. I wanted
to be a part of it. We had worked so long, trained so hard in
the mountains. Roberto, me. But I should never have done
that. I was young and I didn't know better. If I had stayed
home, he would have been all right. I wouldn't have lost her."

Disda got up from the bench and walked back to the bed,
where she stood looking down at Tom, her face hidden in
the blackness.

"I'm haunted by what happened, Tomás. I have dreams
that won't go away. You see, after the headaches began,
Roberto started roughing me up, beating me. I never knew
what would set him off. I would say something or ask him
something and he would get this crazy look in his eye and
I wanted to leave him, but I didn't know how. How could I
go to my father and tell him that Roberto, a faithful soldier,
a man who left his student life to take up the cause, was
hitting me?

"My baby . . . Roberto stayed home with her every day
while I was at work. One day he made a comment about
how I was dressed and I answered him back with a little joke.
He beat me up so badly that I could hardly make it to the
office. It was in the summer, and when I came back home
that evening, he begged me for forgiveness. We made love
that night the way we used to in the Sierra Maestra, tenderly, passionately.

"The next morning, his bad headache was back. I didn't
know what to do and when I told him he should go to the
clinic, he got angry and struck me again. And I apologized.
. . . I apologized to him! I ran to work and by the time I got

there, the comrade police were waiting. They wouldn't tell me what had happened, only that I had to go with them. I saw Roberto, sitting on a chair in the corridor, his hands were attached to the chair. He was weeping, sobbing, his head so crushed into his chest like he was trying to bite out his own heart. In the room, I saw the bundle and I knew in a moment. I knew what he had done and what I had done. He had killed my baby. He had shaken her to death."

"They put Roberto away in the mental hospital, and my life came to an end."

Disda slipped off the shawl that hid her body and slipped back into bed, pressing her body against Tom's.

"I want you to know about me, Tomás. It is important that I come to you as a real person, with a past. Whatever we become for each other, it is important to me that you know who I am."

Many years after she was gone, robbed of her life by a painful and aggressive cancer, Tom would still remember that night she had woken up in bed, screaming, tortured and afraid, fighting the phantoms of the past. He would remember her curled up on the window bench in that apartment in the López Serrano, the cigar smoke curling up from her lips, the chipped wine tumbler in her beautiful, tapered fingers and her voice, so low and so haunted by the deep guilt she felt for a sin that could never be forgiven.

He had embraced her body and her ghosts without fear or hesitation. He had heard her and knew her from that night on. He never had to ask about the bad dreams that possessed her. He already knew.

CHAPTER 19

Nassau, Bahamas, December 1968

Tom Karas emerged from his shower at the Royal Victoria Hotel feeling physically weak, emotionally drained by guilt. Memories of his time with Disda played like a loop in his mind—key moments, frozen images, sounds, words, expressions. He could not help but confront himself with the realization that he had added to this poor woman's suffering. This devastated him because he knew full well that Fidel and Raúl were vengeful men with long memories. Their retribution toward Disda would be far worse for the effort and loyalty she had shown in the Sierra Maestra. Her perceived act of betrayal would shake them to their ideological cores and feed their macho paranoia; if Disda could embrace the enemy, who then could be trusted? They would never forgive her for having taken up with the despised, "enemy," the imperialist, mercenary, two-faced spy, Uncle Sam's treacherous lackey.

The Castros would make sure that she and her family would be ostracized by their friends, fired from her job and, to survive, forced to work, perhaps for the rest of her life, as a menial laborer far from Havana. A few years in the countryside, working in the fields, mucking out stables and pig sties, would be only a small down payment on her debt to the revolution.

He was sitting immobile on the edge of his bed, wrapped in a towel staring off into space when the phone rang. It was the front desk.

"Mr. Karas, American Express wants to talk with you. Something about your credit card. May I put the call through?"

Tom's gut contracted, but, remarkably, his mind quickly cleared somewhat, grasping at a possible concrete problem. American Express? That's all he needed, being thrown out of the hotel. He suddenly realized that the Cubans had never given him his money back and that he was actually penniless without his card, the only one he carried. He steeled himself. "Sure. Go ahead."

"Mr. Karas?"

"Yes."

"My name is Fred Moss and I am a credit supervisor at American Express. Mind if I just make sure that you really *are* Mr. Karas before we go on?"

Any Havana fog that had been clouding his mind vanished instantly. The caller was his Control, Al McIsaacs. Tom felt the warm hand of safety alight on his shoulder.

"No, not at all."

"What is your mother's maiden name?"

Tom told him while fighting hard to stop the release of giddy, emotional laughter. McIsaacs was playing his role perfectly.

"And what is your date and place of birth?"

Tom gritted his back teeth and answered that question, too.

"And, finally, what is your mother's passion?"

"My mother is a painter."

"Thank you, Mr. Karas."

"Anything else?"

"There *is* something, actually. You have not paid your American Express bills for the last three billing cycles. Is there anything wrong? Should American Express be worried?"

"No. Nothing. I'm fine. It's just that I was detained in Cuba against my will for a few weeks."

"I'm sorry to hear that, Mr. Karas. Since you are a valued, long-standing client with an excellent credit record, I will authorize use of your card, provided you tell me when we can expect payment. When do you expect to be back in Montreal?"

Tom swore under his breath; too much, already! McIsaacs was having a wonderful time teasing him mercilessly.

"What's the date today?"

"December six, sir.

"How about December fifteen?"

"Could we make it December twelve?" McIsaacs was suggesting a date for a meeting. "I see from your billing history that you are an equestrian? I believe there is an event for horsemen in Montreal around that date."

"Horsemen? On the twelfth?"

"There is also the billing cycle sir, you know how it is. I cannot let another cycle go by without suspending your card use."

"December twelve it is then." Tom understood. "Thank you, Mr. Moss." He added, "and God bless American Express. I will never ever leave home without it."

Tom's rattled feelings drained out, but this time relief was followed by a certain calm and resignation. The "Disda loop" had been broken by McIsaacs's call. His control's voice brought him back from the edge of irrational and impotent regret. And he also understood that the RCMP "Horsemen" would be waiting for him in Montreal, as well. Forewarned is forearmed.

He realized he was hungry. This surprised him. He had expected his stomach to have shrunk. After all, he had subsisted on not much more than bread, pasta, and water for over two months and, to be truthful, gourmand as he could be, the prison diet had not bothered him at all. Such are the long-term benefits of a youth of wartime deprivation. He returned to the bathroom and stepped on the scale: it showed 135 pounds. The day he was arrested he had been fifty pounds heavier. He now took a good look at himself in the full-length mirror. He had always been slim but now he had the body of a marathoner. His cheeks, though, were gaunt and he discovered, with some regret, that the very last wisps of youth had disappeared from his face. Here was the adult Tom Karas. Clark Kent. Superman.

"Here's a jingle for Weight Watchers," he announced to the mirror. "Want to lose a pound a day? Stay at a Cuban prison . . . and pray!" He laughed out loud and called the restaurant downstairs.

The *maître d'* sat him down at a table on the terrace overlooking the dance floor and he was delighted to find his favorite dish, Holsteiner Schnitzel, with mashed potatoes and cucumber salad, as a special. He ordered a split of rosé.

He looked at the other guests on the terrace, bronzed jet-setters without a care in the world. His eyes turned south-by-southwest, toward Cuba, and he had to work hard to stop the "Disda" loop from re-starting. His food arrived and he fussed over it as a way of distracting himself, but it was no good. Halfway through his meal, nausea overwhelmed him and, against his will, he started to cry.

"Sir, is everything all right?"

The waiter was young, and native to the island. His face revealed his natural, kindly nature, which only triggered more emotions in Tom. Under any other circumstances, Tom would have tightened his face, pursed his lips, and waved off the concern. Maybe he would have been overtly dismissive, but there was something in the waiter's genuine concern that pierced Tom to his core.

"No, I'm . . . I'm . . ." Tom scrambled to assume control of himself. He motioned to the dance floor some distance away.

"I was just looking at the people dancing. They . . . they are so . . . they are having so much fun. . . . They are so close to each other . . . dancing and holding each other." Tom was on the edge now, biting back his tears, trying to control his breathing.

The waiter, like all good people confronted with others' emotional distress, pulled back a bit to give Tom a chance to regain his balance. He followed Tom's eyes to the dance floor.

"Yes, I often think the same. How nice it is that our guests can come here and relax and find each other again."

"And yet, there . . . over there," Tom said, indicating the island held in a stranglehold by two macho, middle-class failures, slaves to an archaic and failed political philosophy, traitors to the true spirit of human revolution. "Less than a hundred miles south of this *paradise,* ten million people are being herded into virtual serfdom while . . . while . . . here I am, sipping expensive wine."

The waiter picked up the split and refilled his glass.

"So, we must drink to them. Drink to their eventual and sure emancipation."

Tom finally looked up fully into the waiter's eyes. There was something of Langley in this young and erudite fellow. Tom raised his glass.

"To their eventual and sure emancipation."

The waiter withdrew discreetly, leaving Tom alone with his thoughts.

"Adisdania Flores, Duque de Estrada," he said out loud, as though to conjure her out of thin air. "I wonder where you are now?" he whispered.

CHAPTER 20

Montreal, December 1968

Even though he had been forewarned by McIsaacs's telephone call, Tom was completely unprepared for the trauma he would have to cope with following his liberation.

It started after they touched down at Dorval Airport, when the steward on the plane informed him that airport authorities had requested he remain on board until all the other passengers had disembarked. He waited anxiously until two "Horsemen"—members of the RCMP's security and intelligence division, came on board and escorted him to a car waiting at the foot of the exit stairs. He was then whisked to the VIP lounge, where his parents were waiting for him. He could not have planned a more awkward and disagreeable return.

While the Horsemen looked on at a respectful distance, his mother, in tears, took him in her arms and whispered while stroking his head, "Thank God you're back safe and sound." His father, standing beside her awkwardly, hand extended for Tom to shake, feigned an expression of emotion that was clearly forced and foreign to him.

"I told you Cuba would mean trouble for you," he said by way of greeting his thirty-three-year-old son, who had just escaped death in front of a Cuban firing squad. "Perhaps now you have learned your lesson. Stay home, work hard, and avoid trouble."

The Horsemen waiting for the right moment drew Tom aside, presenting him with their cards.

"We'll be calling you in soon for an official debriefing. In the meantime, you are not to leave the country and you are to notify us if you plan to travel outside Montreal."

"Right."

Tom and his parents drove home in silence. His father explained, rather shame-facedly, that his detention had attracted the press's attention and that he had been harassed into promising an exclusive interview with his son upon his safe return. Tom looked at his father as though the older man had lost all sense. His mother knotted her handkerchief and pretended to be absorbed by the passing landscape.

"No way!" said Tom. He made his father stop the car a block from his parents' home and walked the rest of the way, evading the press scrum in front of the house by slipping into the alley and in the rear door.

He spent the weekend quietly with his parents and, on Monday, went to the office as if nothing had happened. His right-hand man, Joe Kovàcs, another Magyar who had arrived as a boy in 1956, shook his hand warmly, genuine relief in his eyes. The rest of the young staff were thrilled to see him safely back and welcomed his return with enthusiasm. Not so Harley and the other senior partners.

"Well?"

Tom settled back into his leather club chair, reaching for a thin Cuban panetella. "Well what?" he replied to Harley's prompt.

"Well, how are we going to deal with this?"

Tom was mystified. "Deal with what?"

Harley smiled and shook his head as a gentle admonition.

"We've heard from several clients. Some of them are whining about the 'spy' in our little concern. We're supposed to be discreet. You, above all, have emphasized this. And yet, there you are, arrested in Cuba for lord-knows-what."

Tom lit his cigar, squinting at Harley through the first puffs and waving off the comment. "Let them whine. It'll blow over. Might even attract new business."

Later in the day, another senior partner, Cyril Kiriakedes, handed Tom an invitation to a special partners' meeting the following Friday.

He realized what was coming, and decided he didn't like it. He called in Joe Kovàcs, and together, speaking quickly and quietly in Hungarian, they reviewed the partnership agreement, playing out various scenarios until Tom was satisfied that they had covered every possible angle.

Tom then asked one of the office coordinators to book appointments for the rest of the day with his direct clients. He only had five, but they were among the largest of the firm. The first one he dropped in on was Saul Loewitz out at Huntingdon Mills, about forty minutes west on the city. Diminutive, sharp, gregarious, and a scratch golfer, Loewitz was a politically astute intellectual who had inherited a huge and successful fabric mill from his father and was, with Tom's help, already diversifying. Loewitz hated bullshit of any kind and could be impatient with incompetence.

He was already chuckling as he poured Tom a heavy Czech crystal tumbler of single malt.

"I hope the pussy was worth it."

Tom would not open up to Loewitz about his true feelings for Disda, but rather, played along.

"Ten times over." The two men clinked glasses.

"I heard that you and some of our friends in the Gordon Brown Building were upset with my little Cuban adventure."

Loewitz reacted, perplexed.

"Upset? Jealous, more likely."

"My partners claim you are ready to pull your business."

Loewitz smiled, crinkling his eyes.

"I think your partners are pulling on something, but it ain't business." He laughed at his own joke. "Look, Tom, I couldn't give a shit if they put you in the slammer for fucking a goat. I've been dining off your story for the past month!"

"Glad I could be of service."

Loewitz leaned in, putting his hand on Tom's knee.

"You computerized my payroll, my fucking inventory . . . you have saved me hundreds of thousands. Listen to me. I could not care less what shenanigans you get up to on your own time, you horny Magyar putz!"

"Would you put that in writing?"

The two men clinked glasses.

Contrary to what he had been told, it was the same story with his other four clients. They had no problem staying with his firm, even if he left, as long as their business was supervised by Tom's second-in-command, Joe Kovacs.

The next day he was summoned to the RCMP Montreal headquarters at Greene and Dorchester. The two Horsemen who had met him at the airport greeted him warmly and respectfully, putting Tom at ease. He spent the afternoon providing them with details about his Cuban prison—its routine, layout, and so forth—as well as some background about the people he had met in Havana, especially those who had visited Canada. He did not mention his activities on behalf of McIsaacs, assuming that they already knew about them and wanted to hear no further details.

That evening he contacted McIsaacs and told him about his visit with the Mounties and suggested that their debriefing scheduled for December 12 be postponed for a couple of weeks.

"Why, what's going on?"

"I've got some problems at the office. A putsch by a couple of putzes."

"OK. I'll shuffle around my calendar."

"And, there's one other thing."

Tom could hear McIsaacs sigh over the phone.

"Tom, we can't help her."

"You have assets there."

Silence.

"You can at least find out what happened. Where she is."

Another long silence.

"I'll be in touch." The line went dead.

The Friday senior partners' meeting was brief. Harley, his first and, he thought, most loyal partner, led off with a short, complimentary speech about Tom, the founder of the firm, who, as "Rainmaker," made sure that old clients were happy and that there was always new business flowing in.

"We have prospered under your management and leadership and it makes us very sad to see that our clients, who do not know you as well as we do, feel that scrutiny directed at you by certain government authorities exposes their businesses to unnecessary risk."

"You mean that they are afraid I might snitch on their tax shenanigans?" Tom reposted.

Harley bristled.

"We're not in the business of guessing what they think or fear. We provide a service based on mutual trust." He was getting really upset and could barely control his emotions. "It would appear that trust in our firm has now been shaken by, I am obligated to say so, your selfish lust for sordid adventure, which has caused you to behave in a manner not becoming a professional public accountant. A chartered accountant!"

Harley allowed his anger to get the better of him. "You put us in a po . . . po . . . position," he stammered, "where, where, our firm can only survive if we distance ourselves from you."

Tom's face froze and any warmth that may have been there, vanished.

"What does that mean?"

"We want you to resign with immediate effect and leave." Tom looked around the room.

"Is this a unanimous decision?" He polled them with his eyes, one by one. Cyril Kiriakedes, Brian Connolly, and Saul Levine turned their eyes downward. Only Harley had the arrogant brass to meet his look.

Silence.

Tom waited. Let the four sanctimonious bastards squirm a little. They hadn't complained for eight years while he worked his ass off to bring in new business, supervising the running of the firm and arranging financing for expansion because during those years of plenty they loved the money they were raking in. And they knew very well that the firm's financial success was essentially his making. And yet, if Tom was being honest, there was some truth in Harley's accusations. Tom *was* selfish when it came to his life. He did want more than mere success as a handmaiden to other men's fortunes. Providence lifted its languorous head and squinted its dreamy eyes.

Tom looked up at Harley and said quietly, "Very well. Buy me out. I want $200,000 for my 20 percent share in the business." He got up and walked out. "My parents are waiting for me to take them out to dinner."

Leaving the offices, he stopped at Joe Kovacs' office and whispered some instructions in Hungarian into the younger man's ear. Joe listened carefully, and nodded.

Harley called him on Saturday morning and asked to meet. He wanted to negotiate. They met in one of the badminton and squash club's private conference rooms.

"I thought we were friends, Harley. Am I mistaken?"

Harley was furious and it quickly became apparent that he had been resentful of Tom's leadership for years and was chafing to replace him.

"Don't make this about friendship, Tom! It's about ethics or, rather, your lack thereof!"

"Fuck you!"

Harley leapt out of his chair and began to pace, shaking his finger in Tom's face like a palsied scold.

"No, Tom, fuck you! From the very first days, as soon as we started to have a little traction in the city, you were off. You made the handshake deals and you were gone, leaving us peasants behind to actually do the fucking work."

"So, you're complaining that I made deals that put food on your table and your ass in a Mercedes and fixed your kids' teeth?"

"Don't play stupid with me, Tom. You are never here. Where's Tom? Where's Tom? Tom's in DC! Tom's in Cuba! Tom's in a jail in Havana!"

"What can I say? I like to travel."

Harley sighed and sat down heavily in his chair, rubbing his eyes.

"You refuse to take any of this seriously and that's why you have to go, Tom. We are all, all of us, serious people. We take our job, the ethics of the job, very fucking seriously and you don't and never will. Am I right?"

"There is some truth in what you say, Harley. But we should be able to talk this through, come to an understanding."

"What is there to understand, Tom? You're an ideas man. You had a vision for our firm, I grant you that. But you're a sprinter, at best a middle-distance runner. What we need is a marathoner who will stick to it. A managing director who will be there for the long haul, no matter how boring and banal that is. Our clients expect it and our partners and employees deserve it. Surely you can see that?"

Tom shrugged. "So, buy me out."

"You know as well as I do that we do not have that kind of cash flow on hand. You're asking the impossible."

*

"The treacherous bastard," Tom fumed when he met Leo Rosenberg for a drink at the Ritz's Maritime Bar.

"Money makes people weird, Tom," said Leo blandly.

"It's not about money, Leo. Clearly, the entire situation is nothing more than a power-grab by Harley. He wants me out of the way, but doesn't have the guts to say so directly." Leo signalled the bartender for two more of the same.

"Maybe it's time to move on. Haven't you got enough on your plate, what with helping out our mutual friend and your business in Cuba?"

"My Cuban business is finished. I'm *persona non grata* forever, or until Fidel and Raúl drop dead, may it be soon!"

Leo smiled, twirling the ice in his scotch.

"And how is our mutual friend? I haven't seen him for a while."

Tom knew that Leo was not to know about his work with McIsaacs so he merely smiled. Leo took the hint and chuckled.

"Don't worry. I'll tell him you were discreet."

Tom finished his drink, said goodbye to Leo, left the bar, and hailed a cab.

"Fuck them," he muttered as he climbed in. "They'll pay dearly for their disloyalty."

On Monday morning, Tom went to the office again and was handed yet another notice asking him to attend a special partners' meeting, this one to be held on Wednesday evening. He waited till the caterer had set up the usual dinner in the boardroom before making his first move. When he entered, Tom could not help but notice that Harley had taken *his* usual seat.

"You all know that I met Harley on Saturday and he got nowhere with me," he told the senior partners. He looked directly at Harley. "But, much worse than the bad faith negotiations, you lied to me."

Harley stopped chewing his food as the others lay down their cutlery.

"Be informed, that *my* clients, representing over 20 percent of the firm's annual billing, still have absolute confidence in me." He tossed copies of four letters on the table. "And they have put it in writing. As I told you last week, I will let you buy me out for $200,000, payable up front."

He looked around the table. No one stirred. No one ate.

"Harley said, and I choose to believe him, that you don't have that kind of money. Very well, I'm willing to give you terms and a very small discount. I want $75,000 up front, that's $18,750 each, and the balance in twelve consecutive monthly instalments of $10,000, for a total of $195,000 You will sign a joint and several guarantee for the instalments. In return, I will bend my best efforts to keep my clients with the firm for one year. You have till Friday at close of business to decide. If I don't hear from you in the affirmative by then, I will take my clients with me and start legal proceedings to wind up the firm. Take it or leave it."

He turned and left the room without saying another word.

They caved on Friday afternoon at 4:55 p.m.

*

It took a full week to paper the deal and it would never have happened in as short a time had he not devoted most of his own energy into goading the partners to get on with it and cajoling the financial people into providing the funds needed by his partners to do the deal.

The stress on him cost sleepless nights during which his super-active imagination tortured him with wild scenarios, all predicting doom. No wonder. Despite a major effort to restore some semblance of filial love into his relationship with his aging parents by spending as much time as possible with them, he was failing miserably. They might as well have been living on separate, distant planets. Guilt about Disda's fate was always hovering over him like a dark cloud, and despite his bravado and overt confidence, he was worried sick about his professional future.

To alleviate the stress, he made sure to eat well and to exercise regularly. In fact, by the time it came time to sign the separation agreement with his partners he had regained about a third of the weight he had lost. But sleep kept eluding him.

The signing, to be attended by his four senior partners and four juniors, as well as the notary in whose office the event was scheduled to take place, was called for a Friday evening.

The notary, a slim, stylish, dark-haired, and very striking young woman, needed almost an hour to read out loud, as required by law, the text of the documents the participants were proposing to execute, and another quarter hour to assemble the packages that contained the inevitable last-minute corrections.

Tom waited patiently while his colleagues finished their respective paperwork. When his turn to sign came, he addressed them, pen in hand.

"Let us be clear. We are in this mess together and can extricate ourselves unscathed only if the firm does well. Simply put, the business cannot afford to lose clients, at least not big ones. I'm reasonably confident my clients will stay, even with me gone, provided Joe Kovacs, continues to service them.

Tom made a show of nodding to Joe as the others looked on, puzzled.

"Consequently, it's in our mutual interest to keep Joe happy and the best way to keep him happy is to make him a partner."

He paused and pointedly looked at Harley, then continued.

"Therefore, as my final act as managing partner, I hereby formally move that, before I sign these documents, we make Joe Kovacs not only a partner, but the managing partner."

Harley started to object, but Tom cut him off.

"Let's vote. Who's for Joe?" Harley, Cyril, Brian, and Saul did not budge, but Joe and the three other junior partners raised their hands.

"That's four for Joe out of eight, but as you know, in case of a tie, the managing partner has the deciding vote."

He turned to Harley and gave him a wide, ear-to-ear smile.

"Since I am still the managing partner and since I vote for Joe for partnership, I am happy to inform you, Harley, that your reign is over. You're toast."

CHAPTER 21

Montreal/New York City, January 1969

Tom awoke with a start. His phone was ringing. His watch showed six-thirty a.m., and it took him some time to work out that he was in his apartment in Montreal and that the caller was McIsaacs. Logical—who else would be calling a retired man at dawn on a Monday morning?

"Did you get your cheque from your putzes?" his control asked without preamble.

"In fact, I did, Friday night. I'm depositing it this morning. Is that why you woke me up?"

"Actually, no. Get your ass out of bed and catch the eleven o'clock Delta shuttle to La Guardia. We're staying at the Regency and having lunch at one-thirty. Meet me in the lobby and make sure to bring some spare clothing for a three-day stay." The line went dead.

Tom groaned and heaved himself out of bed.

The Regency on New York's Park Avenue is a luxury hotel. McIsaac's invitation surprised Tom no end because it was uncharacteristic for his usually parsimonious superior to invite him for a weekend-long debriefing session at such an elegant establishment.

Maybe they are happy with what I did for them, after all, he mused as he got his shit together and headed for the airport.

They met in the lobby as arranged. McIsaacs had already checked both of them in so they proceeded directly upstairs so that Tom could drop off his bag. Surprise number two: McIsaacs had booked a sumptuous, two-bedroom suite in which each had his own desk, television set, telephone, music center, and bar. The living room was big enough to accommodate a conference table at which six people could work or eat comfortably if need be.

A knock on the door announced the arrival of a waiter to serve a cold lunch of *homard à la russe* with caviar and potato salad, accompanied by a bottle of Bollinger champagne and *mille-feuille* for dessert.

As Tom gawked in surprise, McIsaacs laughed and faced Tom directly. "You did extremely well in Cuba, sport," he said. "It has not gone unnoticed and the powers that be picked up on it. They ordered me to pamper you a bit."

"With food? You know, I'm not that kind of girl," said Tom, fluttering his eyelids.

McIsaacs laughed, punching Tom in the arm. "This is only the beginning. Come, let's eat."

After lunch, there was a knock on the door and a lithesome, no-nonsense blonde woman entered and set-up a stenotype machine. She didn't say a word to either of them, but perched with perfect posture on a chair and waited attentively. Aside from changing the roll of paper in her machine, she never moved during Tom's debriefing. McIsaacs and Tom made themselves comfortable and, for a long four-hour stretch, McIsaacs let Tom talk about how, where, when, and why he got busted.

By six they were done and, without a word, the stenographer packed her gear and waited. McIsaacs signed a document for her.

"I'll need the typescript tomorrow morning, around ten."

The woman nodded to McIsaacs then caught Tom's eye, nodded again, and left.

McIsaacs stood looking at Tom for a long moment. Too long, as it made the younger man uncomfortable. When he finally spoke it was as though confirming something in this mind.

"All that true? About the girl, Disda?"

Tom raced through his fresh memory of the last four hours of debriefing, trying to spot the land mines he had obviously set for himself. His honesty was being tested.

"I have feelings for her, Al," he said, seeking out his control's eyes and smiling ironically. "Looks like I may be human, after all."

McIsaacs returned the wry smile and mixed them a couple of stiff drinks.

The two men took a break, rested and watched the news. Following an enthusiastic report on the trial flight of the supersonic Concorde, there was a story on Emil Zatopek. The Czech star long-distance runner had been labelled a "public enemy" by Soviet Sport because of his support of the democratic wing of the Communist Party. McIsaacs eyes were glued to the TV and Tom ventured a comment.

"Looks like things are getting interesting in Prague."

"Keep watching," replied his control, ominously.

Dinner was scheduled for eight o'clock at Delmonico`s in one of its private rooms. "Al, I'm impressed by all this conspicuous spending on my behalf, but anxiously awaiting the other shoe to drop," said Tom after they had been seated.

The older man nodded and took a sip of his very dry pre-dinner martini.

"As I mentioned yesterday, you are probably 'blown,' not only in Cuba, but over the entire Soviet Bloc. The other side are very good at this sort of thing. In any case, blown or not, we can't take the chance. Right?

Tom took a stiff gulp of his Tanqueray G&T.

"Therefore, your value to us for clandestine work is, unfortunately, low."

McIsaacs let this sink in. He seemed to take a certain pleasure in playing on Tom's emotional state, especially when the latter tried to maintain his usual poker face.

"However, you are in the first year of your third five-year contract, that's eleven years of service. So, as per contract, we have to give you a choice: you can allow us to buy out the rest of your contract for a lump sum equal to half of what you would earn if you soldiered on." McIsaacs took another sip of his martini and looked at Tom expectantly.

"How much would that be?"

"About $120,000."

"And I would lose my right to apply for an extension or renewal of my contract." Tom emptied his glass. "Am I right?"

"Yes."

"Which would mean that I could combine that money with my 'putsch' settlement and effectively retire completely at the age of thirty-five with a nest-egg of about $300,000."

"If your partners honor their obligation to you."

"And die at forty of terminal boredom."

McIsaacs burst out laughing so hard that he almost spilled his drink. "Not really. You'd still have to work. C'mon, aren't you a CA?"

Tom nodded and put his mind to work.

"Well, a third of the three-hundred-odd-thousand would swim away in taxes and what would be left, let's say about $200,000, would only produce about $1,000 a month in investment income. Not much is it?"

"Tom, tell me. Be frank. What would you like to do?"

Tom took a big breath. The image of a beleaguered Emil Zatopek remained fixed in his mind. It was quickly eclipsed by an image of Disda, perched on her window bench, looking back at him over her shoulder.

McIsaacs was a bit on edge. "Let me be frank, Tom. We'd like to retrain you for more *dynamic* assignments. We think you can do more, stuff that requires direct action. You in?"

Tom took his time thinking before he answered honestly.

"I don't know."

McIsaacs smiled broadly, nodding as though confirming some inner thought. Some cowboys need to be helped back into the saddle.

He held up his glass and Tom took pleasure in clinking it with his own.

＊

During the Christmas holidays, Tom had kept busy attending parties, both for business, and for pleasure. He spent time with his parents and *their* friends, a first in his life, and even attempted to learn how to play bridge. Tom had a lot to think about and many diverse concerns. He had changed since his problems in Cuba and his loss of Disda. For the first time in his life, his usual, casual indifference toward others had evolved into something more gentle and less judgmental. At times, he was uncharacteristically considerate of others.

Often, when sitting with his parents playing bridge, he found himself opposite his father and looking at his face. In the past, his feelings toward the man veered toward pity, contempt, and disappointment. Now, he saw that face as though seeing it for the first time. Each line and wrinkle appeared as a relief map, contouring the old man's successes and failures. His former, comfortable indifference was changing into a discomforting ambivalence. How did he feel about his parents?

When he had returned from his debriefing with McIsaacs in New York, he met Leo for drinks at the Ritz bar, and he did not hold back.

"When the partying is over, I have to confront the fact that I have no real friends or even close acquaintances or even a real social network in Montreal."

"Gee, thanks," mumbled Leo.

Tom waved aside his rudeness.

"No, no, Leo! That's not what I meant, and you know it. I value our relationship, but I have to admit that you might be the only one."

A couple of chirping, stylish society girls took their perch at the end of the bar and Leo raised his eyebrows, but Tom was oblivious.

"My ex-partners, business associates, even my dear clients, are beginning to give me the cold shoulder. Don't blame them I guess. I'm no longer the rainmaker. It was so different in Havana. Such an easygoing life with my Cuban gang."

The society girls were giggling and flirting in their direction and Tom finally noticed, but he wasn't open to the moment. Leo was more receptive and Tom had the distinct impression that there was something going on of which he was unaware.

"Above all, what I miss the most, Leo, and you're not going to believe me, I know, but what I miss the most, is not having anyone in the world who loves me or whom I can love."

Leo put his arm around Tom's shoulders and jostled him firmly.

"I love you, Tom."

Tom smiled dolefully, raised his glass to the flirting girls and muttered, "Fuck you, Leo."

He emptied his drink.

"I betrayed her, Leo. I feel empty. Nothing but shame."

Leo got off his stool. "Stop moping, Tom. Everything you told me about Disda leads me to believe that she'll land on her feet. *C'est le guerre, mon vieux.*" He sauntered over to the giggly girls, leaving Tom to brood.

Tom never stopped trying to find out what had become of Disda through the Canadian authorities, but they wouldn't cooperate. In typical diplomatic fashion they did not want to become involved with him again, too much trouble. McIsaacs's people were stonewalling him. There was something unseemly about an agent with his profile getting all bent out of shape over some foreign trim. It wasn't the done thing.

One evening at the end of January, when he had gone a little too deep into melancholy and a good bottle of cognac, he convinced himself he had nothing to lose and called Disda at her Lopez Serrano apartment. There was the usual delay, the odd, electronic clicks and buzzes, the static and echoes as whoever was on telephone bugging patrol that night put on their headphones, but finally, after dialing three times, he got through. The phone rang. And rang. Until, finally, she picked up.

"¿Hola? . . . ¿Hola?"

Tom held his breath as he realized, in a sober moment of clarity and panic, that calling Disda was not a good thing to do. In fact, it was probably very bad. She was still living in her Serrano apartment, but probably under close surveillance and her telephone was clearly tapped. The silence on the other end was paralyzing. He wanted to hang up, but his hands had lost their function. Finally, she spoke again, low, almost at the end of a breath.

"Hola."

Tom gathered whatever will was left to him at that moment. "Disda . . . yo . . . yo . . ."

There was a muffled sound, as though the receiver had been pushed up against something soft and giving. And then, clearly…

"*No se puede hablar,*" she said and hung up.

He felt awful. A bumbling idiot and guilty as hell!

*

The Montreal winter of 1969 was particularly cold and Tom no longer took any pleasure in winter activities. His skis stayed unwaxed, his skates dulled, the leather cracking. He did walk in the cutting cold, long, tortuous walks over Mont Royal, as though to punish himself for his selfish acts of ego. When he would visit his parent's home they would remark on how pale he was. By the beginning of March, he began to miss the warmth of the Caribbean. Montreal's dreary, gray, and cold winter weather was depressing and this added to his feeling of loneliness.

Toward the end of January, McIsaacs showed up in Montreal unannounced and asked Tom to meet him in the agency safe house near Atwater Avenue. Since the New York debriefing, they had had no contact. According to Tom's file, McIsaacs had proposed a continuing contract for Tom and his *protégé* was supposed to be thinking it over. It was clear to Tom, from the first greeting at the door, that his Control's patience was at the end. McIsaacs directed him into a snug easy chair while he paced and spoke.

"I've never shat you, Tom, and I'm not about to start, OK?"

"I appreciate that about our relationship, Al. What's on your mind?"

"What's on my mind? You! You're on my mind, goddammit!"

Tom was caught off guard.

"I got a call from Leo. He said you are still in a funk over that business with the Cuban girl. He said he dangled two luscious and very beddable co-eds under your Magyar nose and nothing."

This last made Tom squirm and confirmed to him that the fix had been in that evening at the Ritz. Damned Leo Rosenberg.

"And, just so you know, my young princeling, you are the subject of some discussion at the agency and it is not very flattering. No one in our business appreciates *Hamlet*, right? No one likes being put on hold by a talented amateur while he decides if he should be or not be, especially me!"

"I don't know what to say," said Tom quietly. "It is true, I've been having moments of introspection, re-evaluating my life."

"And?"

Tom could not sit there like a schoolboy being lectured on his shortcomings. He stood and went to the TV console where McIsaacs's usual travelling wet bar had been set up. He unscrewed an already open bottle of single malt scotch, noting that McIsaacs had needed to fortify himself before this meeting.

"Drink?" McIsaacs nodded and watched Tom as he prepared two tumblers. "I suppose I don't have a clear idea of what you expect of me, now that my cover is blown. You mentioned files demanding more 'direct action.'"

Tom walked over to hand his control his drink and offered his up for a toast.

"Since we are cutting through the bullshit here, maybe you can elaborate?"

McIsaacs's features softened a bit as he knocked the heel of his glass against Tom's.

"OK. If it helps you to decide," he said, taking a seat and crossing his legs. "Off the record."

Tom settled back into his own chair and nodded.

"A problem has come up in Uruguay. You've no doubt heard of the Tupamaro National Liberation Movement? Well, our sources have revealed that they have penetrated the Uruguayan government to the point where they have a meaningful presence within every ministry, including the police."

Tom nodded. "Yes. I met some of them when I was in Havana. They took special training from the Cubans in insurgency, arms, urban guerrilla tactics. I wrote a report on them."

"I know. That's why you were requested for this file. The Directorate wants an independent and unbiased report on what the hell is going on in Uruguay, and he wants it yesterday."

McIsaacs rose, picked up the bottle of single malt, and refreshed his glass and Tom's.

"The situation appears to be spiralling out of control and our affiliated services, the CIA and FBI, have lost their respective abilities to evaluate the true state of affairs down there objectively. They no longer coordinate their operations. The idiots are too busy fighting each other for turf."

Tom was skeptical. "Surely, you must have someone more senior than me for such a mission?"

"Not really. You have more than a decade of service under your belt, you speak Spanish like a greaser, you are no stranger to corruption, and you are intimately familiar with how Communism, or should we say 'state capitalism,' works. Plus your report on the Tupamaro guerrillas you observed was convincing."

Tom smiled, chuckling. "State capitalism? You mean that, when applied in practice, it unavoidably leads to the absolute corruption of government bureaucracies?"

"It's the only way Communism can survive," mused McIsaacs, eyeing Tom very carefully. "A cynical person, someone with your particular life and work experience, might conclude that free-market systems result in the same situation, right? Except, under capitalism, the rich profit, and not members of an ideological *nomenklatura*."

Tom was being tested and assumed his poker face. What else had Leo Loose-Lips revealed? Tom refrained from voicing his opinion, but he knew that McIsaacs had been tipped off that, maybe, his resolve was weakening, that he was starting to have doubts about being on the "just" side of the fight.

His control read his thoughts. "Your little adventure in a Cuban prison may have softened your perception of what is right and what is wrong, am I correct? You know, as well as anyone, that exposure to fear and suffering does that to everyone. What I want to tell you, Tom, is that this is normal and was expected. It happens to every agent, talented amateur or not. As long as you maintain your objectivity, you will survive. Only ignorant fanatics maintain our system is without flaws. We *are* flawed. But, when you compare it to the rest, it starts to look like the only hope for mankind."

Tom was humbled and inwardly contrite. He could now see how his ego and superiority had run away with his conscience and common sense.

"What's the file?"

"So, let me state the obvious as a way to help you to understand the problem as we see it. The United States considers Central and South America as being part of its sphere of influence. It is bad enough that Castro has provided a foothold to the USSR in the central region, but his influence is now being felt in all the other areas of Latin America, as well." Hence, the need for an on-the-ground assessment in Montevideo, *post haste.*

"I get all that, but I'm still a little ambivalent about this assignment." Tom sounded pensive.

"OK, let me give you some ground rules. Maybe that will make you less ambivalent. I want you to observe and then report only to me. You are expressly forbidden to give advice, either to the Uruguayans or the CIA and especially not to our embassy people. You are there to do what you do best; walk around, meet people, take them for a *cortado*, ask them about their jobs, their families, what they think of the situation, their sympathies, animosities and their views on the USA."

Tom got it. There was an agency turf war going on in Montevideo in which each department was spinning the facts in a way that was most advantageous to its own interests.

He laughed. "Like Joe Friday on *Dragnet*: 'Just the facts, ma'am.'"

McIsaacs squinted at him over his half-moon-shaped glasses, a recent habit he had acquired ever since he had been forced to start wearing spectacles.

"This is not a joke, Tom. We need basic information untainted by secret agendas. But I have to tell you, this is not a file without some risk."

McIsaacs stirred himself and referred to a briefing document.

"Since the early 1960s, Tupamaro Urban Guerrillas have been robbing banks, army and police weapons depots, *and* food warehouses, thereby building sympathy among the population. They have succeeded in intimidating the Uruguayan government to the point where it has retaliated. President Pacheco has suspended parts of the constitution and has been suppressing dissidents. Unless Uncle Sam lends a hand, we fear the government will fail and the country will turn into yet another left-wing dictatorship. We can't afford another Cuba in South America."

"I'm still not clear on my role."

McIsaacs sighed, rubbing the bridge of his nose.

"The FBI has loaned out this guy, Dan Mitrione, to the Office of Public Safety. He's a specialist in policing and torture techniques, and they sent him down there to assist the local police. The director of OPS had no permission, but he acted under his obligations to the Mutual Regional Police and Law Enforcement Agreement. The CIA and State Department are furious. The Tupamaro know all about Mitrione and have ratcheted up their activities and are threatening revenge. All hope for cooperation between the participants in this cluster-fuck has evaporated."

"So what would you like me to do?"

"As I said, discover the truth. We need solid facts on which the NSA can base its objective, informed recommendations to the White House about the position the United States should adopt vis-a-vis the Uruguayan government."

Tom was no longer wavering. He felt flattered and considerably incentivized. He was finally being given an opportunity to help shape policy.

"When do you need me there?"

His Control assumed a more circumspect attitude. "Cool your jets. We've got to come up with a plausible scenario for you, get documentation, arrange some permits, and we need to vet some on-the-ground back-up for you."

Tom's spine was tingling.

"Back-up?"

McIsaacs rose to his feet and walked over to where Tom was standing. He put one beefy hand on Tom's shoulder and spoke to him in a calm, measured tone.

"You got that little medallion I gave you?"

Tom fished it out of his pocket and dangled it. McIsaacs took it and placed it around Tom's neck.

"From now on, you keep this on you. Very close. Assume that, from the minute you land, you will be under surveillance. Everyone you meet, *everyone*, is a Tupamaro agent. They have infiltrated every level and department of officialdom down there. You'll be travelling as a Canadian, with a solid 'legend,' but I want you to be sharp, always. Cover your tracks, be aware that as long as you are there, you could be a target for a kidnapping or worse."

Tom swallowed hard, but he was undeterred.

"I'll be careful."

While waiting for his cue, and with permission from Control, Tom booked ten days at the very chic, exclusive Ixtapa Club Med in Mexico. He found the place full of grasping, un-cool, middle-class, ersatz hipsters trying to screw everything human within their reach within their allotted time under the sun. He arrived in a foul mood and this mindset revolted him.

Eventually, he did find a group of much more laid back and cool travellers, mostly Europeans and South Americans, who enjoyed mocking the sunburnt Americans as much as he did. He got intimate with a couple of French *gentille organisateurs* who showed him several new ways to relax. After ten days, he was feeling almost his old self. Waving a reluctant goodbye to his playmates, Tom boarded a plane to Montreal. When he landed, he found that McIsaacs had sent him a package with his "legend" and another direct warning to watch his back.

CHAPTER 22

Montevideo, February, 1969

This was different, thought Tom as he readied himself for the Uruguayan assignment. This would be the first time that the agency's "talented amateur" would be going deep into subterfuge. During his years of activity in Cuba, he had been himself, a Canadian entrepreneur, ostensibly doing business for the good of the Cubans and himself. His work to help undermine Fidel's revolution was a side job, discreet and organized with little risk to himself. When he was finally picked up, it wasn't for his clandestine activities, though it is possible that they had become known. No, it was for daring to have carnal knowledge of a woman for whom Raúl had the hots.

This was different. This was the first time that Tom would not be "Tom," but a "legend" conceived of and fabricated by others in the NSA. His Control had arranged for Tom to travel to Uruguay under a false identity backed up with a Canadian passport. He was to present himself as a livestock-breeding specialist invited by the Canadian Embassy in Montevideo to help "refresh" Uruguay's cattle herds. To provide depth to this "legend," he would bring with him half a dozen vials or "straws" of bull sperm harvested from a Charolais cattle farm in Valleyfield, just outside Montreal, and carefully packaged in a metal container of liquid nitrogen. There were, of course, far more Hereford and Angus cattle in Uruguay, but Tom thought the "Charolais" touch was an elegant way to distinguish his presence and validate his benevolent Canadian character.

The voyage required careful, somewhat complicated, travel arrangements to maintain the integrity of such a "legend." Tom took Canadian Pacific Airlines from Montreal to Buenos Aires, where he stayed for three days at the modest Hotel Carlton. Following instructions, and by prearrangement, he placed the metal container of bull sperm in the Carlton's freezer and happily played tourist. Then, suitcase and ice cooler in hand, he boarded a vessel of the Buquebus ferry service for the two-and-a-half-hour trip across the *Rio de la Plata* to Montevideo's old port, from where he cabbed it directly to the nearby Ministry of Livestock, Agriculture and Fisheries. There, he met the Canadian Embassy's third secretary, Gaby Walton, in the office of Dr. Elizondo Portuondo, the director of Uruguay's cattle-breeding program and a photographer from one of the city's dailies.

The meeting had been arranged by the embassy purely for protocol and public relations purposes, as an opportunity for Canada to show support for the Uruguayan economy and for Uruguay to acknowledge the gesture. The idea was to say hello, hand over the vials of bull sperm, and then, after a short chat, leave. Walton should have known that, in Latin America, such arrangements never worked out in practice.

True to form, Dr. Portuondo, a large, rotund, and loquacious host, made a big meal of the event by arranging for a small reception party to which he invited half a dozen of his collaborators. It didn't take long for one of these—a dour, unkempt, late-middle-aged, government veterinarian, Dr. Sofia Gonçalves—to discover that the so-called "Canadian livestock specialist" knew very little about the subject.

"You know, the demand for Charolais beef in Uruguay is strictly a niche market. We are all wondering why you have made this gift?"

Tom kept his cool, but inside, his mind was scrambling. Tai Chi time.

"Actually, I believe this was a request from your ministry."

Dr. Sofia overplayed her reaction.

"Really? I don't see how that's possible. We were not consulted and, actually, have no real need for this gift."

Tom tried to catch Walton's eye, but the diplomat was otherwise engaged in a conversation with a reporter.

"Well," said Tom blandly. "You know. Diplomacy."

"As long as it has the BHV-1 certification, I guess there is no harm."

Tom tried to pick up the lead, but fumbled, badly.

"Oh, yes, of course. It has the BVH-1."

Dr. Sofia Gonçalves, reacted, her brows knitted.

"It has BVH-1?"

Tom raised his cocktail to his lips and his eyebrows into his hairline with a gesture meant to be purposefully open to interpretation.

"Bovine   herpesvirus-1?"   challenged   Dr. Gonçalves, incredulously.

The cocktail flew out of his nose as Tom coughed and reached for a napkin. His reaction was turning heads.

"The certification?" he blurted out, recovering quickly. "Yes, yes, the samples have all been *certified* as free of . . . of . . ."

"BVH-1?"

"BVH-1," said Tom definitively as he moved away, calling to Walton.

*

They were in Walton's diplomatic car, headed toward the Sheraton.

"I am under the definitive impression that my cover is blown," Tom said, worried.

Walton squinted into the sunset. "What makes you think that?"

"I got stuck on a technical question by that troll, Dr. Gonçalves. What the fuck is Bovine herpesvirus-1?"

Walton put his hand to his forehead. "Do you think she noticed?"

Tom nodded affirmatively and stared straight ahead, thinking out loud.

"Like she knew what she was doing." He turned around in the backseat, looking out the rear window. "I'd feel better if we made a few evasive moves. I assume that it was your people at the embassy who made the reservation at my hotel?"

"What do you have in mind?"

"Let's check me in and then I'll explain."

The Uruguayan security authorities had initiated control procedures as a precaution against terrorism. By the time they got through the endless bureaucratic check-in process at the hotel, Tom was feeling peckish. Walton took him to dinner at a nearby *churrasqueria*. As they both cut into the excellent, grass-fed Uruguayan beef, served with no seasonings and simple fried potatoes, Walton reviewed the recent developments in the country. Tom put a bridle on his natural tendency to talk, recalling his primary mission: sit, shut up, listen.

"The Tupamaros are principally active in the capital, Montevideo, and they have always had strong support throughout the country." Walton took a sip of the local red they were sharing, a fine yet inexpensive Tannat, and continued.

"What makes the Tupamaros unique is that, instead of relying on seizing control of territory, they favor 'armed propaganda,' a play on the leftist theory of 'propaganda of the deed.' They rob banks and hijack food trucks, redistributing the food and money to the poor. People call them the 'Robin Hood guerrillas.'"

Walton finished his steak and sat back with his wine glass, loosening his tie and scanning the room instinctively.

"The situation is classic. The government has grown frustrated with the insurrection. They have clamped down and not in a good way. With the suspension of the constitution and the torturing, they have escalated the conflict. The Tupamaros, in turn, have become increasingly militant, turning to kidnappings of politicians and foreign diplomats and engaging in shootouts with police and the military. Their growing popularity and increased violence have terrified the government and, as you well know, our American friends, who fear another Cuba in the heart of the continent. Ché failed in Argentina. Failure here is not as obvious."

"How effective are they, really?" Tom asked, mopping up the last of his meal and signalling the waiter for coffee. He tried to keep his face neutral, but, inside, his sense of conviction was being tested and he didn't like it.

"Very. So far, they have kidnapped five diplomats, of which one they released and another escaped. They also kidnapped a US agronomist. They have robbed several banks and continue doing so with monotonous regularity." Walton stopped. "Questions?"

"About a hundred." Tom cut to the quick. "How do they keep getting away with such activities? Where is the police? What's the army doing? Where is the presidential leadership?"

"That's just it. There is none. And when the government does act, they overreact, and piss off everyone. The security apparatus here is not trained to deal with an insurgency. The police look for obvious criminals. The army is looking for organized troops. They are missing an intelligence element that can penetrate the guerrillas. Besides, the Tupamaro are superbly organized and led by professionals, long-time Communists with years of training in subversive activities. And they are everywhere and always find out in advance about police or army activities planned against them, so they get away in time."

"And torture has been used against them?"

Walton sat up as the waiter placed two espressos on the table and cleared away their plates.

"Definitely."

"OK. So, I'd like to tell you what I'd like to do over the next few days."

Walton picked up his espresso. "I'm all ears."

That night, alone in his room, with a nightcap of *grappamiel*, Tom did a quick survey of the day, his reactions, and his feelings for the job ahead. He had botched his exchange with Dr. Gonçalves, but, unless she was on the Tupamaro executive, he didn't think it fatal. He immediately stopped and challenged himself with the possibility that he was still wrong-minded about all of this.

They are everywhere.

Dr. Gonçalves, a frumpy, academic troll, was one of them. Or sympathetic enough to pass on any information that would serve the cause. Walton's driver was one of them. The waiter at the *churrasqueria* had already made his report. The hotel staff who had cleared him through check-in were all in the movement. OK, Tom thought. Without veering wildly into paranoia, if we acknowledge that all of this is not only possible, but likely, what does an intelligent man do?

Tom looked around his room, his eyes scanning all the nooks and crannies where eyes and ears could be planted, all the shadows that might hide a threat. He took a step to the window overlooking the city and, in the distance, *Rio de la Plata*, and thought to himself that, whatever else might happen in the next few days, he was not going to die here.

CHAPTER 23

Montevideo, February 1969

The next morning, Tom got up early and took to meandering in the streets, playing tourist. This was an authentic role he easily assumed and, with each human contact, his anxiety waned somewhat. He told everyone he talked to that he was Canadian. He also made sure to take as many taxis as possible when going from one point of interest to the next because he wanted to interview as many of the drivers as he could.

To his surprise, he found that, in spite of their reputation for cruelty, on the whole, the Tupamaro seemed to be popular with the country's population.

At dinnertime, around ten at night, he found himself at the Old Port. He sought out a tapas bar and tried a few dishes that struck his fancy, then walked up Florida Street, where he bought a small, cheap, canvas duffle bag. He found a café looking out over the port and then waited. The last ferry from Buenos Aires had just disembarked its passengers and, as taxis pulled up, he joined the scraggly group to the Holiday Inn where, on the strength of an HI Loyalty Card provided as part of his "legend" by McIsaacs, and his story about just getting off the last ferry, he wrangled himself a room in which he felt safe enough to sleep for an undisturbed seven hours.

The next morning, Tom checked out early at seven and walked back to the Sheraton. He took the stairs up to his room and entered quietly. Everything was as he had left it . . . almost. He smiled inwardly. Fucking rats. Propping a chair up against the door, he showered with the curtain open and his eyes on his room and prepared himself for the day. He met Walton and his executive assistant, Jorgé Ramos, in the cafeteria for breakfast at eight.

Over ham and eggs and coffee, he reported that, as expected, somebody had searched his carry-on and briefcase the day before. "They were thorough, but careless, on purpose."

"How so?" Walton was surprised.

"They found my tell-tales and lined them up on top of my briefcase. It's a message: we know you are not who you say you are, but we're not yet sure whether you are friend or foe."

"Are you sure? Could it not have been the chambermaid?"

"No, I'm not sure and I've decided that being unsure is the name of this game, right? In any event, we'll have verification by tomorrow morning."

"So you're proposing that we go through with what we've planned the other night?"

"Yes, please."

Tom did not check out of the Sheraton. Instead, he joined Walton at the front door to wait for their car. Walton's assistant left to complete the arrangements they had agreed on over breakfast.

"Jorge?"

Walton smiled. "Medicine Hat, Alberta. Parents were refugees from El Salvador. He played hockey for the Lethbridge Sugar Kings. Degree in poli-sci from McGill."

By nine, Tom was in Walton's car watching him maneuver his vehicle through dense traffic. It took a dreadful half-hour of driving to get out of the city, during which they passed through areas of incredible poverty—shack after shack with no running water or electricity, and raw sewage in the streets. Heartbreaking slums.

Once they got onto *Ruta* 1, the going got easier and Walton was able to establish that they were not being followed. "They go easy on me because I'm a Canadian."

"Who is 'they'?"

The diplomat laughed. "The security services—the police, the army, the CIA. Take your pick."

The idea behind the trip was to validate Tom's "legend" as much as possible, by touring an area, Colonia Province, home to a number of small cattle ranches, one of which was owned by a friend of Walton's. This, it was hoped, would create opportunities for Tom to meet and speak with a number of people representing a cross-section of Uruguayans.

It took them three hours to get there because they stopped for coffee in a couple of small towns on the way to listen to local chatter. At one of these stops. Walton had to make an obligatory call in to the embassy and, when he was done, Tom took the opportunity to make a call of his own. This was the first time he had ever used the number he knew by heart.

"This is the major."

Tom drew a breath, "My name is Barbara."

*

Lunch at Walton's friend's place turned into a lengthy and elaborate affair because the rancher, in true Latino style, had invited a few of his own friends to meet the Canadians.

Tom's fluency in Spanish intrigued the locals, who were unaccustomed to "gringos" who could converse easily with them. Tom had to be conscious of the errant Cubanisms that had crept into his argot. He fumbled at least once and a local rancher reacted, but was too polite to make anything of it. Tom did not have to stretch too far to get the locals to talk about the Tupamaro. After chat about the weather, the rain, the cost of feed, veterinary fees, and BHV-1, the topic invariably turned toward politics. The civility of the guests prevented them from opening up with total candor, but Tom was able to read the body language, the sighs, and the quick glances, and was beginning to form an opinion.

They got back to Montevideo around ten at night. Walton dropped Tom a couple of blocks from the Radisson, his "new" hotel, arranged for him by Jorgé and located across the street from the Canadian Embassy.

Tom had a shower, keeping a chair blocking the door to his suite and the shower curtains open. He called down to room service for a nightcap of *grappamiel.* If Tom's reading of the situation was correct, this entire country was porous, signifying that eyes had been on him the second he landed, which meant that the Tupamaro were, literally, everywhere. The working classes, trade unions, professional guilds, academics, police, army, everyone. How does one defeat such a societal infiltration? The same way that Dale Carnegie taught his acolytes how to win any argument: let your opponents talk until they hang themselves with their own words. In this case, let the Tupamaro operate until the inevitable overreach and then, crack down.

"I'm not going to die here," he said out loud, suddenly seething with anger.

The Tupamaro came for him a few minutes before three a.m. As expected, they had a key to the room to which he was registered. Since he knew they would come, Tom left an overturned chair near the door so that it would have to be shoved aside before one could enter. The noise was to have awakened Tom should he have fallen asleep sitting in an armchair in the adjoining room.

There was no need. Tom was not asleep. He was wide awake, sitting there in his pyjama bottoms. Perhaps more awake at that moment than he had ever been in his life. He was crystalline in his pure awareness that this moment, these next few seconds, would reform and reshape his life forever. There was now no option, no take-back, no do-over. The commitment from this moment on would be absolute and the decision he would make, permanent.

There were two of them, both armed with pistols. The taller had a flashlight and in its beam he saw what looked like a sleeping body in the bed. The silenced .22 snicked viciously as feathers flew up from the bed. It was just a bunch of pillows. The man suddenly felt trapped and dropped to a squat, pivoting on his heel, angry for having been fooled by a vulnerable gringo. He saw the slightly open door leading to the adjoining room and he charged through it.

As the door swung open, it hit another chair placed there in such a way as to fall over between the attacker and Tom. As the Tupamaro stumbled, Tom rose out of the armchair in one smooth motion and raised the silenced ASTRA Constable .380 in the stance of an Olympic target shooter and shot the guerrilla across the bed in the face, not five feet away. It was so automatic, so reflexive that Tom had no chance to be sick.

The man went down. Tom's single bullet had gone through the assassin's eye and buried itself in his brain.

The second man, hugely fat but immensely strong, emerged from out of the shadows and jumped over his fallen comrade, reaching for Tom, and knocking him out of his fugue state and onto his back. Again, Tom reacted without thinking and fired, twice. The Tupamaro dropped his weapon and clutched at his throat in vain. He landed on top of the bed, bleeding heavily from a neck wound, his carotid artery in shreds. Tom rolled him over and watched without emotion as the man on the bed bled out.

Tom quickly took stock of the situation and figured he had at least ten minutes before any back-up would come to see what had happened to the dead men. He dropped the blood-soaked pyjama bottom where he stood, closed the room door, propping the chair against the handle, and ran the shower. Three minutes to rinse off all the blood and douse the bath basin with the bottle of bleach that Jorgé had arranged for him. Tom dried himself carefully, dressed, and gathered up the thick plastic bag and elastic bands that had protected his gun when it was placed by Control in the bathroom cistern. He picked up the damp towels and left the room, stopping only to drop the towels down the hotel laundry chute in the service area.

Weapon in hand, Tom took the service stairs down three at a time, walked through the kitchen, and exited the hotel by the back door. Once in the alley, his sense of detachment kicked in and he stopped to evaluate himself. One side of him was flowing hot blood, like an enraged pit bull. The other side was giddy with an incalculable coolness.

They did not kill me.

There was a heavy grated sewer in the alley. Tom pulled the gun apart in fast, precise movements and dropped the pieces into the sewer, throwing the silencer into a garbage container behind the hotel. Perhaps it was the smell of putrid garbage coming from the container, or perhaps it was his fugue state finally breaking that unleashed his emotions. For whatever reason, Tom had barely a moment to prepare for the explosive and violent bout of vomiting that erupted from his deepest core and nearly knocked him off his feet. He heaved and coughed until he was literally empty and then staggered through the alley and took refuge in the Canadian Embassy across the street, where Walton and Jorgé were waiting.

*

MINUTE ON FAILED URUGUAY MISSION
(February 1969)
Prepared on March 15, 1969, by Alan McIsaacs –
Group Controller

Object: standard intel operation to ascertain the scope and penetration of Uruguay's Movimiento de Liberación Nacional-Tupamaros (Tupamaro National Liberation Movement) into governmental and non-governmental agencies, general popula-tion, civic and social societies and organizations. Conflicting data sets from CIA and FBI determined NSA to do ground-up survey of movement in order to provide current non-biased intel about possible threat to the country and region and information to State Department in order to form policy positions.

1. Our asset's cover was "blown" within four hours of his arrival in the target country, Uruguay. The reason: inadequate briefing by us of his local Minder (a Five Eyes diplomat). The Minder mistakenly introduced our asset to a local who was an expert on a subject with which our asset was supposed to be familiar when, in fact, he was not.

2. Our asset immediately realized that he was "blown" and adjusted his plans accordingly by shortening his stay in Uruguay drastically and devising a plan to:

a   maximize contact, though very little time, with locals to elicit and evaluate public reaction to Tupamaro activity,

b   force the Tupamaro to reveal the extent of (i) its penetration of government institutions and major elements of industry, and (ii) its ability to mount meaningful attacks on targets hostile to it,

c   evaluate local ability to counteract the Tupamaro threat.

Our asset was successful in interviewing a great number of people during his short stay in Montevideo by extensively using taxis and chatting with their drivers and by speaking with a representative number of contacts produced by his local Minder.

Conclusion 1: *On the whole, the Tupamaro are popular and close to winning a sufficient number of hearts and minds to ensure the success of a popular uprising that would chase the present totally corrupt government out of office.*

Conclusion 2: *The circumstances of the assassination and/or kidnapping attempt on our asset are proof that the Tupamaro have a very effective informant network that possesses excellent internal communication systems. The Tupamaro also seem to have a pool of "soldiers" skilled in terror tactics. (Identification of assailants subsequent to their deaths—one university engineering professor, the other a plumber—indicates "soldiers" are drawn from a cross-section of Uruguayan society.)*

Conclusion 3: *The ability to communicate and recruit indicates that the Tupamaro are being assisted by governmental* *organizations such as the police (high penetration likely) and civil service.*

Conclusion 4: *To date, (i.e., to the date of this Minute) the Tupamaro have kidnapped five diplomats and a great number of politicians and wealthy businessmen. They have also carried out dozens of bank robberies without being caught and have, the day after our asset was extracted, killed an FBI police trainer. THUS, THERE SEEMS TO BE NO TECHNICAL ABILITY OR POLITICAL WILL TO SUCCESSFULLY FIGHT THE TUPAMARO.*

RECOMMENDATION: *Military intervention by the us is not an option because Uncle Sam is intensely disliked in Uruguay. Since countering terror with terror has not worked either, the only option that remains is for the US to insist that the present government commence discussions to cobble together a new, somewhat leftist, government that would include members of the Tupamaro.*

CHAPTER 24

Montreal, March 1969

Tom may have been through with Montevideo, but it was clear that Montevideo was not through with him. The nightmares started after Tom's return, and it didn't take a shrink to guess that they were probably triggered by the stimulus of his recent exposure to the deadly Spanish-speaking environments in Cuba and Uruguay.

The scenario was the same every night: he'd go to bed and wait for sleep to come, but it wouldn't, not until early dawn. He'd then sleep a couple of hours and awake feverish, confused, and often shouting. The nightmare was the same; he'd dream that he was in an underground jail cell with a window that gave onto a courtyard. First, Disda would come into view through a side door. Then a Cuban soldier would appear, submachinegun in hand. Tom would start screaming, desperately seeking to attract Disda's attention, but she wouldn't hear him through the thick glass of the cell window. The end was always the same. The soldier would cock his weapon and empty it into the defenceless body of the only woman whose love still haunted Tom, and she would crumble to the ground before his eyes, dead.

Mumbling, "Forgive me, forgive me, forgive me," Tom would awaken, trembling and disorientated.

He stopped eating regularly and took little care of his appearance so that when, buckling under Leo's constant requests, they finally met for a hasty cafeteria lunch, the technician was shocked. When pressed, Tom could barely articulate his inner turmoil and merely mumbled that he was, "not himself."

Leo's next call was to their mutual American friend and, under the guise of the urgent need for Tom's overdue Uruguay debriefing, McIsaacs, stenographer in tow, arranged a visit to the Atwater safe house.

Tom's control hid his dismay at finding his *protégé* in such a psychologically vulnerable state. His "talented amateur" had lost something in that Montevideo alley and his task was to find out if the damage was irreparable. While the stenographer set up, McIsaacs poured a couple of single malts and allowed Tom to relax. Another couple of drinks and the mood seemed right. Tom began in an odd monotone, very much unlike his usual confident voice. His debrief was organized and coherent, which signalled to McIsaacs that maybe all was not lost. When Tom got to the killing, he hesitated and stopped, his voice choked off.

McIsaacs tried distraction. "How did you find the ASTRA Constable.380?

Tom reacted, confused.

"In the cistern, where I was told . . ."

Al laughed, waving him off. "No, I meant, how did you find the gun? The action? We didn't understand why you asked for that gun in particular."

Tom shook off the confusion, his eyes coming up to meet McIsaacs's.

"Oh! Well, from what I observed, it is a common gun in Uruguay. Like the PPK, but less expensive and more available. I recalled it from Langley, a good choice for close-in."

"And the recoil? The silencer?"

Tom sharpened up before his Control's eyes. The stenographer cut McIsaacs a knowing glance.

"Barely felt any kick-back and the silencer was machined perfectly. Like a Kraut did it!"

Now that Tom was focusing better, McIsaacs risked the next question.

"Do you want to know who they were?"

Tom put down his tumbler, but McIsaacs made no move to refill it. He looked up at his Control, his eyes dark, but getting moist with self-pity.

"What right did I have, Al?" he mumbled. "What right did I have to take their lives?"

McIsaacs lit a cigarette and leaned forward. "What right did they have to take yours?"

Tom searched the air for a response.

"I was . . . I was . . ."

The stenographer handed McIsaacs a dossier, which he opened and consulted.

"One was a university professor, civil engineering. The other a plumber. Your would-be assassins."

This information worked its way down deep into Tom's consciousness and came back wrapped in perplexity. He searched for McIsaacs's face as though trying to confirm a poor joke.

"A fucking plumber?" Tom rubbed his eyes.

McIsaacs rose and paced before turning on Tom, bearing down just a little.

"What the fuck is going on, Tom? You've been back six weeks, no report, no response to my requests for a debriefing, *radio silencio*! It took Leo to step in and that is not the way we do things, right?"

"Leo?" Tom was surprised and relieved. So, he *did* have friends.

"Tom, we have this evening to iron things out because I cannot work with an asset I cannot depend on. We are going to straighten this out or we are going to say *adios*, right?"

"Right," said Tom, the shame and doubt creeping up from the pit of his stomach.

McIsaacs poured them both another drink as the stenographer lit a cigarette and waited.

"Spill it."

"I thought I could," said Tom, stumbling over his thoughts and words. "But, now, I'm not certain anymore. I'm not sure about . . . about what we are doing. A plumber, for fuck's sake."

McIsaacs lit another cigarette and nodded his head as he paced back and forth as though confirming his own suppositions. He took up a position near the window, his back against the wall, in the shadow dropped by the curtains, and spoke without emotion.

"Plumber. History professor. Journalist. Schoolteacher. Student. Writer. Failed monk. Businessman. Novelist. Farmer. Accountant. Stenographer. Day laborer. Taxi driver. Petty criminal. Army officer. Drug pusher. Hijacker. Assassin. Marxist. Maoist. Leninist."

Tom was paying attention.

"All the banal, small-minded, egocentric salon revolutionaries, pushing their mimeographed pamphlets, trumpeting a new world order, who think they know better how to run the world."

McIsaacs sat down on the coffee table, uncomfortably close to Tom. "You need a tune-up, my friend." McIsaacs sought Tom's eyes and held them with his own.

"*Propaganda of the deed.* That's what your Uruguayan plumber believed in. I'm sure you have read up on it. Insurrection. Anarchy. Violent acts to show the impotence of government. To show the people that revolution *is* possible."

Tom nodded his head, his eyes focused intently again.

"Do you know how this works, Tom? There was never a moment in the history of the world when the average citizen was as free as right now. Say what we like. Do what we like, live and move as we like. Fuck as we like. We are free to live as we like and make stupid errors about everything."

Tom was now spellbound by McIsaacs. His anxiety receding.

"For the vast majority of ordinary citizens, there is no surveillance. There are no knocks on the door at 0200h AM. No gulags where one is officially 'disappeared.' No show trials. And, in the Western hemisphere, we take that freedom for granted. But not everyone, for there are bad actors everywhere, Tom."

Tom shivered. "You don't need to tell me about 'bad actors.'"

"I know I don't need to tell you, but sometimes we need to be reminded. Bad actors can always find reasons to resent the freedom of others. Because they know better."

McIsaacs rose to his feet and extended a hand to Tom, who took it. His Control pulled him to his feet and led him over to the window. "This is what freedom looks like, Tom. A democratic haven where you and your parents found refuge from the jackboot of totalitarianism. Here it is, Tom. All the values. All that is good and imperfect."

Tom reacted at the word.

"That's right, I said, 'imperfect.' It's not, but perfection isn't an absolute. It's relative, right? Churchill said it, 'Democracy is the worst form of government except for all those other forms.'"

Tom was smiling wryly as he turned away from the window to face McIsaacs, who continued. "So you have to ask yourself one question: is this worth defending? Do democracies have the right to defend themselves?"

Tom was skeptical and gestured toward the world beyond the window.

"But what I did down there, had nothing to do with *this* democracy."

McIsaacs smiled indulgently. "Tom, after all that you have lived through, how can you be so naive?"

McIsaacs left Tom at the window and went to pour himself another finger. He leaned up against the commode. "You have bombs going off in mailboxes right here. People have already died and, according to the Agency, it is only a matter of time before we see kidnappings, murder, hijackings. You know, the Defence Department, has this initiative, Project Camelot. They listed Quebec as one of the 'troubled spots' of the world in 1964."

Tom was incredulous, his expression evidencing his complete confusion with the pure light of sudden revelation just creeping in. McIsaacs noticed and clamped a heavy hand on Tom's shoulder.

"Why do you think I am even up here?"

Tom's mouth opened and then closed. He felt like a complete idiot. Where had his mind been? McIsaacs relented.

"Tom, I'm a lifelong Kennedy democrat. What we are confronting is bigger than anyone's politics or ideology. Freedom has no color. It is the desired state. You, above so many, must see this."

Tom nodded his head, feeling less stupid.

"Down in Montevideo, it wasn't some bearded, frothing-at-the-mouth, banana republic guerrillas who were after your skin. It was people like you. Fine, middle-class people, with education and social advantages. A plumber and a university professor. With tenure!"

Now Tom could laugh. McIsaacs gestured at the window. "And who do you think is running things up here? Sure, some of the shock troops and the fall guys are working-class bums, drunk on fantasies of the 'class struggle.'"

Tom reacted. "No, Al, that's where you are wrong. Here, it's cultural and linguistic. You've heard that phrase, '*Les Nègres blancs d'Amérique*'? "

It was now McIsaacs turn to laugh, spit-taking his scotch. "What is that, a joke? You can't be serious, Tom!" he laughed, wiping down his shirt front. "That's marketing strategy! That's how they are selling their revolution to the cultural elites. Tom, it isn't about, '*Frères Jacques*!' It's about power! It's always about power, Tom."

"Al, with all due respect, I think the agency is wrong on this."

McIsaacs smiled and shook his head with conviction and a touch of condescension.

"OK. In this case, let's agree that there is a basis of truth in what you say, I'll give you that. It is true, the population has shifted and the old ruling elites are disenfranchised from the masses. After your 'Quiet Revolution,' a new elite has emerged—professional, secular, academic—and parallel to their emergence is a cohort of impatient, disenfranchised ideologues who want change now."

Tom considered McIsaacs words carefully.

"Maybe that's why Montevideo shook me up so much. I have turned a blind eye to what has been happening here and now I know why. The violence of those men coming for me. Their arrogant disregard for my life, any life. I've seen men like that before, as a kid, in Budapest."

McIsaacs put his heavy arm around Tom's shoulders and steered him away from the window. Tom sat down heavily on the sofa as McIsaacs remained standing. The stenographer's ashtray was filled, but she kept on, a cigarette hanging out of the corner of her mouth.

"Once, a few years ago, I came home to find my mother sitting in the salon. The television news was on, and she was crying and my father was shouting at her to pull herself together. She was white with fear over a news report of some FLQ attack on an armory. They had seized some weapons, explosives. I tried to calm her, but she just kept repeating, 'Again, it is starting again!'" Tom stopped.

McIsaacs nodded his head emphatically. "The ideology will come from the few working-class heroes and social failures who have read and misunderstood *Das Kapital* and Mao's Red Book. They will throw the flaming cocktails and do the crimes and, in time, might even be forgiven for them. But the real change will come from the bourgeoisie. The middle classes."

Tom looked up at McIsaacs, his spirit calmer than it had been for weeks, his resolve aligned for a pure evaluation.

"So, the question we all have to ask ourselves is: When the radicals turn to violence instead of the ballot box, do democracies have the right, the responsibility to defend themselves, or not?"

*

The stenographer gathered her things. McIsaacs saw her to the door and they exchanged a few words that Tom could not hear. McIsaacs locked the door behind her.

In the weeks that followed his return to Washington, McIsaacs received two reports inspired by that evening with Tom. The first was from Magda Koves, the short, round, and unkempt "stenographer" who was, in reality, a Hungarian ex-pat and doctor of psychology. Koves's psychological evaluation suggested a slight case of post-traumatic stress disorder, and prescribed a regimen of physical training and ideological motivation if Tom was to continue in his capacity as an NSA asset.

The second report was written by Jorgé Ramos, of Medicine Hat, Alberta, former defenceman for the Lethbridge Sugar Kings, former student in poli-sci at McGill where, following a lead from Leo Rosenberg, McIsaacs had contrived to meet and recruit him. Currently assistant to Gaby Walton, third secretary, Canadian Embassy, Montevideo, Jorgé had been assigned to shadow Tom Karas from the moment he set foot on Uruguayan soil. Jorgé had never let Tom out of his sight and had followed him to the Hotel Radisson. It was Jorgé who had placed Tom's ASTRA Constable.380 in the toilet cistern. As it turned out, the "talented amateur" dispatched the professor with aplomb, but was in serious trouble when the immense plumber crashed into the room. Jorge had to admit afterwards that, under the circumstances, Tom had been very lucky that his far-too-hasty shots at the unfortunate plumber had killed him.

And it was Jorgé's report on the incident that McIsaacs now perused with pleasure and satisfaction.

*

On the third day of March, after McIsaacs's cathartic visit, Tom visited his mother to help celebrate her birthday. The popular news had been full of foreboding coverage anticipating further FLQ attacks and violence but, strangely, his mother was calm, causally brushing off the news hysteria.

Gingerly waltzing around the subject, Tom presented her with his gift, a beautiful Hermès scarf he had found at Holt Renfrew. She admonished her son for his extravagance and as she cooed and wrapped it around her neck, Tom wondered aloud if, perhaps, the news wasn't upsetting her? Wasn't she worried?

His mother kept admiring her reflection in a nearby mirror and remarked tersely, "Tom, after all I have lived through, what do I have to be worried about?"

Tom looked up to find his father watching and listening to their exchange with a discernible glint of smug vindication in his aging eyes.

The next day, Tom called his Control and told him he was ready for retraining. Without another word, McIsaacs ordered him to report to Harvey Point within seventy-two hours.

CHAPTER 25

Hertford, North Carolina, 1969

The Harvey Point Defence Testing Activity facility, a campus of the Department of Defence, is located on a peninsula near the city of Hertford, North Carolina. Agencies such as Alcohol, Tobacco and Firearms, the CIA and the FBI, use the place for the comprehensive training of assets such as Tom, relating to overseas counterterrorism and asset-protection formation.

The Point was very different from Camp Peary, the site of Tom's first training tour, in that it offered "individualized" service to the assets detailed to it. Tom had his own room and phys-ed trainer who got him into shape within a month, exercising with him for a couple of hours in the mornings and in the afternoons. Two nights per week were spent meeting with a psychiatrist as McIsaacs had ordered as a result of their meeting in Montreal. The rest of his time

Tom spent on the required reading about the geopolitical situation in Central and South America and the Caribbean. He had no close contact with people other than the trainer, the doctor, and McIsaacs, who visited him once a week.

One of the required papers Tom read with great interest was a CIA report entitled *Cuban Subversive Activities in Latin America: 1959-1968*. It posited a theory, which Tom had also developed from personal observation, that Castro was a compulsive revolutionary, who saw himself as another Simon Bólivar, and was chosen by destiny to bring freedom and unity to Latin America by liberating the continent from US domination.

After analyzing Castro's recent attempts to foment uprisings in the region in detail, the paper concluded that Fidel had attributed Ché Guevara's recent failure and subsequent death in Bolivia to insufficient indigenous financial and tactical support and, therefore, what was needed for success was an organism that could provide those two facilities from the outside with no need for support from the inside. The ideological irony of exporting revolution into regions where there was no popular support for it never seemed to have occurred to *El Lider Maximo*.

Consequently, frustrated by the lack of revolutionary progress, Castro had ordered the creation of a Havana-based organization within the Ministry of the Interior (MININT) that would carry out sophisticated guerrilla activities wherever it deemed to have identified fledgling movements that showed promise of becoming meaningfully successful. In this context, MININT was granted sweeping powers: it was authorized to requisition assistance not only from the treasury and the army, but also from the recently revitalized Cuban merchant navy.

The paper's ominous forecast was that the military capabilities of the countries in Castro's sights—Nicaragua, Venezuela, Guatemala, Colombia, and Bolivia—were incapable of mustering successful resistance to the guerrilla onslaught that Castro was planning, and that, therefore, the US needed to intervene militarily, but not overtly, to thwart Fidel's plan to convert the continent into a seething cauldron of communist unrest, uniformly hostile to the US.

*

On the fifth Sunday of his "vacation" at The Point, McIsaacs invited Tom for dinner at the facility's private dining room. He was surprised to find that seven of his co-inhabitants, whom he had met only casually, were also present.

After steak and kidney pie, beer, and cheesecake, coffee was served and McIsaacs stood up to speak.

"I'm sure you've probably seen each other around before so there'll be no introductions. You have all read the CIA report, *Cuban Subversive Activities in Latin America,* so you know that Fidel is planning to intensify guerrilla activity in that area. The US now has no choice but to help Fidel's targets to defend themselves. We intend to do so, but discreetly, by providing these targets with trained paramilitary *advisors,* multilingual, non-US citizens, under contract with the NSA. You're the first batch of such advisors."

McIsaacs looked around the room, meeting each person eye to eye. "I don't think I need to mention what all of that means. If there's anyone here who wants out, speak up now." No one said a word.

*

For the next four weeks, the eight advisors were given intensive training in infantry tactics, counter-guerrilla maneuvering, on-land and in-water demolition science, and advanced, practical spy-craft. The latter included behavior-modification techniques. The men also spent time on the firing range to hone their ballistic skills. As before, Tom was found to be an average leader and motivator, but a crack shot. If anything, his eye had improved.

The physical training was complemented by intense sessions in theory and ideological practice, led by a sweaty, red-faced, bald-headed, physically imposing Green Beret on temporary assignment from his post in Vietnam. His specialty was insurgency suppression and he barred no holds.

"Your fuckin' role is that of *advisor* and not that of combatant. Do you read me?"

None of the eight assets stirred from their note-taking. The Green Beret snatched the clipboard out of Tom's hands and broke it over his knee.

"Do you read me!?!"

"Sir! Yessir!" the eight assets barked back.

"In country, you are there to guide, not lead. You are there to explain and not order. They won't follow your fuckin' orders anyway, do you read me?"

"Sir! Yessir!"

"Your mantra is sacred, solid, and inviolable: 1) embed yourself in a unit of the host country's army, 2) get to know the indigenous soldiers you are there to help, but, 3) leave the fuckin' fightin' to the soldiers. Do not, I repeat, do not participate unless you absolutely have to. Do you fuckin' read me?"

"Sir! Yessir!"

After a couple of weeks of field exercises using different weapons, the men opted unanimously for the standard helmet, Kevlar vest, Uzi 900 machine pistol, the weapon favored by the US Secret Service, and the standard US Army Colt 19 as a side-arm. These choices were validated as the gear most suited for the type of work the advisors would be required to perform,

Unfortunately, all the training and physical exertion and the twice-weekly sessions with the agency psychologist had no impact on Tom's nightmares. They continued unabated, depriving him of much-needed sleep and progressively exhausting him, reducing his ability to perform at optimum level. This deficiency did not go unnoticed and it was only McIsaacs's direct intervention that allowed Tom to go out into the field. The day before the group was mustered out, McIsaacs came to visit.

"It's time to say goodbye," he said as he handed Tom a bottle of Calvados as a going-away present. "Your unit will be shipping out to Venezuela tomorrow. From now on you'll be reporting to the regional unit commander responsible for the theater in which you will be operating."

"A new boss?"

"Yes, every time you are posted to a new theater. Your theater of operation during the foreseeable future, or at least until your present contract ends, has been defined as being Latin America."

"When and where will I be meeting him?"

"He'll be waiting for you guys in *Puerto la Cruz* when you get there."

"And you?"

McIsaacs allowed himself a little smile of pride.

"I am being promoted to Deputy Assistant Director of Plans for Latin America, so don't worry," said McIsaacs, cuffing Tom on the shoulder. "Indirectly, you'll continue to be working for me."

CHAPTER 26

Puerto la Cruz, Venezuela, April 1969

The city of *Puerto La Cruz,* originally called *Puerto de la Santa Cruz,* or Harbour of the Holy Cross, is home to one of the largest oil refineries in the world. It is also the hub for a number of Venezuela's important pipeline terminals and, therefore, merits a significant military presence.

Tom's people, all Spanish speakers, were billeted in the army barracks near the refinery. Three days after having settled in, they were called to a morning briefing attended by a contingent of soldiers and led by a Venezuelan army captain, Emmanuel Rivero. Rivero had the looks and demeanor of an oily weasel, caught in a uniform that swam on his rounded shoulders.

"We are here to advise, that's all," said Tom in his first meeting with Rivero. "Our orders are very specific in that regard. I'm sure you understand."

Captain Rivero sat back in his chair behind a heavy wooden desk, eyeing Tom in a manner as to invoke a bad, silent screen villain.

"What I understand is that your superiors expect much of us. We are the bulwark against assaults on American hegemony in this sphere."

Tom smiled, blandly.

"And yet you are reluctant to commit to, as you say, 'boots-on-the-ground.' Why is that?"

Tom sighed and replied in a gentle voice. "These are political decisions that are taken far above my pay grade."

This seemed to mollify Rivero, who sucked a bad front tooth, wincing with discomfort.

Tom spent the next couple of days wandering innocuously around the base, sometimes dressed in his civilian clothes, like an errant tourist. After the first day, no one noticed him and he found that he had surprisingly easy access to every corner of the base. He noted that there was a lot of coming and going of civilian cars and trucks and noted the delivery to the base of food, laundry, and other material, but also trucks leaving with large and small crates and equipment on pallets.

He entered the helicopter machine shop, asking with all innocence if he could use the bathroom. A good-natured army grease monkey pointed to the facilities. Tom lingered in the back for a good twenty minutes, during which time he observed odd exchanges of goods and material all supervised by a sergeant quarter master who had that furtive look Tom knew so well. As he left, he stopped to thank the friendly mechanic who was under the guts of a Huey UH1 helicopter.

"Thank you!"

The mechanic pushed out from under the copter.

"*De nada*! You OK?"

Tom placed his hand over his stomach, wincing with embarrassment.

"*Turista*!"

The mechanic laughed. "Better stick to the local beer!"

Tom bent down, pretending to be impressed by the mechanic's work.

"You service all the 'copters on the base?"

"When I can get the parts."

"Oh? Is that a problem?"

The mechanic eyed Tom with fresh interest and shrugged. "Shouldn't be, but it is."

"So, what do you do?"

"I rebuild a lot of the parts myself. The pilots don't like it, but what can you do?"

Tom spent the rest of the day closely observing the traffic around the base and concluded that someone was running a very nice little business in stolen army equipment and supplies. He decided to write up his suspicions and bring them to Rivero's attention at the briefing called for the next day.

*

"Last Saturday we got a report from *Machurucuto*, a small town in the state of Miranda along the northern coast between Caracas and *Puerto La Cruz*," said Captain Rivero, referring to a large map on the wall. "We've spotted a Spanish-built, state-of-the-art Cuban fishing vessel called the *Alecryn,* named after some kind of fish, lurking off *Cabo Tuerto,* the little promontory about ten miles south of the village. The Cubans use these supposed 'fishing' vessels to land guerrillas."

Rivero looked around to make sure everyone understood, stopping for a moment when he caught Tom's eye.

"A line of coral reaches out toward the sea there. The village overlooks the bay, which has fair-sized coral heads. The area doesn't seem like a good landing site, so we figure the Cubans are crafty enough to use it precisely for that reason. We're sealing off the area within twenty miles landward of the promontory. It is a guess, a gamble."

"But definitely worth a try," this from Tom. "I understand you have some guerrilla activity in the area as well, near *Valle de Guanape.*"

Rivero nodded, impressed by Tom's insight. "The *Alecryn* is currently fishing off *Cabo Tuerto,* drifting closer and closer to shore. This makes sense. Our weather forecast indicates a local depression in the area and, by nightfall, there should be lots of rain, thunder, and lightning. Then the wind will reverse direction and begin to blow from the south. The *Alecryn* will legitimately seek shelter from the waves by heaving to north of the line of coral, less than a mile from shore. But even that close, we may not see her because of the darkness and the rain squalls."

"What's the plan?"

"We will head out to *Cabo Tuerto*. We'll hide four Jeeps with about twenty men behind a bluff at the center of the beach," said Rivero, indicating the position on the map. "Two of the Jeeps will be mounted with heavy machine guns, fifty caliber."

"That's two squads," said Tom, nodding.

"Correct, but we will also have you, *Señor Tomás*, and a radioman, a driver, and a bodyguard for you in a command car."

"And where would the rest of the company be deployed?"

Captain Rivero turned back to the map and drew the positions.

"In a semi-circle on the landward side of *Cabo Tuerto*."

"What mobility?"

"Six more Jeeps and three trucks, all with radio." The captain paused and turned away from the map. "We will wait till the *Alecryn* drops her delivery and intercept, with prejudice. Any more questions?"

There were none.

"Good. Suit up and be ready to roll at 1400 hours."

Tom fingered his carefully folded written notes containing his observations of a potential black market in army material at the base, but decided that it was not the right moment to bring his suspicions to Rivero. There would be plenty of time after this operation, which he considered a minor policing effort, one he could safely and benignly observe.

*

The Cubans came ashore, under the shelter of the night and the storm, in two inflatables. There were eight of them— large, lean men, professionals, all armed for lethal engagement. Tom's team never saw them come ashore, but found out later that they had landed with considerable skill on the beach below the bluff. The night was so stormy and the rain and the thunder so noisy that the team never heard their outboards.

In fact, after waiting for hours, Tom and his platoon of eight, four in an open Dodge WC24 Command Car (DCC) and the other four in a Jeep with a mounted Browning M1919 machine gun, began to think that the Cubans had aborted. Following a hunch, Tom suggested that the DCC double back south, get down to the beach below the bluff, and drive north. The Jeep with four men and the Browning M1919 were to follow. Tom didn't know that by then the Cubans had landed and split into two groups of four. One squad, the diversion, disappeared behind the dunes and began to work their way inland, where they were quickly spotted and taken prisoners by Rivero's men.

The second Cuban group headed south along the beach, almost right into Tom's unsuspecting arms. The beach was very narrow for about 300 yards immediately below the bluff. The four Cubans, on foot and loaded down with arms, were just about past this narrow stretch when Tom's DCC came roaring around the corner, lights blazing and tires kicking up beach pebbles. The DCC was moving at speed, exercising no caution because Tom was convinced that the Cubans had not come ashore.

The Cubans knew at once they were trapped. They couldn't outrun Tom's vehicles, nor could they hide, as there was little natural cover. However, they had the advantage of having seen Tom's DCC first. They threw themselves on the ground, positioned strategically and hunkered down. One of the Cubans waited for the DCC to come up to less than fifty yards before rising in a half crouch and firing his grenade launcher right down the pipe. The grenade hit Tom's vehicle, killing the driver and his bodyguard instantly and wounding the radioman, who managed to get away from the overturned and burning DCC.

Tom was the luckiest of the four. He got thrown clear and landed in the surf about ten yards from the burning vehicle. He was dazed with a slight concussion, but in one piece. He patted himself and was relieved to find the Uzi still strapped to his shoulder and the Colt in a holster on his hip. Tom squinted through the brine in his eyes and the dust that had been shaken loose in his head and tried to place the Cubans' position on the beach.

Lying in the water and somewhat shielded by it, Tom cocked the handle on the Uzi and watched the Cubans rise up like ghosts out of the sand and begin their advance on the four bewildered soldiers in the Jeep, which was coming up fast. The Cubans split up, two men on either side of the burning DCC, stepping low. The terrified men in the Jeep scattered, except for one, who stayed behind at the mounted Browning M1919 machine gun. He let fly with a long burst in the general direction of the Cubans and appeared to have tagged one, but the DCC was in his line-of-sight, burning fiercely in the middle of the strip of beach. The flames lit up the area blinding everybody except Tom who, from his position in the surf, didn't have to look through the flames and could see what both the soldiers and the Cubans were doing.

The Cubans had two choices: stay and fight, or cut and run. But the machine gunner had, in fact, hit one of the Cubans. Tom saw him lying on the sand, another Cuban bending over him. The downed Cuban did not move and Tom assumed rightly that the injury was serious. The Cubans followed standard defensive positioning covering each other and decided to fight it out. They could not have known the strength of their opposition and erroneously assumed that the DCC was the only vehicle tracking them. They did not expect another Jeep full of soldiers behind it, but they did not panic. Their training in Cuba had made them stoic and fearless.

The Venezuelan soldiers lying in disarray on the beach and firing away blindly were not doing much good. However, the man who stayed with the Jeep and the machine gun was banging away through the flames of the burning DCC, strafing the area where he sensed the Cubans were regrouping, forcing the guerrillas to keep their heads down.

Neither side knew much about the strength of the other and there was a moment of comic irony when Tom felt weirdly detached, like a referee at a football game, waiting for the two teams to come out of their huddles.

The Cubans had to silence the machine gunner. A strategic thinker, the Cuban commando with the rocket-propelled grenade began to work his way seaward so as to have a clear shot at the Jeep. It never occurred to him that Tom, or anyone else in the burning DCC, had survived, so he never bothered to glance in Tom's direction. When he raised himself into a kneeling position to fire his RPG, he presented Tom with a substantial target. Dizzy and still half-blinded, Tom shot a first Uzi burst that missed. The Cuban pivoted quickly and caught Tom in the shoulder with an expert shot from his Soviet-made APS Stechkin pistol. Tom recoiled in agony from the shoulder wound, but resurfaced in time to see the Cuban resume his stance and let lose his RPG at the Jeep. Tom's Uzi spit out seawater and death at the Cuban just as his grenade blew away the Jeep and the machine-gunner. That left two Cubans and five soldiers, including the strategically situated but now painfully wounded Tom, lying in the water to the side, still more or less in the shadows.

Tom didn't waste any time. He charged out of the surf and shot the Cuban crouching in the marl closest to him and screamed in Spanish at the last one to surrender. He did, and Tom signalled his side to stop firing. They disarmed and tied up the Cuban and then looked around. The situation was pretty bleak for an *advisor* team.

They had lost four men dead; the radioman was wounded, but not too badly, although he would never hear again as the concussion had ruptured both his ear drums. They patched him up as best they could and used the jeep radio to call Captain Rivero, who was standing by in a Command Car on top of the highest rise two dunes away.

Tom turned his attention to the two surviving Cubans. He couldn't be too rough on them; he needed at least one alive to tell him where the other Cubans who had come ashore were headed. He chose the Cuban whose right leg was a mess where the bullet had shattered it. During the fire fight, his buddy had applied a tourniquet and, aside from the leg, the guerrilla was not in too bad shape. He was conscious, anyway. Tom used his Cuban-accented Spanish to ask where the rest of the Cubans were heading.

The Cuban smiled a little, hearing Tom's use of Cuban jargon but shook his head. Tom dispassionately loosened the tourniquet and both men watched the arterial spurts of blood seep out onto the beach. The man looked up at Tom, his eyes pleading.

"*¿Cual es su objectivo, socio?*"

"Barcelona," the Cuban whispered bitterly and fainted.

One of the Venezuelan soldiers was already applying a compress on Tom's shoulder wound. The APS 18mm round had passed clean through beneath the clavicle, but there was a significant loss of blood and Tom was fading. He could hear another soldier calling in for a medical evacuation.

Tom's mind went back to Harvey Point and that bald, red-faced Green Beret barking over and over, "Do you read me!?!" He felt a bit of a fool. It would have been easy for him to have stayed beside Rivero, safe up on that bluff. He had allowed himself to be assigned a front-line position and for no real reason. He could hear a Huey coming in from far off.

His thoughts drifted for a moment as he lost track of time, conscious only of his breathing and the ebbing pain in his body. And then his mother, sitting admiring her reflection in the mirror as she tried on the Hermès scarf and his father, standing back, eyeing his son with a critical frown.

The air around him suddenly felt compressed and heavy as the old Huey UH1 hovered and then landed onto the beach one hundred feet off. The soldiers carried Tom carefully to the waiting medics aboard. The rotors whipped and the copter started to rise. In his delirium, Tom looked at one of the medics shouting, "Did you get the parts?"

The medic could not hear Tom above the rotor wash and bent low over the wounded man.

"¿Qué pasa, socio?"

Tom, almost delirious with pain, raised his head and shouted, "Did you get the parts?"

Barely fifty feet off the beach, the Huey blew a tail rotor pitch cam and started to spin out of control. Within seconds, the copter crashed onto the beach and burst into flames.

BOOK TWO

CHAPTER 27

Northern Quebec, 1980

The Metroliner took off dead on time at five p.m. from Chibougamau Airport and headed south. It was the afternoon milk run for Nordair, a small, Quebec-based aviation company that provided transportation for goods and passengers between the bustling mining region of northern Quebec and the vibrant city of Montreal in the south, with an intermediate stop in Jonquiere.

The twin turboprop aircraft, built by Fairchild Industries, was economical to operate because it was self-contained. It needed no loading ramp and was certified to carry nineteen passengers with a crew of only two. The co-pilot could act as steward during the flight and, if necessary, assist with the loading and unloading of freight and luggage at stopovers.

The flight from Quebec City to Jonquiere would take about forty-five minutes, followed by a half-hour break to load and unload. The flight would then continue on to Montreal, a journey that usually took about an hour to an hour and a quarter, depending on air-traffic congestion at Dorval International.

Captain Greg DiMauro was in charge that particular day, with his childhood friend Mike DeAngelis riding shotgun in the co-pilot's seat, both of them thirty-four.

Products of Montreal's "Little Italy," the two had been friends since early childhood and shared two overwhelming passions: sailing and flying, to the point where neither completed a university education, choosing, instead to enroll in flying school after junior college. They shared a third passion of which their families were only dimly aware: freedom. They loved the Square Mile of their youth. They loved their families, but both men had been stung early on by an overarching desire for infinite horizons and freedom. Any wall, any limit on what they could achieve was to be overcome, ignored, defeated. The two men were as one when it came to the pursuit of unbridled freedom; hence, the passion for sailing and soaring.

Since DiMauro had finished the course six months ahead of DeAngelis, he would forever be "senior" to his buddy according to the inflexible rules that govern rankings for pilots belonging to the Canadian Airline Pilots' Association. As a result, whenever they flew together, DiMauro occupied the left seat in the cockpit.

DeAngelis didn't mind because his turn at being *el supremo* would come every time they sailed together, which was often.

Mike's uncle Alberto, his mother's bachelor brother, had been in construction and, after making a small fortune, had bought a thirty-four-foot Nautor Swan sailboat, which he kept in North Hero in Upper New York State. He docked it at a small country house along the shore of Lake Champlain, about fifteen kilometers south of the US-Canadian border.

After suffering a serious heart attack, Uncle Alberto moved into a long-term-care facility in St. Leonard and left the sailboat and the cottage in Mike DeAngelis's care, together with a dilapidated old panel truck used for carrying "stuff," sails, and suchlike back and forth between North Hero and Montreal.

There was a tacit family understanding that, in the fullness of time, Mike would inherit the lot.

Mike and Greg would spend most summer weekends in North Hero, sailing and partying with a revolving door of likeable but not serious-minded young women. Then, each September, Mike would have the sailboat de-masted and stored on blocks for the winter. But not that September.

"Wheels up," ordered Greg, and Mike obediently pulled the appropriate lever then went aft to see if someone wanted a drink. There were no takers from the half-dozen passengers on board, all of them heading no further than Jonquiere.

Mike returned to the cockpit. "We're set to go," he reported and slid into the right-hand seat.

Greg was sweating. Nerves. "Where is the gold and how much of it is there?"

Mike grabbed the manifest off the shelf above him and flipped through it.

"I stored it behind the passengers' luggage, so it'll be easily accessible as soon as the suitcases and whatnot are unloaded."

"Any other freight?"

"The usual mix."

"How much gold?" Greg asked again, his voice strained.

Mike found the freight waybill.

"The standard average amount, just as we expected." Mike lit a cigarette and continued reading. "Forty Good Delivery bars, each weighing 400 troy ounces, or about eleven and a third kilos. Total weight, 16,000 ounces. Total value for insurance at $1,500 an ounce: $24 million."

Greg whistled and wiped his forehead. Mike continued.

"Standard wooden packing crate on skid. Total weight in is about 500 kilos."

"Just another day at the mill, right?" chuckled Greg.

The gold had originated at the Globex smelter used by the Chibougamau region's gold miners to convert their product, gold ore of varying purity, into standard Good Delivery bars containing 99.999 percent gold and weighing eleven and a third kilos. The smelter shipped these bars via air freight to Montreal at irregular intervals, relying heavily on security keeping shipping dates a strictly guarded secret. Only Brinks, which accompanied the gold to and from the relevant airports, had twenty-four-hour advance notice of shipment dates.

And Brinks leaked, at least to Greg DiMauro, whose cousin, twice removed, was married to a woman who worked for the company.

After an uneventful landing at Jonquiere, Greg taxied the Metroliner as close as possible to the twin Beechcraft 58 Mike had flown up from Montreal two days earlier. As usual, the ground crew was short one man, so Mike had to help unload the luggage and the freight destined for Jonquiere. Over the years, this situation had become so routine that his driving of the forklift aroused no suspicion.

There was little luggage, but some freight, including a wooden crate loaded with bricks that Greg had sent to himself in Jonquiere. Thus, diverting the relatively small box of gold into the Beechcraft's hold presented no problem for Mike as he shuttled deftly back and forth among the Metroliner, the terminal, and the Beechcraft. Had he been challenged about loading the gold into the Beechcraft, he could have claimed that he had mixed up the two boxes.

Meanwhile Greg disabled the Metroliner's transponder, buttoned up the aircraft and sauntered over to the Beechcraft. Mike got in beside him and tied a hankie in front of his mouth to disguise his voice. He then called air traffic control in Montreal, obtained clearance for take-off and piloted the aircraft into the air, upon which Greg switched on the transponder they had installed in the Beechcraft a few days earlier.

The transponder was calibrated to the frequency identical to that of the Metroliner, so that, to ATC in Montreal, it looked as though the Metroliner had taken off on schedule for Montreal from Jonquiere.

An hour later, and moments before landing at Montreal International, they diverted to Cartierville Airport, a small abandoned strip belonging to the now-defunct Canadair Aero-engine Testing Company situated next to the main airport. They pried open the crate containing the gold and, using a wheeled dolly that had also belonged to Uncle Alberto at one time, ferried the forty bars across to the old panel truck they had parked next to the strip the night before.

It took them only eight trips.

Ninety minutes after landing at Cartierville, they were crossing the US-Canadian border on a side-road with no border guards near Champlain, New York. Another quarter hour had them at Mike's chalet, where they stashed the gold under the floor boards of the Swan, hid the panel truck in the garage and motored sedately south in the un-masted vessel, toward the south end of Lake Champlain to the canals, locks, rivers, and lakes of the Intercoastal Waterway, with $24-million worth of gold as ballast.

The authorities fumbled around for half an hour before locating the missing plane and another hour reconstructing the crime. The following morning detectives began interviewing the DiMauro and DeAngelis families. They were Italian-Canadians who cooperated with the police in their own way—that is to say, they answered all questions, but volunteered no additional information.

The cops stumbled onto the existence of the sailboat only four months later by accident because the panel truck and the chalet were all registered in the name of Mike's maternal uncle, whose family name was Bianchi, not DeAngelis.

By that time, the gold and the Swan and Greg DiMauro were safely tucked away in David, a small town an hour and a half's drive south of Panama City, Panama. Greg had ditched his Canadian passport and was travelling on a valid Italian passport in which his name appeared as G. Roberto Mauro. The "Di" had disappeared, and Greg's second middle name, Roberto, was now being used, courtesy of a "careless" clerk named Cristina Bianchi who worked at the Italian Consulate in Montreal and who just happened to be Gregorio DiMauro's cousin.

However, Mike DeAngelis was no longer around.

The trip down the coast of Florida had been uneventful. Mike was a conscientious captain and had plotted their course carefully, mindful every minute of the load they were carrying, their future, their destiny, their freedom. He had noted the weather reports of a small storm rising up between Jamaica and the Cayman Islands, but had felt that there was a margin of safety and so had no hesitation ordering Greg below to catch up on some much-needed sleep while he took the first watch.

Greg was exhausted—from not so much the physical effort of the past week, but the nervous tension that had seized his body and mind. As soon as he hit the bunk below he was out and only came to several hours later when a violent swell tossed him up against the bulwark. It was a black, moonless night and Mike's small storm had bloomed into a violent squall. Stumbling up on deck, Greg discovered Mike was gone, his tether snapped, clearly knocked over while trying to handle the swinging boom by himself. Maybe he had called out for Greg or maybe he really felt he could handle the storm by himself.

Greg immediately instituted a search, fired several flares into the inky black, motored ineffectively against the surge in diminishing circles, but without success. The darkness and the strong winds had been just too much for him. When the storm cleared, he lingered in the area for several days, listening to the maritime broadcasts for any news of a rescue or an unknown body washed up on a beach. At the time the cousins had planned their heist, they had made a pact that, if anything should happen to one, the other would carry on as best he could. Reluctantly, Greg moved on. All he could hope for was that Mike, who was wearing a life vest, would be picked up by a passing vessel or perhaps that he would drift ashore somewhere while still alive.

CHAPTER 28

Panama City, Panama, 1982

The view from Alejandro Samos's eighteenth-floor office in the *Torres de las Americas* complex in Panama City was truly breathtaking. The panorama-sized windows overlooked the spectacular *Corredor Sur* Highway skirting the beach of Panama Bay and, beyond it, the Pacific Ocean in its full, sparkling glory.

However, it was not the view that held Alejandro's rapt attention, it was his own reflection in the floor-to-wall window, which revealed to him *omnino hominum,* the man in full. Alejandro Samos, the former Tom Karas. Samos, a meticulously dressed CPA who affected thin, almost invisible glasses with steel-wire frames and who spoke English with a slight Latino accent, was the managing director and sole owner of ISC, International Services Corporation. The company provided facilities for forming and domiciling bearer-share Panamanian shell companies.

Samos stepped closer to the window, his reflection in the glass forming a palimpsest of the past and present. The plastic surgery after the helicopter crash had been painful beyond description, but well worth it. McIsaacs was, after all, correct. He did have more to live for and the man standing in front of him had been a blank canvas on which the "Tom Karas" within could paint and form as he wished. A better version of himself?

Better? What's that all about, anyway?

For the better part of nine years, Alejandro Samos had cultivated a deep and resistant back story that was, for all intents and purposes, bulletproof. True, it had taken much longer for his wounded and scarred face to find its final form. The dozen or so operations with the accompanying side effects of inflammation, swelling, tissue displacement, and the delicate bone grafting had taken years to settle and solidify and stop aching. Samos had not been idle during this time of healing. The agency had scoured birth and death records in Panama until they found the correct child death notice from a family that had effectively disappeared. Assuming the identity of this unfortunate infant was child's play, and not even particularly illegal, given the Panamanian laws in the matter. The name and background fit him like a glove. It was this appropriateness, this "fit" that impressed Samos no end. If he was being honest with himself, there was always something about Tom Karas that he did not like: his detachment, his hardhearted attitude toward women, and his self-absorption. Karas had the need to make sure everyone in the room knew how smart and successful he was. Samos had no such desire—quite the opposite. Samos's greatest social joy was when someone unknown to him discovered what a clever and nimble-minded person he was and stood in awe of the fact.

So it was now, with the long, lush-bodied, and mature woman who sat in the consulting chair opposite his large, cleanly modern desk. She had come to Samos a couple of years ago through a Brazilian consular friend for whom the CPA had done some important work and had revealed herself as an archetypal, PEP, a *Politically Exposed Person*. She was the secretary-general of Brazil's largest teachers' union and had asked Samos to set up an offshore retirement fund for her into which she had deposited very modest amounts over the past two years.

She had asked for one of her twice-yearly consultations, excusing herself for taking up so much time. Samos would not hear of it and stepped out of his somewhat narcissistic reverie to address her present concerns. He turned to the green-eyed woman who, due to her confidence and maturity, appealed to Samos.

"So, are you pleased with our OFC services so far?

The woman had a dazzling but somewhat smutty smile that stirred Samos.

"All these acronyms," she mumbled. "How do you keep them straight?"

It was Samos's turn to smile as he took the chair opposite.

"Yes," he drawled in English, because his Portuguese was weak. "It is annoying, isn't it? OFC, Offshore Financial Center. It is a good thing for the region that Panama became on OFC."

"Business is good?"

"For people who are *offshore*, like you, it could not be better."

"Like me?" asked the woman as she drew out a long, Brazilian panatella and fired it up. Samos slid a heavy, clear crystal ashtray closer to her chair.

"Like you," said Samos, smiling. "Your international transactions have tax-exempt status and we are very friendly toward commercial and financial operations."

"Friendly," murmured the woman, fragrant smoke circling her lush mouth. The lovely perfume of the cigar tempted Samos, but he had been advised by the reconstruction surgeons to stop smoking, so he rarely indulged.

Samos had to reposition his legs to hide his growing erection. "As a result, Panama has attracted great amounts of foreign capital and, right now, we are one of Latin America's largest financial centers."

"And secure. Security is very important to me, you understand, given where the money is coming from," the woman whispered, holding Samos's lidded eyes with her own.

"Are you concerned? Compared to our neighbors to the north and south, we have had several decades of proud, solid political stability. Your money and securities are in the Bank of Nova Scotia, a Canadian bank. And your monthly statements will never be known in Brazil."

The woman seemed satisfied. Her hands dropped to the sides of the Eames chair, sliding over the black leather, enjoying the sensation. If he squinted, Samos could almost see the young woman she must have been thirty years ago.

"You will note an important increase in the amount of money I will be sending you. I'd like you to open a separate account for this, under the same conditions as my retirement account."

"Of course, my dear."

Expensive real estate, this one, he thought. Not his, but one didn't have to own to appreciate.

"The money that I will be sending to you, will be coming . . ."

"I don't need to know!" said Samos sharply, raising his palm to stop her. "In fact, much better that I don't know."

The fact was, that, due to his connections inside the US consulate in Brasilia, he already knew that this luscious banana split of a woman had started skimming off the nation's teachers' pension fund, a hedge against the upcoming elections, which might unseat the incumbent government. He expected her new deposits to be substantial indeed.

"I will set up the new account for you and you will have the number and the security protocol to wire money whenever you wish. I will receive your statements and manage the funds exactly as before."

"Same management fees?" she asked without any shyness.

"There will be some one-time costs, but, yes. But, if these new despots are *important*, I am willing to lower my percentage a smidgen."

The woman raised herself up to address him more directly.

"My future happiness is in your hands, Señor Samos." She grew thoughtful. "I feel . . . what I want to say is that I appreciate everything you have done for me. Life in Brazil now is very difficult. You have made me feel so much more secure. I'd like to think that if there were ever anything I could do for you, you would ask."

Her eyebrows were raised expectantly and the implication was clear. Samos came around from his desk to take a seat next to his client. She leaned in, as did he.

"Actually, I wanted to ask your advice about the upcoming November elections."

This was not the response she was expecting and her eyebrows went up another couple of millimeters, but she was also intrigued and leaned in closer.

"The November elections?"

Samos played it a little shyly.

"Yes, you see, I have some clients—friends really—with serious business interests in your country. They are concerned about a possible change in your government."

The woman smiled widely and sat back. She understood very clearly what she was being asked.

"Well, you know that the National Renewal Party has changed, right? They are now called the Democratic Social Party."

"Yes," replied Samos. "I guess they felt threatened by the surge in popularity by the Brazilian Democratic Movement Party?"

The woman was practically purring in delight by how brazen Samos was behaving.

"Right. So, what is it your *friends* are concerned about?"

Samos feigned discomfort.

"The unions will hold a lot of sway over the results of the election. We have heard that some of the larger ones, like the Central Unica dos Trabalhadores . . ."

"The CUT," said the woman, interrupting and laughing. "And the Confederação Nacional dos Trabalhadores da Educação."

"The CNTE," Samos interjected, joining in the acronym competition. "With their millions of members, they could decide the next government."

The woman stopped laughing and stood up abruptly, straightened her blouse over her impressive form, brushed the wrinkles from her tight skirt, and bent down to place her lips close to Samos's ear.

"The CNTE is voting DSP," she whispered breathily. "There will be no change in the government, except the name of the party."

With this, she put her hand under Samos's chin, turned his face to hers, and planted a long, wet kiss on his mouth, her tongue sneaking out to taste his lips.

As she straightened up, she looked down at Samos and asked, "Will that suit the *FOS, meu lindo*?"

"FOS?"

The woman headed for the door with a jaunty air.

"Friends of Samos!"

After seeing her out with a promise to meet again that evening for dinner, Samos sat down and composed a memo of the encounter that he would send to his control, Scott Prewitt, at Foggy Bottom. He would ask for the usual authorized "error" of US$30K to be deposited in the Brazilian's existing account at the Bank of Nova Scotia. When she asked about it, he would tell her it was an error and to ignore it. But the error would stay in the account and, eventually, would be conveniently accepted and forgotten. Accounts paid in full.

Samos sat back and considered the last and only time he had met with Scott Prewitt. A desiccated New Englander, Prewitt could trace his American family roots back to the witch-burning Puritans of Salem, Massachusetts, and had replaced Al McIsaacs some time ago. In line with his inquisitionist pilgrim pedigree, Samos found Prewitt had no sense of humor, was less than qualified and definitely not *sympatico*.

Scott Prewitt, rake thin and angular, like a praying mantis, was more of a diplomat than intelligence officer who, it was obvious to Samos, had never operated in the field. He was high-ranking, with first class connections both in the NSA and at Foggy Bottom. Samos had deduced from their first face-to-face conversation over brunch at Joe's Stone Crabs on South Beach, during which Prewitt actually declined to eat, that Prewitt was way high up, because he was reporting directly to the Director of the National Resettlement Operations Center (NROC), a spanking new Directorate under the NSC (National Security Council) umbrella.

"We're quite independent of the CIA and the NSA," Prewitt had told Samos. He was soft-spoken, blue-eyed, red-haired, and middle-aged, with an elegant bearing helped along by his spare body. Presumably Ivy League educated, the man was comfortable in his own skin and had an easy way with words. Samos estimated that he was in his late fifties—his own age, more or less.

"First things first," Prewitt said, by way of breaking the ice. "I confirm that the transfer of your file to NROC has now been completed and, as I told you in my last signal, I am honored to become the minder of such a distinguished and experienced warrior as you." The flattering words were spoken as if by rote, with no genuine sincerity behind them, giving Samos some doubts. Too much honey from someone with Prewitt's austere, Calvinist, New Englander genes.

To test his theory Samos opened with the standard flattering gambit. "Harvard or Yale?"

Prewitt barely looked up from the notes carefully compiled and organized in his worn leather, Filofax.

"Neither. Brown."

Bingo, thought Samos. He's a graduate of one of the oldest American universities, exclusive as hell and boasting of at least four U.S. Secretaries of State, dozens of Cabinet officials, and a bunch of Congressmen among its graduates.

Connections, connections, connections!

"Undergraduate or graduate?" he asked, probing for brain power.

Prewitt allowed himself a quiet chuckle. "I hold a doctorate in *PoliSci* and my special area of interest is South

America." He looked up from his notes as though to gauge Samos's reaction. "Why do you ask?"

Prewitt was obviously familiar with the game. Samos had not wagered on the American's forthright challenge. Prewitt's pale blue, slightly bulging eyes, held Samos's far longer than was comfortable and didn't drop as he explained the situation. "I've been in my present position for a couple of years now and I was hoping to pick up some practical pointers from you that would help both of us to further our joint interests more effectively."

Samos felt emboldened to up the ante. "Is there a problem?"

"On the contrary," said the New Englander, dropping his eyes and leaning back, all smiles. "You've been so damned effective that you got the powers that be thinking about replicating your kind of operation in some other part of the world, like, say, the Balkans."

Samos was inwardly pleased and gratified, but remained cool. "You don't say."

The waitress appeared, filled their glasses with fresh orange juice and then took their orders. After emptying his glass, Samos looked across at his new Control with renewed interest. "So, where do we start?"

"Perhaps you could give me examples of how you identify useful contacts and then recruit them."

The request surprised the ersatz Panamanian. It spoke volumes about his Control's lack of familiarity with his file at NROC and trade-craft in the field. Samos had expected a more technical discussion rather than a review of sensitive information in the open air. Some years later he would come to regret that he had not paused to question why his Control was so interested in familiarizing himself with the personal details of his network's members.

At that moment, his was not to question why, so he launched into an elaborate tale more than half of which was fiction.

"The process is lengthy and requires patience because one needs to establish oneself as a trustworthy and discreet professional in the community in which one wishes to operate."

The waitress, a mid-thirtyish *Cubana* with a figure that resembled a cello from the rear, and breasts that were truly spectacular when viewed in profile, began to hover. After refilling their coffee cups, she departed but not before cutting Samos a sidelong glance affirming a mutual interest. Samos continued with his story.

"Of course, picking the right community is also a serious consideration. In Latin America, the possibilities are limited to Uruguay, Panama, and Costa Rica, as far as confidential, private banking is concerned. Reasonably safe operations are legally possible, under a tax-exempted regime, without local government interference. In the islands, there is Grand Cayman to the south and Bermuda in the north, both doing business under British-type, stand-alone—or, if you prefer, independent—legislation.

"How about the Bahamas?" asked Prewitt, jotting down notes.

"Too dependent on US mainland influence."

"And Europe?"

"Well, as you know, Switzerland, Lichtenstein, and, to a degree, Luxemburg."

Prewitt shook his head. "You should know that these so-called European 'safe havens' hiding offshore money will be coming under intense pressure by our Treasury Department. We anticipate that the smart money will turn away from them and seek refuge elsewhere."

Samos's ears picked up. This was news, though not quite unexpected, for him. He wondered if Prewitt's connections were far more wide-reaching than he'd imagined. Were his new Control's simplistic-sounding inquiries, in fact, more calculated?

"Such as where?"

Instead of answering the question, Prewitt delivered himself of a lecture, the point of which, Samos realized, was the real agenda behind the American's desire for a face-to-face conference.

"Cyprus, for example, for the rich residing in Russia and the Middle East, and Hungary for the Balkans."

Samos could not believe his ears and was careful not to react. Inwardly, he voiced his shock. *They've lost their senses!* Samos was aware that Prewitt was scrutinizing him for a reaction. "That sounds kind of unlikely—at least, to me."

Prewitt shook his head. "I really don't think so." He wiped his mouth with his napkin, folded it, and put it on the table. Game over, for now.

CHAPTER 29

Key West, 1982

Greg DiMauro, now traveling as Roberto Mauro, and Mike DeAngelis, now traveling under an Italian passport under the name Gino Fantigrossi, had taken three months to get to the Bonanza Bay Marina at Key West. Along the way, the "Swan" had been rechristened the "Shirley," and was sailing under the Australian flag. As was their routine, the boys headed for the nearest modest-looking eatery offering reasonably priced food. They had disciplined themselves to keep a low profile and never to flash money.

After lunch, they cleaned up the vessel and glanced through the pages of *The Key West Citizen*. Their attention was drawn to an article describing the latest problems facing Moe Hunter, the perennially broke treasure hunter and discoverer of the *Our Lady of Attoche* shipwreck.

"He's going to be at a breast cancer fundraiser tomorrow," noted Greg.

"Then that's where we'll meet him."

The following day, they sought out Hunter at the brunch fundraiser and, after handing over a respectable cash donation, invited him to visit them on board that afternoon. Hunter was savvy enough to take the proffered bait.

"Why are you always broke?' asked Mike waving the newspaper article around as the other two men laughed and cracked open some beers. "I mean, it looks like you found one of the fucking richest wrecks out there, and this article says you can barely pay your fucking crew!"

Hunter pulled hard on his ice cold beer before answering. He didn't know who these two guys were, but they spoke like goombahs from the hood and if they had any money, which he suspected they did, there was no reason why they couldn't be persuaded to invest in his operation.

"That's a fucking great question Roberto."

Mike stopped him, pointing at Greg.

"He's Roberto. I'm Gino."

"Right, right. Gino," said Hunter, by way of an apology. "Well, like I said, great question. You see, we have begun to 'mine' the wreck, but I'm required by the authorities to deposit the objects we bring to the surface in a bonded warehouse pending a decision by the United States' Supreme Court as to who really owns the *Atoche* treasure—Hunter Explorations, Spain, or the state of Florida?"

"So you're saying that you might wind up owning no treasure at all," Greg cut in.

"That's unlikely. What is possible though is that I'll only get a sort of a finder's fee for locating the stuff."

"And how much would that be?"

"Well, let's see," said Hunter, warming to his favorite subject. "Based on what we know from Spanish historical archives, the *Attoche* sank in 1536 on her way from Latin America to Spain. She was transporting a load of gold worth anywhere from $200 million to $300 million. I am hopeful that the court will award me at least a 20 percent finder's fee."

Greg was intrigued. "Then you're hoping for a $40-million payday, right?"

"At least," said the diver, taking another refreshing pull of his beer. He turned the bottle and noted that it was a Molson Export, from Canada.

"And you're financing current diving operations from the sale of participations in that payday, right?"

"As well as the legal costs of the proceedings, yup."

"How much of the participations have you sold so far?" asked Mike.

Hunter was used to answering such questions. "We started a few years back by getting friends together and raising a million bucks. In return, they were given a 25 percent stake. Two years of salvage operations at the general area of the wreck conducted before we found the wreck itself yielded a couple of million dollars' worth of gold and artifacts. We used these funds to buy out the original stakeholders, who were glad to double their money because they were unwilling to wait for the jackpot."

"A bird in the hand."

Hunter raised his almost empty bottle to Mike.

"How did you continue financing operations?"

"We jacked up the unit price to $80,000 per unit representing a 1 percent stake and sold ten participations."

"And you have just about spent the $800,000 you raised?"

Hunter sighed and finished his beer. "I'm afraid that's so. I'm now forced to offer another 10 percent for sale. I want to raise the unit price, but, under present economic conditions, this may not be possible."

Mike nodded agreement. "If the court awards you no more than a 20 percent finder's fee, the total package would come to forty million bucks, 1 percent of which is a maximum of $400,000. Therefore, if you sold participations at $100,000 a crack, people would get back only four times their money, not enough to entice them to take on such a high risk."

"Gino, you just nailed it, right on the head." Hunter checked his watch as though he had someplace to go. An old ruse, but it was important to appear as a man in demand. "Sorry, boys, I gotta go, but thanks for the beer."

They all got up. Just before reaching the gangplank, Mike turned to Hunter.

"If we came up with an alternative money-raising solution, would you be willing to try it?"

"Of course. As long as it's legal. With the Feds watching me, I gotta walk the line."

Mike revealed little, just nodded. "Let me sleep on it before I say any more."

They agreed to meet the next day for an early breakfast in the cafeteria.

The next day, Mike stayed behind to supervise the work of re-installing the Swan's mast while Greg met Hunter for breakfast. The two spent an hour and a half in carefully guarded conversation, during which Hunter impressed his visitor with his knowledge of political and economic conditions throughout the region.

He also seemed to know everybody who was somebody in the Bahamas, Cuba, the Caribbean, and Central America, having tried to raise money from them for his venture, and was particularly taken by the possibilities that Panama offered.

"You must absolutely check out the place on your way south," he said when Greg told him he was thinking of heading for Argentina. "And if you do, look up my friend Alexander Samos, who is definitely the go-to person in Panama."

After some polite but tough negotiations, Greg, Mike, and Hunter worked out an arrangement that suited all of them. Hunter was to prepare a letter attesting that "Roberto Mauro" had purchased two standard gold bars from the treasure hunter. Hunter was then to send this letter to his attorney in Grand Cayman with instructions that it be handed to Mr. Mauro against a payment of $8,000 in cash, which was about $5,000 short of the money Greg and Mike had left from the war chest they had withdrawn from their banks before committing the bullion robbery.

In reality, Hunter had sold nothing to Greg. No gold bars. No gold anything. The transaction was a fiction, but one that netted Hunter $8,000 in cash and provided Greg with a paper backup for at least two of the gold bars that he and Mike needed to sell in order to complete the heist.

Greg and Hunter also agreed verbally that this arrangement could be repeated in the future at any time the "boys" had $8,000 to spend.

CHAPTER 30

Panama City, Panama, 1982

Alejandro Samos had made a great success of the business that he had founded half-a-dozen or so years earlier. At least, as far as Greg could judge, based on the impressive directory board next to the entrance to the man's elegant offices that listed over a hundred entities for which ISC provided domicile and administration.

Greg was accustomed to making decisions in concert with his cousin, but Mike was gone and he was going to have to make the important evaluations alone. Looking at the gold-chip surroundings, Greg's first reaction was to cut and run, but he checked his impulse. Moe Hunter had told him that Samos was the go-to guy in Central America if you wanted to get things done safely and Greg meant to find out.

Alejandro Samos was all business. "I must remember to thank Moe Hunter for thinking of me. He has been a steady source of new business for us." He took a sip of his espresso. "Now, you must tell me how I can help you."

Greg was ready. "First, I need a bearer share company, preferably administered from here, but resident in Cyprus."

"Why Cyprus?"

"I'm essentially European," Greg lied shamelessly. "Cyprus is closer."

"You mean to Italy?"

"Exactly."

"No problem. A bit more expensive, but feasible. What else?"

"I need Panamanian banking facilities."

"That could also be arranged for a fee."

"Excellent. I bought some gold from Moe, which I now want to use as collateral against a bank loan."

Samos's eyebrows did not flinch and his lidded eyes remained in their sockets, placid and blandly responsive. "You don't say? How much?"

"About a million dollars' worth."

Samos made a note and then looked at his visitor with renewed interest. He took him in for a full thirty seconds and noted the sail-scarred hands, the wind- and sunburnt complexion, and a caution behind the pugnacious bravado.

"You must be joking. Moe Hunter is not allowed to sell anything before getting clearance from the US courts. And it takes ages to get permission, which, by the way, is seldom granted."

Greg had been looking for the opening. "Here's a letter from Hunter." He threw the treasure-hunter's document across Samos's desk. "Call him, if you wish. The gold he sold me was brought to the surface before Hunter had actually found the mother lode, so it's not subject to the seizure. He had it refined and is now selling what little of it he has left to continue financing his operations."

Samos instantly perceived what his visitor was about. Moe Hunter was not an idiot. He would never have taken historic archaeological gold, worth its weight but also worth its historic significance, and melted it down as ordinary trade ingots. This fellow's gold was obviously of dubious origin, and most likely, there was more of it than the two bars to which Hunter's letter referred.

No matter. Samos felt that as far as the laws of the jurisdiction of Panama, were concerned, he was on safe ground. If Moe Hunter confirmed that he did sell two gold bars to Mauro, Samos would have satisfied the requirement that he exercise due diligence when dealing in precious metals.

Samos's bank would lend this Roberto Mauro money on the gold, he was sure of that. If not, Samos could easily finance the operation himself—he had plenty of money. Converting Mauro's original gold into freely tradeable bars would be a problem to solve with the assistance of his lover and business partner, a very senior executive at the Mexican National Mint.

In very few seconds, Samos could see how it could be achieved. It was all just a matter of paying off the right people.

He turned on the charm. "I'm sure I can help you with securing such a bank loan, but I'm afraid that I will have to charge a substantial fee to cover the cost, if you understand what I mean."

Greg returned Samos's smile with all the sincerity he could muster, trying hard not to show that he felt like strangling the vulturous bastard.

"No, actually. I don't know what you mean. How much?"

"One third of the face value of the loan right off the top."

"That's far too much."

"How do you figure?" Samos seemed amused, sure of himself.

Greg took a deep breath. Samos had no idea who he was or what he had been through since leaving Key West. But the sloe-eyed Panamanian appeared to be sizing him up with unnerving intuition. Greg needed a friend right now and it was his turn to turn on the charm and switch to negotiating mode.

"Let's assume that a standard bar of gold is worth $600,000. Surely, someone like you, a well-known and respected businessman, would have no difficulty obtaining a $300,000 loan from one of the banks with which you deal, secured by such a bar of gold."

Samos knew he was being played, but accepted the compliment with a slight bow of his head. "Thank you for your confidence in me. But we both know that even *I* would have to provide a certificate confirming that the bar assays at 99.999 percent pure gold, that it is the proper weight, and that it is not—how should I put it diplomatically?—of dubious origin."

Greg had a ready reply. "You have Moe Hunter's letter to cover that point. You know him, so call him."

"That's true, but my banker doesn't. Therefore, the loan would have to be in my name."

"So?"

"This would mean I'd be guaranteeing *your* loan, and would have to charge for it."

"How much?"

"One percent per month."

While Greg considered this last option, Samos checked his math. He'd deposit Mauro's gold bar worth $600,000 with his bank, then borrow $300,000 against it, which the bank would be happy to lend. He'd then charge Mauro an overall fee of $75,000, which meant that he'd have to give Mauro only $225,000 of $300,000 loan. The rest of the money— $75,000—would be his net profit from an operation requiring absolutely no money from his pocket because it would be financed entirely by OPM: Other People's Money.

If the Italian skipped or defaulted after one year, he would sell the gold and by doing so would almost double his money in twelve months.

Samos took a deep breath. "Make it 12 percent interest on the loan and not 6 and you've got a deal."

"You mean you want to charge me 25 percent off the top?" cried Mauro, incredulous at Samos's chutzpah.

Samos nodded—he was impressed. Mauro was quick.

The Italian shook his head. "I won't pay a cent more in fees than $66,000, and that's final."

Samos held out his hand. "Make it $75,000 and you've got a deal."

Greg shook his head. "Not so fast. The deal is conditional on four things. One: I'll pledge two bars, not one, on which you will lend me $600,000 less the agreed-on fee. Two: we complete the transaction within seventy-two hours. Three: I can retrieve my gold during the next twelve months at any time by paying you back $600,000. Four: you'll give me $50,000 at closing *in cash* because I don't want to have to wait for my money while your cheque clears."

"And if you don't pay me off within a year?"

Greg was expecting the question and had worked out an answer he felt would satisfy Samos.

"Let's just say that's highly unlikely." He leaned over the banker's desk and gave him the hard look of a tough kid from Montreal's Little Italy. "Neither of us is crazy, Mr. Samos. Gold's value will increase over the next year. When the time comes, you and I will sell one or both of my bars and repay you from the proceeds. Meanwhile, I will use the money you will be lending me now to buy more gold from Moe Hunter at a discounted price."

With this last, it was Greg's turn to hold out his hand. Samos hesitated for only a split second before taking it. This Roberto Mauro character was still a mystery, but Samos was reassured. He felt that his new client knew what he was doing.

Greg, on the other hand, was glad he had found a method of "liquefying" his entire stash of gold bars over a period of time. He changed his mind about taking his money and running. He felt he understood and could handle the usurious Panamanian.

Of course, at that time, Greg DiMauro, now Roberto Mauro, did not know who Alexander Samos really was. He did not know Samos was an ex-advisor of the NSA, and now a key player in its hush-hush "Not Much" operations department. He did not know the deal that Al McIsaacs, Samos's "Control," had struck for him with the NSA's employee protection program. He did not know that Alexander Samos was shielded from being grabbed by *un-friendlies*, who would have loved to painfully milk him for details about black operations that would embarrass the US if they found their way to the popular media.

CHAPTER 31

Panama City, Panama, 1982

Alejandro Samos had met Maria-Isabel Echenique at a US embassy cocktail party in 1980. She and her husband, the Mexican minister of finance, a senior member of the *Partido Revolucionario Institucional*, the notorious PRI, the political party who'd ruled Mexico seemingly in perpetuity, had been visiting Panama in a semi-official capacity. Echenique, a vivacious brunette, five feet two inches tall, with a figure that was made for modelling her Thierry Mugler suits, exuded intelligence, *joie de vivre*, and sex appeal, which Samos found compelling.

He would discover later on that the feeling had been mutual.

Their animated chat had soon turned to personal generalities, and when Samos explained what he did for a living, she called her husband over to join their conversion. At the time he had ascribed this act to a polite brush-off on her part to avoid further involvement.

The following weekend, Samos had been invited to dinner at the US chief of mission's home. Echenique was also a guest, but her husband was not. During the meal, the chief told Samos that *la señora* had asked for references on Señor Samos's company and had then asked if Samos were willing to meet with her on business.

Samos, convinced that her request was more a prelude to an *affaire* than *business*, said he understood and would be glad to oblige.

He was then somewhat disappointed when, during their first meeting in his office, she made no sexual overtures, but, instead, asked him to explain how offshore companies worked.

"As you know, I am a Mexican citizen and a senior government bureaucrat," she said. "I work at the Republic of Mexico's mint. My job is to supervise the logistics of the mint's precious metals trading operations. By the way, I am a CPA, like you, Mr. Samos."

Samos was impressed and said so. "Really? Where did you take your degree?

"Brigham Young. My husband and I are Mormons."

Samos was intrigued: something didn't add up.

"Mormons. But didn't we share some interesting insights over some excellent champagne at the chief of mission's house the other night? And I could have sworn you asked for seconds of his excellent coffee."

Echenique smiled awkwardly. "We're Mormons, not fanatics."

"I see. So, you buy and sell gold for the mint?"

"No. The buying from domestic producers is done by the Economics Department. We almost never buy gold or silver from foreign sources. My job is to supervise the acquired gold's conversion into marketable objects and their subsequent sale."

"Such as?"

"Gold and silver coins, bricks, and rounds. We compete in the world's precious metals markets with these. You may not know it, but Mexico has plenty of gold and silver mines. In fact, Mexico produces 20 percent of all silver mined in the world."

She took a sip of the mineral water Samos's secretary had brought her.

"You are probably asking yourself why I would be interested in offshore companies. Am I right?" She gave him a warm smile.

"Frankly, yes." Some vague suspicion was floating around in the back of Samos's brain, but he stifled it for the time being.

"Let's just say that my husband and I are not geniuses. I do have a CPA, but, let's face it, I graduated near the bottom of my class. My husband was no academic success either. Mr. Samos, we are political animals. Our job security depends on our loyalty to the political party in power."

"You work for the PRI and they have been in power for a long time."

"Quite right. My husband's and my families have been staunch supporters of PRI for generations. But you already know that."

Samos was able to express genuine surprise. "How would I know that?"

She smiled again. "Because the US government knows, and you are close to that government."

It was time for the well-practiced denial.

"You are absolutely wrong," Samos said firmly. "I am a Panamanian-born citizen of this country and I am not close to any particular foreign government." He fixed her with his sleepy, lidded eyes. "Certainly not the US government."

She seemed puzzled. "But you're friends with the US chief of mission?"

Samos chuckled. "My dear Señora Echenique, don't be so naive. Don't tell a soul, but most of my clients come from referrals by diplomats, people who have noted, for many years, that I am precise, reliable, and well-connected. Do you know my nickname? 'The Tomb.' I never talk about my clients to anyone, above all not to government. Any government! And I work hard to be effective at being of service."

Mollified, Echenique relented and became flirtatious. "And charming."

"When I have to be. I cultivate diplomats, as many diplomats as I can, without prejudice. Otherwise, I would starve. Besides, diplomats are a fountain of information and information is power—everywhere."

He rose and fetched a couple of pamphlets from his desk and handed them to her. "Look through these; one of them outlines how off-show companies work, the other tells you about my firm, which was founded almost a decade ago."

He watched as she began to read and was surprised by how the expression on her face changed when she was concentrating. There was something savage that he sensed in her being. Or was it just total selfishness? He couldn't decide.

She looked up and their eyes locked. She smiled sheepishly. "Would you mind terribly if I asked you to walk me through this literature?" She held up the pamphlet about offshore companies. "I told you, I graduated near the bottom of my class. . . ."

It was obvious to both of them that she was lying.

After an hour of close tutoring, she tasked him with incorporating a Panamanian bearer share company, of which she would be the sole owner and for which Samos would act as its resident director. She also requested that the company open a US dollar bank account and rent a large safety deposit box at the Bank of Nova Scotia.

*

That evening, following standard operating procedures, Samos settled down with a glass of dry sherry and sent an encoded Telex to Prewitt, his dour superior at Foggy Bottom, informing him of the acquisition of yet another PEP, on behalf of Maria-Isabel Echenique, a senior executive of the Mexican Mint who happened to be the wife of the Mexican minister of finance.

CHAPTER 32

Panama City, 1982

Contrary to what the parties had hoped for, it took Samos a week to get the paperwork for the Mauro deal completed, which of course included a contract and an assay of the two gold bars that Mauro had delivered to him. Another three days were taken up by securing the cash necessary for closing.

While Samos had completed the necessary paperwork, Mauro had become increasingly cagey with Samos. The man had spun him a tale about having been born in Italy, validated by his authentic Italian passport, and having reached the ripe age of thirty-three, and having the ambition to circumnavigate the planet, he had bought a boat second-hand from a down-at-heels American at the Club Med in the Bahamas where Mauro had been employed as a temporary *"gentil organisateur."*

"I'm crazy about sailing and I like solitude," he told Samos. "So, for me, boating is the life I prefer."

Samos's hooded eyes betrayed only passing interest in Mauro's story, but his mind was racing because, the more Mauro spoke, the more a distant bell rang in his memory.

"How will I contact you then when the paperwork is completed and the cash assembled?"

"How about me calling you in three days' time?"

"Deal," said Samos, sure of his ability to wrap up the paperwork quickly. Mauro had already given him two gold bars to be assayed as to purity.

Mauro flew to *Puerto Pedregal*, in the Panama district of David, Chiriqui Province, and took a cab back to his boat, which he had left moored at the Las Olas Beach Resort. The next day, he sailed for Golfito Bay in Costa Rica, a country with which Canada had no extradition treaty. *Better safe than sorry*, he thought to himself. Mauro was impatient and young, but also a realist and he knew that, in Latin America, everything took longer than planned. He had done his research and was aware that Panama *did* have extradition agreements with Canada. He was not comfortable with the idea of having to wait for a week or perhaps longer in Panama, temporarily almost penniless, while Samos finished papering their deal.

It took Mauro five days to sail from David to Golfito and another full day of exploring the area before finding the ideal mooring for his boat: the Banana Bay Marina, five kilometers south of Golfito airport, from where he could fly to Panama City in a couple of hours.

Back in Panama City, Samos wasn't too happy about the situation either. He had arranged to have Mauro followed to Costa Rica because it had made him uneasy to be getting involved with someone without a fixed address. He liked Mauro, admired his aplomb and ambitions, but there was something about him that needled, something familiar that he could not put his finger on. And then, with the sputtering illumination of a cheap flashbulb, it finally fired.

Mauro was as Italian as a first-generation son of immigrants could be, and yet, there it was, that telltale verbal tick, the Montreal accent. Perhaps Samos had been too long away from the island city. Or perhaps his ears had been dulled by the rapid, droning Spanish all around him, but, yes, it was undeniable. The blunted consonants, clipped vowel endings. As Montreal as Ben's smoked meat.

CHAPTER 33

Panama City, 1983

The account statements that Samos had begun to receive from the Bank of Nova Scotia in his capacity as the resident director of Avro Industries Ltd., the corporation he had formed for Maria-Isabel Echenique, were initially unremarkable. During the first five months of its existence, the company's bank account balance at the end of each month showed an amount equal to her original deposit: $5,000.

The first day of the sixth month, Echenique sent word that she would be visiting Panama within the week and wondering whether Señor Samos would please have cocktails and dinner with her the following Friday at her hotel, the Intercontinental Dream Spa and Resort at Playa Bonita. "I'm staying over the weekend, so come early and bring your bathing suit," she added with direct simplicity.

Samos had an idea of what was up, but he never liked to get ahead of himself in matters of sex. Echenique had been an intriguing and beguiling combination of coolness and personal frankness, which was like catnip to someone with Samos's background and tastes. Samos was far too clever and respectful of his "rice bowl" ever to make assumptions about any of his female friends, clients or not. This cautious respect was the key to whatever success he could claim in that department. He always could assume the mantle of "he-who-was-taken-by-surprise."

Echenique met him at the pool and he could tell she was already a little bit high from a pitcher of *seco* cocktails. He had never seen her so undressed; she wore a high-cut bathing suit suited to her shapely legs, the halter top cradling beautiful, store-bought breasts of the highest quality. Her mouth was parted in a permanently wry smile, but it was her eyes that Samos found compelling and a bit unnerving. Later, he would describe them as "shark eyes," slightly wide apart, dark, almost black, as though the pupil took up most of the surface. She did not blink, another unsettling revelation. When she stared at Samos, it was as though she was dissecting him, flesh off the bone, in order to get to his deepest self.

The *seco* cocktails were potent and, as they flirted and watched the succession of perfect bodies drift around the pool, pair up, and float off, the focus of their discourse narrowed. Echenique fixed her unmoving, unblinking black eyes on Samos and suggested they get to her room and change for dinner. He concurred and the two stood unsteadily, leaning on each other, becoming aware of the heat coming off their bodies, and headed toward the elevator. Once inside her perfect suite, the situation become charged. They never made dinner.

Samos was taken by the erotic combination of her petite body and her powerful femininity and tried to embrace her. Echenique titled her head back to suck in his mouth while reaching down to slip her hand into his waistband and grab his testicles with all the confidence and finesse of a seasoned dealer shuffling the deck. Satisfied with her hand, she dragged him into the bedroom, knocked him back onto the bed, and inhaled his cock into her mouth, stiffening that which was not already rampant.

Pulling aside her high-cut crotch, she guided him into her without taking off her bathing suit and climaxed loudly almost as soon as he began to thrust up into her. He withdrew and she rolled over on her side, helping him to slip off her bathing suit. He felt her black, unblinking eyes on him again, this time above her cock-eyed smile. She then knelt down and took him into her mouth again, her tongue caressing his penis as she moved her head and both small hands back and forth, urging him to explode. Helpless against such a determined assault, he ejaculated into her mouth as she pushed her finger into his anus, pressing his prostate.

This was not enough. Echenique rose to her feet and cracked open another bottle of chilled *seco* and poured it into a highball glass filled with ice cubes. She took a long swallow and passed it to Samos, who did likewise. She then grabbed his hand, jammed it between her thighs, and held it in place with fierce strength and rubbed her clitoris against it until, with a scream, she climaxed twice in rapid succession. Temporarily spent, she dropped to the bed, rolled herself in the sheets, and fell asleep in his arms.

Not so Samos. On the contrary, his mind was running wild.

He had never expected the degree of animalistic sexual behavior Echenique had exhibited, though he had an inkling that she was a woman capable of great passion. Her intense focus as she discussed her business interests in his office that first time had hinted at a relentless determination to have her way at all costs.

Was this wanton, shameless behavior an act laid on for his benefit or was it the manifestation of deep and repressed animal drive, a genuine need to satisfy her desires? Samos did what he always did: he remained detached, on guard, and non-committal.

*

Samos awoke at the crack of dawn on Sunday and slid out of bed noiselessly, careful not to wake the woman still sleeping at his side. He headed for the balcony and watched the rising sun paint the horizon red above the sea. From where he sat, he could clearly see the line of ships waiting to enter the Panama Canal.

The hotel on Playa Bonita, near Panama Pacific International Airport, was located on a spectacular beach-front property about twenty minutes from downtown Panama. An upscale establishment, its specialty was cater-ing to families seeking a comfortable weekend escape from working drudgery. He made himself a cup of coffee, went back outside on the balcony, and sat down to contemplate his future by reviewing the past.

He realized with sudden insight that he had once more reached a crucial point in his life and, quite naturally, his thoughts turned to Adisdania Flores, Duque de Estrada.

Disda.

She had finally managed to leave Cuba with the rest of the Marielitos in 1980. When he discovered that she had immigrated to the US, he'd had to fight hard to resist seeing her, even if only from afar. He noted with some bitterness that she never attempted to reach out to him. But then, as he had learned over the years, in life, there were those who reached out and those whom one reached out to. Disda was not the type to reach out. He somehow managed to keep his distance, but the emotional struggle to deny himself a last encounter left him so deeply depressed that it took him months to recover. Surreptitiously, he had kept track of her through contacts in Atlanta, where she lived with her sister.

The news of her death from cancer two years later had wounded him like a knife thrust into his heart. Against McIsaacs's express orders, he threw all caution to the wind and flew to Atlanta, and wept uncontrollably as he watched her funeral from a safe distance. At least, so he thought at the time.

The half-dozen years that had followed had not been easy. He had to constantly re-imagine himself as "Alejandro Samos," and learn to think the way Samos would think, react the way Samos would react. It was years before it became second nature. A vestige from his previous character remained: the perceived necessity to live without emotional entanglements. That had been really tough and he had not succeeded entirely. Along the way, Samos found himself getting emotionally involved in short-term liaisons—but, luckily, none had lasted for more than a few months and for this he was grateful, but also more than a little concerned. As a corrective to this tendency, Samos threw himself into the task of building a business that required his social engagement with a wide network of contacts, of which an integral part were members of the Panamanian diplomatic corps.

As for his business activities, they were gradually becoming too stressful for his tastes. Not only did he have to service his clients as their Panamanian manager, but he also had to make time to "influence" them to head "in the right political direction," whenever the request to do so came down from Washington. Of course, "influencing" cost—either money or favors.

Influencing a *P*olitically *E*xposed *P*erson through a payoff of money was relatively easy. When necessary, Samos would arrange for Washington to "create" a deposit in the PEP's bank account. This "creation" would be made to look as if it were an error. Samos would then draw the PEP's attention to the "error" and tell him not to do anything about it. It was a wink and a nod to indicate that the erroneous deposit was theirs to keep.

Favors were always far trickier. Most requests for favors were motivated by the need for political or business contacts, or for objects or information that would otherwise be difficult to obtain. Invariably, the fulfillment of such favors would require extensive research to identify how and by whom they could be fulfilled. Digging out the relevant information required the involvement of experts and a very extensive network of contacts of all kinds.

Samos ceased his musings and reverted to reflecting on the situation at hand.

His sleepy, hooded eyes revealed nothing, but inside, he was smiling at himself cynically. At the moment, as far as Echenique was concerned, he was emotionally uncommitted, but the more he thought about her, the more he felt vulnerable. Part of the insight that had crept up on his unsuspecting mind was the acknowledgement that there had been recent moments when he had felt lonely and had yearned for someone with whom to share his life. He shook his head as though to discard the thought. "You better watch yourself with this one, old boy," he muttered to himself.

He had just ordered a bottle of Pommery and breakfast for two from room service when he turned around to find a glowing Maria-Isabel standing stark naked in the doorway of the bedroom with a towel around her head. He had not heard her in the shower while he was on the phone.

She opened her arms and hissed, *"Fóllame bien, mi pequeño macho."*

CHAPTER 34

Playa Bonita, Panama, 1983

They were having breakfast on the balcony, both wearing the luxurious, wonderfully soft, thick, sparkling white bathrobes provided by the hotel. Maria-Isabel's Eggs Benedict yolk was running down her chin.

"I am a woman of passion, used to having my way and I owe no one any apology for my behavior."

Samos motioned to the egg on her chin, laughing. Maria-Isabel looked like a kid as she used her linen napkin self-consciously, smiling at Samos sexily.

"I'm sure you know the story. My husband is much older than me and I have decided that I need a fuck-buddy. And a business partner, preferably both rolled into one."

"And you thought I was a likely candidate."

Samos couldn't stop laughing. He felt happy. Happier than at any time since he had become what he had become.

And no wonder. He was enjoying a delightful, post-coital breakfast with a handsome, sensuous woman in beautifully pleasant surroundings. The arresting view of the Pacific Ocean from the terrace contributed mightily to his sense of well-being.

"No, *querido*," said Maria-Isabel. "You are not *a* candidate, but *the only candidate,* the one I have chosen." Her wide-set, black, unblinking eyes were boring into his, demanding that he pay heed to what she was saying.

Samos sobered up quickly. "Surely you are not serious."

"Surely I am, *Licenciado* Alejandro Samos, resident director of my so-called offshore company. I fancied you from the first, at that boring reception where we met, and I knew that the feeling was mutual. I engineered the business meeting with you. You were not only courteous, but also patient and respectful, rare qualities in this region, where men are macho pigs who live to belittle and ignore women." A small smile lit up her face.

"Admit it, when you got my invitation to meet again, my *pequeño macho,* you were sure that I was angling for a little fuck. Yes?"

Samos said nothing, but smiled.

"Answer me," she commanded.

Samos was unaccustomed to being bullied, physically or verbally, and took control. "Yes, and I was very disappointed that all we did was to talk business. Can you blame me? But you have me all wrong. I may have wanted you, but I would have continued to respect the professional tone you appeared to appreciate. After all, business is business . . ." he paused for effect. "Up until the moment you grabbed my balls."

They both dissolved into uncontrollable laughter, left the breakfast table, and went inside.

She led him to the plush leather sofa that afforded a lovely view of the sea. They settled in comfortably.

"Let me start by confessing that I spent the last six months informing myself about you. I checked your professional reputation in the diplomatic community here, I talked to some of your friends and clients, and everybody said you were very discreet, qualified, and reliable."

Samos was genuinely surprised. "What friends? I have no friends, only acquaintances."

Maria-Isabel slid a little closer, whispering intimately into Samos's ear. "A couple of your ex-lady-friends."

Samos was startled.

"Don't fret," she hurried on. "They, too, confirmed that you're a straight-shooter. Strangely enough, they all expressed regret that you dumped them. I found that some-what encouraging."

Maria-Isabel helped herself to some coffee from the jug. "The only thing about which I couldn't find anything was how you were in bed."

"So, you thought a frontal attack on the family jewels was the best maneuver?"

She slid even closer, holding his head between her small and perfectly shaped hands, and dared him to look into her eyes as black as the waters of a lake on a moonless night. "Do you blame me? I can't afford to waste any time. I had to know what kind of lover you are. I'm a sensuous woman and I find that, lately, my needs are urgent and great."

CHAPTER 35

Of course, while she was checking out the goods, Samos was learning all *he* could about Maria-Isabel Echenique. She was born in 1948 into a wealthy, politically influential family, living on a hereditary estate in a mansion in Lomas Altas, the most exclusive district of Mexico City.

After attending a posh private high school with her sister, Elvira, four years her junior, she graduated *magna cum laude* from high school. A strong-willed and independent-minded woman, she convinced her father to allow her to study political science at a US university. She picked Brigham Young to be near the Mormon power-brokers where she obtained a double Masters in Business Administration and Political Science.

Returning to Mexico, she enrolled at the *Universidad Nacional Autónoma de México,* where she took her CPA. At age twenty-six, she married a man fourteen years her senior— a rising star of PRI and protégé of her father. Foreseeably, her husband ended up running for political office and was elected, thanks principally to the impressive campaign that Maria-Isabel had mounted and managed for him.

They tried to have children, but without success, which led to a certain cooling of passion and both of them seeking partners outside their marriage.

Maria-Isabel found the vacuous life forced upon her as the wife of an important politico maddening, and she cajoled her husband, by this time minister of finance, into getting her a job interesting enough to save her from dying of boredom. When he finally relented. she found herself at the Mexican National Mint as its logistics manager, a key, politically sensitive post.

*

After lunch, Maria-Isabel preened about the hotel suite under Samos's hooded eyes, chirping like a parakeet as she related her life's story, unabetted by any prompting. Clearly, she had left out the most important quality in the candidate she hoped to make her business partner and lover: the ability to listen. Maria-Isabel had a lot to say and expected Samos to hear her every word.

"I've been at the mint for six years, the last three as the person in charge of supervising the conversion of the precious metals bought by the mint from producers into marketable objects and their subsequent sale. As such, I have to do business directly with the smelter that physically does the conversion."

Samos was mesmerized by just how petite but womanly she was. Maria-Isabel pretended not to notice his eyes fixed on her boobs or her divine Spanish bum.

"The job has serious complexities," she said with a sigh, begging silently for Samos's interest.

"Really? Such as?"

Maria-Isabel leaned in, warming to the subject.

"The precious metals arrive at the designated smelter in the form of standard bars and are checked for purity. One of my jobs is to decide which smelter gets the conversion contract."

"And who are the suppliers?"

"Principally Mexican mines. They have small smelters of their own. To reduce delays, I instituted a protocol of pre-approved suppliers to make sure that most of the products that arrive at the mint's smelter qualify."

"Who does the pre-approval screening?"

"I do," she replied with some pride. "Well, most of the time."

Mauro's gold, thought Samos. How serendipitous could this be? Almost too good to be true. Now, it was Samos who was warming to the subject.

"And what is the required standard?" he asked nonchalantly.

"Standard: 99.999 percent."

"Standard. Right."

"Once the bar is tested, the supplier is issued a payment order that he can deposit in his bank. The payment order is as good as money. I get a weekly report of how many bars have been tested and bought. On the basis of this report, I determine what combination of products the smelter is to manufacture for me. Of course, I also consult with the marketing department and coordinate with them to make sure we make items that people actually want to buy."

"Sounds like a lot of work fraught with dangerous accountability. I hope it's worth it?"

Maria-Isabel shook her head. "The pay is lousy."

"I don't understand. Your husband . . . ?"

"You know Mexico and Mexican men. When I complained to my husband about the low pay scale, he said that, as a woman, I should consider myself lucky that I have an interesting job, and not rock the boat. In other words, if I want to earn more money, I have to find additional sources of revenue in an 'imaginative Mexican' way, just like everyone else."

Samos gestured to their surroundings, the suite, the panoramic view.

"So, all this is about money?"

Maria-Isabel laughed and playfully cuffed Samos under his chin.

"Don't be silly! I don't need additional sources of income. I already have a family trust fund."

"Oh?" Samos found himself betraying how annoyed he was. What was she on about?

"I want to talk to you about that later, *querido*."

Maria-Isabel walked over to the bar and poured each of them a tumbler of vodka on ice. "You know, one of the things I like about you is that you really listen. Or, at least you pretend to! I appreciate you listening to my family problems, but how about *your* family? I'd like to hear about them if you care to tell me."

Samos sensed that she was unsure about how much she wanted to trust him and was playing for time. He allowed himself to appear modest and touched by her interest in his life and launched into the cover story his minders had developed for him.

"Well, I have no wife, never been married, nor any children," he started. "But that you know, I'm sure."

She nodded.

"I don't know who my parents are or were," he sighed and made himself look wistful. "You see, I'm a foundling."

"What's that?"

"A foundling. I was found at the door of the church by the local priest in San Isidro, a small village near Peña on the coast. The priest arranged for me to be accepted at an orphanage run by the Carmelite nuns, but I was never adopted."

"You poor thing," cooed Maria-Isabel.

"I stayed there until I was twelve. Then I won a scholarship to a Jesuit high school in Colon and from there went to the University of Southern Florida, also on a scholarship."

Maria-Isabel had slid back up against him on the sofa, curling her lithe legs under her. She reached gently under his shirt collar and caressed his neck.

"What about these scars?"

"I was in an automobile accident and was badly burned."

Maria-Isabel's perfect, womanly hands were now on his face, her fingertips tracing the ridges and metal plate tectonics just under the skin. Samos pretended to be sensitive and stiffened a little.

"Did you have plastic surgery on your face?"

"Extensively."

"No wonder you look so young and handsome." Maria-Isabel seemed relieved. "Forgive all these questions, but I am about to place my future into your hands and I can't afford to make any mistakes."

Samos was casting about for a way to get away from further questions so he simply turned the tide of the conversation. "And, what horrible secrets do you have in your background? Or are they the usual petty deeds of corruption that most Mexican politicians have?"

Maria-Isabel had fixed him for a few long seconds with her unblinking, pearl-black eyes, and made up her mind.

"You really want to know? OK, here it goes. PRI's grip on Mexican politics is weakening. Their eventual fall is an historic inevitability. My husband and I foresaw that this would happen and began to set aside some extra money the 'creative Mexican' way. Do you understand what I am saying?"

"The 'creative Mexican' way."

"Yes."

"How?"

"It's quite simple, really. My husband is on the mint's board. Two years ago, the board authorized the production of gold briquettes that would be of 'commercial' grade for retail users, such as, for example, jewellers. For reasons of logistics and security, instead of 99.999 percent purity, the briquettes would be 99.5 percent pure. That way, there would be no confusion about the origins of the gold. As you know, the standard gold bar traded internationally is the 400-troy-ounce Good Delivery bar. At 99.999 percent purity, these bars, when converted into briquettes, yield 400 briquettes weighing one troy ounce each."

Echenique paused. "Are you with me so far?"

Samos nodded.

"The bars supplied to the smelters by the authorized Mexican mining companies are 99.999 percent pure. If the smelter is asked to convert the bars to briquettes that are only 99.5 percent pure, the yield per bar is 402. I arrange for those two extra briquettes to be accounted as a 'manufacturing loss' in the smellter's books and 'gifted' to me to ensure that the mint keeps on doing business with that particular smelter."

With this, Maria-Isabel reached into her bag and tossed something small, rectangular, and shiny at Samos, who caught it in mid-air. He didn't need to look. The density, weight, and warmth told him all he had to know. Even as a small briquette, gold was intoxicating.

Samos held the gold up to the light. He was well ahead of his new lover and was just doing the mental arithmetic.

"So, you've been accumulating briquettes for the last two years and you want to sell them now as discreetly as possible, preferably without revealing your connection to the transaction."

Maria-Isabel reached out to place her petite, perfectly manicured hand on his inner thigh. "I knew you would understand."

Samos stood up and paced, giving himself a little time to think.

"Where is the gold now and how much of it is there?"

Maria-Isabel sat back, keying her approach back to "all business."

"On average, I get five briquettes per month, which I have been storing in my safety deposit box at the Bank of Nova Scotia, which you so efficiently arranged, here in Panama."

Samos was not shocked. Through his contacts at the bank, he was well aware of the monthly visit—he just did not know exactly what was being deposited. But he had assumed the truth. Now, the proof was in his hand.

"That's a stash worth about $180,000, and growing at the rate of about $8,000 per month." He looked up at the woman. "How long do you expect to stay in your present job?"

"The PRI has just been re-elected, though with a substantially reduced majority. My husband figures we're safe in our jobs for the next four years."

"Both of you?"

"Yes," said Maria-Isabel, suddenly evasive, almost shy.

"My husband is fifty-two. Fourteen years my senior. We've been married for ten years and are no longer in love, that's for sure. Divorce is out of the question; he has ambitions of running for president. As for sex, he screws around so much that I'm afraid to let him come close without a rubber."

Maria-Isabel rose and approached Samos, her robe falling open. She slid her body up against his, the heat coming through like a wave as she placed her lips close to his ear. She took the gold briquette from him and tossed it on the bed.

"He won't fuck me with a condom, so we're kind of at a stalemate. You can see, it's been a while; hence, what I already told you. I had urgent needs when I grabbed you." With this last, her hand was already hunting inside the folds of his robe.

*

They were lying in bed side by side, watching the shadows form on the wall opposite. "You are asking me to liquefy over half a million dollars' worth of gold during the next four years, gold of dubious origin. This is not going to be easy, quite frankly."

"Will you try?" said Maria-Isabel, propping herself up to gaze into his eyes.

"I'll need some time to think about it."

"How much time?" Back to business.

"Not so fast, m'lady. You're leaving Panama tomorrow morning. You're not giving me much time."

Maria-Isabel rolled her lithe, almost weightless body on top of Samos and started to crawl up his torso, her vagina tantalizingly close and swaying.

"That was the plan before you fucked me so well," she giggled. "I changed my reservations to Tuesday evening. So, *mago financiero*, you have plenty of time to fulfill all my needs, *sí*?"

CHAPTER 36

Golfito, Costa Rica, 1983

Samos and Roberto Mauro were having beers with their club sandwiches in the cockpit of Mauro's boat moored at the Banana Bay Marina complex in Golfito. Their choice of venue was dictated by their desire for discretion. Samos noticed that the boat has been repainted and most of its fittings replaced by new ones. It had also been rechristened the "Shirley." Samos wondered if Mauro was preparing to do a flit, but decided it was unlikely. At least, not quite yet. Mauro was not the type who gave up until the very end.

He had left Maria-Isabel, sex drunk and sleeping it off, in bed at the hotel in Panama City, very early Monday morning. He had no time to go home and no proper travelling clothes so he had tipped the night manager of the Playa Bonita Hotel a hundred dollars to let him into the hotel's clothing store, where he bought a pair of slacks, a jacket, and a shirt.

From the hotel, he went straight to the airport to catch the charter he had booked, arranging a meeting with Mauro for Monday at noon in Golfito.

The trip between the Aeropuerto Pacifico de Panama and Golfito on board the Beachcraft that Samos had chartered, took just a bit more than an hour. The pilot was told to stand by for three hours and then fly his passenger back to Panama.

Polishing off the mediocre club sandwich, Samos had to talk fast.

"The last time we spoke we agreed that the problem with large quantities of gold was twofold. One, that when time comes to sell, very few private buyers have $600,000 on hand to purchase a bar of gold."

Mauro's body language was clear. He was readying himself for a quick "thank you and goodbye." Samos ignored the signals and plowed on.

"And, two, that the purchasers for gold bars of dubious origins will only buy them, if at all, if they are given the time to have the gold assayed for purity. And even when proven 99.999 percent pure, these types will only sell at a huge discount. Right?"

Samos took a sip from his bottle. It was a weak, tepid *Imperial*, a Costa Rican beer. Mauro hadn't moved, so Samos prompted him. "Am I right?"

Mauro was in a belligerent mood, convinced that Samos's insistence on an urgent meeting at short notice meant trouble for him and this repetition of what they both already knew was tapping on his last nerve. The repayment date for Samos's loan was fast approaching and Mauro had reason to suspect that Samos was "engineering" delays so that the loan would default.

"Yeah, yeah, so what else is new? Look, if you are fucking me, you might at least buy me a soda!"

Samos was caught between a loud guffaw and the standard withering look he bestowed upon recalcitrant clients. "Enough of your paranoia, young man. I came here to help you. Do me the courtesy of hearing me out with respect."

Mauro breathed out the pent-up tension in his chest. There would be time to kill this clown, if necessary. For now, he smiled and mimed locking his lips.

Samos began to speak without raising his voice, enunciating each word with great care. His hooded eyes bored into Mauro's, and when the younger man met his gaze, he noted, with some disquiet, absolute emptiness.

"According to the terms of our loan agreement, we are fewer than three months from when you are supposed to repay me." Samos kept the sound of his voice neutral. "You are, of course, under no obligation to do anything for the next ninety days. If you default, I keep your gold, you sail away with nothing, and all is good with the world."

Mauro could not resist and mimed unlocking his lips. "And fuck you, too, man."

Samos had to laugh at the younger man's chutzpah. Not a bargaining chip in play and he still strutted like a henhouse cock.

"OK, fuck me. Fuck me all you want, but I'll still have your gold."

This time it was Mauro who had to smile and mime the locking of his lips again.

"*Ostinsto*, listen to me. Very recently, I have been made aware of a situation that, if properly handled, may just solve some of the problems I think you may be faced with."

Mauro was surprised. He did not expect an offer to help, just the contrary.

"What problems?"

"I'm talking about whatever you and your friends are involved in." Samos made a dismissive gesture with his hand. "You might be interested in an arrangement that would take care of three of your biggest problems: one, the sale of bullion with doubtful origin in large quantities; two, internationally acceptable certification of the purity of the gold; and, three, the problem of converting gold bars into smaller gold units, such as briquettes, for example, thereby making the sale of the metal easier to finance."

Samos tossed the gold briquette at Mauro, who almost fumbled it. The young man palmed the gold piece, turning it over and over in his hand with obvious wonder.

Mauro's thoughts raced. This could be the solution to his long-term woes. He would have the freedom to do whatever he wanted and the cash to make the freedom worthwhile.

He put the gold briquette up to his ear as though listening to a sea shell. "Start talking."

Samos looked at his watch. "I have exactly two hours before I have to leave, so listen carefully. Like all things that appear simple, it's complicated."

*

"Can you forgive me for having skipped out on you this morning? You were sleeping so deeply I didn't have the heart to wake you up."

"You are forgiven." Maria-Isabel rewarded the apology with a radiant smile. "Your note explained everything, except the whereabouts of my little baguette."

Samos smiled and flipped it in his hand like a coin and then to Maria-Isabel, who pressed it to her bosom with a lusty laugh.

"I have ordered dinner for two to be served at six, in our suite, just as you requested."

"Great. Let's have a drink on the balcony. We have time." Samos was pretty tired, but excitement kept him pumped. He enjoyed living on that line where his grasp exceeded his reach.

"Let me start at the beginning," he sighed contentedly, and took a grateful sip of the gin and tonic Maria-Isabel handed him. Maria-Isabel curled up like a cat in the plush, comfy lounge chair, listening.

"I have a client, let's call him 'Mauro.' He's a young man, very bright, very sharp, and in the middle of a trip around the world aboard his sailboat. Recently, he bought a couple of gold bars from this Florida treasure-hunter, Moe Hunter—do you know him?"

Maria-Isabel nodded. "Of him."

"Right. Well, Mauro bought the gold from Hunter at an incredible discount because Hunter needed money to continue hunting for the wreck of the *Santa Maria de Atoche*."

He looked up at his girlfriend. "I presume you've heard about his story."

"I certainly have. I read that he is still working at finding his jackpot, his *El Gordo*."

Samos nodded. "Now, Mauro left Florida with the gold bars and then got into a little financial trouble. Nothing dramatic—rather banal, actually, but he suddenly needed money so I loaned him half-a-million-dollars and he pledged the bars to me as security. They are in my possession."

Maria-Isabel's face was glowing in the early evening light. Her widely spaced black eyes were fixed on Samos in a manner that another man might find unnerving. Samos found her focus arousing.

"I met Mauro this morning to find out how he was doing and whether he was going to be able to repay me on time. He told me exactly what I expected him to say." He paused.

"He had to default on the loan."

Samos smiled and shook his head slowly.

"No. I told you, Mauro is young and very sharp. He told me that it would be easier for him if he could mint his two gold bars into smaller pieces. He felt certain he could find buyers much more easily. There were not many willing to take entire bars."

Now, it was not only Samos who was getting aroused. Maria-Isabel changed her position, leaning toward Samos, planting her perfect feet on the terrazzo and allowing her tanned, firm legs to part just slightly. Samos kept his *élan,* but it was getting a little crowded in his pants.

"Given our own conversation yesterday, I thought of Mauro's problems and his desires as an example of divine serendipity. And I thought of you, my dear."

Maria-Isabel cooled her ardor with a healthy gulp of icy G&T, her depth-less eyes never leaving Samos's face, which was getting hotter by the second.

"I let him talk, express his frustrations, and then I suggested that I might know someone who could help."

Samos's little speech was cut off suddenly by the intrusion of Maria-Isabel's white hot tongue deep into his throat. They nearly rolled off his chaise lounge as their mouths glued to each other like limpets. Maria-Isabel fished his penis out of his pants and eased it into her, straddling him in her favorite position.

"C'mon, *mi genio financiero*, you've got my undivided . . . don't leave out any detail."

Samos moaned like a man on death row as the woman's vagina contracted like a slippery fist around his erection. But if she could last, then so could he.

"One thing led to another and we ended up thinking that it would not be such a bad idea if the two of you went into the retail jewelry business in Central America and the Caribbean."

Maria-Isabel stopped her subtle movements and relaxed her internal grip, a puzzled look clouding her face.

"Retail jewelry? *Mi querido amante*, I was not made to worry about stores and employees and who was diddling the books and stealing the goods!"

Samos pulled her closer, his lips at her ear, whispering.

"You are also not made to live even one second in prison."

Maria-Isabel rose up, giving Samos an opportunity to roll her over, putting himself on top. He kissed her lips hard and deeply before rising up and sitting back on his haunches.

"Listen to me and be smarter than anyone. You need to make gold from a dubious source disappear, and leave nothing but cold, hard cash in its place. One way to do that is to pass it through a legitimate market."

"Jewelry. Retail jewelry."

Samos pulled the woman up so that she was sitting in his lap, his erection burning up into her belly. She appeared to like this position.

"You could wipe the floor with the competition because you'd have a supply of gold that would cost you well below market."

Maria-Isabel was now all ears as well as eyes. "How much below?"

"When cornered, Hunter would go on selling you and Mauro a gold bar at 40 percent below market."

The business part of the woman's brain, inspired by self-preservation and fuelled by greed and lust for power, switched into high gear. "Does this Mauro know anything about making gold jewelry?"

"We discussed that, too, and I made the suggestion that you should market jewelry manufactured by local partners."

Maria-Isabel stopped moving, and then gingerly raised herself off Samos and walked naked toward the wet bar, tossing over her shoulder, "You lost me completely."

Samos raised himself up, wondering what line he had just crossed.

"I'm boring you."

"No, no, on the contrary," she protested vigorously. "It's just that you seem to have this scheme with your 'Mauro' character so well thought out, I'm having some difficulty understanding my role."

"After I described the advantages, Mauro wants you as a fully committed and equal business partner. We discussed opening a dozen very high-quality, snobby, jewelry stores, each in partnership with a local jeweller and exclusively at ports of call frequented by upscale cruise companies, not the discount rabble. The company that I would set up for both of you would own one half of each store. The supply of 'cheap' gold that you and Mauro would provide exclusively for the chain would indenture the chain to you and keep it from breaking apart."

"Your 'unbeatable competitive advantage.'" Maria-Isabel's eyes were sparkling with excitement as she made her way back to where Samos was sitting on the bed.

"Mauro and I ran the numbers. It will take about $600,000 to start such a business. That's about 200 ounces of gold, or 200 gold briquettes weighing one ounce each. You already have 150 such briquettes in your safety deposit box. That's worth about $225,000. So, to go into business with Mauro as an equal partner, you'll have to put up your stash of gold briquettes plus $75,000, which, if you don't have, I will lend you. Mauro, too, will have to put up 200 briquettes, which he will do after you will have helped him to convert one of his gold bars into briquettes."

"And how will I do that?"

"I'm going to incorporate a company that Mauro wants to call Tango Metal Industries, TMI for short. You and Mauro will own it, fifty-fifty. Mauro will do the legwork to set up the first half-dozen shops and you, my dear, will be responsible for the logistics of supplying the business with gold."

Maria-Isabel climbed back aboard Samos's lap and worked through the mechanics.

Samos gritted his teeth and continued. "You will preapprove TMI as a supplier of the mint. Mauro will lend you one of his gold ingots and you will deliver it to the mint. The mint will convert the ingot into 400 briquettes and, after charging for its services, which of course will include testing for required purity, will then return the ingot in briquette form marked as emanating from the Mexican National Mint to TMI. TMI will keep 200 briquettes as Mauro's contribution to the formation of the company and return the other 200 to Mauro."

Samos eased the lithe woman's body up and settled it back down, earning the appropriate response.

"I've got the idea, keep going."

Samos resumed a slow and steady grind.

"As for the gold TMI will need for operating the business in the future, it will buy it from you and Mauro as required. Both of you will be paid the market price, less a discount of 40 percent."

Samos stopped his movements and looked his girlfriend in the eyes. She focused once again on him with a penetrating look.

"A word of caution," said Samos. "You are aware of the origin of your own briquettes, so when you offer them for sale to TMI, you can state truthfully that they are from the mint. However, when Mauro sells his gold to TMI, you should ask him to have a letter ready from Moe Hunter certifying that he sold the gold to Mauro."

Maria-Isabel stopped moving and focused again on Samos.

"So, to make things crystal clear, this whole arrangement you have cooked up is to enable Mauro to convert a large amount of gold into cash, with me benefiting from the system *en passant,* correct? "

"Frankly, yes."

"And my exposure?"

"If ever there were an investigation, your exposure depends entirely on what position the mint would take. So, I suggest that maybe it would be wise for you to have a minority interest in TMI, rather than an equal position."

"Why?" asked Maria-Isabel, her eyebrows arched with suspicion.

"That way, you can always claim that your principal interest in participating was that you are a born marketer, in love with fashion. You could admit to a fascination with jewelry and say you had exercised reasonable care to ensure that the gold you were handling had proven origins."

"The Moe Hunter letters."

Samos nodded and then paused, frowned, and pretended to have just thought about something new. "Do you travel on a diplomatic passport?"

"Yes. Why?"

"Well, this might not be your style, but you could save yourselves a lot of time and money if, instead of TMI *shipping* the bars of gold it will be selling to the mint, *you* transport the gold both ways. Every time you visit Panama, you could easily carry Mauro's briquettes from the mint to TMI in your personal luggage and on the return, Mauro's gold bars to the mint in Mexico. A standard gold bar weighs eleven and a third kilos, less than half the limit of what you are allowed to travel with in business class. Of course, you would be entitled to a fee for this service."

Maria-Isabel had stopped moving again as Samos continued musing.

"There's another advantage to your position. Your luggage can be considered diplomatic baggage, not subject to inspection."

Maria-Isabel closed her eyes and cuddled into Samos's shoulder. "I need to think this through," she murmured. "I'll let you know within the week. I need to check out a few things with the mint and the smelteter we're doing business with."

She bent her head back, her lips parted. "And when will I have to pay you back for the money you have lent me?"

Samos ran his mouth over her open, generous lips.

"When TMI pays you the first dividend."

Maria-Isabel caught fire and returned Samos's kisses with fierce lust.

"OK, this is our last night. Stop talking and start fucking. "

Ten days later, Samos had his answer. Maria-Isabel called him in the middle of the night. When he answered, she simply asked: "When do we start?"

"The next time you come to Panama," Samos replied and hung up.

CHAPTER 37

Grand Cayman, 1986

Like celestial bodies in opposing orbits or distant black planets rotating around ebony stars, Samos always felt that there were operatives like him, people who were half-forgotten, working quietly and diligently in the far-flung corners of the American empire, but he rarely, if ever, met them. From time to time, he could feel their operational pull on him and his activities. He could sense them eclipsing the faint light that still fell on him from Foggy Bottom, casting him momentarily in the deepest shadow, only to slip away before he could put a name or a face onto these charmed bodies.

Jack Longhurst was such a charmed body. A man who now had to steel himself against the emotions that threatened to overwhelm him as he walked toward the arrivals hall at Grand Cayman's Oral Roberts International Airport.

Longhurst had strongly resisted being assigned a file involving the Cayman Islands, but his immediate boss, the Assistant Secretary of the US Treasury, had insisted: if he wanted to remain a Special Consultant to the Treasury Department he had better get on with the task he had been given. And Longhurst needed to keep his job, not for the money, of which he had plenty, but because he knew that the only thing that was keeping him from going mad with grief was his work.

He trudged over obediently to the queue for arriving passengers and waited until his turn came to pass through Immigration and Customs Control.

"Mr. Longhurst," said the officer on duty, all smiles, "Nice to see you back."

Longhurst recognized the man from his previous visits to the island and pulled himself together.

"Nice to see you, too, Dilbert."

"I see you haven't brought the missus. How is she anyway?"

"Fine, just fine," the soon-to-be-forty Longhurst answered automatically as he retrieved his passport. But Mrs. Longhurst wasn't fine, was she? She wasn't at all fine because some carrion-eating, Russian bastard had pressed a button that launched a 2K11 Krug missile into the skies over Ukraine, where it intercepted a Malaysian Airliner on its way to the US from Bali, where Mrs. Longhurst had taken a well-deserved vacation, blowing it and Mrs. Longhurst out of the sky to rain down in bits and pieces over the Ukrainian steppes. So, no, Mrs. Longhurst was not fine at all.

After retrieving his luggage, Longhurst took a cab to the Hyatt, arguably the best hotel on the Caymans. Might as well be comfortable, he reasoned. He was on assignment for Uncle Sam and Uncle Sam had plenty of money.

Jack Longhurst was the Boston-born son of a wealthy father with extensive real estate holdings, and an aristocratic mother, an Astor. Jack had gone to Exeter and from there to Harvard, where he majored in business administration and graduated *magna cum laude*. The MBA was not enough for him, so he continued his studies and became a CPA. When time came to choose where to spend his required two-year indentured apprenticeship, he made a bold choice and opted to work for KPMG in George Town, their Cayman Islands office.

His gamble paid off. As the international money-laundering scandals of the 1980s became more and more frequent and shameless, triple-threat professionals like Longhurst with pedigrees of an MBA, a CPA, plus experience in important tax havens, became much sought-after by the authorities engaged in fighting against the monumental rip-offs conducted by banking giants worldwide.

Longhurst had enjoyed his two years in the Caymans. He learned a lot, swam a lot, sailed a lot, and partied a lot. Toward the end of his stay, he met Penelope—Pippa to her friends—a fellow Bostonian and software engineer with a degree from MIT, with whom he developed a relationship that soon led to love, and eventually, to marriage. When he returned to the mainland, he established an independent consultancy and, through his high-powered connections on both his father and mother's side, developed a small but high-profile clientele.

Happily married and thoroughly enjoying their professional lives, the Longhursts were considered to be a young power couple definitely on their way up. Life was good.

After three years of truly wedded bliss and, with both approaching their dreaded forties, they decided to have a last fling at travelling the world before trying to have children. They booked tickets for a trip to Bali and spent two weeks there having great fun. The only cloud on the horizon was Pippa's need to get back to Boston a day earlier than planned because she had been called, out of the blue, to address a prestigious seminar at MIT on the subject of software engineering, a venue she could not afford to miss.

The Longhursts hastily rearranged their plane reservations, but, unable to find two seats on the same flight home, agreed that Pippa would fly first, with Jack following the next day. And thus, the wheels of fate were set in motion and Pippa's number was called. Unpredictable. Random. Capricious. Unforeseeable. Chaos.

Longhurst would never forgive himself.

CHAPTER 38

West Bay, Grand Cayman, 1986

"One-eyed" Frank picked Longhurst up in his dilapidated truck at seven-thirty on Sunday morning. They drove to Jacques Scott's warehouse, where Longhurst bought a couple of cases of beer before they headed off for the West Bay wharf, where Frank, and most of the other day-charterers, kept their boats.

Born with a defective left eye, Frank Bodden was north of sixty, one of the old-time charter captains. He had fished for a living when young and then switched to day-chartering in the seventies when the tourist business picked up in the islands that time forgot. He'd run his boat from West Bay into the North Sound, dived for conch with the tourists he had on board, at times visiting "sting ray city," but mostly avoiding it. He preferred to head for Rum Point, where he'd build a little fire on the beach near the hotel and prepare conch salad from the catch of the day. He and his clients would then sit around the fire in the sun, eating and conversing, and listening avidly to Frank talk about how life used to be in the Cayman Islands during the good old days.

"We were supplied by a schooner that called once a month. People would watch out for the ship's arrival, and when they'd spot it on the horizon they would pick up a conch shell and blow in it to get people to come down to the harbor."

Frank would stop and look around to see if he had his audience's attention. Invariably, someone would say that it must have been tough to be so isolated from the rest of the world. "It had its advantages," Frank would grin, then add, "We only found out that World War II had broken out a month after Britain had already declared it!"

"So, what did you do?" a tourist would invariably ask.

"We were a loyal British Crown Colony, so we sent a contingent of young volunteers to fight for the king. Some of them died on the battlefield."

As he got older, Frank found it too much to navigate and simultaneously dive for conch, so he'd hire a young local mate from time to time to help with the work. In exchange, the mate would be allowed to bunk on board his boat during the nights.

Longhurst was surprised to find that, this time around, the mate was not a young local, but a disturbed, mostly mute, sun-burnt, desiccated, thirty-odd-year-old mainlander, already in his second season with Frank.

"Don't mind him," Frank told Longhurst. "He's a bit off his rocker. I fished him out of the water about four years ago. Fell off some boat and spent a long time in the sea. He was half-dead and badly sun-stroked. See that scar around his neck?"

Longhurst saw the wide, callused wound that furrowed around the poor creature's neck. The wheezing and the muteness were thus explained.

"That's a rope scar. Almost cut his head off when he went overboard."

"Where's he from?"

"Nobody knows. Can't speak, memory almost gone, but I taught him how to dive and spear fish. We call him Mike. Mike the Mate."

The addled creature reacted to his name with a crooked smile and a rasping wheeze.

"How does he communicate?"

"He's got that little blackboard around his neck. Chalks up his answers."

As usual, the Sunday outing to Rum Point turned out to be a great success. In addition to Longhurst, there had been six tourists on board: a family of four from Houston, and a couple from Switzerland, temporarily living in Grand Cayman. The wife said she was a personal trainer, the husband claimed to be in what he called "private banking." When Longhurst did not volunteer his reasons for visiting the islands, the Swiss remained friendly, but somewhat guarded.

In the evening, Frank, drove Longhurst back to his hotel, while Mike the Mate stayed behind to tidy up the boat.

Frank, characteristically, said almost nothing during the drive. When time came to say good night, the older man turned to the American with tears in his eyes.

"I heard about your wife," he whispered. "Bloody bad luck." They embraced and Longhurst had to fight hard not to break down.

When he got to his room, he found a slip of greasy paper slipped into his day bag that raised the hairs on the back of his neck: LOBBY MONDAY, TEN P.M. MIKE.

CHAPTER 39

Longhurst was not looking forward to the meeting he had been asked to attend on Monday morning. Experience had taught him that Caymanians could be bloody-minded, especially when it came to negotiations involving their sacred independence and lucrative livelihood.

Given the news that Longhurst had for them, the islanders had good reasons to be prickly, The Cayman Islands are an autonomous British Overseas Territory governed by a locally elected Legislative Assembly headed by a Governor, representing the Queen. The place became a tax haven in the 1960's when the governor hired two attorneys, one from Calgary in Canada and the other from Miami, to cobble together a generously liberal tax code backed by a strong Bank Secrecy Act, and straightforward companies' regulations that made the Caymans very attractive for those who wanted to avoid paying income tax or hide their money.

Monday's meeting, hosted by the financial secretary at the request of the US Treasury Department, was at the Glass

House, the headquarters of the islands' various administration departments. Those present included the directors
of the five so-called Class A "clearing" banks," plus the
island's police commissioner and, surprise, surprise, the
Swiss banker Longhurst had met onboard Frank's boat on
Sunday. Apparently, he was there to represent the interests
of the Class B banks, which numbered over a hundred and
accounted for the bulk of the Cayman banking industry.
Banking had become the bread and butter of the islands'
lawyers, accountants, and estate administrators, and, therefore, of the entire country.

Another reason for Longhurst's reluctance to take on this
assignment was facing an almost impossible task: convincing the Cayman government to acquiesce to US Treasury
requests to suspend the regulations of the Bank Secrecy Act
in cases where these were being used blatantly to shield the
taxable income of US citizens.

As expected, those present were professional and civil
and allowed him to make his case in detail with the help
of charts, statistical tables, and economic studies. By lunchtime, however, the overt consensus was that this request
was but the thin end of the wedge, a veiled threat that if
cooperation was not given, there would be serious economic
consequences. The US government meant business, and that
was bad for *business*.

Lunch proved to be a painful effort at joviality that failed
miserably and did not lessen the acrimoniousness that followed the debate after the meal.

By late afternoon, the situation had deteriorated to the point where the Cayman Financial Secretary decided to cancel the planned dinner. Everybody went back to their hotels or their homes except the Swiss banker, who volunteered to drive Longhurst back to his hotel. Once there, the American invited the Swiss for a drink at the Hyatt's bar.

They ended up having dinner together, during which the Swiss provided a short history lecture.

"We Swiss invented bank secrecy in 1934, when we introduced the so-called 'numbered account' concept. It was designed to protect the identity of an account's owner. The concept was a success because all kinds of people, mostly in Europe, feared the consequences of the war that everybody knew was coming, and needed a safe place for their money, regardless of who won. Of course, the place had to be neutral, not one of the potential belligerents."

"Right," prompted Longhurst. "And of course you guys had a tradition of remaining on the sidelines."

"And so did the Swedes," countered the Swiss, defensively.

"And both countries grew rich as a result."

"Yes. Neutrality, in times of war, is always profitable," the Swiss said smugly. "Today, however, there is not going to be a war fought with tanks and bullets, but with trade and commerce and the ammunition will be the means of exchange, money."

Longhurst took the lead. "Do you know, approximately, how much money is hidden offshore in the world's various so-called 'tax havens'?"

"Hard to estimate." The Swiss really wanted to know. "What's your guess?"

Longhurst scratched his nose. "A total of approximately one billion non-cash business transactions take place every day worldwide. Add to that two billion cash transactions and you get three billion. Now multiply this number by 360 and you're at more or less one trillion transactions per year, worldwide. That's my estimate of the total offshore money sloshing around on our planet. And everybody is out to get as much of it as they can."

The Swiss man didn't move or challenge Longhurst's estimate, but rather sat quietly, ruminating over their conversation. He made no move to leave as he lingered over his *eau-de-vie*.

Longhurst signed the bill, stood up, and tossed some money on the table for a tip. "Of course, the big boys—the US, the Brits, the Germans the Russians and the Chinese—are getting most of it."

"*Natürlich*," replied the Swiss banker, his focus a long way off.

On his way back to his room, Longhurst felt himself being shadowed by someone on the patio. At first he took the figure to be a local and braced himself to be hit up for money, a drink, what have you. Then he saw that it was Frank's mate Mike, about whom Longhurst had totally forgotten. The man stepped shyly out of the shadows, already scribbling on the tablet around his neck. Longhurst had been anticipating the comfort of his bed, but, sighing, led the poor man to the bar at the semi-deserted pool area. They sat down at a table and Longhurst signalled for two beers. Mike showed Longhurst his tablet. "You polise?"

Longhurst shook his head. "No. Why?"

Mike scribbled and Longhurst read out loud, "Help me. Shobogomo gold. Statue of Lebetry when?"

A waiter placed two beers on the table and left them alone. Mike grabbed his beer and guzzled it, sloppily.

"I don't understand," said Longhurst, shaking his head. "Do you want to go to the States?"

Mike nodded vigorously, beer dripping down his chin.

"OK, do you have any money?"

Mike shook his head and then wrote: "Gold."

"Gold? You have gold?"

Mike nodded, polishing off the last of his beer and gazing thirstily at Longhurst's.

"Where is it?" Longhurst asked. Mike pointed again to the tablet

"Shobogomo," read Longhurst, his patience coming to an end.

Longhurst stood up, rubbing his forehead. "I'm sorry Mike, I can't help you tonight. I'm too tired. Let me think about it and I will contact you tomorrow."

Mike was breathing rapidly, angrily, as he scribbled, tears forming in his eyes. He thrust the tablet at Longhurst, who strained to decipher the words: "I know you no help. Nobody help."

The lost soul turned on his heels and left, sobbing.

Longhurst stood and watched Mike slink off like a beaten dog avoiding the next cruel blow. He finished his own beer and left the table.

"Shobogomo," he murmured, almost laughing to himself. He took one final look back, but Mike the Mate was gone, the night having swallowed him whole. Longhurst's eyes lingered for a moment, then settled back down on the table he had just left. The two empty bottles of Red Stripe beer were glistening in the harsh patio light. Something was bothering him, that itch that one can't help but scratch.

Walking back to the table, Longhurst stuck his index finger into the neck of Mike's beer bottle and carried it carefully to his room, where he emptied the remaining drops and then carefully wrapped the bottle in toilet-tissue paper, which he then secured with surgical tape from the small first-aid kit he always had with him when he travelled. He slipped the wrapped bottle into one of his socks and placed the little package in the bottom of his suitcase.

Then he went to bed, promptly forgetting about it.

CHAPTER 40

Panama City, Panama, 1988

Alejandro Samos was mildly annoyed. It was Saturday and he had hoped to spend the entire day with his client and lover, Maria-Isabel. She had come from Mexico to visit for the weekend carrying a shipment of gold briquettes for Mauro and trailing her sister Elvira, four years her junior.

Elvira was nice enough, but possessed a very weak, almost comically receded chin. She had refused to do anything about it, even though Maria-Isabel had left the offer of plastic surgery on the table. Along with her weak chin came a passive, dull personality. She was taller than her older sister and had a beautiful body and good fashion sense, which drew attention, of which she was mostly oblivious.

"Man proposes, God disposes," Samos said to himself, though, of course, he did not believe in God. The bedside call he had just fielded from the chief of the US Mission in Panama, his principal diplomatic contact and significant supplier of new clients, had forced him to change his plans radically. Instead of remaining in contented post-coital stupor in his wonderfully comfortable, luxurious, king-sized bed, he was being asked to meet an important visiting "fireman" from the US Treasury Department.

Samos could not afford to refuse the request.

He kissed Maria-Isabel, his half-awake lover, heaved his body out of bed, and shuffled toward the bathroom, cursing all the way.

It was Saturday, so he decided to dress down and forgo the formal shirt, tie, and jacket. Instead, he put on a pair of designer jeans and a stylish light pullover. He slipped into a pair of comfortable loafers and took the elevator down from his penthouse apartment to his office nine floors below.

He had hardly had time to warm up the espresso machine before his visitor arrived. As Samos opened the door, there was an awkward moment of mirth. The two men looked at each-other up and down and simultaneously burst out laughing. They were dressed in almost identical clothing, both style and color-wise.

Samos glanced at the card his guest had handed him, reading it out loud as a way of welcome.

"Jack Longhurst, CPA, special assistant to the secretary of the United States Treasury."

Impressive, but Samos cautioned himself to keep it friendly and switched on his fail-safe *I-am-your-newest-best-friend* smile, laughing as he sat back to listen.

"Apologies," said Longhurst. "I'm sure I'm messing up your plans for the day."

Samos noticed with approval that the man was sporting a Rolex Explorer.

"Don't mention it," replied Samos, waving off the concern. "Can I offer you an espresso? I switched the machine on just before you got here. My secretary does not come in on weekends."

"Yes, thank you, if it's not too much trouble."

The friendly smile on Longhurst's clean-shaven, all-American face disarmed Samos in spite of his determination to keep the meeting short and impersonal.

"No problem."

"You have a Rouault print," said Longhurst, indicating the wall above Samos's desk. "Is it a signed?"

"Yes, a gift from one of my wealthier French clients."

"Always reminds me of Chagall. I have one at home, but it's not signed."

"Where is home, Mr. Longhurst?"

A slight hesitation slowed Longhurst's response.

"Georgetown, Maryland."

Samos got up. "Come, let's fetch our coffees from the kitchenette."

Samos waved his hand as they passed through the office space. "Look around, see where we labor."

Longhurst was impressed. He had counted twenty work stations. "Looks like business is good."

"Too good."

"Actually, business is what I want to talk to you about."

It took a full hour for Longhurst to fill Samos in on his own background and mission, an hour during which the ersatz Panamanian listened attentively, saying almost nothing. When Longhurst finished, Samos checked his watch.

"Would you excuse me a moment?"

Samos left Longhurst sitting in his office and went out into the cubicle farm where he sat down at a desk, picked up the phone, and called Maria-Isabel.

"Would you and your sister like to have lunch with us in half an hour?"

"Who is 'us'?"

Samos could see Longhurst waiting for him in his office.

"This tall all-American from Treasury."

Marie-Isabel hesitated.

"What's going on?"

"I'm not sure. He made an appointment through our friends at the American Mission. I couldn't refuse, but he is talking some very serious shit here and I'd like to get your take on the man."

Again, Maria-Isabel hesitated. "I've got Elvira with me. We've got some girl stuff to do today."

"Bring her. You'll have time after lunch."

They met in the building's atrium and Samos took them to the nearby sake restaurant for sushi. Maria-Isabel liked Japanese food and while they savored the sea urchin and flying fish roe, Samos became aware of a change in Elvira. The woman sat up straight, her eyes glued to Longhurst as he reiterated his polished pitch about America's need to regulate offshore banking. Samos chuckled to himself that the American seemed to have reached a part of Elvira where no man had gone before.

"You know, Maria-Isabel is the director of commercial distribution for the Mexican Mint," said Samos, by way of introduction. "Her husband is the minister of finance."

Longhurst reacted, impressed.

"Well, then, our project will be of direct interest to both of you," he continued, sitting back and finding his pace.

"There is far too much black money circulating offshore to be ignored and the US Treasury feels that the time has come to exercise more control over it. In response to our concerns about money laundering, the Treasury, in collaboration with a number of other Western countries, is forming a task force to counter this threat to the international banking system and to financial institutions."

Maria-Isabel and Elvira were cutting glances back and forth with Samos as the American, oblivious to their exchanges, helped himself to some tuna sashimi. Samos glanced at his lover. He was becoming uneasy about the direction in which the conversation was going and decided to push back just a little.

"You mean, Treasury wants to lay its hands on some of the 'black money.'"

Longhurst did not react to the challenge, but remained cool.

"As far as the likes of tax cheats are concerned, for example, yes."

"The thin end of the wedge."

Longhurst smiled. "I wouldn't worry. It will take time to develop the program, but sooner or later, the ax will fall on the so-called 'anonymous numbered accounts' industry. So, a word to the wise: be prepared."

"Just like a good Boy Scout. How much time?" Samos pretended concern, though he knew full well that his important clients would never be affected. The McIsaacs and the NSA would see to that.

"And why am I being singled out by you for this friendly warning?"

It was Longhurst's turn to be Samos's *newest best friend.*

"Because your friends at the Mission have told me that you have always been very helpful to them." Longhurst finished his sake wine, and dipped the last sushi on his plate into the wasabi infused soya sauce.

"My assignment is to visit the major offshore tax havens to soften the blow in advance of it being struck, thereby cushioning its impact somewhat. I have already spread the word to sympathetic friends in the governments of Bermuda, the Bahamas, and Grand Cayman and, now, Panama and…"

Longhurst raised his sake cup to Maria-Isabel and Elvira.

"Mexico?"

Maria-Isabel replied with polish and serpentine evasion, her wide-set black eyes unblinking and cold.

"I'm here on a weekend break, Mr. Longhurst. If you want to make your pitch to my husband, he does have an office coordinator. I can give you his number."

Longhurst realized he had overstepped and back-tracked. "Of course, my apologies. I would consider your help with contacts as a personal favor."

Samos stepped in, curious but cautious. "And where are you headed from here?"

"To Montevideo," replied Longhurst, his eyes stopping lightly on Samos. "I understand they are trying to establish a reputation for safe offshore banking for Latin American clients to compete with you guys here in Panama. I was hoping you might know someone in Uruguay with whom I could speak."

Samos felt an ice-cold flush in his guts, but laughed out loud, and although it took him tremendous self-control, kept the expression on his face friendly.

"Now, why would you think I'd know someone in Uruguay? You're obviously too intelligent to be one of those Americans who thinks all banana republics share common borders?"

There was an uncomfortable moment of unease as the women cut glances at Samos to see the telltale signs of a joke. Longhurst's expression remained neutral.

Samos was firm. "Uruguay is very far from here and, as far as I know, the country is not politically stable. Such a state of affairs is not particularly attractive to nervous money."

"I guess I'll just have to fish around there as I did here."

"Meaning?"

"I'll go to the embassy and ask for help from the commercial attaché."

Longhurst called for the bill and absolutely insisted on paying. "The three of you have been more than kind. I really appreciate your spending so much time with me," he sighed. "I wish I could reciprocate the favor, but I'm leaving tomorrow evening."

He looked at Elvira, who, to Maria-Isabel's surprise, returned his look with an open invitation. "Perhaps you would let me put things partially right by inviting you to join me for a light lunch tomorrow."

Elvira didn't blush, but unconsciously thrust her chin out and smiled as though to balance her face. It was obvious to all that Longhurst seemed to have been quite taken by her and had sensed that she reciprocated his feelings. She looked questioningly at Samos, but before he could reply, Maria-Isabel cut in.

"That's a splendid idea. It'll give Alejandro and me an opportunity to catch up on some long-overdue correspondence." Then, realizing that she had spoken out of turn, she added hastily. "That is, if my sister has no other plans."

Elvira finally spoke for the first time during the entire lunch. Her voice was low, throaty, and compelling as she fixed the American with eyes that, while not as effective as her sister's, were nonetheless dark and dewy with anticipation.

"I'd love to."

Samos stretched out a fine trip wire.

"Then it is settled. You two should definitely have lunch tomorrow. But, you could do me a favor. On your way home from Montevideo, perhaps you could swing through Panama and tell me about the political situation in Uruguay. I'd like to know how they react to the Treasury plan."

"I will definitely try, but I'm not sure how the office has booked my return," said Longhurst as they shook hands. He kissed Maria-Isabel on the cheeks and gave a happy nod to Elvira. "I'll pick you up in the lobby tomorrow at two?"

Maria-Isabel and Elvira went off, chatting like budgies about Longhurst while Samos returned to his office. He spent the next four hours worrying about Longhurst, wondering whether the man's inquiry about Montevideo was an unfortunate coincidence, or a calculated attempt at signalling that his cover was known. For reassurance, he sent a very detailed report about the meeting to McIsaacs at the NSA and requested confirmation that Longhurst was not a "Hunterman," trolling for information outside his official purview.

He received a reassuring answer within twenty-four hours, which he did not entirely trust—too quick. As though someone had just been waiting for his inquiry and had the answer cued up in the fax machine. His gut told him that McIsaacs would have needed more time to check on the matter in depth.

Obviously, something was up and he decided to watch his step. He felt it wise to protect his hard-earned assets so he gave Maria-Isabel a heads up about his unease, but did so by dropping enough oblique cues, thereby allowing her to figure out things for herself.

"Why were you so quick at getting Elvira to lunch with the American?" he asked once they were cozily wrapped around each other in bed.

His lover laughed. "Because Elvira is . . . Elvira! She is getting old and has no boyfriend. It is high time she found herself a suitable husband and I have rarely seen her react so hormonally to any man."

"But we know practically nothing about him," Samos protested. "Aren't you a bit too quick to start thinking about wedding bells?"

"*Querido*, you are definitely turning into an old fart. What are you, blind? Did you not notice how much the two were attracted to each other?" She became pensive. "Besides, I liked this American. I can tell that he comes from good stock."

CHAPTER 41

Montevideo, Uruguay, 1988

Longhurst completed his notes on his frustrating day with the Uruguayans, locked his papers into his dispatch-box like attaché case, and descended to the Hyatt's mezzanine bar to have a drink and dinner with his newfound friend, *Licenciado* Juan Gonzales, a partner at the TMR GROUP, an organization that offered corporate hosting in Uruguay for non-resident-owned companies.

After the second round of Glenfiddich twelve-year-old and careful probing, Gonzales, whom Longhurst had met at the TMR offices that morning, opened up just enough for the American to get a rough idea of the lay of the land.

"This has been a bear of a day, my friend," moaned Longhurst, hoping to stir some empathy in his Latin associate. "I understand the old 'Yankee go home!' attitude, but I thought we were past that."

Gonzales smiled politely but did not mince words. "People have long memories, Mr. Longhurst, and it has only been eighteen years since the 'Mitrione' affair."

Longhurst was caught up a bit short. He knew the story, but not the details.

"Another time, another administration," he said, by way of apology. "Might as well be another world."

Gonzales settled in his chair and leaned closer, visibly ill at ease.

"Allow me to put into proper perspective the somewhat unfriendly reception you experienced when you visited us this morning. We agreed to meet with you because we did not wish to offend your embassy's third secretary, who is working hard to ensure that Uruguay is given the funding our country so desperately needs from the World Bank." Gonzales hesitated then went on. "We are acutely aware of the US's influence on the bank's decision-making process, so we bend over backward to cooperate with the embassy when it asks for a favor."

Longhurst was beginning to feel put upon and frustrated. "Are you telling me that you are not interested in what I have to say? That you only listened to me to be polite?"

Gonzales laughed. "Before I answer that question, I want you to promise that you will let *me* be your host for dinner." He held out his hand and the American had no choice but to shake it.

His gesture seemed to break the ice.

They ordered dinner—a generous portion of *bife*, of course, with all the trimmings, and copious glasses of red wine to go with it.

By the end of their meal and a spirited exchange of ideas, it was clear that they would not find common ground. Uruguay resented US meddling in its affairs, and was irrevocably committed to becoming a Swiss-style tax haven for South Americans.

"After the dark days of the Tupamaros, we have finally managed to stabilize the political situation in our country to the point where our neighbors have confidence in our economic, financial, and legal infrastructure." Gonzales lit his after-dinner cigar. "Why should we fritter away this advantage by agreeing to join this Financial Action Task Force thing you are proposing?"

Longhurst took a deep breath and consciously removed the anger from his voice.

"Well, principally, to be a bit crude, because North America and Western Europe's financial centers have already agreed that they would join. Eventually, you, too, will need to join to be able to enjoy the advantages of a secure, integrated, and just money-management system."

"But Russia and China have not," said the Uruguayan dryly. "And nor will India and Japan."

"That's true. For now." Longhurst folded his napkin and placed it deliberately beside his empty wine glass. "Look, this has been a long, unrewarding day."

Gonzales picked up the cue, signaled for the bill, and then did a very curious thing. Without any fanfare, he dipped into his inside suit pocket and removed a folded paper, which he handed to Longhurst. The American unfolded it and scanned the list of names quickly.

"These are the companies who are already offering offshore financial services to Uruguayans. Most of them have offices in Montevideo. Why don't you visit with some of them to see what they have to say?"

Longhurst was caught for a reply, his eyes going from the list to Gonzales's face and back again. Gonzales was unsuccessfully hiding his delight at having been able to surprise Longhurst. "I've written to some of them about your visit and most of them will be happy to speak with you."

Longhurst was about to express his gratitude one last time when his eyes got snagged on one name in particular. He placed his finger on the name, showing it to Gonzales, who smiled.

"ISC, International Services Corporation?" Gonzales puffed on his cigar. "Alejandro Samos. One of the best."

CHAPTER 42

Mexico City, December 1989

Maria-Isabel was absolutely adamant. "I want to organize a colossal bash at Christmas."

Samos was skeptical. "And where and when do you want to do that?"

"In Mexico City, at the Hacienda San Angel, on, December twentieth."

"You're out of your mind."

"No, I'm not, querido. *Atiende-me*, pay attention to me. We'll have the party to which we'll invite about a hundred people at the Hacienda on the twentieth. Then we'll have a family Christmas party for fifty people, only family, on the evening of the twenty-fourth at my mother's house. This way, we'll achieve two things: repay our social obligations in one fell swoop, and get you to meet my various cousins, nephews, uncles, and aunts, something everybody has been clamoring for."

Maria-Isabel was in full flight, highly stimulated by her plan.

"Imagine," she added. "We'll be done with Christmas social obligations within a week." She gave Samos a hug. "And do you know who else will be at the Hacienda Christmas party?"

"Who?"

"Your friend Jack Longhurst. Elvira has already invited him." Samos was surprised and a bit sickened at the same time.

"Really."

"They have been corresponding regularly and Elvira has also visited him in Washington twice during the year. Did he mention it?"

"We're business friends, my dear one."

Samos shuddered mentally. Festivities, especially family gatherings, always meant innumerable questions from curious friends and relatives. The stress not to trip up was considerable, but he was not that concerned. Been there, done that, and survived.

As he watched Maria-Isabel getting all damp about Christmas, his heart went out to her. He was amazed at how adept she had been at converting an almost unbearably stress-ridden life into a happy one. This forty-two-year-old kid had made life bearable for him for almost a decade, loving him physically and nurturing him emotionally. He felt safe with her because, although both of them had secrets, he knew hers, but she did not know his.

Their relationship had gone through several iterations: clients to lovers to confidants to companions and, finally, after she left, but did not divorce her estranged husband, to soulmates. Each stage had its highs and lows, but the highs had outweighed the lows by a generous margin. The most difficult part of their relationship for Samos, the real challenge, had been coping with the tight-knit nature of Maria-Isabel's own family.

They were all very close to each other and this represented a real danger for Samos. When struggling with the decision to change his "persona" from Karas to Samos, he realized, of course, that he would be cutting all ties to the past and embarking on a lonesome road. And he had done so successfully. But a decade is a long time and cohabiting with the wonderful being that was Maria-Isabel, even part-time, had eroded his resolve to never love or trust anyone. In fact, that vow lay tattered and torn at the very bottom of his concerns. For the first time in his life, and perhaps far too late, he had learned to put the needs and desires of someone ahead of his own. And this, he knew, was dangerous.

Now that their lives seemed to be moving along without a hitch, their relationship solidified as it matured, they were having fun, living in a partnership that was constantly evolving for the better. Their gold problem had been resolved years ago. Mauro had been as good as his word and had supplied them with a dozen gold bars every year. Their jewelry company had opened a half-dozen stores throughout the Caribbean, turning gold of questionable provenance into clean, honest cash. Now, a new challenge appeared on his horizon: Jack Longhurst.

Try as he might, Samos could not pinpoint what bothered him about the American. He knew, because it was his business to know, that the Financial Action Task Force, or FATF, which Longhurst was promoting, was going to be an international body established to set banking standards and implement effective measures for combatting money laundering, terrorist financing, and other related threats to the integrity of the international financial system. These, unfortunately for Samos and his clients, included tax evasion.

But not tax avoidance, which would remain legal.

"My dear, the difference between evasion and avoidance is open to interpretation," he explained to Maria-Isabel as they prepared to meet with Elvira and Longhurst for a late supper. "We can, how can I say, accept Longhurst into our social circle . . ."

"Do we have a choice?" interrupted Maria-Isabel with a wry smile.

"No," Samos conceded. "But we have to exercise extreme caution when discussing business in his presence. He can never know the source of your supply of discounted gold."

Samos watched as Maria-Isabel primped in front of her mirror. "How could he possibly find out about that?"

"I've done some casual research and I have discovered that Elvira's boyfriend is not only involved in creating FATF, but is also slated to be the head enforcer of its regulations in North, Central, and South America, as well as in the Caribbean."

Maria-Isabel let out a long, low whistle, catching Samos's eyes in the mirror.

"What's that expression? Keep your friends close?"

"And your enemies closer," said Samos, completing her thought.

As he mulled the situation over, Samos could not stop himself from laughing. What was he to do? Uncle Sam, on whose behalf he was supposed to act, was being extraordinarily duplicitous: on the one hand, he was encouraging evasion if it helped create cooperative *politically exposed people*, and, on the other, wanted full disclosure when it came to undeclared income.

A classic case of sucking and blowing at the same time!

CHAPTER 43

Mexico City, December 1989

La Hacienda San Angel, an old Carmelite monastery founded in the seventeenth century, had been converted, in 1963, into a well-known restaurant in the popular park called *Bosque de Chapultepec*. Its Mexican-colonial architecture and interior decorations, spacious gardens, and fountains lent a touch of exquisite elegance to those who dine there, especially in the month of December. The *crème de la crème* of Mexico City society vied for the opportunity to host Yuletide parties in its main banquet hall, which can accommodate as many as one hundred diners. Some of these events succeeded in duplicating the splendor of bygone years when viceroys, their consorts, and the aristocracy would celebrate the Christmas season in the Hacienda's halls.

Maria-Isabel Rodriguez Duque de la Mancha's family, being near the top of the political and social pile, enjoyed first dibs on the main banquet hall of the *Antiguo San Angel* every year for the Friday night preceding Christmas ever since the Hacienda became a first-class restaurant in the early sixties. This year, Maria-Isabel had made it clear that she expected Samos to be there, as her husband, recently released from his marital responsibilities by mutual accord, would not.

For his part, when faced with this subtle ultimatum, Samos had to fight hard to control his fight-or-flight instincts. Part of what made Samos good at his job was his ability to disappear into the landscape, like a camouflaged sniper. He was continuously aware that the more public his persona, the more likely it was that someone, anyone, might catch him on an obscure fact, or an unlikely association, or note that tiny fleck of *lúdláb* on his chin, and his jig would be well and truly up.

To avoid such complications when he began seeing the still-married Maria-Isabel, and finding himself visiting her regularly in Mexico City, Samos decided to maintain a small suite at the Hotel Camino Real across the street from Mexico City's largest park, the *Bosque de Chapultepec*. The park contains several lakes and excellent museums, as well as the homes of Mexico's high and mighty. The current presidential residence, *Los Pinos*, is within its four-square-kilometer territory as is a former imperial palace, the *Castillo de Chapultepec*. A popular destination, it is packed with tourists and locals during the weekends.

Sunday is the park's big day, as vendors line the main paths and throngs of families come to picnic, navigate the lake on rowboats, and crowd into the museums. The Museum of

Anthropology is world-class. Of course, there are a number of fine restaurants in the park, as well, ideal places for lovers to meet without creating unwanted gossip.

Christmas dinner at the Rodriguez-Echenique mansion in Lomas Altas turned out to be an incredibly elegant affair, far surpassing the formality of the party that Maria-Isabel had organized at the *Hacienda San Angel* the previous Friday at which gentlemen were required to wear tuxedos and the ladies cocktail dresses. No sit-down dinner had been served, but rather a sumptuous buffet had been offered, featuring, among the many delicacies, mountains of Beluga caviar on ice and unlimited Cristal champagne.

At the Rodriguez family mansion, the men were required to wear tails and the ladies full-length evening gowns. The seating arrangement had been carefully worked out in advance. Gold-edged place cards on which the guests' names had been beautifully calligraphed in gold letters were placed in a way to make sure that no guest would find himself sitting next to his or her partner.

There were no children present. They'd been banished to a separate room where, supervised by their nannies and governesses, they were allowed to romp around to their spoiled hearts' content.

Samos located his place card and found himself seated on his left beside Maria-Isabel's first cousin Omara, a rather shy conversationalist, and on his right, Ilona, the vivacious wife of Uncle Octavio, who, as it was revealed, was the attorney in charge of customs at the city's international airport, a politically high-octane position.

As soon as they sat down, Ilona, a handsome, mature woman with jet black hair, porcelain white skin, and emerald green eyes and whose rich, glowing *decolleté* was a joy to behold, told Samos that she was thrilled to be sitting next to, "my good friend Maria-Isabel's mysterious Panamanian friend about whom I have heard so many nice things."

As the dinner got underway and after some elaborate toasts had been offered, Ilona confessed that her family was originally from Hungary, a truth that Samos had already quietly noted. As soon as he had realized that he was bantering with a fellow Magyar, Samos made a special effort to reply in firm, Panamanian-accented Spanish, complete with some vulgar street expressions. So odd, thought Samos, to be speaking Spanish with this sexy, sensual woman, while the Hungarian rose irrepressibly in his throat only to be suppressed by the clenching of his jaw.

"I escaped to Vienna in 1966, and from there I immigrated to Canada where I started a pastry shop," Ilona laughed. "Hard work, but lucrative. I concentrated on making cakes from recipes I learned in Austria."

"And how did you get involved with Uncle Octavio?" Samos asked politely as he nodded and raised his glass in salute to Ilona's much older husband sitting some distance away. Samos was already bored and they had barely finished the soup course.

"He was the Mexican ambassador to Canada and a widower. I conquered him," replied Ilona proudly, her chest puffed up.

Traditional Christmas Eve fare in Mexico differs in various regions, but the usual main dishes are *Bacalao a la Vizcaina,* made from salted cod, or *Pavo,* roasted turkey. However, truly memorable Mexican Christmas dinners begin with *Pozole,* a must-have soup, flavored with green chilies, cumin, garlic, and lime. The meal dragged on interminably because two main courses were served, the fish *and* the bird.

Much to Samos's relief, dessert finally arrived, starting with *buñuelos,* a dessert made from fried dough covered in cinnamon sugar. Samos was about to tuck into his portion when the waiter moved it to one side and placed a slice of Sacher Torte, the archetypal Viennese chocolate cake, in front of him. As a child it had been his favorite dessert. Shocked, he turned to Ilona to find her gauging his reaction with some interest. Sobering quickly to hide his true feelings, he struggled for an appropriate comment, but, luckily, she impatiently cut him off, thereby saving him from revealing his own European origins.

"You probably are not familiar with this cake, yes?" she asked proudly. "It's Uncle Octavio's favorite ever since tasting it for the first time in Vienna."

Samos found Ilona titillating but he was obliged to feign interest as he was fully familiar with the torte's history. "And what is it called?"

"Sacher Torte," replied Ilona, who then launched into a long-winded explanation from which Samos could only escape when coffee was being served and Jack Longhurst came over to speak with him.

He had spotted the American when he had arrived with Elvira on his arm. Samos could not help but notice the sudden change in Elvira. Whereas, prior to meeting Longhurst, she had been dull and tedious, now, after seeing him for almost a year, she was simply scintillating. There was no other word for it.

"I'm sorry about not having called you earlier, but I have literally just gotten off the plane in time to rent some evening tails for this shindig."

He smiled engagingly at Ilona. "I'm sorry to interrupt you, but since I must head for home the day after tomorrow I wanted to discover if Alejandro could find the time tomorrow."

He turned deliberately to Samos. "I know it's an imposition on Christmas Day, but could you meet with me for an hour or so?"

The hairs on the back of Samos's neck prickled and a warm flow of blood threatened to redden his face. Fortunately, the low light in the room helped hide his reactions. "Sure, if it's that important and urgent."

"It is. How about at your hotel tomorrow, at eleven?"

"Maria-Isabel will crucify me," said Samos, shaking his head regretfully.

"Again, I apologize." Longhurst looked extremely uncomfortable.

"So be it," said Samos, fighting hard to sound off-hand, but seriously concerned.

CHAPTER 44

Mexico City, Christmas Day 1989

An immaculately dressed Longhurst, wearing a charcoal bespoke suit from London's Gieves & Hawkes in Saville Row, a sparklingly white shirt, and a dark red tie with matching pocket square, arrived dead on time. Samos had arranged to have breakfast served at a secluded table of the Azulejos Restaurant in his hotel, the Camino Real. He did not want Maria-Isabel anywhere near him as he conversed with the American, knowing full well that Longhurst was bound to be a bearer of bad tidings.

His guest sat down and eagerly accepted the cup of cappuccino Samos offered him. Longhurst appeared to be nervous and tired and seemed to have aged years since he had gone to Montevideo, when Samos had last seen him.

"We have a lot of ground to cover," Longhurst commented through almost clenched teeth, his jaw muscles flexing involuntarily. His eyes were missing their usual luster and they seemed to be having difficulty meeting Samos's reassuring but inquiring, gaze.

"Allow me to speak uninterruptedly to set the scene." He swallowed hard and then continued, putting Samos on high alert. "Don't worry, I'll answer all your questions after I've finished."

Samos nodded wordlessly, his stomach knotted tight like the turnbuckle ropes around a boxing ring. He practiced breath control, willing himself to appear calm, relaxed, and friendly. When he was younger, his ability to detach his emotions had been great, but as the years went by, to do so under stress was becoming gradually more difficult. Having to pretend, every second of the day that he was someone other than his real self had become second nature, but as he grew older, the tension simmering under the surface of his ego caused him to tire easily and to worry more.

Longhurst began with the chance meeting at the Grand Cayman Hyatt with One-Eyed Frank's new mate, Mike.

"I had forgotten about the beer-bottle because it was in an inside pocket of the Tumi suitcase I rarely used. I came across it again four months ago, barely recalling what it meant to signify and sent it off to Interpol to be tested for fingerprints."

Longhurst's eyes never left Samos's face.

"You understand, it was a purely benevolent thing for me. I saw this poor guy, clearly the victim of some kind of trauma, maybe an American, stranded in the islands, with, perhaps a family back home who were looking for him. When we met for that one time, he had kept on muttering to me about something that sounded like 'Shobo-gummo' and for some reason it stayed with me. The results came back from Interpol two weeks ago. It seems that Shobo-gummo means *Chibougamau*." He stopped talking.

As fast as thought itself, Samos put it all together, even as he was inwardly chiding himself for being so stupid and, at the very same time, applying a super-human, wilful effort to not react at all! Mauro's blunt, Montreal north inflection, the seemingly endless supply of gold ingots, the sailboat, "shobo-gummo," all added up to form a fresco in his mind of a desolate minefield of shit, pain, horror, and scandal. Samos was much better at keeping his poker face than he knew because Longhurst, who was watching carefully for any *tell*, searched in vain.

"And what's that?" asked Samos finally, assuming a mildly puzzled mien as he forcefully distracted his thoughts by focusing on Longhurst's shirt, which he concluded, judging by the cut of the collar, had also come from London, probably from Turnbull and Asser. At the same time, the inner, "know-it-all" showman hidden deep inside him was fighting to blurt out that he knew all about Chibougamau, a gold-mining center in Northern Quebec.

Longhurst's face, on the other hand, could not hide his cautious skepticism.

"You've never heard of Chibougamau?" he said, as he continued staring.

This time is was Samos who put hardened steel in his eyes, raising his normally heavy, disinterred lids as an act of defiance.

"Nope, but why do you ask?"

Longhurst finally broke his gaze and sipped from his glass.

"I thought that maybe you had heard of it. In 1980, two pilots, both Canadians of Italian descent, literally sailed away from Chibougamau airport with forty gold bars worth about $24 million, and disappeared without a trace. The gold belonged to one of the smelter companies in the area."

Samos began to temporize. "Surely, you mean 'fly away,' not 'sail away.'"

"I meant 'sail away.' They had a boat."

"So?" A look of incredulity and amazement was allowed to flash.

"According to Interpol, the fingerprints on the beer bottle I picked up in Cayman belong to one of the pilots."

"So you think this Mike-the-Mate fellow is one of the pilots?"

Longhurst nodded, his eyes fixed again on Samos, who now pretended simple-mindedness because he began to sense the direction in which his visitor was heading. "But you said the man was down on his luck and eking out a hard-scrabble living on a fishing boat."

"I did."

"So he *has* no money and certainly no gold."

Longhurst nodded. "No, something must have happened, an accident or maybe a betrayal. *Mike-the-Mate* had nothing, but what of his partner in crime?

"And where is *he*?" asked Samos, showing how much he was enjoying this mystery.

"That's the $64,000 question." Samos watched as Longhurst's body language suddenly changed. The man had begun to sweat a little and he leaned forward, making Samos do the same, bringing their faces closer. The friendly, tight little smile almost always present on Longhurst's face had disappeared and was replaced by a troubled look of bewilderment.

"Here is the thing," he continued, almost stammering. "I find myself in an untenable position. As you know, I am involved emotionally with Elvira and we've been seeing each other regularly during this last year. We . . . uh, I've . . ."

Obviously finding it difficult to continue, he waved to a passing waiter and asked for more coffee. Samos stopped the waiter, held up two fingers and added, "*Corretto.*" The waiter nodded and moved off.

While waiting for the "corrected" espressos, Longhurst somehow pulled himself together. "Maria-Isabel and Elvira are close and they talk. In fact, they share just about everything. And of course Elvira shares a lot with me about her family."

Longhurst was watching Samos's face once again, as though expecting this last bit of revelation to provoke a reaction but, again, Samos chilled his emotions as the thunder clouds of impending disaster roiled like a fist over his head. Longhurst took a deep breath. "She told me about Tere's jewelry business and her business partner, *Mauro.* The one who lives on a boat. In Costa Rica."

Samos held back the storm forming around him with a smiling counterattack. "But what has all this got to do with me?"

Longhurst didn't blink, but responded with devastating, assured, bluntness. "Elvira told me that the man in Costa Rica, *Mauro*, was your client and that he and Maria-Isabel were successful because their business had access to very cheap gold through him."

Samos relieved the tension somewhat by leaning back away from the American, placing his fingertips together and allowing his eyes to hide, once again, behind his heavy lids.

"And you now postulate that my client Mauro is the other pilot and that he is sitting on a pile of stolen gold."

"I have to ask as it has been driving me a bit mad," said Longhurst delicately. "Did you vet this Mauro character? Did you look into his past?"

It was time for Samos to put on the mask of the wounded.

"Jack, there was no need. He presented me with his valid Italian passport. Roberto Mauro, a citizen of Milan. No red flags, nothing to indicate that he wasn't who he said he was."

"And the gold?"

"That I did follow up. He had a signed letter from Moe Hunter in Florida, a bill of sale for two ingots. I confirmed this with Hunter's lawyer."

"Moe Hunter?" Longhurst's face had turned red. He was obviously very uncomfortable. "I should be ashamed of myself for suspecting that a member of my fiancée's family, a family of prominence, is fencing stolen goods. And, frankly, I am." He stopped talking and began fiddling with his heavy gold cuff links. They were engraved: JAL, for Jack Arthur Longhurst. "I have been struggling with this problem for a couple of weeks now and I'm lost. I need your help."

"What do you mean?" ventured Samos, cautiously.

"There must be some way, through you and I working together, to find out whether my suspicions are justified without alerting the powers that be and precipitating a horrible scandal."

"Not to mention an end to your future happiness."

"Exactly."

Both men stopped talking for a while and listened to the sound of tinkling cutlery and the murmur of conversation, interrupted by the shrill laughter of young children from time to time. Behind his heavy-lidded eyes, Samos marshalled his thoughts, going rapidly over each possible scenario.

After a couple of minutes that seemed like eternity, Samos broke the uncomfortable silence. He caught the eye of a waiter and asked for two Calvados chasers, then turned to his guest.

"This is all coming at me from out of the blue, Jack. I'll need some time. but once I've had the opportunity to look into the matter, I am sure I'll find that the gold-trading arrangements of the people you mentioned will prove to be well within the boundaries permitted by Panamanian law."

Longhurst reacted. "Panamanian law? But that's not what I'm concerned about."

Samos cut him off just as the waiter put the two glasses of liquor on their table and left. "I recognize your need for more than just verbal assurances from me. Believe me, I do. Let's be frank, this touches me also, right?"

He knocked back the Calvados chaser and leaned back in his chair, the picture of relaxed insouciance. "I promise to find out whatever I can, and promptly," he said, giving Longhurst the most radiant, 'I'm-just-an-innocent-bystander,' type of smile of which he was capable. "How much time do you give me?"

"I'd say a maximum of four months?"

"Four months then," confirmed Samos.

A much relieved Longhurst wiped the sweat off his brow with a handkerchief as red as fear. "I'm returning to Washington tonight, some family Christmas commitments there. Then it's back to the office in mid-January, so I don't much have to respond to Interpol before the end of April."

He pushed back his chair and got up to leave. They shook hands and said goodbye. Fortunately, both his and his visitor's palms were wet enough with perspiration that neither could tell whether the other was also nervous.

"There it is, then," said Samos to himself while signing the bill and leaving a few pesos for the waiter, "A direct threat to just about everything."

He looked around. The place was filling up with families eager to be seated for the special Christmas-day brunch offered to *aficionados* of the beautifully airy, blue-tiled— hence, *azulejos*—restaurant.

On his way up to his suite where his Maria-Isabel was probably still asleep, he mused about how to broach the subject in hand with her. Being an experienced and embittered realist, he fully expected the situation to develop into a major disaster unless he immediately intervened decisively and drastically. An investigation would almost certainly reveal his own real identity, or at least that Alejandro Samos was a perfect confection of the NSA, and that Maria-Isabel's business partner was not the Italian national, Roberto Mauro, but *Greg DiMauro*, formerly of St. Leonard, Montreal, Canada, and "the other pilot," who floated away with forty bricks of pure gold from under the nose of every important law enforcement body in the world.

Nothing that Longhurst had said was a revelation and, again, Samos had to curse himself for his temporary weakness and denial. He should have known that this moment would come. His training had prepared him, but, screw the NSA training! His own, war-sharpened instincts had let him down. Samos had suspected Mauro from that very first meeting when the Italian's "Montreal accent" had given him away. When he never got a reply from Foggy Bottom to his direct request for information on any gold thefts in North America or Europe, he should have pressed the question. But, he hadn't. Why? Because he already knew, and didn't care.

Of course Mauro was the other pilot. Why else would a young man, making the kind of money he was, live on his boat almost twenty-four-seven, in a country with no extradition treaty with the US or Canada? What remained of the stolen gold bars was obviously hidden on board. The story about Hunter selling bullion to Mauro was probably a special arrangement that had been conceived to cover up the origin of the gold for a fee. The perpetually broke treasure hunter needed money to fund his diving operations, and Mauro had negotiated a clever win-win.

As for legal or criminal liability, the situation was fraught with complications. Of course, as long as Mauro stayed in Costa Rica, he was safe, except if his secret got out and bounty hunters or insurance recoup agents tracked him down. Samos was unconcerned about his own dealings with Mauro; he still had the original signed Hunter letter-of-sale in a safe place and even a copy of his telephone bill showing his call to the treasure hunter to verify that Hunter really *had* sold those gold bars to Mauro.

No. The real problem lay with Maria-Isabel, who had vouched that the gold bars she was sending regularly to the Mexican Mint for conversion into briquettes were legit. Unless her company could produce a Hunter-like letter for each such transaction, she could be accused of dealing in stolen goods—inadvertently or purposefully, it made little difference in law. There was very little legal light between "knowing," and "should have known," between due diligence and wilful ignorance. To make matters worse, an investigation of her affairs would also reveal her little cozy, corrupt kickback deal with the Mexican Mint.

And there was his anger to resolve, as well.

Never trust, never love, his life's mantra.

He had betrayed himself, made himself take unconscionable risks, and for what? Great sex? Companionship? A feeling of belonging, of family? Emotional baubles, trinkets to delude and betray. Hard as he tried, Samos could not wrap his subtle, sophisticated and experienced mind around it. How could Maria-Isabel have been so stupid, so incautious and reckless? How could she have revealed their most intimate business affairs to her naiveyounger sister? Why? To what end?

Of course, even as he asked himself these questions, he knew the answers. A lifetime of surviving by seeing deeply into people's souls, their desires and motivations and recognizing their essential self-centeredness, revealed the answer to him. Sisters. Fucking sisters. Maria-Isabel, beautiful, smart, social, comfortable in her own skin, the Queen Bee around which the world turned, and her low-achieving, dishwater-dull sister, Elvira. Tall, but stooped, big-footed, awkward, socially inept, ordinary spinster, unaccomplished, and always in second place.

That was the way of the world until *he* came along: tragic, lonely, wounded, handsome, accomplished, powerful, Jack Arthur Longhurst. And suddenly, the order of Maria-Isabel's universe changed. Under Longhurst's careful and gentlemanly seduction, dishwater Elvira, the ugly *pata,* raised her cow-like eyes and blossomed into an alluring *cisne,* and it drove Maria-Isabel crazy. Order must be restored! And what better way to put her dull, younger sister in her proper place than to share intimate little secrets about her fabulously successful business? Maria-Isabel could not have helped herself if she tried. She had to be admired and worshipped by everyone, especially her younger sister.

However, understanding what happened and why she did it did not remove the barb of pure, red rage that drilled deeply into Samos's heart and clouded his mind. His own ego could only see Maria-Isabel's indiscretion as a betrayal of himself! How could she have done this, to *him*! How could she have created a situation where he was, for all intents and purposes, called onto the carpet by Longhurst and told, in only lightly veiled terms, that his deal was blown!

Samos walked softly to the mini-refrigerator in his suite's kitchenette, fished a couple of ice cubes from their container, and threw them into a crystal glass. He then grabbed the Calvados bottle that he kept in the freezer and walked glass and bottle to his desk, where he sloshed four ounces of the burnt amber liquid over the cubes, lifted the glass to his lips and inhaled the content in one giant gulp.

One thing was certain: he would not hang alone for this. He had come too far, suffered far too much to be treated like some Budapest street boy, a petty criminal punching above his weight. A picture of him cringing in a ditch that ran alongside a tobacco field in Cuba's *Pinar del Rio* province flashed through his mind. He was hiding from Fidel's militia, scared shitless, while waiting for his men to finish poisoning the tobacco crop.

"Just like the good old days," he whispered to his empty tumbler. "The Calvados in my canteen fuelling my courage then and fuelling it now."

He squeezed into a corner of his sofa and waited for the knot in his gut to dissolve, hoping fervently that Maria-Isabel would not wake up before he stumbled on a solution to their problem.

But this was not likely.

CHAPTER 45

Mexico City, Christmas Day, 1989

Maria-Isabel, quite besides herself, was pacing, the tears running theatrically down her high cheeks, though her face was quite frozen, like a death mask. "Stupid, stupid, stupid," she kept repeating, "I should never have talked to Elvira about my business, ever."

Samos watched her passively as she went through the throes of regret, thinking less and less of her and wondering what feminine alchemy she had used to disguise her base inanity from his eyes for all of their time together.

"What happened, happened, and cannot be undone," Samos said, finally, all business. "It was an unfortunate coincidence that Longhurst got involved with Elvira so soon after he had been to Grand Cayman. And who could have predicted that fate would bring him and this *First-Mate-Mike* character together, and that he would be so touched by the poor soul's predicament that he would follow up with a fingerprint inquiry and discover the crime?" He sighed. "Maria, nobody could have foreseen this."

Still in her nightgown, Maria-Isabel sat down on the sofa beside Samos, shivering, but more from shattered nerves than the cool air. Samos deliberately put his arm around her shoulder, almost as a test to himself that he could still do this without wanting to strangle her. "Does Elvira know about your various arrangements with the mint?"

"No."

"Then what does she know that could hurt us?"

"That Mauro is buying gold cheaply from Moe Hunter, in Florida."

Samos put a hand under her chin and turned her face to his.

"Why should that hurt us? That's not against the law and we are covered if we can document that Mauro did, in fact, buy the gold from Hunter at a reduced price." Samos was beginning to feel more and more positive about the overall situation, if even more angry with Maria-Isabel.

"I presume that, as I suggested, you obtained a letter from Hunter every time you took one of his gold bars to the mint for conversion into briquettes."

"Yes, I did, but now," she hesitated and looked down, avoiding Samos's eyes. "I'm not sure if they were really signed by Hunter."

Samos pulled away, incredulous. He stared at the woman as his guts constricted, the nausea rising. He could not keep himself from blurting, "What the hell do you mean by that?"

"Keep your voice down, please. Let me explain."

Maria-Isabel got up and poured herself a drink from the Grey Goose vodka bottle in the freezer. She was so accustomed to always wearing the highest of heels, her Achilles tendons had shortened so that, when barefoot, she had the tendency to walk on her toes. Samos watched her tight, lush body move under the thin nightgown, her irresistible ass tilted seductively, and was stirred despite his anger. He absently noted that the vodka bottle was almost empty and began to wonder about who was drinking his liquor. Perhaps it was he, himself, and he did not realize how much he was drinking these days.

Or was it his girlfriend?

Or both. It was Christmas, after all.

Maria-Isabel knocked back her drink and sank back into the sofa cushions again. "Over the last five years, Mauro sold our shops sixteen bars. I got a Hunter letter from Mauro covering each and every one, like clockwork. Except for the last one, which we bought in early December."

The tears began to course down again. "The trouble is that when I asked for the letter, Mauro took a week to get it, and it was dated ten days after Hunter had died."

"Jesus." Samos was almost giddy as he watched the wheels slowly coming off their wagon.

"Hunter could not have signed it."

Samos was now easily able to predict what was to come. "And, of course, the signature on this last letter matched with all the other previous letters you got, right?"

"Absolutely."

"So now, this makes you suspect that all the other signatures on the letters were forgeries, too."

Fresh tears and, finally, the few nerves in her face not already in the grip of her monthly Botox injections revealed themselves and crumpled her beautiful face into something much less beautiful.

"Yes."

"And this confirmed to you that, aside from the first two bars, which I bought, and for which I *do* have a genuine letter of sale, there were really no sales of gold by Hunter to Mauro, right?" With a silent nod, Maria-Isabel acknowledged that this was so.

"And now we know where the gold really came from. And so does Longhurst."

"*Querido,* I no longer know what to believe." She looked pleadingly at Samos. "I beseech you, don't be cross with me."

Samos looked at the woman and felt the divided loyalty that tore at what was left of his heart. What on earth was he doing, he asked himself. Why was he giving her a hard time, hurting her? And yet, there was a reckoning, there had to be. Like a fish-wife at the market, he assembled the weights of the sins stacked against her and threw them onto the scales of judgment.

Was she not the only family he had in this whole damned world? But, when all was said and done, what was family worth?

And had she not stood by him through thick and thin during the last eight years? And had she not been handsomely rewarded, beyond all proportion?

When he caught a bug on one of his business trips to Bogota and almost died from the pleurisy he had developed in the high altitude, did she not come to fetch him and bring him home and then nurse him back to health? But then, would not anyone do the same to save their rice bowl?

When her family criticized him for being no more than a ruthless money shark and begged her not to have anything to do with him, did she not staunchly defend him when they kept on making him feel, whenever the occasion arose, that he was just a low-born Panamanian foundling? Which, given his true origins and his singular success in almost every endeavor, and his lining of her purse, was that not laughable? Coming, such as it did, from a gang of inbred, corrupt, petty grease-ball, bourgeois bums, scratching for whatever ill-gotten crumbs came their way?

And, above all, was it not *he* who had encouraged her to do business with Mauro when all his instincts told him that the man's gold was toxic? But then, was it not Maria-Isabel, with shark eyes wide open, who had hungrily seized a way to meld her own corrupt, thieving plans with the opportunity he offered?

Shame on him. Shame on her. Was there any light between them? Something had been broken and that he could not forgive. Betrayal. Weakness. Indiscretion. A reckless disregard for what *he* had done for her. And all just to put her idiot sister back in her place.

The image of Maria-Isabel, on her toes, her divine form revealed by the light raking through her sheer nightgown, banished any hesitation for now. For now, he had to play the part as Longhurst had written it.

He took her in his arms and kissed her tenderly on her lips. "I take full responsibility for this whole mess," he whispered into her ear reassuringly. "Don't worry; I know exactly how to fix the problem."

She held him close. "Are you sure?"

Seeing the fear reflected in her beautiful, wide-set, unblinking, coal-black eyes, glittering with tears, he lied without hesitation.

"I am absolutely certain," he said, knowing full well that this affirmation obligated him to resolve the situation one way or another, even if it meant that some people would no longer need rice bowls.

CHAPTER 46

Panama City, February 1990

The parcel, suspiciously heavy, was addressed to him personally at his office and marked Private and Confidential. On
closer inspection, however, Samos was relieved to see that
the sender was *"Pasteleria Vienesa,"* with a return address on
Avenida Paseo de la Reforma, in Mexico City, right opposite
the US Embassy.

"Of course," muttered Samos, greatly relieved, "It must
be from Ilona, Uncle Octavio's wife."

He opened the package. It contained a small wooden box
with a delicious-looking chocolate cake sealed in an air-tight
cellophane envelope to maintain its freshness. Under it was
an envelope with a letter from Ilona.

Dear Alejandro, it read. *On Christmas Eve I promised to
send you one of my famous Sacher Tortes. I hope you'll enjoy
eating it.*

I hear from Mari-Isa that you and she will be coming to Mexico on her birthday. I would like to meet you there to discuss a matter relating to so-called offshore banking, something that you know a lot about.

Please don't talk about this with M-I. There is enough gossip about this sort of thing within the family and I don't want to add to the flow.

Do not write, do not call. I will call you on February 10 to tell you where to meet me for lunch.

Ilona.

Samos was not surprised. The PRI had recently been voted out of power in Mexico and those who had been involved with it now found themselves under the microscope of the new regime, which was certainly not a comfortable place in which to be.

Maria-Isabel's family had been a traditional supporter of PRI for decades, so, unfortunately, its members became prominent targets of the new inquisitors.

Hence, Samos thought, Ilona and her offshore problem, for which she was now looking for a solution.

But why from Samos? Surely, her husband, Uncle Octavio, a senior member of the distinguished Rodriguez-Echenique family with an impressive diplomatic career behind him, possessed a wide range of powerful international contacts through which he could solve whatever problem his wife may have involving so-called offshore banking.

Provided that he wanted to or, more importantly, she had wanted him to.

Or, perhaps he did not even know about these offshore problems, which would mean that Ilona had not shared them with him.

And why not?

Samos reread Ilona's letter. Her instructions not to write or call or speak with Maria-Isabel were worrisome and forced him to conclude that the woman was somehow deeply and dangerously compromised and wanted desperately not to be found out.

And if this were so, would it be wise for him to get involved, thereby perhaps complicating his own life? He suddenly remembered one of McIsaac's favorite sayings, "When in doubt, cover your ass."

Samos had developed his own variation on this: "When in doubt, there's no doubt." He shrugged inwardly and sent a coded message to Prewitt in Washington.

He had his answer within twenty-four hours:

URGENT CONFIDENTIAL - exercise extreme caution

Re: yours re: Ilona Rodriguez (59), née Keszthelyi .

Keszthelyi is the estranged second cousin of Vince (Vincent) Olah, political activist and a prominent leader of the 1956 Hungarian Revolution. Subject is an ex-lover of Peter Lakatos, ex-Hungarian minister of defence and member of the Hungarian Security Directorate during the two decades following the said Revolution. Suspected of having ties with the NKVD (KGB) and the GRU that she developed through her ex-lover.

Left Hungary in 1966 with her lover's help.

Her wealth (if any) is of dubious origin, probably acquired through graft during the Communist regime. Probe carefully whether she is really estranged from her cousin and then report.

CHAPTER 47

Mexico City, Mexico, February 1990

"A pastry chef's life is not easy," said Ilona Rodriguez in her fluent, Hungarian-accented Spanish. "When you're at the retail end of the business, I mean. When you not only manufacture the goods, but have your own store to sell them in, your work day is very long, literally from dawn to dusk, often twelve hours at a stretch."

She sighed, kicked off her shoes and waved her arms. "This place is only a couple of blocks from my store on *Insurgentes* so I can break up some days by sneaking over here and catching a few winks after lunch."

They were sitting in a small room at the Hotel *Geneve* on *Calle Londres* in the centre of Mexico City's *Zona Rosa*. The *Geneve*, an elegant establishment with a history that went as far back as 1902, was in a beautiful building boasting a breathtaking stained glass dome above its atrium. Ilona was picking away at the shrimp salad the room service waiter had delivered a few minutes earlier and watched Samos bite into his *perro caliente.*

The room contained a sofa, probably a hide-a-bed, and two comfortable armchairs facing it across a sizable coffee table.

"You rent the room year round?" Samos asked. "Must cost an arm and a leg."

"Not really. I pay for the room with pastry. The hotel is my best client." They both laughed and Samos took a sip of his Corona Extra, the Mexican beer he liked best. Then he turned to his hostess.

"Enough of this idle chatter. Your note said you needed my help and it also stressed that I should be extremely discreet, especially when it came to members of the Rodriguez family."

Ilona handed him a sheet of paper. "Before I tell you my problem, let me give you some background information, but first I want you to sign this document, it's in English. I hope you don't mind, my written Spanish is very bad. It says that you will not tell anybody what I am going to tell you, especially not the Rodríguezes."

Samos looked at the paper. It was obviously drafted by Ilona herself without the help of an attorney. He signed and dated the writing and gave it back to Ilona, who put it away in her purse.

"I left Hungary for Vienna in 1966," she began while making herself comfortable in one of the corners of the sofa. "When I was thirty-six, I broke off a lengthy, on-again-off-again love affair with a married man who happened to be the Hungarian minister of defence. He arranged the papers I needed to leave the country."

"Why did you go to Vienna and not America?"

"Because, even as a small child, I always wanted to become a world-famous pastry chef and Vienna was the nearest place I could learn how. When I turned forty, I emigrated from Austria to Canada. I settled in Ottawa and opened my own pastry shop, which became an overnight success."

"When was that?"

"1971."

Samos nodded, impressed by the woman's determination and ability to focus. There was clearly more to her than her lush, chestnut cream exterior. "What happened next?" he asked.

"As I told you, I met and married Uncle Octavio in Canada and that was well over ten years ago. He made me sell my business because, as a senior diplomat, he wanted a woman at his side who knew how to run his formal social life."

"So you sacrificed your dream to accommodate him."

Ilona shook her head in vigorous disagreement. "Not at all. We agreed that I would run his official life for three years, at the end of which he'd retire and I'd open a *patisserie* in Mexico City. And that's exactly what I did and do. He, on the other hand, was called out of retirement and was named head of customs at Mexico's international airport, a very remunerative job."

Samos ignored the observation; he knew when to keep his mouth shut. The job was highly "political."

"So, you feel fulfilled and content with your present life," he remarked, after a few moments of silence.

"Yes, of course."

"What, then, am I doing here?"

Ilona gave him a sad smile. "Patiently waiting while an old woman tries to work up enough courage to endanger her future by trusting you with information that could totally ruin her and her loved ones."

Samos was surprised. "Old woman? My dear madame, you do yourself a disservice. Do you have children?"

"No, thank God, but Octavio does. Luckily, they're all grown up and have families of their own." Ilona sighed, sat up straight, and poured herself a glass of water.

"Let me get you another beer. This is going to be long and painful."

CHAPTER 48

Budapest, 1965

Peter Lakatos was scared out of his mind. He had just been named Hungarian Minister of National Defence by his buddy Prime Minister Erno Kadar, because Kadar wanted a friend and ally to head the portfolio responsible for handling relations with the Soviet Army's High Command in Hungary.

And this meant constantly 'massaging' the high-ups in the GRU, the USSR Army's Military Intelligence Unit, a bunch of nosy and frighteningly efficient intelligence officers.

Lakatos, who was thirty-nine, like Kadar, five years his senior, was a long-standing Communist apparatchik, with broad familiarity with the ins and outs of the communist bureaucracy. He had survived the '56 Revolution and several purges, advancing steadily by manoeuvring from one ministerial post to the next, all the while trying desperately to avoid either the Interior or the Defence portfolios. Experience had taught him that getting involved with either of these was inevitably fatal: Interior was death by NKVD, Defence by GRU. So, of course, his old friend had made his worst nightmare come true; Defence. His new job was fraught with danger. He clearly realized that even a small misstep, real or imagined, discovered by the Soviets or any one of his colleagues, most of whom resented his youth and his close friendship with the Prime Minister who was also the First Secretary of the Hungarian Communist Party, might easily be exaggerated to the point where he would become the subject of yet another show trial. Petty, party envy like this had prematurely ended the life of László Rajk, a true Communist.

Peter tried to argue his way out of the posting, but Kadar was adamant. Lakatos had, therefore, no choice but to develop a well-financed escape route and nest egg, in the form of a secret pile of money kept, preferably, outside the country, should the proverbial shit hit the fan.

But, for the time being, duty called. So Peter dragged his ass over to the Defence Ministry on *Balaton Utca*, and was in the process of organizing his office with his secretary's help when his phone rang. It was his girlfriend, the vivacious, clever, and sumptuous Ilona Keszthelyi. "Are we on for tonight?" she asked.

"Definitely, but only for dinner."

"Oh, trouble at the office?"

Wary of telephone surveillance, Peter remained cagey. "Nothing I can't handle."

"Then let's meet at the Kis Pipa at eight and show the flag."

The Kis Pipa Restaurant on the second floor of a building on *Akácfa utca* in the old Jewish district just off *Erzsébet Körút* was the favorite watering hole of the "sophisticated" press and, therefore, a good place to make sure that whatever indiscretion one committed there got reported in the papers, and no later than the following weekend's gossip columns.

As planned, Lakatos faked a spectacular row with his Ilona and, by the weekend, everyone knew that the relatively young new minister of defence was looking for a new liaison. It was further whispered that his heartbroken girlfriend of many years was preparing to leave the country.

Exitus Ilona.

Intrabit Caligula!

CHAPTER 49

Mexico City, 1990

"When I got to Vienna in 1966, I found a job," Ilona continued. "Dishwasher in a restaurant called *Zum Weissen Rauchfangkehrer*, The White Chimneysweep, on *Weihburggasse* near *Steffl*, the famous department store. I got the job thanks to pure luck."

"How so?"

Samos watched the woman fidget on the sofa. Either she was finding it hard to continue, or was having a hard time pretending.

"The distance from Budapest to Vienna is only about two hundred and fifty kilometers, two and a half hours by train today. But, in those days the trains sure did not fly. To start with, there were only two every day and they made a stop at Győr, a town half-way between the two cities. That's where the Hungarian border guards came on board to check on who was travelling. And they were very thorough. They made sure that everybody on the train had the proper exit papers and that nobody was smuggling out valuables."

"And were you?"

"Yes. I had $5,000 sewn into my sheepskin overcoat that my lover, Peter Lakatos, the Hungarian defence minister, had given me with detailed instructions as to what to do with the money and when." Ilona shuddered. "I was in a cold sweat while the guards went through my luggage and clothing, but they found nothing except a bottle of Kosher Szilva, plum brandy, which they asked me to 'gift' them."

"Five thousand dollars was a lot of money in those days. Where did your lover get that?"

Ilona let out a puff of air from her pursed lips. "You know, I never asked him. I just didn't want to know."

Samos made a mental note to follow up on this rather unusual statement.

"The Austrian border guards came on board at *Nickelsdorf* and made short shrift of their job, so that we arrived more or less on time after four hours of train travel."

"My dear woman," Samos protested very gently. "All this detail, is it necessary?"

"I think so," replied Ilona, as she pondered the question. "Yes, very necessary."

Samos shrugged, lit a *Cruzero de Panama* Churchill cigar, and settled back on the love seat as Ilona gathered her thoughts.

"In Vienna, I stayed for free for a week with a classmate who had left Hungary before me, and used this time to obtain the papers necessary to stay and work in Austria. On the seventh day, I decided to take it easy and do a bit of sightseeing. As I was passing the *Zum Weissen Rauchfangkehrer* restaurant, I saw someone fasten a notice on the window next to the door. I spoke some German—it was compulsory to learn it in elementary school. The restaurant was looking for a dishwasher. I went in and applied to the maître d'. His mother turned out to be Hungarian and I got the job."

Ilona stopped talking and closed her eyes. Samos realized that his hostess had arrived at the point of no return in her story. He waited, drawing on his cigar, not uttering a word, allowing the woman time to vanquish the demons of uncertainty that appeared to be tormenting her.

She began to speak again without opening her eyes.

"One year into my job, in 1967, when I was no longer a dishwasher but, miracle of miracles, the assistant pastry chef of the *Rauchfangkehrer,* I cut open the lining to my coat and removed the tight bundle of American dollars and a letter from Peter. Following his detailed instructions, I applied for ten days' vacation and took the train to Zurich. Once there, I made an appointment with a man named Dr. Alfred Hauptmann, an account manager at a private bank called *Julius Bär.*" Ilona's eyes opened. "Have you ever heard of it?"

"Of course I have. It is one of the oldest and most reliable private Swiss banks. If I remember correctly, it was founded sometime in the 1890s. The head office is on the famous *Bahnhof Strasse* near the *Fraumünster* Church, right?"

"Quite so. Have you ever done business with it?"

"No, but some of my clients have."

"Do you know anyone who works at that bank?"

"No, why do you ask?"

"Because, in 1967, following Peter's wishes, I gave Dr. Hauptmann $3,500 to incorporate a company to be called CH.FEG.GmbH. The CH would stand for Confederation Helvetique, which means Switzerland, and GmbH, the abbreviation in German for 'Private Limited Liability Company.'"

"What about the FEG?"

"No idea. Peter never explained what he meant by it."

"And who were to be the shareholders of this GmbH?"

"Two bearer shares were to be issued, one of which would be Peter's and the other would be mine. These two share certificates were to be placed into a safety deposit box belonging to the company. To open the box would require two keys, one of which would be given to me and the other to Peter. Peter and I were to sign letters of instructions to the bank stating that, in case either of us died, the other would inherit his or her share and would have the right to open the box with only one key, the survivor's."

"What would be the GmbH's principal business?"

"Anything and everything, but principally trading in cocoa futures."

"Cocoa futures? And who would manage the company?"

"Peter alone until he became certifiably incapacitated or was relieved of his duties by the two shareholders jointly."

Ilona stopped talking, reflecting on the past, letting it flow through her.

Pretty complicated arrangements, Samos mused, as he tried to digest the information he'd been given. The difficulties of respecting the proposed arrangements raced through his brain. How on earth could two relatively sane people, who had loved each other until recently, and who had just finished breaking up, manage to live harmoniously under the proposed regime, especially since they would be separated physically?

Furthermore, Samos added silently to himself, though ownership was fifty-fifty, the proposed arrangement definitely favored Peter: control was, for all practical purposes, his.

He decided to probe more deeply. "And did the company make money?"

Ilona's laughter was genuine. "I have no idea. I paid Dr. Hauptmann $3,500 to get the paperwork done. This included the incorporation of the company, its maintenance for a year, the rental of a safety deposit box for a year, and the opening of a numbered bank account into which he was to deposit $500. I asked him how long the paperwork would take and he said I should come back with my partner in a week to sign the papers."

"Did you go back to Vienna?"

"No. I rented a room in the *Gasthouse Heinrich* on Urania Strasse above the restaurant and asked if the pastry chef would take me on as an unpaid *stagiaire* for the week, just to learn how things were done in Switzerland. I had a reference letter from the *Rauchfangkehrer* and they agreed. You know the Swiss, they fall for anything if they think that it's really free. In the end, they allowed me one staff meal per day in return for which I taught them some new tricks. When I left

I asked for a reference letter. I found out that you can never have enough of those, and they were very glad to write one."

Samos looked at Ilona with renewed interest. He had to admit that the woman was naturally smart and had guts. There was something more. She was a *cliché*, the bosomy, wide-hipped, broad-shouldered, full-faced Magyar wench, but despite all of this, his professional coolness aside, he found himself being stirred.

"At the end of the week, I met Dr. Hauptmann as planned, signed my share of the paperwork, put the bearer shares into the safety deposit box, locked it with two keys, put the documents and Peter's key into a thick manila envelope and sealed it. I printed CALIGULA in capital letters on the front of it, then handed the envelope to Dr. Hauptmann. I told him that someone called Caligula would pick up the envelope within the next twelve months, but, if no one showed within a year, he was to destroy the papers and close the file."

Silence.

Samos's curiosity was aroused. "And that was that? Do you know if Caligula ever showed? Or if the company ever operated?"

"No idea. I never ever went back to the bank again and I didn't hear from the company either. The same goes for Dr. Hauptmann. In fact, I forgot about the whole affair until just recently."

Here we go, said Samos to himself, now very much on guard. "Really?"

"About a month ago, a man—well-dressed, elegant in the Italian style and very European-looking—came into the bakery. I was standing behind the cash register and I noticed him because he kept wandering around looking lost. I asked if I could help. 'Yes,' he said. 'I am looking for Señorita Keszthelyi.'"

Samos noted that Ilona was watching him intently, but Samos had the lids down, his eyes slightly hidden. No tells.

"I almost fainted," Ilona breathed.

He knew she was testing him and he played her hand.

"Why? Who is she?"

"Oh," answered Ilona, pretending to look muddled. "Of course, I never told you my maiden name."

Samos waited.

"I didn't know what to do. I told him that Señorita Keszthelyi no longer worked at the store, but I could tell he did not believe me. He then asked whether I knew where he could find her, if I knew where she had gone, or if she had taken a job somewhere else. I said no and asked him what he wanted with her. He looked me in the eyes as if he knew that I was lying and said, 'If by any chance she does come by again, please tell her that her friend Dr. Hauptmann had her results and that he was trying to get in touch with her.'"

Samos was taken aback. He had written off Ilona's Cold War adventure as a lost cause.

Ilona continued. "The next day I found a hand-delivered letter in the store's mailbox addressed to me and marked Personal and Confidential. All it contained was this."

Ilona handed Samos a piece of paper. It was a copy of an obituary in Hungarian that had appeared in one of the

Budapest dailies announcing the passing of Peter Lakatos, ex-Minister of Defence in the Kadar Government.

Samos was on full guard and, sensing another test, pretended that he could not read the text. "I don't read Hungarian," he said, and watched Ilona's expression change.

"How come you knew that the text was in Hungarian?" she asked with a victorious smirk.

"I didn't," he replied with a tight smile. "I just guessed because, on the top of the page, it said Budapest. What does it say?"

The smirk dissolved into a pout as Ilona took back the clipping. "It's a one-month-old obituary announcing the death of Peter Lakatos, ex-Hungarian minister of defence in the first Kadar government."

"You don't say." The Panamanian pretended to be floored. "So what are you going to do?"

"I'm going to Switzerland." Ilona was defiant. "And I want you to come with me. I'm too afraid of the consequences to face them alone."

*

Samos had to admit that he took no small pleasure in announcing to Maria-Isabel that he had been engaged by Ilona, one of her best friends, a family member, to accompany the woman on a trip to Switzerland. She watched him carefully as he packed his bag.

"What about our problem?"

"You mean, the 'Elvira' problem?"

"Our problem," Maria-Isabel repeated, with some emotion, her black, wide-set eyes fixed on him with such intensity that he could feel them on the side of his face. "And Elvira will no longer be a problem. That, I can guarantee."

Samos looked up inquisitively.

"We had a very *intimate* conversation. She now understands things very differently."

Samos sighed, no longer hiding his deep disappointment with the way things had gone.

"My love, I am working on a solution. Believe me. I just need more time."

"And yet, you have the time to fly off to Europe with that old Hungarian cow on some wild mission."

"How unkind! My love, that's dear Uncle Octavio's wife you're talking about. The woman you yourself sat me beside at your Christmas supper." And now the little prick. "Besides, she's not that old."

Maria-Isabel became quiet and approached the bed side on silent feet, her eyes no longer drilling exploratory holes in his cranium. She was actually rather chastised.

"Are you punishing me? For being so inexcusably stupid?"

She looked so lost, so hurt and worried, he could do nothing but take her in his arms and stroke her hair.

CHAPTER 50

Zurich, Switzerland, March 1990

The Hotel *Zum Storchen*, located on the Limat, the river that flows into the lake called the *Zürcher See*, is one of the oldest hostelries in Zurich. Some claim that the original building had been on the city's tax roll as early as the mid-1300s.

Samos and Ilona reached their respective rooms around two o'clock on a rainy spring afternoon after a fifteen-hour journey from Mexico City, including a two-hour stop-over in Amsterdam. They flew first class on KLM to placate Samos; he had seemed very reluctant to undertake the journey, but, in reality, Samos was finding Ilona more and more interesting.

This was odd, for the woman was hardly his cup of tea. Ilona was a *háziasszony,* or what the Germans call a *hausfrau:* big boned, lushly padded with arms and shoulders toned by her work as a baker. She wasn't intensely dark like Disda or

Maria-Isabel and guile was not one of her innate talents. She was open, frank, and emotionally available.

They were bone tired and agreed to rest and to reconnect in the lobby for dinner at eight. For old times' sake, they went to the Urania Restaurant, a place that specialized in venison, and where, of course, Ilona had helped out the pastry chef over two decades earlier. Unfortunately, no one on the staff remembered her. The food ended up being mediocre and the service nothing to write home about, so when they got back to their hotel, they repaired to its famous bar for a nightcap and consolation.

Kirshwasser seemed the appropriate *eau de vie* to wash down the aftertaste of their banal supper and, within a short time, half the bottle was gone and the temperature of the air between them had risen.

"*Miért színlelsz?*" she said breathily, hoping once again to catch him out. "*Az inged eleje gulyásfoltos.*" ("Why are you pretending? The front of your shirt is stained with goulash.")

Samos easily fended off the parry by taking one of her beautifully manicured, strong hands and placing it over his erection. "I don't know what you're saying, but it is having the desired effect."

It was only a short distance from the bar to Ilona's room, but it took them a good half hour to get inside due to them stopping every few steps to grab each other's bodies and neck furiously, only to break, holding themselves at arm's length, assuring each other that "This must stop! It cannot happen!"

Perhaps it was Ilona's extreme "otherness" when he compared her to Maria-Isabel. Or maybe it was the idea that he was about to fuck dear old Uncle Octavio's trophy wife? Or maybe it was just his way of settling the score. Whatever the reasons, Samos was finally only too willing to set aside the ancient admonition, "*Wann der Putz steht der Kopf geht!*"

Inspired by Ilona's breathtakingly beautiful breasts and her Hungarian exhortations at moments of mutual ecstasy, Samos, inflamed by Ilona's demands, which he continued to pretend not to understand, surpassed himself by performing sexual acrobatics the likes of which he never suspected himself capable.

"Show me!" he had kept repeating in Spanish, "Show me!" And she did, over and over again, while a stream of the most suggestive, filthy, and erotic pleas spilled from her mouth in torpid Hungarian.

The following morning, shy and ashamed and still drunk with lust and fatigue, they slept in and only got around to telephoning Dr. Hauptmann after lunch. Samos left the woman still in bed and only just stirring.

While shaving back in his room, Samos reviewed what he called "the film." He still had an excellent memory, kept sharp by constantly exercising his brain, because, apart from the requirements of his rather complicated double-edged job, he also had to keep remembering during his waking hours that he was really somebody other than who he appeared to be.

The "Ilona film" that unspooled in his mind reflected his interaction with the woman in great detail, starting with the *Sacher Torte* incident at the Christmas dinner. Then came the parcel containing a cake and a letter demanding strict confidentiality. The mystery deepened when he read

Washington's answer to his inquiry about her. She had then tested him about her maiden name during their conversation in her "escape" hotel room in Mexico City. And what about handing him an obituary written in Hungarian? A trap, of course, but why was she so desperate to prove his Magyar identity?

He switched off and reviewed what had happened the night before. Who had seduced whom? Was it he who had started things or had it been her? He smiled and then began to chuckle, recalling her screams of ecstasy in Hungarian! And, why not in Spanish, after having lived in a Spanish-speaking country for decades?

He started to ruminate about the source of the original $5,000 Ilona had said that she had received from her lover before emigrating. How would a Hungarian Communist party apparatchik get his hands on five large, US? And the instructions she had been told to follow once she got to Switzerland—Samos was sure that she had never written them down, afraid that someone might find her notes, however well hidden. And if she had memorized them, how come she had never thought about the complicated affair during all these years? After all, legally, she was a 50 percent partner? Did the money mean so little to her?

*

Dr. Hauptmann's office at 36 *Bahnhof Strasse* was impressive, a prestige place situated on the third floor of the building, a corner suite overlooking the intersection where the *Bahnhof* and *Sanktpeter Strasse* met.

Ilona and Samos were escorted to the elevators from the ground-floor reception desk by a liveried assistant who delivered them to a secretary waiting at the elevator door upstairs. Entrance to Hauptmann's suite was through a small but handsomely furnished waiting room decorated with remarkable oil paintings depicting landscape and hunting scenes. The door facing them led to the secretary's office. *Doktor* Hauptmann's office lay beyond it.

They were offered a choice of tea, coffee, or hot chocolate and biscuits. They had hardly sat down when a middle-aged, somewhat unsteady-looking man appeared in the doorway. He had a full head of dark hair, a formidable beard, and strikingly blue eyes. "*Fräulein Keszthelyi*," he called out in German, beaming. "How very nice to see you again after so many years. You look stunning."

"Dr. Hauptmann?" Ilona hesitated, taken aback. Age had been kind to their host. Hauptmann noticed. "I know, I know, I don't show my age," he said and flashed her a huge grin, running his hand through his full head of hair. "Runs in the family." He turned to Samos. "You must be Señor Alejandro Samos, my Panamanian competitor. Come in, come in."

In his office, he led them to two comfortable antique armchairs and then rolled an expensive-looking, ergonomically adjustable leather rocking chair into position facing them across a beautiful mahogany coffee table.

Samos looked around and saw Hauptmann's immense desk behind the man. It also was an antique. The place exuded money, very old money.

The banker began. "I'm glad you decided to call on me in the afternoon rather than in the morning." After a questioning glance at Samos who nodded, Hauptmann continued in English. "This will give us more time to lay the foundations for the work we'll have to accomplish." He took a sip from one of the cups of espresso the secretary had placed on the table on an antique silver tray. "My plan is to get the legal formalities out of the way this afternoon and then spend two days to acquaint you with what has happened and what is happening now, as we speak, with CH.FEG.GmbH. We refer to it in house as FEG, for simplicity's sake."

That was the moment Samos realized that he was being drawn into a situation far more complex and potentially dangerous than he had signed up for. He decided to speak up. "Forgive the interruption, *Herr Doktor*, but before we continue, could you give us an indication of the magnitude of the situation?"

"Certainly. We will be talking about cash and investments in marketable securities worth in excess of $15 million, plus two operating subsidiaries of the company that require constant supervision."

"Caligula!" Ilona gasped, went pale, and almost fainted.

CHAPTER 51

Samos had moved quickly to catch Ilona's torso before it slipped out of her chair. She came back to her senses very quickly and the doctor called for a bracing round of schnapps, which revived the new millionairess promptly. After making sure that Ilona was all right, the trio got down to business.

Samos suggested that the two bearer shares evidencing ownership of FEG be immediately converted into nominal ones—that is to say, to share *certificates* with their owners' names on them. To his great surprise, Hauptmann enthusiastically supported his suggestion. Thinking like a CPA, Samos further proposed that, to avoid tax complications in Mexico, only one of the shares be in Ilona's name and the other in the name of a non-Mexican resident and citizen. Ilona would sign a notarized side agreement in which said person would agree to sell their share back to Ilona on demand for $1 million. Samos explained that such an arrangement would enable Ilona to claim that she had no financial control of any offshore company, since 50 percent was not considered control. The tax advantages of this type of arrangement were perfectly legal and significant.

This suggestion was discussed at length. Ilona wanted Samos, a Panamanian, to hold the second share certificate, but Samos hesitated. He felt that the arrangement would jeopardize the independence of his professional relationship with Maria-Isabel and her side of the Rodriguez family. He had already begun to feel quite guilty about what had happened between him and Ilona the previous night and was trying to figure out how to avoid a repetition.

After she insisted for the third time, he agreed to accept, provided first that the agreement be reciprocal, and that Ilona would *have* to buy his share from him on *his* demand for the same amount of money and, second, that the two share certificates were to be kept in the safety deposit box at *Julius Bär* under Ilona's control, with the proviso that, should she ever want to move one or both shares somewhere else, he would be promptly notified by the bank. As for succession in the event of either party's death, the deceased party's successors would abide by the same arrangement. Hauptmann listened and approved and arranged for the documents to be drawn up.

The next morning, they signed and sealed the documentation required to put into effect what they had agreed on the previous day and locked the shares up again in the safety deposit box.

After lunch, they started a review of the contents of the files relating to FEG's activities. They discovered that FEG was only a holding company acting as banker for its two operating subsidiaries: FEG Nicaragua, and FEG Spain.

"Allow me to explain how the present setup developed," *Doktor* Hauptmann proposed. "The original company that *Señorita Keszthelyi* had me form in May of 1967, let's call it FEG Switzerland, was initially dormant, while, as directed, I waited patiently for Caligula to make himself known. In March 1968, he did, and as you both know, his real name was Peter Lakatos."

The banker continued. "Lakatos signed the required documents, deposited more money, $5,000, into FEG Switzerland's bank account, and told me to expect money via wire transfers from various parts of the world from time to time. I was to use these moneys to build an investment portfolio along moderately aggressive lines. He also told me that he intended to visit three or four times a year to see how I was doing with the investments."

"And how *did* you do?" This from Ilona.

The banker smiled, referring to the audited balance sheet. "I dare say that I didn't do too badly. Of course, it helped that money kept on dribbling into the account from all over the world. By the end of the next calendar year, the portfolio was worth over a million dollars, but he was such a dour Communist, I could never tell if Caligula was satisfied with my work."

"He never thanked you?"

"No, he didn't, Señor Samos." A belittling smile appeared on *Doktor* Hauptmann's lips. "But he seemed to be satisfied because he left me to get on with managing the portfolio during the following four years without much interference, except for the occasional tip he passed on to me." He stopped talking, blew his nose vigorously, and then picked up the narrative sounding pensive.

"You know, in retrospect, it is uncanny how the great majority of the tips he gave me worked out spectacularly well." Hauptmann shook his head in wonderment. "He must have had inside information," he said softly, almost as if he were talking only to himself.

"But to act on such information is forbidden by law," said Samos, not liking what he was hearing.

Hauptmann made an almost impatient gesture with his hand, by which Samos felt chastened.

"Today it is, but not then, at least not in Switzerland." *Doktor* Hauptmann was beginning to look tired. "Why don't we pick up the story tomorrow at noon? Allow me to invite you to a working lunch in our executive dining room." Then he added as an afterthought, "As you can see from the statements I gave you earlier, the portfolio was worth approximately $10 million by the end of 1973."

Laughing, he stood up. "Let me give you some homework, Señor CPA." He handed Samos a thick envelope. "Here are the bank statements showing the cash movements in and out of the FEG Switzerland bank account from inception to the present time. Why don't you have a look at them at your hotel tonight and tomorrow morning? It might help you to understand how Caligula transformed FEG during the last years of his reign."

Ilona was mystified. "Transformed? What do you mean?"

"Caligula ran the show until 1987. In January of that year, he had a mild heart attack, resigned his post as minister of defence, and turned over the management of FEG to Caligula Number Two."

CHAPTER 52

The dining room of Zurich's *Kronenhalle* shared this in common with all great bourgeoise eateries in Europe—it was cozy, intimate, and casual, but scrupulously serious about what it put on the table. Samos's attention was divided in three: his continuing guilt over having rogered Ilona like a buck stud the other night, the Byzantine structure of FEG and its various satellites, and the deeply comforting food and wine on the table before him. Samos was, like so many other children of wartime deprivation, moved by food because during his formative years, there wasn't any. However, he did have a duty to the 'rode-hard-and-put-up-still-damp' Ilona, so, he ventured gingerly into the financial swamp.

"I am beginning to see patterns in the operation, but, to tell the truth, I need much more information before I can be sure that I'm not climbing up the wrong pole," Samos mused out loud as he sipped his half-cup of delicious green pea soup.

While he waited for *Herr Doktor* to digest this, he allowed the waiter to clear the table for the main course, a delicate *bouché a la reine*, filo pastry filled with chicken in *béchamel* sauce. The wine accompanying the chicken, which Hauptmann had selected, was a Chasselas Rosé called *Oeil de perdrix*, "eye of the partridge," he translated for Ilona, an earthy wine with a pretty salmon color—hence, the name.

Samos was delighted. He loved good wine.

"I'm not quite sure about what you mean," said Hauptmann as he tasted the wine offered by the *sommelier*. He was pleased. He, too, was a wine enthusiast. "Perhaps you could elaborate."

Samos wiped his mouth. "From what I have been able to glean, during its first five years of its existence, FEG Switzerland received, on average, about half a million dollars each year from three or four sources. I'm going to take a wild guess and suggest that these remittances were probably *honoraria* paid to Caligula for his intervention in the awarding of contracts to suppliers of the Hungarian army."

Hauptmann nodded in agreement. Samos continued.

"According to your extensive records, during the next five years, which brings us to 1978, the same pattern continued, except that the amounts and the number of contributors grew year after year, so that by the end of that year, the portfolio stood at $20 million. And it is clear that this amount is in no small way thanks to your skill in exploiting the tips Caligula kept providing."

Hauptmann put down his cutlery to focus more intently on Samos's *resumé*.

"Then, in 1981," the ersatz Panamanian continued, "something changed, and rather radically. There was a $10-million outlay from the portfolio, the first payout of substance. I presume that's when FEG Switzerland acquired either FEG Nicaragua or FEG Spain?"

"You are correct," Hauptmann conceded. "That's the year the company acquired FEG Nicaragua, a manufacturing company near Leon in Nicaragua."

Now it was Samos who quietly placed his knife and fork on his plate.

"I know the answer to this question, but I think it is important for Ilona that she hear it from your lips. What does FEG Nicaragua manufacture?"

Hauptmann was not a squeamish man, nor was he unnecessarily burdened by ethics—at least not when it came to business. He addressed Ilona directly.

"Originally, FEG Nicaragua made precision locks and keys and now, weapons. Specifically, small arms, including Kalashnikovs."

Hauptmann picked up his cutlery and piled a well-crafted portion of chicken on the turned down tines of his fork. "As I understood it, Caligula secured a license to manufacture these arms from the Russians."

Samos carefully calculated his level of his righteous indignation. He kept an eye on Ilona, who, he noted with some dismay, had not reacted, as though she hadn't grasped the significance of this discovery.

"Are you telling me that the company, of which *Señorita Keszthelyi* is now virtually the sole owner, is manufacturing and presumably marketing the weapons most sought after by terrorists and mercenaries? Surely, this is playing with fire!"

Samos was authentically beside himself and turned to Ilona. "I insist that you sell the company immediately."

Hauptmann intervened gently, but firmly.

"Señor Samos, with all due respect, there is more to the story, so I beg you, calm down and hear me out."

Samos played at being chastened and, after glancing at Ilona, who remained apparently, unmoved, nodded to the older man.

"As you no doubt noted, '82 and '83 were not particularly successful from the cash-flow point of view. FEG Nicaragua required financial assistance from time to time as it struggled to establish a market for its products. In fact, the value of the investment portfolio dipped below $5 million by the end of 1983."

Hauptmann took a sip of wine and sighed. "Caligula had his work cut out for him to get that operation to begin generating income. I can vouchsafe for that!" Then the banker became enthusiastic. "But he did, and brilliantly so, but the stress on him had been considerable."

"How did he engineer the turnaround?" Samos asked, his eyes never leaving Ilona's face as she, in turn, had her eyes fixed on *Herr Doktor*.

"It was a canny, if not brilliant, move. In late 1983, he swapped 40 percent of FEG Nicaragua for 60 percent of a leaf-spring manufacturer in Spain, which he then converted into an arms manufacturer, using his Kalashnikov sub-licensing rights."

"And?" Samos, uncharacteristically, indicated that he was lost.

"Don't you see? The swap made of the FEG Group an intercontinental player in the armaments business, which made it possible for it to circumvent arms embargoes."

Samos turned to Ilona and shrugged, feigning ignorance. He needed to know how deeply Hauptmann was in this scheme. *Herr Doktor* noted the insouciance and sighed heavily.

"Do you remember the Iran Contra affair?" Samos asked Ilona.

"Of course. It was only a few years ago. What about it?"

"If you remember, the plan was for Israel to ship weapons to Iran, for the United States to resupply Israel, and for Israel to pay the United States. This complicated process would not have been necessary had the FEG Group already been in existence at that time."

Hauptmann turned to Ilona. "Strategic arms problems such as the Contra affair are occurring more and more frequently throughout the world. The existence of a reliable *and* neutral—I repeat, *neutral*—arms manufacturer is making it possible to avoid them." These last words were addressed to Samos, who sat back, playing at taking it all in.

"Did the flow of business increase?"

"Dramatically, Señor Samos, and so did profits. Especially after Caligula instituted a special profit-sharing scheme for those whom he called 'persons of influence.'"

Ilona came to life, enthralled. She loved talking about money. "And how did that work?"

"Let me give you an example." The banker was beginning to sound professorial. "Caligula, as Hungarian minister of defence, could influence the choice of every supplier, down to who would be awarded the contract for making blankets for Hungary's soldiers. Caligula would come to Zurich at the end of every calendar quarter, examine the sales reports of the two FEG subsidiaries, Nicaragua and Spain, and then hand me a list of bank account numbers to which I was to wire money and how much—always US dollars, of course. When I asked, he called the owners of these bank accounts 'persons of influence,' who directed business to FEG."

"No names?" queried Samos.

"Never. He kept the names strictly to himself."

"Have you kept the lists?"

Hauptmann was irritated, but put a chuckle behind his retort. "Of course I did. That's what I get paid for. I am the custodian of all documentation and especially papers involving financial transactions. Would you like to examine them?" He seemed to be challenging Samos, who laughed to ease the building tension.

"No, thank you, not just now, but perhaps some time in the future. But I am curious about one thing: who is the entity that now owns 40 percent of both FEG manufacturing plants?"

Hauptmann calmed down and assumed his avuncular demeanor.

"The Spanish business was originally owned by a rich family in Bilbao. They were easy to deal with because they allowed Caligula a free hand and never interfered as long as they got dividends regularly. Then, a couple of years later, they needed cash for their real estate business and sold their interest to a Swiss holding company, the owners of which are not known to us."

"And they never ask questions?"

"Never. They are happy as long as they get their annual dividends."

Samos found this interesting, but did not dare to rustle Hauptmann's feathers further. He went on. "I am very grateful for your *exposé*. It explains the plethora of wire transfers featuring in the bank statements."

Their host was mollified. "They're overwhelmingly numerous, aren't they?"

"They sure are. Over a dozen at the beginning, and now over twenty, I believe."

"Twenty-seven by my last count." The pedantic Hauptmann sounded very proud. "And I suspect they cover at least ten countries."

"How do you get that number?"

Hauptmann's answer was pure common sense. "Each transfer has to end up in a financial institution eventually. Therefore, the SWIFT code number of the institution to which money is being sent via wire transfer has to be part of the transfer order. This list of bank codes is accessible to the public. By consulting this list one can determine the name and the address of any participating bank.

"Of course," interjected Samos, "knowing the bank's address does not necessarily mean that one knows where the account holder lives, especially if it is a numbered account."

"True, but the exercise is useful to give a general indication of the number of countries with which we are dealing."

"And you say, *Herr Doktor*, that Caligula was the only one who knew the identity of these 'persons of influence' with whom FEG was dealing?"

"Correct."

Samos hooded his eyes and turned up the corners of his mouth just a little as he looked at Hauptmann, but it was Ilona who broke the silence.

"You liked him, did you not?" Ilona whispered, near tears.

"Yes, I liked him," sighed Hauptmann from a place of real emotion. "And I admired him and I am sorry that he's not with us anymore." There were tears in Hauptmann's eyes, too. Then he shook his head. "I never understood for whom and why he had created the FEG Group of companies. What was the end *Ziel*—the end goal, as they say?"

"Perhaps he just couldn't bring himself to stop," mused Ilona.

Samos ventured in softly. "Perhaps he tried, but was not allowed to stop." He was letting his suspicious nature get the better of him. "And who is Caligula Number Two?"

The banker's answer stunned both of his guests profoundly. "I have no idea."

CHAPTER 53

In her hotel room, Ilona was trying to pack her bag for her early-morning return flight and was making very little progress. Every few moments she returned, again and again, to Samos and his reluctance to do what she thought was so painfully obvious. For his part, and for reasons he thought equally obvious, Samos deflected her every plea. The anger and sexual tension between them was intense and Samos felt adrift, his emotions roiling as he pedalled frantically away from this overbearing woman, while, at the same time, marvelling at the compelling life force within her.

Their differences about how to deal with the inheritance left behind for her by Caligula and how to cope with the issue in the very near future, were driving them crazy. They had tried to resolve them during an alcohol-fuelled dinner, but without success, and the clock had run out. It was midnight and Ilona had to pack. She was scheduled to leave the hotel at seven in the morning.

"As I've been trying to tell you, from my point of view, you have only two choices," repeated Samos for the umpteenth time. "Either sell FEG Switzerland as is and run, or remove Caligula Two and take over the management yourself."

Ilona turned the full passion and power of her glimmering Magyar soul on him.

"And *I* have told you ten thousand times, there is a third choice! We keep the *status quo* and allow Caligula Two to run the fucking company and not interfere unless profits started to decline."

Samos shook his head, dead set against that scenario. "We? No, you! You'd be flying blind. You don't even know who he is and he could seriously harm you by getting FEG involved in some illegal operation about which you'd find out only *post hoc.*"

"Stop with all that Latin garbage, I've had enough of it!" cried Ilona.

Samos calmed himself and tried another tack. "Ilona, my dear. What do you want? Please, tell me." The woman would not be mollified and rode her emotional wave against him.

"What I want is to keep on making money! That's why I have you and *Doktor* Hauptmann working for me. It's up to you two to find a way to protect me. And don't keep telling me that I have two choices acceptable to you. I have only one, because *you*'re unwilling to take over management from Caligula Two and I have nobody else but you whom I trust."

Samos could not decide which gambit to play, flattered or insulted. While deciding, he kept his cool and, instead of blowing up, he bade the frustrated woman "good night," and left for his room.

He was in his pyjamas, brushing his teeth when there was a knock on his door.

Ilona was standing in the doorway wearing nothing but her bra and panties and a pair of kitten heels. She stormed past him, slammed the door behind her, then pushed him toward his bed. "My mother taught me, never go to bed angry."

*

The following morning, Samos awoke with a slight headache and his back aching again from the strenuous sexual acrobatics of the sleepless night. Instinctively, he groped for Ilona at his side, but she was gone. No wonder, his watch showed ten past eight. The note in Spanish on his night-table was brief and to the point. *Me he ido al aeropuerto. Que duermas bien. Te quiero.* "I've left for the airport. Sleep well. I love you."

I love you.

Samos stared at the cursed twowords as though they were an oracular omen of trouble ahead.

As for *his* flight, he saw that he was going to miss it, so he called the concierge and asked to have it changed to the next available Lufthansa flight to Panama via Frankfurt.

He ran a hot bath and crawled into it, covering his face with a steaming hand towel, breathing deeply, and reviewing the mess in which he had placed himself. Since she did not wake him before leaving, Ilona was obviously taking the cowardly way out, unwilling to reach accommodation about what to do next. Her KLM flight to Mexico City via Amsterdam was departing at ten and would reach its destination fifteen hours later. His re-booked Lufthansa flight, the concierge reported, was scheduled to take off at eleven that night and arrive at Tocumen Airport in Panama at noon, local time, the following day. This meant that he had about seven hours in Zurich to study the material he had been given on FEG, and to consult *Doktor* Hauptmann, if need be.

After his hotel's continental breakfast of croissants and delicious *brötli*, the small, bread-like pastry that the Swiss baked so well, jam, honey, marmalade, creamy butter, and a couple of cups of strong *latte,* he wandered over to the reception desk and arranged, for a generously large tip, to be allowed to keep his room until five o'clock p.m.

Six hours into his studies, during which he forced himself not to think about his complications with Ilona, and interrupted only long enough to wolf down an omelette for lunch, he felt he knew enough about the FEG Group's operations to form a cohesive plan of action.

As he lay down his mechanical pencil, one thing was very clear: the FEG Group was operating very profitably.

The Nicaraguan subsidiary showed an annual profit averaging close to $3 million. Sixty percent was remitted religiously to FEG Switzerland in the quarter following each year-end. Forty percent went to the minority shareholder. According to the annual report, the unit was ably managed by a highly skilled employee who had escaped from Transylvania five years earlier and spoke Spanish, Romanian, and English, in addition to his mother tongue, which was

Hungarian. Samos deduced that the man must have been one of Caligula's original hires, probably recruited personally.

The FEG Spanish operation was being run by a very talented East German defector and former tool-and-die-maker who, in addition to his native tongue, spoke Russian, English, and Spanish. FEG Spain produced an average annual profit just shy of $5.5 million, of which 60 percent was also sent to FEG Switzerland at year's end and 40 percent to the minority shareholder.

Samos's calculated summary indicated that FEG Switzerland's gross income was around $5 million. From this amount, it had to pay *Bank Julius Bär*'s annual maintenance fee of $480,000, which presumably included *Doktor* Hauptmann's salary, plus Caligula's salary in the same amount, plus another $1,700,000 to twenty-seven "persons of influence," which, *alle zusammen,* represented 20 percent of FEG's overall profit.

There were additional expenses of smaller amounts: $100,000 for travelling expenses, plus unspecified, "administration" charges of $10,000 a month. That left about$2 million of profit.

Samos silently congratulated Caligula's business acumen. FEG Switzerland's investment in its Nicaraguan and Spanish subsidiaries, for which it had paid a total of $10 million, was yielding a steady $2-million profit, or 20 percent per annum, and all tax free.

And what was FEG selling?

Death.

"Unbelievable," he murmured to himself. Playing with FEG's balance sheets and annual reports had realigned Samos's mind, blowing away the cobwebs spun by Herr Hauptmann's financial fables and the carnal shenanigans with Ilona. For the first time since he had discovered Maria-Isabel's stupid betrayal of his trust, he was thinking clearly and sharply, and the specter of truth that his newly pellucid vision revealed made him uncomfortable. Things were not making sense.

For one, Samos was finding it increasingly hard to accept that the Hungarian-born wife of an obscure Mexican diplomat would suddenly find herself the majority owner of an international, and seemingly independent, arms manufacturing group worth millions. Such things happen in cheap pulp thrillers, but in real life? Unheard of.

"Of course," he reasoned with himself out loud. "The FEG group is small, its gross annual turnover must be between $100 million and $120 million. Day-to-day control rests not with the unknown, absentee owners in Spain and Nicaragua, but with the mysterious Caligula, who directs daily operations through two general managers who are intimately familiar with the small arms industry and the major players in that field."

"And these major players know them as well, and tolerate them," he added as an afterthought. It then dawned on him that FEG, because of its size, nature, and geographical locations, could be useful to the big boys as a tool to circumvent embargoes by being able to operate under the radar.

As for leadership, the original Caligula had been ideal and his successor, Caligula Two, was very likely of the same ilk, so Samos speculated. The two managers—the Kraut defector and the Transylvanian Magyar escapee—had been hand-picked for their language skills and backgrounds in manufacturing and metallurgy. Caligula knew that such men from the Soviet Bloc when let loose and supported within a pure capitalist environment, were like unbridled engines of energy, initiative, and devotion. Caligula Two had to be cut from the same cloth.

Or was he?

CHAPTER 54

What had *Herr Doktor* Hauptmann said about Caligula? Samos remembered it verbatim.

"Peter Lakatos, the first Caligula, was hands-on. He visited at least four times a year, looked at financial, sales, and production records the subsidiaries sent me, analyzed, and at times sharply criticized my work when he felt I should have gotten better yields on the securities we invested in."

And then, that which Samos had let slide the first time, now came back as one of those silent specters.

"Caligula No. 2 never came to visit."

This had puzzled Samos and now that he had the opportunity to see the old man alone before his flight home, and, without Ilona's vibrant hormonal perfume clouding his judgment, he pursued the point again.

"So, how was the changing of the guard handled?"

Hauptmann had not expected to see Samos that day, assuming he had caught his morning flight and was out of his hair, at least until Ilona had made her decision about the future of FEG. He noted a change in Samos, a sharpness and impatience that had not been there the past few days and decided that he would not mention the call he had received that morning from Ilona. Hauptmann had made time in his schedule for this last minute meeting with Samos mostly because he thought if he hadn't, it might look as though he was avoiding the Panamanian.

"In December 1987, Lakatos visited me for the last time, looking seriously distracted. He had just been diagnosed with a hole in his heart and a fluttering heart-valve and felt he would need all his energy to fight for his health. He presumed that I could look after the financial part of FEG's business and did not expect me to get involved in the running of the two subsidiaries. His managers could take care of the subsidiaries themselves."

"And what was your reaction to all of this?"

"The news that Lakatos had an incurable illness affected me greatly, Señor Samos. As I told you, I liked the man and although we only met a few times a year over a decade and a half or so, we had developed a relationship that went beyond just being in a business together, so to speak. So my first reaction was immense pity for a relatively young man, about my age, sixty-five, who had just been handed a death sentence." The banker paused. He appeared to be struggling to control his emotions.

"After the initial shock," he continued, "I confess that selfish thoughts took over. Who would run the subsidiaries? Would a new Caligula take over or would the FEG be sold?

Would he dispense with my services? Could the bank lose a profitable account? Would my pension be affected?"

Samos sympathized guardedly, surprised to see that the cold, calculating banker was, after all, human. "So what happened?"

"We ordered four fax machines, one for me, one for Caligula, and one each for the subsidiaries. I remember, at that time, they cost $20,000 apiece. He streamlined the group's reporting system; the quarterly reports were not to exceed twenty pages in length. He then gave to me a copy of a book called *Three Men in a Boat*, and sent a copy to each of the plant managers.

"Whatever for?" Samos played dumb.

Hauptmann held up his hand. "Let me finish. Each one was a copy of the book's rare English edition published in Moscow."

"OK."

"The books were to be used to ensure, through book code verification, that the faxes emanated from authenticated sources. For example, instead of saying 'I am missing $5,000,' the sender would get his copy of the book, find the word 'am' in it somewhere, let's say on page 16, at line 4, word 7 and then write, '16,4,7' for 'am.' The person receiving the fax would go to *his* copy of the book and locate the word. Every fax sent had to start with the addressee's code number."

"Pretty cumbersome," murmured Samos, pretending ignorance.

"Agreed, but secure. Besides, you didn't need to encode a long text, just a personal identification code agreed to in advance and changed from time to time by Caligula. In this manner, he was assured that he was communicating with his people and, of course, with me."

Hauptmann formed a steeple with his fingers, leaned back in his chair, and smiled. "You see, it was made known to me that Caligula Two wanted his identity kept strictly secret. The secure fax system eliminated the need for him to visit me or, for that matter, to visit the plant managers. The two men would send *me* their twenty-page quarterly reports by fax, I'd look them over, make annotations, and send the whole package, including *my* report on the investment portfolio, by fax, to Caligula Two. He would then do what he needed to do with it, then send me my instructions."

"How about the plant managers?"

"He would communicate with them by fax directly, with copy to me."

"And you still remained responsible for paying the 'persons of influence'?"

"Quite so."

Samos was once again both impressed and uneasy. "You said you never met Caligula Two, but, surely, the original Caligula must have arranged to have you meet his successor in his presence at your office."

"You are right, Lakatos wanted such a meeting, but Caligula Two could not be persuaded to attend. Frankly, I've never seen such a security-obsessed person in my life."

Hauptmann allowed the springs of his ergonomic chair to bring his torso forward. "Lakatos had no choice but to stay on for an extra six months, though sick, to make sure that all glitches were fixed and that the system was functioning properly. I believe this hastened his death."

CHAPTER 55

Samos flew to Frankfurt, had dinner at the airport during his stopover there, then boarded his flight to Panama and fell asleep as soon as his head hit the pillow on his seat. He was totally spent.

Ilona had left Zurich that morning temporarily sexually sated and ecstatic. She was an independently rich woman now, even if she did nothing more than cash out FEG Switzerland's investment portfolio and place the money with Samos for handling. What did Hauptmann say the portfolio was worth? She couldn't remember.

To do what she wanted and live the way she wanted was something she had often dreamed about. As for good old Uncle Octavio, who had started to have trouble getting it up and expected Ilona's help via a once-a-week fellatio, well, she'd start saying no to him until he finally let her go.

And then, and then there was Samos, that horny Latino. Forbidden fruit, so tasty and easy and accomplished. She admitted to herself that part of the thrill in seducing him was making a cuckquean out of her niece, that horrid little snob Maria-Isabel. In the limousine on the way to the airport, just thinking about him made her all restless.

At KLM's check-in counter, she was told her flight would depart forty minutes late so she went to the first-class lounge and called her Swiss banker.

"If we liquidated the portfolio, how much cash would the company have?"

Hauptmann was taken aback by the question and decided to play for time. "I would have to make some calculations, but I think that in an orderly liquidation of the securities we own, that is, if we took our time, we could probably raise about $15 million. Why do you ask? Are you contemplating another acquisition?" He was being purposefully vague, probing.

"No, no. It's just that I might like to withdraw a few dollars next month. I have my eye on a rather expensive house in Palm Beach." He had to admit that she sounded quite charming over the telephone.

"Of course. That could be arranged." Hauptmann was relieved.

She's just like the others, these *nouveau-riche* bitches, he thought. As soon as they get their hands on some money they want to become jet-setters. Emboldened, he asked, "Have you come to some conclusion about how you intend to continue operations?"

"As you saw, *Herr Doktor*, I don't seem to be able to convince Señor Samos to take charge of the subsidiaries. So, I have decided to change absolutely nothing and carry on as is, but only for the time being. I´m sure that I will be able to change Señor Samos's mind within a couple of weeks." She sounded out of breath. "*Au revoir*, and thanks for your help. Must run, they're calling my flight."

She hung up.

CHAPTER 56

Panama City, mid-March 1990

After eight hours of deep sleep in his comfortable first-class sofa-bed, Samos awoke well rested and hungry. His watch showed that he had completed about half of his trip and that local time in Panama was 4:27 a.m.

Too late for dinner and too early for breakfast.

He was hungry, damn it, and now deeply troubled. His meeting with Hauptmann had only consolidated his feeling that there was a dissembling veil over everything having to do with Caligula and FEG, through which his instincts and intellect could not penetrate. Compounding this feeling of unease were feelings of guilt over what he had done to his relationship with Maria-Isabel by going to bed with Ilona. It was unpardonable, and even worse, Ilona was a client! *And* a member of the Rodriguez family.

What an unholy mess.

His hunger panged him, so, to ease his conscience, he ordered an early breakfast and a shot of Pedro Domecq brandy in his coffee.

His plane landed precisely at noon, dead on time, and by twelve-thirty he had retrieved his luggage. Maria-Isabel had said she'd come to pick him up, so he went outside onto the arrivals quay, but he couldn't spot her cream-colored Mercedes. Obviously, she was late, as always. He called her car phone, but there was no answer. After hanging around for another ten minutes, he called his office.

No answer, which was strange, because it was an ordinary weekday so someone should have been manning the phones. It was lunchtime but his employees would never go out *en masse,* leaving no one behind to take care of the office.

He went back out again to the arrivals quay and scanned the passing cars. An odd feeling came over him, as though she was coming up behind him. He turned on his heels, but there was no one. The crowd of people leaving the terminal had thinned, leaving Samos quite alone and an odd stillness drifted down from above. In the broad daylight of a fine Panamanian day, Samos was aware of another faint tug on his orbit.

Upset, he hailed a cab and headed for home.

The trip from Tocumen Airport to the *Torres Las Americas* complex where he had his office and in which he also lived with Maria-Isabel in a luxurious six-bedroom penthouse apartment, took half an hour or so, but, this time, traffic seemed to be unusually heavy and got even heavier as they approached the complex. Idly, he noted that there were a number of emergency vehicles, police, fire, and medical, that kept passing his cab with sirens blaring.

When they got off the *Corredor Sur*, the traffic became bumper to bumper and it took ages to reach the complex's main entrance. Samos was surprised to see a fire truck and police cars stationed at the entrance. As he tried to enter the complex through the chaos, he almost collided with a police lieutenant, Carlos Del Santo, whom he happened to know. Seeing Samos, Del Santo's face turned white as a sheet. He put his hand on Samos's arm quite firmly and pulled him away from the street to the shelter of the portico that formed part of the plaza complex.

"Carlos, what's going on?"

The lieutenant tried to block Samos's view with his body, but refused to meet his eyes.

"Carlos?"

The policeman bent his head and stammered, "Señor Samos, I have very bad news. There has been an explosion in the garage."

Samos could have left then and there because his mind and training had already filled in most of the blanks, but he willed himself to remain still and calm.

"Speak to me, Carlos."

"Your car." He stopped, not knowing how to go on. "Somebody rigged your car to explode and when your wife started it, the bomb went off. I'm sorry, Señor Samos, but Maria-Isabel Echenique is dead."

Samos stared at the man, absorbing carefully what he had just been told. "But that's impossible. How do you know this? She has her own car," he said, fighting to keep his voice low and assured.

"We have the concierge. He was wounded, but he saw it. He spoke to her. Her car was low on gas and she was running late. She asked the concierge for *your* car keys because she wanted to be sure to get to the airport before you arrived. So she took your car and. . ."

At the words "low on gas," Samos's innards turned to ice. Maria-Isabel had a fetish about filling up as soon as the tank was half empty. It had been fixed. Obviously, the bomb had been meant for him. He was under attack; somebody was trying to kill him. No wonder. But who were they after? Tom Karas or Alexander Samos? Karas, for the many blood enemies he had made due to his own past sins? Or, Samos, for his hard-edged financial dealings, or, for the number of men he had made cuckolds? In any case, his cover was blown and he had to flee.

Training took over, but Samos didn't understand how much he was in shock and how much it was affecting his decision-making. He was fixed on putting as much space as possible between himself and Panama City and, for some odd reason, the figure of Longhurst kept creeping into his thoughts. He knew that an operative like Longhurst was unlikely to be behind this attempt on his life unless he felt threatened or had gone rogue. First things first, he thought: Get outta Dodge!

He asked Carlos for a police officer to accompany him and they took the elevator to the forty-sixth floor. Leaving the uniformed cop on watch in the hallway, Samos entered the bedroom of the apartment and swung the tall mirror on his dressing room's wall outward, revealing a full-sized safe behind it. He applied his thumbs to the digital sensors at its front. The heavy safe door sprang open. Ignoring the equipment ranged on the top shelf, he lifted out a large box-like attaché case from underneath and opened it with one of the keys on his key chain.

He checked the contents: $20,000 in cash; a Canadian, a US, and a Swiss passport, each in a different name; a pair of beige Chinos; a shirt; underwear; socks; a cap; a light sweater; toothbrush and paste; a small bar of soap; and a Glock 17 pistol in its shoulder holster with two spare clips of ammunition and a silencer. He found his silver medallion inside. He closed the safe door, swung back the huge mirror, and sat down at his desk. Snatching up the receiver, he punched in the phone number he had never forgotten. The reassuring sound of an American phone exchange calmed him.

A male voice answered, "This is the major."

Samos almost broke down with relief, but steeled himself. "My name is Barbara."

"Alias?"

"Frosty the Snowman."

"Go ahead, the line is secure."

"I've been compromised. Cover blown. Self-extracting. Touch base in twenty-four."

The voice on the other end hesitated for a beat. "That's a negative on self-extraction. I have your twenty. Make your way to the AE."

"Negative on AE. Compromised. Repeat. Compromised. Touch base in twenty-four."

Samos hung up the phone wondering if, perhaps, extraction via the American Embassy wasn't such a bad idea, after all. He knew that whoever had planted the bomb might have eyes on the complex, but on the other hand, they may have thought they had succeeded and would have vanished. Samos decided to listen to his gut.

He changed into jeans and a windbreaker and was out of the apartment in fifteen minutes. Bidding goodbye to the uniformed policeman, he exited through the garage on foot at the back of the building and caught a cab to Panama City's alternate airport at Paitilla, the base for private aircraft. His friend Evaristo Martinez and Jaime Perez, his partner in both senses of the word, ran a small, discreet air charter business using a four-seater Cessna Skyhawk and a six-seater Beechcraft Baron 58P.

Samos was in luck. It was three o'clock in the afternoon, business was slow, and Martinez was bored. Samos asked him for a price for flying him to Golfito in Costa Rica, about one hour's flying time in the Beech, overnighting in Golfito, then flying from Golfito to Managua in Nicaragua, about an hour and a half flying time the next day, and then flying back to Panama the same way.

"You paying for the hotel both ways, yes?"

"Absolutely, and for the food, as well."

"When do you want to leave?"

"How about 5 p.m. or thereabouts?"

"Today?"

"Yes."

Martinez stroked his goatee. "That'll be hard, but let me talk to Jaime and see what we can do." Samos had helped Martinez and Perez financially in the past. Martinez sensed that Samos was in need of help and he was glad for the opportunity to return the favor.

The pilot went to his office and Samos to the telephone in the waiting room. He made two calls: one to Mauro, telling him that he wanted to have dinner with him in Golfito at eight p.m., to talk business The other was to the Nicaraguan minister of the interior's secretary. Samos was the minister's secret, offshore banker. He asked the woman to arrange for the minister to receive Samos and a new and very good friend of his the following day at noon. He made her repeat the message to him and, when he was satisfied, he hung up.

The message for the minister was in code. The words *new* and *very good* meant that Samos had come across yet another opportunity of getting a substantial bit of graft going for the minister.

As for the secretary, Leticia, she had her own arrangement with Samos. Every time she managed to arrange a short-notice meeting between Samos and her boss, she got $500.

CHAPTER 57

When the Beechcraft landed, Martinez taxied to a quiet corner of the small aircraft section at Golfito airport. He and Samos were already carrying their bags toward the terminal and the small customs and immigration counter when the Costa Rican duty officer crossed their path, his attention on a clipboard. It was an old routine.

"*¿Algo que declarar, guapo?*"

Martinez raised his hand, which hid a $100 US bill, and high-fived the officer.

"*Nada.*"

"*¡Qué tenga un buen día!*"

Mauro met them outside the terminal in a black SUV, a burly, thick-necked Costa Rican who, Samos assumed, was armed, at the wheel. They drove to the modest, six-floor hotel in the Banana Bay marina complex that housed Mauro's office and permanent residence. In the ten years that Mauro and Maria-Isabel had been working together, their firm had grown in size and status and had the outward appearance of a legitimate business. Sure, there were whispers and rumors; how did they manage to provide such excellent, artistically designed gold jewelry at a discount? Success, however, had not changed Mauro's sense of vigilance; hence, the bull of a man who shadowed his every move. He was still the same taut wire who had showed up unannounced at Samos's door so long ago. That alertness was on full as he showed his guest into the hotel.

Mauro lived in the penthouse suite from where he could see his boat, the "Shirley," night and day. The old boat was in top shape, painted, gleaming, and now it bobbed beside a considerably larger one, which Mauro had bought recently. Martinez was left to register. Samos knew that business had been good for Mauro and Maria-Isabel, and then he checked his thoughts abruptly.

A wall rose up in front of him as the finality of the situation sunk it. Maria-Isabel was gone. Gone forever. There would be no last words, no last moments. He would never be able to say to her what he had wanted to say, confess his licentious behavior with Ilona, rid himself of the guilt. Maria-Isabel was gone and, with her, Mauro's connection with the Mexican Mint. Therefore, in fact, Mauro's business was temporarily halted.

They boarded the "Shirley" and made themselves comfortable in the cabin. The shadow remained outside, vigilant but relaxed. Samos could feel, but could not spot, other eyes on him. Mauro was thorough and still a very careful fellow.

"You'll be comfortable at the hotel."

Samos opened his windbreaker, and when Mauro saw the Glock in its holster under his visitor's armpit, he paled. "Dude, what's with the hardware?"

Samos was almost embarrassed and quickly drew his jacket closed.

"Look, I've got some bad news, and maybe some good news," said Samos, his eyes lifting up to Mauro's. "Greg."

The Canadian was stunned, but then smiled as he sat down opposite his visitor.

"Took you fuckin' long enough! How did you find out?"

Samos shook his head, thinking carefully how to unfold this story.

"Well, I had an idea after our first meeting."

"Oh, yeah?"

"Your accent. St. Leonard?"

Mauro laughed deep and hard. When he caught his breath, he said, "Ville Émard."

Samos allowed a tight smile. "Montreal, anyway."

"So, you made me, like ten years ago?"

"No, I didn't. I had an idea, but I never followed it up. You might have trouble believing this, but trust me, it is true. There's an American treasury agent, by the name of Longhurst."

Mauro reacted, his eyes narrowing. "Why do I know that name?

Fucking Maria-Isabel's sister! Samos shouted inwardly, but then he chastised himself and pressed his lips tightly.

"Wait," Mauro continued. "Isn't that the guy who's shagging Maria-Isabel's sister? She told me Elvira had finally landed a man, an American, government big shot."

Samos nodded. "He's heading a task force to pull various nations into a program to shut down money laundering and illegal offshore accounts."

Mauro whistled. "And he's sleeping with the sister of . . ."

Samos cut him off. "About five years ago, he was touring the Caribbean, trying to get the region on-side for this initiative. He stopped off at the Cayman Islands, where, by pure coincidence, he met this odd fellow, almost mute, not quite in possession of his own mind. He works on a little charter fishing boat. They call him 'First-Mate-Mike.'"

"Mike? . . . DeAngelis?" whispered Mauro, eyes widened with surprise. "Mike DeAngelis? He's alive?"

Samos nodded, his heart melting a little seeing the joy in the Canadian's face.

"What happened when you two left the Keys? How did he end up in the sea, half-dead?"

Mauro had his hands pressed to his forehead like he was losing his mind with joy. "He insisted on taking the watch at night. I woke up when the swells threw me out of my cot. His tether had snapped, he was gone. I spent a week cruising the area, asking anyone if they had seen or heard . . ." Mauro stopped and for the first time since Samos had met him, saw the younger man choke up with emotion.

"Mike, fucking Mike! Couldn't kill you, no fuckin' way!" He looked up at Samos. "Dude, we gotta get there. I gotta see him, get him back with me."

"Too dangerous. I haven't told you everything."

"Listen, the statute of limitation on robbery has run out on our *alleged* crime. Besides, there is no extradition treaty between Canada and Costa Rica. I'm safe as long as I don't leave this country."

Samos rose to his feet to pace the deck, his head lowered. From the dock, the thick-necked fellow had his eye on him, stone-faced.

"So, you didn't hear?"

"Hear what?" asked the Canadian, an annoyed edge to his voice.

Samos lidded his eyes as he turned to face Mauro. He wanted to watch the younger man's face. "Someone planted a bomb under my car, set to go off when I turned the ignition."

Mauro's jaw tightened. "Jesus."

"And it worked, but it wasn't me who started the car. It was Maria-Isabel."

Mauro's mouth fell open and, in an instant, Samos could see the panoramic tapestry illustrating the consequences of his late wife's death flash across the Canadian's eyes.

Samos shook his head. "I do not know who is after me, or why, but, there are several notable contenders."

Mauro walked over to place a consoling hand on Samos's shoulder. "You're safe here. I've got Ricky out there, a few more good men. You'll be safe for as long as you need."

Samos was touched, but he was under no illusions about how long such kindness would last. He needed to set the Canadian back on his heels in order to realize his plans.

"Thanks to Longhurst, I know all about the robbery and you should understand this: he has got your scent and he's the kind that follows through."

This caught Mauro up short. He nodded as he listened, as though he had already heard Samos's words in his own mind for years.

"And you need better legal advice. There is no statute of limitation on indictable offences in Canada. As for being safe," said Samos, indicating to the armed guard on the dock. "When this thing gets out—and, believe me, Longhurst will make sure it does—a dozen 'Rickies' won't be able to stop the bounty hunters. They'll come after you. And good old Jack Longhurst will be there like your favorite uncle, just waiting with an offer to turn yourself in."

He could see that he was finally breaking through Mauro's self-confidence. He changed the subject. "How many bars are left on board this boat of the forty you two stole?"

"About half."

"And how many one-ounce gold briquettes can you lay your hands on?"

"Here and now?"

"Yes."

Mauro shrugged, "About a hundred?"

"Good. You and I are flying to Managua tomorrow morning. Bring sixty-four briquettes with you, thirty-two for me and thirty-two for your savior. Do you have any liquor on board?" he asked. He was beginning to fade and needed a pick-me-up. Fatigue and stress were starting to affect him.

"I have half a bottle of brandy left here, Carlos Quinto?"

"I think you need one, too"

While Mauro was rummaging around for the bottle and glasses, Samos could not stop himself ruminating about Maria-Isabel.

"I am contemplating two problems to the exclusion of all others, Mauro: how to survive the next twenty-four, and how to find and punish the person who killed her."

"Look, Samos, I'm sympathetic. I liked M.I. We were excellent business partners and, if I can help you find who killed her, I will. But, I will be frank with you. My priorities have to be myself and now Mike, and the business."

Cold-hearted but totally correct, thought Samos. It would be his own attitude if he were not so emotionally involved. Score one for the Canuck.

"If what you say is true," Mauro continued, "this had nothing to do with our business. You said it yourself, they were out to get you, right? What does all the rest have to do with me? Why are we flying to Managua?" Mauro poured a second round.

"Like I said, Longhurst met Mike on the Caymans about three years ago and he felt sorry for him. He has a big heart for a WASP prick and he wanted to help, maybe repatriate a down-on-his-luck American. He sent a fucking beer bottle with Mike's prints on it to Interpol to help find out who he really was. This gave Interpol a huge hard-on because now they had a reason to reopen the unsolved robbery file. Mike is destitute and suffers from almost total amnesia; he cannot even speak intelligibly."

Samos knocked back his drink and continued. "Naturally, when Interpol figured out Mike's identity, they briefed Longhurst about the robbery and now it is Longhurst who has got the hard-on."

Mauro poured another round, shaking his head. "It's a great story, Samos, but, again, what the fuck does it have to do with me? I say we hire your Beechcraft, swoop down on the Caymans, and get Mike the fuck outta there!"

Now it was Samos who girded his guts. "Mauro, let me ask you something. Do you believe in *kismet*?"

"*Kismet*?"

"Fate. Destiny. You know, '*It is written . . .*'"

The Canadian sat back on the cabin sofa.

"Yeah, as a matter of fact, I do." He took a deep slug of the brandy. "It was destiny that Mike and I grew up together. That we both wanted to fly. That we had access to a sailboat on Lake Champlain. Sure. And it was fate that put the opportunity in front of us, legs spread wide and damp." He took another slug, draining his glass. "It is a sin to ignore your destiny."

Samos held up his glass to toast the younger man.

"Destinies do not exist in isolation, without touching those of others, right? Your destiny. Mike's destiny. Maria-Isabel's. And now, mine."

"They intersect."

"Right," nodded Samos, feeling the soporific, but bracing effects of the booze. "If we could only see the orbits of those whose destinies intersect our own. Oh! how better off we would be, right?"

"Fuckin' A."

Samos leaned in toward Mauro.

"So, how about this for fate: three years ago, this pesky agent from the US Treasury Department, stinking of Secret Service juice, comes to see me at my office. This tall drink of water found me via some mutual contacts in the American foreign bureaus and he wants to chat about offshore banking and the people who indulge themselves. He's a friendly cunt and he wants to warn me of the changes his government is bringing down. This is just after I introduced you to Maria-Isabel."

Samos looked up to find Mauro holding up two fingers and he named them, "You, Longhurst . . ."

Samos chuckled. "By the time I'm done, you might have to take off your socks! Anyway, I realize that it is getting time for lunch, which I promised to Maria-Isabel, and I can hear Longhurst's guts gurgling, too, and I think that, maybe, Maria-Isabel would like to hear what Longhurst has to say. So I call her and she's dying for sushi and, sure, she'd like to meet my new American friend and, could she drag along her big-footed, goofy, younger sister, Elvira?"

Mauro added two more fingers, "You're fucking kidding me? Maria-Isabel, Elvira . . ."

"And wouldn't you know it, that drip of a dishwater dull younger sister takes one look at Longhurst and perks up like she sat on a cattle prod. Mauro, I shit you not, her nipples jumped up and stayed hard all through lunch. And Longhurst could not take his eyes off her."

Mauro was rubbing his face, incredulous.

"Don't tell me."

Now it was Samos's turn to pace. "Maria-Isabel was many wonderful things, but she was a Queen-Bee and jealous. The idea that her sister had landed a man like Longhurst was an intolerable insult. So, like sisters do, they chatted and chatted and M.I. just had to brag about her incredibly successful and profitable business, how she had made deals to undercut every jewelry merchant in the Caribbean and Central America and it was due to a supplier who had access to discounted gold."

"Jesus, no, she didn't!"

Samos merely nodded and sat down heavily, reaching for the bottle Mauro offered.

"Fuck me," moaned the Canadian.

"The fact of your destiny is that Longhurst now knows about your business and suspects you as being one of the robbers."

He held out his glass for another shot of brandy. "And that, my friend, is all the bad news."

Samos lifted his glass to eye level and looked through it while contemplating what little joy his miserable, lonely, uncertain future might hold, if any. Once more, he was totally alone in the world. *Ni travail, ni patrie, ni famille,* as the surviving foreign members of the Toulouse Resistance, fighting against the Nazis during the Second World found themselves when they returned from their respective concentration camps: ignored and ostracized.

"So, what's the good news?" asked Mauro, a sardonic smile twisting his mouth. Samos snapped out of his reverie.

"Because of his respect for Maria-Isabel, my late beloved, and his desire for Elvira, and to avoid any family scandal, Longhurst came to see me before telling Interpol about his suspicions about you, leaving us some room to make this right."

CHAPTER 58

At the crack of dawn the next morning, Martinez flew Samos and Mauro to Agusto Cesar Sandino Airport in Managua, where they landed at 8:32. Once again, Martinez escorted them off the tarmac and into passport control, where he undertook a series of very warm, dollar-loaded handshakes with several duty officers who blithely stamped Samos and Mauro's passports, welcoming them to the land of lakes and volcanoes.

They left Martinez at the Airport Inn with instructions to stand by for a mid-afternoon flight back to Golfito. On their way to the capital on Highway 1 in a rented limo, Samos asked the driver if he played chess. The man said yes.

"Do you know where I can buy a couple of decent-looking chess sets?"

"You a collector or just a player?" the driver asked.

"A collector."

The driver half-turned in his seat to look more fully at Samos, as though not quite believing his ears. He shook his head.

"This is very fortuitous. I know of a collector who died not so long ago. He had over a dozen sets and his widow wants to sell them, but she's asking a fortune and, today, nobody has money in Nicaragua for frivolities."

"Where does she live?"

"In town, near the *Lago de Tiscapa* in the *Barrio William Diaz.*"

"Can you call her?"

The driver stopped at the next gas station and when he returned to his car he was all smiles.

"All set. Señora Flores still has half a dozen sets left, but she warned me that she wants a lot of money for them."

The chess sets were all impressive and the Widow Flores knew the value of what she possessed so Samos didn't bother haggling. Besides, it wasn't his money, it was Mauro's. Samos picked a magnificent, hand-decorated ebony case containing a set of exquisite hand-carved ivory figurines depicting the Shah of Persia and his acolytes, each housed in its individual silken slot. He also bought an unusual set made of plywood inside and covered by water-proofed leather outside, with two handles that made the set look like an attaché case when closed.

Señora Flores kindly gave them some package tape and tissue paper and went off to count her money. Samos and Mauro closeted themselves in the dining room, where they replaced the pieces in both sets with the gold briquettes they had brought along with them, making sure to tape them securely in place. Thirty-two briquettes went into each set. The ivory figurines were wrapped in tissue paper and placed in a linen shoe bag given them by their hostess.

Punctually at noon as agreed, Samos and Mauro were in Minister Santiago's outer office. His secretary, Leticia, a handsome, mature woman, received them warmly. She had harbored an unrequited and not-so-secret crush on Samos for years and was all smiles.

She ushered them straight into Santiago's plush, modern office. The air conditioning was purring faintly, and the floor-to-ceiling windows were filtered by clever hanging vertical blinds. The minister had taste and style. The walls of the office were decorated with very fine examples of Nicaraguan modern art and some excellent examples of folk art, both pre- and post-Colombian. Samos's eyes were drawn to a primitive nude in a stunning *art nouveau* frame.

After brief introductions and the ceremonial consumption of the inevitable espresso, during which Samos expressed his regrets for having disturbed the minister on such short notice, he placed the expensive chess set and the bag containing the ivory figurines on the minister's desk. "*Mea culpa,* but opportunity was pressing," he added humbly, opened the set and turned it toward the minister so that the man could see what was in it.

Then he came to the point.

"*Licenciado,* my client, Signore Mauro, is an Italian citizen living in Costa Rica, and he owns a chain of high-class jewelry stores in Central America and the Caribbean. Perhaps you have heard of them, *Tidre*?"

The minister was impressed. "But of course! My wife is a frequent client."

"Mr. Mauro wishes to open one in Nicaragua. For this he needs a work permit. Since he has a spot already picked out, it is essential for him to obtain such a document as soon as possible because he wishes to acquire the property quickly before it is bought by a potential competitor."

The minister was happy. "Señor Samos, I am delighted to hear that you are bringing new investment to my country. We certainly need it."

His eyes were scanning the row of briquettes, his brain doing the math: he was looking at about $50,000 worth of gold. There must be more to the matter than urgency, he said to himself. Nobody pays that kind of money for a work permit.

"How urgent is the matter?"

"We flew in this morning especially for this and are hoping to return home this afternoon." Samos took a deep breath. "We understand that the document we seek requires the fingerprints of the holder." He looked the minister squarely in the eyes. "Unfortunately, Signore Mauro suffers from a serious skin disease. He is very allergic to the ink used during fingerprinting. It creates a painful rash all the way up to his elbow. Could it be arranged that the permit be issued with the prints of a substitute?"

Samos held his breath. The minister's eyes flitted over to Mauro, whose face remained pleasant and unconcerned.

The minister understood everything immediately and hesitated. Then he smiled. "No problem. We'll issue the permit for a month. Will that be agreeable?" Greed had won over ethics.

Samos started to breathe again. "That will be just fine. Where and when could we pick it up?"

And just as he started to breathe again, he stopped. Why did he stop? That primitive nude that Samos kept staring at had a little plaque at the bottom. He had ignored it initially, but now he was a little closer and could actually read what it said; "*Desnuda lánguida*" 1958, de *Rodrigo Peñalba*—Compliments of FEG Industries. Samos barely heard the minister's instructions.

"Give my secretary Signore Mauro's coordinates and let her have an hour to get things organized, then come back here." Mauro saw that Samos was somewhere else and stepped forward to shake the minister's hand. The minister saw them to the door.

"Thank you again, Señor Samos, for thinking about us." They shook hands. "Hopefully, we will see each other again soon."

"You OK?" asked Mauro once they were outside.

Samos's mind was already racing, but he fronted calm confidence.

"Yes, sorry about that," he shrugged back toward the ministry. "I got a little lost in my thoughts. I'm still a little shook up."

Samos and Mauro had the driver take them to a nearby McDonald's, where they freshened up and destroyed a Big

Mac each. At 2 p.m., they picked up the work permit. Samos then asked Leticia for a sheet of notepaper and an envelope and wrote a short note to Longhurst:

"I enclose a Nicaraguan Work Permit that my client Roberto Mauro obtained in order to open a branch of his business in Managua. His certified fingerprints are on the document. Have Interpol check his background as needed."

Samos then put the note and the work permit into an envelope and gave it to Mauro under Leticia's carefully oblivious regard. "Longhurst is going to show up sooner or later. Give him the envelope when he shows."

Samos then slid a thousand dollars into another envelope and handed it to Leticia, gave her a radiant smile, and left with Mauro in tow. On the street, he told Mauro to take the limo back to the airport.

"I might not see you ever again, but my office is still your management firm. Ask for Jaime Balart, he's my second-in-command and he is familiar with your file."

Mauro hesitated, but only for a second before sweeping Samos up in a crushing hug. At 3 p.m., Mauro and Martinez, now $5,000 richer from the Canadian's pocket, were en route home in the Beechcraft.

CHAPTER 59

Samos had watched Mauro leave in the rented limo till the vehicle was out of sight before returning to Minister Santiago's outer office. Leticia's surprised look and wry smile revealed her inner hopes, but Samos burst her bubble, miming the need for a telephone and a quiet corner. Leticia pointed to an empty office with a desk and phone.

Closing the door behind him, Samos once again dialed the number he knew so well and waited. A male voice answered, "This is the major."

"My name is Barbara," replied Samos, keeping his voice down.

"Alias?"

"Frosty the Snowman."

This time there was a delay of a few moments.

"Go ahead, the line is secure."

"Managua. Twenty-four-hour check-in."

"That's affirmative. How can we be of assistance?"

"Any news on interested parties following Panama City?"

Another delay of a few moments filled with odd electronic noise.

"Frosty, you are instructed to make your way to Managua AE for extraction at 2100 hours."

"Negative on AE extraction. Repeat. Any news on interested parties?"

No delay this time.

"Negative interested parties. You are instructed to proceed to Managua AE for extraction, 2100 hours."

"Negative. Check-in twenty-four hours."

As he terminated the call, Samos sat back in the empty office, ruminating. Once again, he felt the slight pull of celestial bodies, these ones not-so-charmed, tugging on his fate. FEG. What impish deity placed that sculpture in Santiago's office? Was it only to enrage or was it meant to focus his attention. His blood was up and in his eye. Blood for blood.

Samos approached Leticia at her desk with his most disarming and casual smile. "My dearest, what can you tell me about FEG?"

*

From the Ministry of the Interior, Samos took a cab to the Metrocentro shopping centrer near the Intercontinental Hotel and began the laborious process of covering his tracks. He was worried that carrying around two attaché cases made him look a little conspicuous and he had to plan his next move. He found a small café and ordered a *café negro* while he mused. He knew he had made a clean escape and that no one was expecting him in Nicaragua. He was in a perfect situation to lay low for a few days and figure out what to do, though, if he was honest with himself, he didn't have that many options.

And then there was FEG. What he had preached to Mauro on the nature of destiny and fate seemed to have come around to bite him in the ass. Of course, he now remembered that FEG Nicaragua was based near León, the Second City of Nicaragua. What to do? Ignore fate and bum around Managua for a few days before allowing the Agency to repatriate him? Or, should he follow the tides and currents and allow himself to drift toward FEG so as to see, first hand, what kind of operation it was? He could not decide.

He wandered among the shops for a while and when he was sure that he was not being followed, he walked up *Avenida de las Naciones Unidas* to the *Rotonda Rubén Diario*, cut left on Pista Pablo II, and, on a capricious whim, hopped into a cab. He took it to the inter-city *UCA Managua-Leon* terminal, where he boarded the next bus to Nicaragua's *Leòn*. In his experience, interurban bus travel was one of the safest ways to go to ground.

So, León it was.

During the two-hour trip, though bone tired, he reviewed his situation. He understood that for the past twenty-four hours, though fronting very well, he had been living on nerves and adrenaline. He was also aware that the shock of the attempt on his life and losing Maria-Isabel were stirring his deep psychology. He put himself on the couch and talked himself into setting immediate priorities.

Finding a place where he could go to ground and sleep safely was priority one. The bus dropped him at the *Mercado Central* in *León*. From there he took a tuk-tuk taxi to the Hotel La Perla, recommended highly by one of the passengers on the bus. He was pleasantly surprised; the place suited his needs perfectly. He registered using his Canadian passport. After checking that the air conditioning was working, the doors were solid and the locks functioning in his room, he jammed a chair against the door-knob and lay down on the bed with his Glock under his pillow.

But sleep eluded him. Was it because the hour was early, after all, it was only seven in the evening. Or did he need another self-therapy session to quell his inner torments? He could not tell. It had been a long time since he had been so afraid, so alone in the world, and hunted.

Maria-Isabel, his only close companion during the last five years, was gone forever. Once more, the finality of the event hit him hard. There are no second chances. There will be no do-overs. Members of her family will now have reason to back up their negative opinion of him. They will shut their doors to him, even those for whom he had done service. His employees and clients will surely distance themselves from him as time goes by. His business would disintegrate because nobody would want to deal with an organization the owner of which was an absentee fugitive, however innocent of any crime he may be. On the other hand, he had faith in Jaime Balart, his number two. He was a good man and, over time, the face of the business, which was very viable, could just as well become his.

He could not stop himself from laughing out loud. The only two beings in the world he could think of who might be willing to help him in the short term were Longhurst and Mauro.

And, perhaps, the boys in Washington. Which brought his mind around to his two recent contacts. "Extraction." Why so eager to extract him? Well, for one, an attempt had been made on his life. Sure, professional *noblesse oblige*. Or, were the brethren at Foggy Bottom nervous about having a remote but still active asset running around with state secrets in his addled pate? This had to be unlikely. In his current situation he was of no further use to them. For the past few years he had often felt like *Pascali,* the Turkish agent in Unsworth's novel, a spy who sends his intelligence reports with religious devotion to a master who has not replied in decades. Clearly, there was something about all this he was simply not getting.

As for his would-be killers, the list was not long. He could think of no more than a half dozen people who might want him dead, but his crimes against them occurred so long ago. The question was, who would be motivated enough, or mad enough, after so many years, to go to the trouble of mounting an operation to eliminate him?

A novel thought wormed its way past his fatigue and the last ribbons of the shock that had rattled his brain. Maybe, it was a *new* enemy?

Exhausted, he never noticed that he had fallen asleep.

*

He awoke the next morning at seven by the bells of *La Catedral de Leòn* a few blocks away. His head was clear, his mind rested, his instincts sharp. Twelve hours of sleep had restored his resourcefulness and his desire to fight. The maid took his clothes to the laundry and solemnly promised to have them back by the evening. Dressed in his spares, he had breakfast on the terrace, a virgin *Macuá* followed by *huevos rancheros* and strong coffee. Then he went shopping for more clothing, a backpack, binoculars, a bathing suit, and a wide-brimmed sombrero with a strap. A cheap camera, slung around his neck, completed the picture of the average gringo tourist.

According to Leticia, the FEG establishment was located in a hamlet called, of all places, *Ernesto Ché Guevara*, off the highway connecting *Leòn* with *Las Peñitas*, the popular beach resort on the Pacific Ocean less than twenty kilometers away.

Back at his hotel he slid his briquettes into a canvas shoe bag, which he placed into the backpack, then stuffed his windbreaker and binoculars on top of it. He regarded his Glock and wondered why he might need it. He was a tourist, just walking around, seeing the sights and getting lost. No one would think ill of him. Once again, on a pure whim, he slipped the gun into a side pocket of the knapsack. He took a deep breath. The script he was currently living had not been written by him.

Leaving his attaché case and leather chessboard in his room, he sauntered over to the cathedral and bought a pass allowing him to walk on the roof, a popular pastime for curious tourists, and, for him, an opportunity to sight-see while planning his next move. It was also a chance for anyone watching him to dismiss him as another gringo looking to get his nose sunburnt.

He left the roof just before noon and melted into the crowd milling about in the market in front of the church. He found a tuk-tuk taxi that looked sturdier than the average and talked the driver into taking him to the beach at *Las Peñitas*. During the trip, the driver told Samos that if he wanted to stay overnight, he should choose the Lazy Turtle Hotel as his abode on the beach. "It's located a bit south of the town center, near a spectacular inlet, so it's quiet. Next to it there is this fabulous seafood restaurant, *La Barca de Oro*," he had raved, no doubt earning his kickbacks from both places.

Two thirds into the half-hour trip, Samos saw what he had been looking for: a sign pointing to the road leading to the hamlet, *Ernesto Ché Guevara*. His heart quickened and then, through force of will, slowed.

CHAPTER 60

Las Peñitas, March 1990

Samos followed his driver's advice and checked into the Lazy Turtle Hotel, rented a bike, then pedalled over to *La Barca de Oro,* where he made a reservation for dinner. He kept going and started biking around the horseshoe-shaped inlet the driver had mentioned. At the horseshoe's head, the beach came to an end at the 150-yard wide estuary of a stream that seemed to originate well inland. There was no bridge in sight for crossing it.

The stream appeared to be navigable, though he could not judge the depth of its waters. Nor could he see, even when using his binoculars, the direction from which the stream originated because he could not see beyond its sharp bend to the right, about a thousand yards upstream,

Back at the hotel, he bought a swimsuit, a T-shirt, and underwear, changed, and went down to the beach bar. He ordered a proper *Macuá* from the waitress on duty and engaged her in banter when she brought him his drink. Finding her accented Spanish very familiar, he asked where she was born, but he knew even before she answered.

She laughed. "Everybody asks me that. I can't help my accent. I was born in Cuba. My husband and I left the country in 1978 with our ten-year-old."

"Your husband?"

"Yes. Well, we met in Cuba, but he is originally from Transylvania, the part that was Hungary. He came to Cuba and worked at the glass factory that socialist Hungary gave as a present to socialist Cuba. In '78, we came to this place because we wanted to continue living in warm climates."

"But why Nicaragua? I would have thought that both of you had had enough of living under dictatorships?"

She shrugged. "You know how it is. My husband is a specialist tool-and-die maker; Hungarians are famous for this kind of expertise. He heard from our government contacts about a factory here that was looking for a manager, so he applied and got the job."

Samos's mind had stopped on the word "manager." This intersecting of fate was getting a bit absurd. He tried to talk himself out of it—after all, why would the wife of an FEG manager be working as a waitress in a beach-side bar? No, there was no coincidence here, but, for the sake of his own amusement, he continued to chat.

"And how did things work out for you?"

"Very well. My husband had a well-paying job, so I could stay home and look after my young son."

"Pretty boring."

"Yes, and that became a problem."

"Huh?"

"When my son became a teenager, he no longer needed looking after and I was stuck at home, slowly going crazy. We had a maid and I literally had nothing to do all day. There is very little social life with people of the same—how can I say this?—education. The most interesting people are the tourists. So I looked around for something to do away from the house at least once a week."

"And?"

"I declared Friday as my day off from home. I got a job here as the pool waitress in the morning and, at night, while my husband plays poker with his friends, I work for a couple of hours as the bartender at a nearby restaurant. I also act as a receptionist here on Monday mornings."

The woman then asked "Where are *you* from?"

Samos had to think fast. He was travelling under the name of Thomas Bellon on a Canadian passport. He had shown it to the hotel's receptionist when registering. The woman might check him out at reception so he had no choice.

"From Canada," he answered. Luckily, he still remembered the legend attached to his Canadian passport, memorized long ago as a matter of routine training.

"Lucky you. Your lot is known for playing it straight."

"What do you mean?"

"When my husband got the job here in *León*, he needed to get a residency permit for us. He had a connection at the Ministry of the Interior whom he bribed to get the job. Panama."

Samos nearly blew his drink all over her face. What the hell was going on?

The waitress, seeing what she took for a perplexed expression on his face, burst out laughing. "Panama? That's what they call bribery in Hungary. It goes back to when they were building the Panama Canal. There was plenty of bribing there."

As she walked back to the beach-bar, highly amused, she called back over her shoulder, "By the way, my name is Aurora."

*

The *Barca de Oro* was an upscale beach restaurant catering to a crowd that had money to spend. Its building resembled the cross-section of a huge barge that had three levels; hence, the name: one on the road, another below, halfway to the beach, and the third, on the beach itself. Samos had reserved a corner table on the halfway level that had an unobstructed view of the level below and of the inlet itself.

"Would you like a drink to start with, señor?" inquired the maître d', who was ushering him to his table. "A mojito, please, but do you have *hierba buena*, and sugar cane syrup?" answered Samos hopefully.

"In other words, a real mojito," laughed the waiter. "Of course we do. Right away, *señor.*"

"Make it a double," Samos called after him.

He was happy with the table he had been given. Sitting away from the crowd near the railing in a corner that was in semi-darkness allowed him to survey the crowd around him and, at the same time, to see the water of the estuary glittering with stars reflected from above. It was relatively early; the moon had not risen as yet.

"Your drink, *señor.*" The busboy, a child, looked no older than fourteen. He placed the drink and several bowls of peppers, olives, and wedges of warm tortilla on the table.

Samos took the glass from the tray and, on impulse, chugalugged the cold, delicious cocktail. "Bring me another," he commanded the astonished boy, then sat back and waited for the rum in the mojito to hit him, which it did almost immediately. His meager lunch of a solitary *nacatamal* was a long way behind him.

Looking seaward over the crowd, it struck him that he was the only person in the place sitting alone. This depressed him. Too preoccupied during the past two days with trying to keep alive, he had been forcing himself not to think about Maria-Isabel. But now that he felt temporarily safe, no doubt due to the effect of the mojito, he suddenly realized with a pain that hurt as if someone had driven a dagger into his heart, that his loving and faithful partner for the last decade was gone forever.

That hateful finality.

And there was no way he could beg for forgiveness for having betrayed her love and trust in him.

"One of the many sins I will have to go on living with," he muttered and with tears coursing down his cheeks, whispered: "I killed you."

A shadow fell over him and when he looked up, he found that Aurora, the waitress who had served him at his hotel on the beach, was standing in front of him, his second drink on a tray in her hand.

"*¿Qué pasó?* Are you all right?" She appeared genuinely concerned.

Afterward, he could never fully explain why he uncharacteristically confessed to her, an utter stranger, the gut-wrenching, deeply hurting emotion that tortured him. "No, I'm not all right, not all right at all." He shook his head.

She put his drink on the table. "What's wrong? You're pale. Are you ill?"

"No," he said in Spanish, breathing deeply to regain control. "I'm not ill. I am just incredibly sad and lonely."

CHAPTER 61

Las Peñitas

Samos finished his beer, burped discreetly into his napkin, and turned to his hostess. "I haven't eaten chicken *paprikash* with *nocchi* for a long, long time. To tell the truth, I had forgotten how good it tastes when prepared with the right ingredients by capable hands." He patted his stomach. "Tonight, you hit it out of the ball ark."

They were finishing Sunday night dinner on Aurora and Emilio Kiss's terrace. The couple's very comfortable, well-appointed house on the beach next to the *Oasis Hostal* was not far from where Aurora worked in the mornings as a beach-bar waitress at The Lazy Turtle Hotel, and as a bartender at *Boca de Oro* once a week at night, whenever her services were required.

On Friday night, seeing her new friend in emotional distress, she had felt intensely sorry for him. "I spoke with my husband about you and we decided to ask you for dinner tomorrow night," she told him at breakfast the next day. "It's Sunday and I'm not working, so I'll cook something real Hungarian to cheer you up. My husband taught me all of his mother's recipes! Will you come?"

He couldn't believe this serendipitous streak. And he didn't trust it. Things just did not happen this way. From the little Aurora had told him, he was almost certain that her husband worked at the FEG factory. Was he the manager? It was doubtful. Of course he accepted.

Aurora was serving coffee and Samos felt he should pretend being expansive. "It's a funny thing, but, although I have only been here for three days, I feel comfortable in *Las Peñitas*," he said to her. "Thanks to both of you."

Kiss poured him a thimbleful of Tia Maria. "Where do you live, anyway?"

From the moment he entered their home, Samos had tried to size Kiss up, searching for any tell that would give him insight into his host's character. Kiss was moderately tall and very fit, rail thin, wiry, and intense. He had massive hands, muscled and veiny, but it was his face that provoked Samos's thoughts. Unnervingly symmetrical, an aquiline nose, sharp, narrowed eyes behind ultra-thin prescription eyeglasses, high cheek bones, a hard, square chin. It was a face that shouted *"Magyar!* But tight-lipped, tight-jawed, and vigilant.

"In Mexico City," Samos replied.

"How come? Aurora said you're from Canada."

"I was born and brought up in Montreal. My father had immigrated to Canada from Toledo, Spain, in the late twenties, my mother in the early thirties. She was also Spanish. They met in Montreal in the mid-thirties, fell in love, and got married. When I finished college, I bummed around a bit and tried my hand at having my own consultancy. Then I got a job with a pharmaceutical manufacturer. It's called Apotex."

Samos had carefully rehearsed this little presentation and, as if on cue, produced a business card from his shirt pocket and handed it to Kiss. "They needed a Latin American sales rep and I fit the bill. I spoke Spanish as well as I can speak English."

Kiss was nodding, his eyes fixed on Samos's mouth so firmly, the older man thought he might have a piece of parsley stuck between his teeth.

Samos took a sip of his Tia Maria. "And what about you, Emil? Aurora told me you work in some sort of a factory here?"

Samos deliberately used the word "work" as bait for a prideful man who might be a manager but Kiss didn't bite. He avoided answering any questions. "So you set up your headquarters in Mexico?"

"Yes, it's halfway between Montreal and my territory, which is all of Latin America, a huge area. I had to find a way to reduce travelling time, so I moved to Mexico City." He lifted his glass. "This is delicious. Could I have some more?"

They continued chatting for a while, but Kiss revealed little about his work. Before leaving, Samos stopped in the vestibule and took both of Aurora's hands in his own.

"Thank you so much for your hospitality, fine cooking, and sympathy." Then he added, jokingly: "It's funny, you know. You've been so kind to me and I have spoken so much about myself. I wanted to ask what part of Hungary Emil is from?"

"Oh, he is so shy." Aurora looked back furtively over her shoulder to confirm that her husband was still in the salon. "He is from Arad, which is now a Romanian town, as you probably know."

"Arad," said Samos with a disarming shrug. "No, never heard of it."

And now the bait that he left dangling for the husband was snatched up by his prideful wife. She checked on Emil's whereabouts once more and then stepped closer to Samos

"And, he doesn't just work at FEG," she whispered. "He's the manager!"

Samos waved his hand as though to erase an error, "Of course, yes, you told me." He raised one of her hands and kissed it. "I hope he was not offended?"

The woman blushed, her eyes lingering on Samos, who carefully kept his own hooded as he took his leave.

On the short walk back to his hotel, Samos felt as though he was walking on air. He felt giddy, lighthearted, and ener-gized. He also felt the elliptical forces of heavenly bodies in their orbits intersecting and exerting their pull, but, at that moment, he did not resent it. He mastered it.

He had never mentioned FEG the entire evening.

CHAPTER 62

He got up late on Monday, somewhat disoriented and still bewildered, his head ringing with the music of the spheres. How was it possible that, of all the places he could have wound up, it was at the home of the man who was probably the heretofore anonymous manager of FEG Nicaragua? It was as though he were a string puppet in some absurdist child's pantomime. At any moment, he expected to hear a chorus of kids' voices shouting, "Look out, he's behind you!"

The various disparate elements were falling into place: Kiss's Hungarian background, his opportune posting in Cuba, the move from Cuba to Nicaragua, the comfortable house on the beach in a choice location, the key job within the FEG organization, and the reluctance to talk about it, a reluctance shared by almost every regular resident of *Las Peñitas* that Samos had met during his stay in the town. People either pretended not to recognize the name or merely shrugged, smiled, and moved off.

He considered his options carefully and then followed his gut and, feigning innocent ignorance, approached Aurora at the reception desk after breakfast with coffee still in hand.

"No one here seems to know anything about Emil's factory. What was it you said last night? FED?"

She made light of his question. "Not FED," she giggled. "FEG."

Aurora had what he now identified as a furtive tick, a habit of looking sharply back over her shoulder, but she also had an urge to talk to Samos.

"When Emil took on the job of running the FEG factory, it was making locks and keys. Then, I think a deal was made with the Somoza government and Emil started making guns. Since Chamorro came into power, the government is no longer involved. Too dangerous."

"This is fascinating. What kind of guns?" he asked, playing to her sense of pride.

"Rifles, handguns, all kinds of guns, Kalashnikovs, whatever . . ." she said, casually.

"Kalashnikovs? But those are Russian."

"FEG has a sub-licence from the Russians."

"But, what is FEG?"

"It's a Hungarian factory, silly. *Fegyver- és Gépgyár, F.É.G.,* which means, Weapons and Machines Manufacturing company," she laughed. "FEG are *the* head licensors for Kalashnikov in Central America," she cooed proudly. "That's my husband."

Samos finished his coffee. "Too complicated for me," he said, feigning total disinterest. "Thank you, Aurora."

"Where are you off to?"

"I thought I'd look for a place to stay in *Las Peñitas* for a while. I like it here. See you later."

Still dressed as an everyday tourist, Samos got on his bike and headed for the town's center, where he visited a couple of real-estate agent offices. He was looking for maps of the area, which he found at one of these offices. From *Las Peñitas,* he biked north along *Autopista Nacional 14* until he reached the intersection with the road leading to the hamlet *Ernesto Ché Guevara.*

At the corner gas station, which was also a bus stop complete with shelter, bench, and public telephone booth, Samos made a couple of long-distance calls, the first to his office in Panama to reassure Balart that he was safe and just away for a few days' rest to recover from the tragedy that had befallen him. Balart reported that the press furor had died down and, contrary to Samos's fears, clients had been concerned by the bombing, but no one had asked to close down their accounts or withdraw their custom.

The second call was to the number on the business card he had given Kiss the night before. The number was that of a private phone line connected to a sophisticated voice mail system. After composing the number, Samos waited for the "welcome" message to play and dialed 1017. The system went into message playback mode and recited the list of new calls since the last playback, including hang-ups, incoming messages in their entirety, text, caller's telephone number, name of caller, country, town, and the street address from where the call had originated.

As he expected, the box reported only one message emanating from a phone number registered to Emilio Kiss in *Las Peñitas*. Obviously, the Hungarian was checking up on him.

Samos hung up, and then dialed the number he could never forget. A male voice answered, "This is the major."

"My name is Barbara," replied Samos.

"Alias?"

"Frosty the Snowman."

"Go ahead, the line is secure."

"*Las Peñitas*. Twenty-four-hour check-in."

"That's affirmative. How can we be of assistance?"

"HX urgent on one Emil Kiss, Hungarian national. Current small arms manufacturer. Company, FEG, repeat: Foxtrot Echo Golf, *Ernesto Ché Guevara*."

"Roger that, HX on Emil Kiss, Foxtrot Echo Golf, *Ernesto Ché Guevara*."

"Frosty prepping for self-extraction."

"Frosty, you are expected at Palm station."

"Affirmative, Palm station."

"Do you need assistance?"

"Negative. Check-in twenty-four hours."

Inside the gas station he bought an energy bar and a bottle of water. The couple running the gas station spoke to him in perfect continental Spanish, but to each other in a dialect that he could not place, though he was able to listen for several long moments before he had to exit.

Samos went outside, where, pretending exhaustion, he collapsed theatrically on the bench in the open shelter. He mused on what he had heard inside the gas station. It wasn't

Slavic, not Germanic, not Romance-based, and yet, it was familiar. Catalan? Yes, probably Catalan.

As he ate his energy bar and pretended to consult a tourist map, he confirmed that the couple was acting as gatekeepers of the road leading to the *Guevara* hamlet. Whenever a motor vehicle—car, truck, or motorbike—turned on to the road heading toward the hamlet, the man or woman would pick up a Motorola walkie-talkie and say a few words. Samos suspected that they were keeping the factory security gate up the road abreast of approaching traffic.

Pretending to look for a place to relieve himself, Samos left his bike at the pumps and walked up the road toward the hamlet until he came to a small clearing to the right of his, about twenty yards into the bush and surrounded by robust trees, some climbable. Just to make sure, he unzipped and urinated long and happily against a tree. He then turned and walked back to his bike with a lively cadence.

A man on a BMW motorcycle had appeared from seemingly nowhere. Samos kept up his happy camper attitude, but his ears were perked. The motorcycle man obviously knew the couple because he was conducting an animated, somewhat heated conversation with the husband in the language Samos could not identify. It looked as though the man would not be leaving for a while, so Samos got on his bike and pedalled away. That's when he noticed that he had grown a tail; motorcycle man followed him at a professional distance, not only all the way back to *Las Peñitas*, but also around town. Samos, playing the *ingénue*, gave him a run for his money by circling around town aimlessly for a quarter hour.

While motorcycle man kept a discreet distance, Samos ate a sandwich at two-thirty and went to his room to rest for a couple of hours.

Gazing down from his window, he could just spot Motorcycle Man waiting for him in the shade of a roadside restaurant. He had a sudden attack of nausea and backed away from the window, his forehead suddenly beaded with pearls of cool sweat. He saw an image in the theater of his mind, a file folder dropping down on a desk in some forgotten basement office in a nondescript grey brick building in Foggy Bottom. He turned his face back to the window. "Fuck this. I'm not going to die here," he said.

At half past five, he took everything out of his knapsack except his money, his gold, his gun, his four passports, and his windbreaker. He sprayed his body, face and head generously with insect repellent, put on his cap, shouldered his bag and took a long look around his room. Something cool and steely was growing in his gut, leaving a metallic taste in his mouth, which he ignored.

Samos stepped out of the hotel with the same goofy tourist cadence of the afternoon. Waving through the reception windows at the front desk staff, he got on his bike and pedaled strongly, cruising back to the gas station, hoping that his tail would follow him.

Motorcycle Man did not fail him and followed at a respectful distance.

The sun had set and it was getting dark by the time Samos turned right at the gas station, heading up the small road toward the hamlet of *Ernesto Ché Guevara*. Spotting the motorcycle out of the corner of his eye as it closed in, he accelerated, and when he reached the clearing, he squeezed the brakes, skidded to a stop like a kid, laiythe bike on its side beside the road, and entered the clearing. He placed his knapsack against a tree trunk so that it could be seen from the road, extracted the holstered, silencer-equipped Glock, slung it under his armpit, and climbed the sturdy tree he had peed on in the afternoon.

He did not have to wait long.

Within a few moments, as dusk was deepening, Samos heard the idling, unmistakable put-put of the BMW as Motorcycle Man rode slowly toward his position. When the man spotted the bicycle lying on the ground he cut his engine, dismounted, and took something out of the box behind the seat.

Was it a gun?

It was. Motorcycle Man walked through the clearing with his weapon in his left hand.

Samos squeezed the branch on which he was sitting with his thighs, leaned back against the trunk of the tree to steady himself, and drew his pistol. He took aim and when the man bent down to examine Samos's knapsack, he squeezed the trigger twice, Mossad-style. His first shot missed, but the second hit the man in his shoulder spinning him around like a top and making him drop his gun. Motorcycle Man scrambled to pick up his weapon, but by the time he was able to raise it, Samos was on the ground and shot him twice in the chest.

CHAPTER 63

Palm Station (South Beach), Miami, end of March 1990

The street was full of practically naked young female bodies swirling around in a mad, purposeless melée. On foot, roller skates, and bicycles, and in convertibles, the young, college-aged animals of all kinds and of every sexual orientation were hell-bent on having fun whatever fun may be: booze, sex, weed, or white powder.

Welcome to South Beach during spring break.

The populace was enthralled by the sight of voluptuous young women flaunting their newfound freedom by prancing along Ocean Drive skimpily dressed. Nobody took notice of the middle-aged man on the Betsy Hotel's terrace dressed casually in elegant designer shorts, matching short-sleeved shirt, and Gucci loafers worn without socks, all purchased within the last hour and at great expense at the hotel's clothing shop for gentlemen.

Samos was feeling very hungry and had just ordered breakfast: grapefruit juice, bacon and eggs sunny side up, buttered toast, marmalade, and coffee.

The Betsy, an upscale place favored by the Long Island crowd when slumming it down to Florida for the odd long weekend, was popular because it had a delightful pool on its roof, access to which was strictly limited to registered guests and their invitees. This restriction was carefully enforced without exception for two reasons, the first being that the hotel's owner insisted on it and the second, because the wing adjacent to the pool was a safe house operated by the NSA.

Samos had flown in from Managua the night before, arriving at the safe-house at two a.m., very, very tired, mosquito-bitten with deep scratches all over his arms and legs, the result of his tree climbing adventure. He had gone to bed immediately after signalling his keepers in Washington that he needed an urgent, friendly, and senior debriefing, code for his having important information to be revealed only to someone high-ranking he knew personally. He thought that this might be problematic because he had had no physical interaction with National Reconnaissance Operations Center personnel for the last ten years.

He was finishing his coffee when the hostess told him that the party he had been waiting for had arrived and was waiting for him in his suite. Samos signed his bill, left a five-dollar tip and took the pool lift upstairs. He noted that he did not need to press his floor's button, it was done for him by a fit-looking, hard-eyed young man wearing the hotel's uniform, which included a loose-fitting canvas jacket.

Security had also been doubled on the sixth floor. Instead of one, there were now two male secretaries in his anteroom. He went through and found an elderly man seated in one of the armchairs next to the coffee table.

The man got up and held out his hand. "Hello Tom," he said, causing Samos's gut to twitch in panic. "Remember me? I was Al McIsaac's boss. My name is Richard Grabowski."

"Of course I remember you. I'm just a little shocked. I thought that Prewitt would come down. I'd assumed you had retired years ago."

Grabowski crinkled his eyes with pleasure. "Ah, no. Every time I think about it I break out in hives! I'm a man born to serve. Besides, what else would I do?"

Samos was truly moved and lost for words. Grabowski coming down to debrief him was unprecedented. He tried to place some order around the chaos of the last week, but failed. What the goddamned hell was going on?

"I remember the day very clearly. It was one of the most remarkable days of my professional life. McIsaacs found a way to get you out of bed after the helicopter accident. He tasked you with creating the PEP influencing network idea. I can still see you, your body wasted from the enforced bed rest. Your face . . ." the man stopped and shuddered. He looked around at the other agents in the room, drawing them closer as he pointed his hand at Samos.

"But, this wounded man stood up there in our conference room, like a wraith, like a righteous demon of liberty and he drew a blood line in the sand. There were thirty raw agents in that room and he gave them the stick, you did!"

The younger agents murmured their admiration as Samos blushed and shook Grabowski's outstretched hand. He managed to stammer, "Whatever happened to him?"

"McIsaacs? His wife died four years ago and he retired early a couple of years later when he hit sixty."

Samos was saddened. "He was a decent guy and good to me. Where is he now?"

"He lives in Switzerland, near his daughter." Grabowski saw that Samos was surprised. "His wife was originally from there, didn't you know? When she died his daughter went to live with her grand-parents in Zug and Al followed her."

*

It took Grabowski a couple of hours to astonish Samos into a state of silence and awe as he summarized the activities of his errant agent over the last ten years, culminating in his very recent adventure with the BMW-riding motorcyclist in the sleepy tourist town of *Las Peñitas,* Nicaragua.

Grabowski noticed the agent's complete and utter submission and perplexity and thought to ease his mind.

"When McIsaacs passed you on to Prewitt, I thought I'd maintain a quiet overview of your dispatches just to make sure there was an easy transition. Not that I didn't have faith in Prewitt, he's a good man, but, as you probably gleaned, a desk jockey."

"Doesn't like dusty shoes," muttered Samos.

"Well put," chuckled Grabowski. "In any case, you may have felt adrift, but you never were. There were people in Foggy Bottom who were paying attention."

Samos was still overwhelmed by the senior director's intimate knowledge of his clandestine life. "I just don't know what to say, sir. It's like you've been in my life, my home, my business…" A penny was stirring in the deep recesses of his mind. When he looked at Grabowski's face, the director had a tight, crinkly grin.

"Why did you hire Jaime Balart?" The Director asked,

The penny slipped a little.

"Jamie? Well, he had an impressive resume, CPA from Georgetown, post grad work at McGill." Samos stopped. "McGill?"

"We knew that would catch your eye. Your work was too important to us to let you fly without a net. Balart was the last recruit that Al ever made and he is cut from the same cloth as you and I. Did you guess he was an Argentinian Jew?"

"He always told me he was born in Chile."

Grabowksi nodded. "His legend. His parents were murdered by that dog, General Videla's goons during the Dirty War, for 'progressive activities.' Progressive. They ran a free medical clinic for the poor in *La Boca.*"

"So, you waved him under my nose and I took it, hook, line and sinker," smiled Samos, marvelling inwardly at the subtlety of the spy-craft. "Hell of an accountant as well!"

"He was placed to keep an eye on you, assist you and report to us, just in case."

Samos nodded, understanding so much more.

At that point Grabowski, who seemed tired, suggested they stretch their legs, so they went for a half-hour walk. They crossed Ocean Boulevard and headed north on the

Boardwalk. When they got past 15th Street, Grabowski began speaking again.

"When your car exploded, Balart made contact and waited. When you showed up, there was a team in place to keep an eye on you. In fact, we had eyes on you in *Golfito, Managua,* and *Leòn.*"

"Makes me feel all warm and fuzzy inside."

"On the other hand, I knew that you were probably in a state of shock and needed to work things out for yourself. I didn't expect that comedy with the motorcycle guy."

"It was him or me. But, how he made me, I have no clue. There was no way. I was travelling under my Canadian legend, didn't put a foot wrong."

As they walked, Grabowski seemed content to allow Samos to clear the muddle from his mind.

"I know I'm missing something, but it is just out of reach. I keep on trying to figure out who would profit most from my death. My activities during the past few years have been passive. I did my best to avoid open controversies."

"Passive? Avoiding controversies? Is that what you call it? Those noisy shenanigans with the Hungarian/Mexican woman, Ilona Keszthelyi ?"

Samos was once again shocked into silence, his mouth left ridiculously half-open like a stunned carp. Grabowski was enjoying himself.

"C'mon, Samos! We've had eyes on all the former communist apparatchiks since forever. Especially now since the wall came down. They scurried off like cockroaches when the lights came on, except people like *Peter Lakatos* and his known associates, of course. And, when you wired Prewitt for intelligence on Ilona Keszthelyi, believe me, all the red lights came on and sharp!"

"Caligula," sighed Samos. "So, Ilona? Is she tainted? Was she playing me? You know I agreed to becoming a co-share-holder of her company. And she is pressuring me to take over management of the FEG Group."

"FEG." Just saying the name caused Grabowski's jaw to tighten and twitch. "Yes we know. Hauptmann has been drip-feeding us intel on Lakatos for decades. But then you came along and fucked up everything."

Samos put his hand to his chest in the gesture of total innocence. Grabowksi put his hand on Samos shoulder as they walked.

"Keszthelyi had been content to be blissfully ignorant of Lakatos's fate for decades. That much may be true, with a big 'maybe.' When Lakatos died, I think the intention of Caligula No. 2 was to keep the status quo. Or, maybe, cut the woman in for a few *forints*. No one ever counted on Keszthelyi coming to you for help and then *coming on to you*!

"Kismet," muttered Samos, the very marvel of the inter-secting orbits of fate baffled his mind. "She would not be denied."

"Well, old boy, it takes two to tango and you and Ilona really pissed off Caligula No. 2 big time."

Grabowski turned around and headed back. Samos fol-lowed, as did his entourage: two young men wearing jackets with bulging arm pits.

"There was something about the game that bothered me. Something I could not understand but, I had let it go, along with Ilona Keszthelyi. When I landed in Managua, I just wanted to set a client straight.

"The Canadian, DiMauro."

"Right. But then I realized where I was. I had to go to ground anyway and *Las Peñitas* seemed as good a place as any. I had no idea I would flush Caligula out."

"And you did, didn't you?"

Samos was circumspect. "Maybe."

Grabowski, an astute reader of people, heard the uncertainty in Samos's voice. "You still not sure?"

"How did he make me? How? He had no reason to expect to see me in Nicaragua. As far as Hauptmann was concerned, I had refused to take over the management of FEG. I told him so. There was no threat. So, how did Caligula No. 2 manage to organize a strike against me so fast? In fact, two strikes," Samos wondered.

"With *Doktor* Hauptmann's unintentional or intentional help," said Grabowski. "You're not considering the timeline."

Grabowski led them over to a bench on the boardwalk. The accompanying young men, trying hard to look casual, took up standard defensive positions.

"Lakatos, the original Caligula, who was also one of only two shareholders, dies. Hauptmann informs Caligula No. 2 and starts looking for the other shareholder, Ilona Keszthelyi .

Samos interjected. "He has no choice—the instructions left behind by Lakatos compel him."

Grabowski nodded. "Hauptmann finds Ilona Keszthelyi in Mexico City, but getting her to come to Zurich takes, let's say, a month. Caligula No. 2 had about thirty days to prepare for probable changes, but hoped there wouldn't be any."

Grabowski stopped and turned toward Samos, placing a hand firmly on his shoulder, drawing him to his feet. "And then you turn up with Ilona Keszthelyi at Hauptmann's office and she insists that you take over management. Hauptmann knows you by reputation—an expert on offshore banking and the creative camouflaging of financial assets.

"He joked that I was his 'competition,'" mused Samos.

"And, you were. At least that is how some people might see you. The fact that every stool pigeon in the hotel heard the two of you going at it, hammer and tongs, in three languages, confirmed to the interested parties that you were a united front, and, therefore, a threat. Thereupon, Hauptmann provides this news to Caligula No 2, together with your coordinates and probably a photo."

They crossed Ocean Boulevard and entered the Betsy.

"We believe it's at this juncture that Caligula No. 2 decides on a pre-emptive strike against you. He knows from Hauptmann that you will be heading home in a couple of days." Grabowski and Samos reached the lobby elevators. "Hitting you in Switzerland was too risky, so he sets you up to die when you get back to Panama. He could never have predicted that Maria-Isabel would use your car."

A working lunch, consisting of club sandwiches and beer, had been laid on for them in the suite, which made it easier to discuss matters without having to bother with waiters.

"To summarize," said Grabowski while unwrapping his serviette, "I estimate that Caligula No. 2 had at least a month to plan an attack and then three days to launch it when the time came."

Samos was intrigued, but remained unconvinced. "Maybe. And he would have had a worldwide network of operatives to carry it out, through FEG."

Grabowski nodded. "I have to agree with that, so let's work things backward. Tell me, with the greatest possible detail, what happened after you had shot your man."

"I winged him, right shoulder, slid down the tree, and hit the ground hard, almost dropping my Glock. He was hurt, but not enough because he was reaching for his weapon. By the time I steadied myself, he had retrieved his gun and was raising it up toward me. I moved on him, fired at close range, and hit him twice in the chest. He fell on his back, moaning and bubbling blood, still holding his weapon. I kicked it out of his hand. He was coughing up blood, gasping. I tore open his shirt and saw the blood oozing out of his chest.."

"What make was his gun?"

"I expected it to be a Tokarev, maybe a PSS, but it turned out to be a Makarov."

"Standard Russian army issue. He would have been accustomed to it. They make them at FEG."

"Yes, for NCOs and tank crews." Samos continued: "After ejecting the magazine, I threw the pistol as far into the bush as I could. I went through the guy's pockets—keys, wallet, chewing gum, over a hundred US dollars and a wad of *Cordobas* worth about three cents each. He had a Spanish passport and a Nicaraguan work permit card. I threw the lot into my knapsack, started the BMW, and got the hell out of there."

"How did you get to Miami so fast?" Grabowski was curious. "I was told you got here around two a.m."

"*Las Peñitas* is about 120 kilometers from Managua. It took me an hour and a half's ride on the BMW to get to *Augusto Sandino* airport. Arrived there at around eight-thirty. The daily flight to Miami was leaving at nine p.m., and I bribed my way on it at the last minute, using my Swiss diplomatic passport. We landed at Miami International at one, and I cabbed it here, sent the message to control, and passed out."

Grabowski called for coffee and waited while it was being served.

"Let's review what we know," he said, as the room service waiter left. One of the young men guarding them approached with a file folder and stood while the older man spoke.

Samos understood why Grabowski had been the youngest Assistant Deputy Director ever. He had heard about his razor-sharp analytical mind and elephantine memory. Now, he had his proof.

"You got involved with a Hungarian refugee woman, Ilona Keszthelyi, living in Mexico, whose lover created a business manufacturing weapons *sub rosa* under licence from Kalashnikov."

The agent with the file folder placed photos of Ilona and Lakatos in front of Samos. He also dropped what looked like a microfilm print of a Hungarian licensing agreement between FEG and the Izhevsk Machine-Building Plant for the production of Kalashnikov and other arms.

"The business consists of a Swiss holding company and two manufacturing units, one in Spain and the other in Nicaragua.

The agent placed photos of the exterior of both FEG plants on the table.

"The holding company owns 60 percent of each manufacturing company and an unknown entity, domiciled in Switzerland, but banking in Cyprus, owns the other 40 percent. The FEG holding company is currently owned by you and Ilona Keszthelyi and is run, day to day, by Hauptmann, a Swiss banker. Both of the manufacturing companies are currently under the control of a mysterious man, or woman, known as Caligula No. 2."

Grabowski stopped to sip his espresso. "Have I got the picture right?"

"Yes."

"So let's simplify. We have two camps: the owners who have no control over operations, and Caligula No. 2, who controls operations, but has no ownership." Grabowski gave Samos a radiant smile. "Mr. CPA, with your decades of experience in business, does that make any God damn sense to you?"

Samos shook his head ruefully. The obvious irrationality of the situation came down on his common sense like a heavy, stinging blow.

"Can you imagine under what circumstances such an arrangement *would* make any God damn sense?"

Samos opened his mouth, but his brain had not yet engaged. The answer was there, in the shadows, on the tip of his tongue, but he could not formulate it.

"Come on, *commendatore*! McIsaacs said you had the most subtle mind of all his operatives. What is the only possible answer?"

And then the truth seeped in. A tiny crack in the darkness, split with a blue light.

"Caligula No. 2 *is* the unknown entity that owns 40 percent of both manufacturing companies." Samos looked up at Grabowksi, who sat back, knitting his aged fingers over his stomach, a satisfied grin on his face. "Is that likely?"

"Very," said the older man. "Especially if we imagine that after the attempt to kill you failed, he probably circulated your photo and profile to all FEG concerns worldwide. He could not know you were headed to Managua, but, just like Caligula No. 1, he was uncannily thorough. He might have thought that you had figured out that the bombing of your car was authored by FEG. And, of course, Kiss reports directly to Caligula and would have been in the loop."

"Uncanny," Samos admitted. "And I walked straight into his area of activity, and he had the human assets needed to eliminate me. So, there is no mystery about how a Spaniard got into the mix in Nicaragua. He could have come from FEG Spain."

Grabowski left the table, stretched his legs, and headed for the terrace, removing a slim cigar case from his inside pocket. He held it out to Samos, who accepted the long, thin Cohiba panatella. The two men lit up on the terrace overlooking the busy boulevard below.

"It would be consistent with the profiles we are building of Caligula No. 1 and No. 2 that they would use Spanish security personnel at both facilities, in Nicaragua and in Spain. It's easier to enforce security protocols if all the participants trained in the same place. You never got near Kiss's plant, so you have no idea how big it is or how the entrance is guarded."

"I do have some idea," Samos insisted. "The turn-off to *Ernesto Ché Guevara* is watched closely by the couple who run the garage station at the entrance. They were in constant touch via walkie-talkie every time a vehicle approached. I tried to catch the signals that went back and forth, but, I have to admit, either it was some sort of code language or a regional dialect."

Once again, Samos found himself under Grabowski's amused scrutiny.

"What?"

"Think about it. You just said that you thought the couple at the gas station spoke some strange code or a regional dialect right?" The Director's eyes lit up. "Can you think of a Spanish dialect that may sound like the language these people were using?"

More bright blue lights went on in Samos's mind, nudging aside the darkness. He sighed, exasperated. "Stupid of me. Of course. Basque, northeastern Spain."

"And would you happen to know where the Spanish FEG facility is located?"

"In the Basque country, near Irun." Samos scratched his head, mildly embarrassed. "So you think Caligula may be using Basque security personnel?"

Another sharp and obvious revelation. "No, not just Basque operatives. ETA!"

Grabowski looked at Samos with pity in his eyes. "My friend, I'm afraid that it might be far worse than that. I think that, following a singular, extraordinary long-term plan set in play by Lakatos and now pursued by Caligula No. 2, ETA has somehow become the 40 percent minority owner of the two FEG production facilities."

Samos's face revealed his reluctance to accept this as true.

The Director sighed. "Don't you see? You told me the minority partner never interferes with running the business, never requests meetings or clarification. He is content to be a silent partner because this provides him with the cloak of invisibility a respectable, impersonal, and impenetrable Swiss parent company provides."

"And Caligula No. 2?"

"He's immovable as long as he is in control of operations and, by all the evidence, probably mortally afraid of you."

"But why?"

"Because he now knows about your influence over Ilona Keszthelyi. She wants you to take over the management and he knows how persuasive she can be. He fears that as soon as you take over and find out the complete picture you'll convince Keszthelyi to wind up the operation and cash out, thereby eliminating not only one of ETA's important income sources, but also its access to weapons."

Grabowski continued his musing. "He will go to great lengths to make sure this never happens. You'll see."

Samos prepared himself for the worst. "What you're telling me is that it's now up to me to find him ASAP and then eliminate him."

Grabowski smiled tightly.

"Only if you want to go on living."

"I'll need help. Will you provide it?"

The older man took a long, luxurious puff of his contraband cigar. "What did you have in mind?"

CHAPTER 64

Fort Meade, March 1990

The OPS2A building, the tallest building in the National Security Agency complex and the location of much of the agency's operations directorate, is accessible from the visitor center. A dark glass Rubik's Cube lined with copper sheeting to prevent snooping from the outside, the facility's "Red Corridor" houses non-security operations such as concessions and the drug store. The name refers to the "red badge," which is worn by people without a security clearance. The NSA headquarters includes a cafeteria, a credit union, ticket counters for airlines and entertainment, a barbershop, and a bank. NSA headquarters has its own post office, fire department, and police force.

Samos was given a blue badge, which meant that he could access areas for visitors with low security-clearance as long as he was accompanied by an "orange badge' or higher.

Grabowski's rank – Assistant Deputy Director of Plans and Chief of Division AX – entitled him to a green badge: top security clearance.

Grabowski used optical recognition to open the door of the special elevator that whisked them up to the top floor in Building 2B. Two women and a man, the FEG team, as Grabowski called them, were waiting for them in his spacious office.

"Here is what we have found to date," Jim, the man, reported. "Josephine, our passport expert," he nodded toward the older of the two women, "ran the passport that Samos took off the assassin. It was issued in Madrid and is genuine, but its holder is not. He was born in Syria, real name Hamed Al-Assad, and he acquired the passport when he fled from Damascus, from whom and how, we do not know. Essentially, all he did was substitute his own photograph for that of the original owner."

The younger woman, Elizabeth, picked up the story. "I specialize in satellite surveillance and, following your request, have looked into FEG Nicaragua and FEG Spain. The Nicaraguan installations, situated about five kilometers east-north-east of *Las Peñitas,* are surrounded by dense bush and consist of a machine shop, a warehouse, and a small office building in a clearing. It can be approached on land by a good road, a kilometer long, that connects to Highway 14. It can also be approached by boat on a canal dug through an estuary of a nameless river that seems to be navigable for barges with shallow drafts—less than ten feet. Loading and unloading facilities are at a dock about two kilometers upriver from the sea, visible only from the air. The river widens there to form a small lake. The warehouse is on the river bank. Two barges run up and down the river and out to sea regularly to load and unload material to and from ocean-going vessels anchored offshore. I estimate that the warehouse contains one-hundred thousand square feet of space. The machine shop is somewhat smaller."

Samos nodded. What the woman said squared with some of what he had seen.

Elizabeth continued. "The facility in Spain is substantially larger, a 300,000-square-foot, bunker-looking building in an industrial park in a small community called *Vera de Bidasoa* in Basque country, Northern Spain. It has excellent access by highway, the N-121-A."

Jim took over. "The Spanish FEG not only manufactures weapons, but also leaf springs for cars, trucks, buses, and railway rolling stock, a continuation of the original concern before 60 percent of it was acquired by FEG Switzerland. The two FEG facilities combined have a maximum capacity to produce about 60,000 Kalashnikov AK47 assault rifles a year. This is no small potatoes. Production is constantly sold out."

Samos interrupted. "Who is buying all this stuff?"

"Of course, the FEG Group doesn't produce exclusively AK47s, but other weapons, too, such as pistols, heavy machine guns, and rocket launchers, plus accessories. I am just using the AK47 to illustrate my point. And, for your information, about one million new such weapons are produced every year worldwide and there are close to 70 million floating around five continents already. No wonder it is called the 'Peoples' Gun.'"

"And who and where are FEG's principal clients?"

"In the Middle East, Africa, and South America. I regret to say, its principal client, in addition to ETA, which accounts for about a third of the weaponry manufactured by FEG, is the Quds Force and its affiliates, such as Hezbollah. In this connection it is worthy of note that the Spanish firm, contracted to provide security for both the Nicaraguan and Spanish facilities, is rumored to have ETA connections." Jim stopped talking for a moment, allowing this information to sink in. "But then, who knows what is true and what is false in Basque Country, given the constant turmoil?" he added as an afterthought.

Grabowski was lost, deep in thought, his fingers knitted, supporting his chin. A slowly raised index finger prompted the junior agents to gather their briefing material and leave the room.

"I'm afraid that your situation is far worse than I thought," Grabowski began with carefully measured words. "For you to stay alive, we must immediately find out the identity of Caligula No. 2, neutralize him, and then wind the FEG Group up." Grabowski was dead serious. "And for this, we need not only your cooperation, Samos, but that of Dr. Hauptmann and Ilona." Samos saw that the Director felt ill at ease about having to continue. "To complicate matters, I must tell you that we cannot assist you much longer because your case is borderline. It falls outside our remit."

Samos was shocked. "I don't understand."

"The NSA is not the police. Now that we have identified the probable reason for your having been targeted, we must decide whether the FEG problem is worthy of further attention by us. We are inundated with situations similar to yours and our resources are stretched to the limit. Therefore, bureaucratic caution dictates that we now thank you for having drawn our attention to the FEG Group, and kick the can farther down the road by passing it to the CIA."

Grabowski rose and began to pace, putting his hands into his pants pockets. "As for you, the best we can do is suggest that you seek personal attention and protection from the Panamanian police where the crime, the murder of your partner, took place. I understand that, due to the financial services you render, you have some status with the officer class in the country."

Incensed, Samos, who could not believe his ears, rose to his feet, about to interrupt vehemently. Grabowski held up his hand to stop him.

"Tom Karas, the man who worked for Division AX, and for whom we were responsible, is officially dead. Alexander Samos, on the other hand, reports informally, and on a voluntary basis, to NROC, the National Resettlement Operations Center."

"If DAX wants nothing to do with me, how come you hauled ass down to Florida to see me?"

Grabowski smiled, his lips parted, as he looked at the floor.

"Because you were partly my creation and definitely our best advisor, and because you continued serving in your new capacity as PEP handler for, let's see, ten additional years."

"What's next?" Samos asked, totally lost, with fear start-ing to gnaw at his loins. His mind raced as myriad survival strategies flooded in.

Grabowski sensed it. "Don't worry. I have a plan—admit-tedly risky, but definitely worth trying."

"Which is?"

"Ever since you sent out your SOS to your handlers at NROC, we've been monitoring your phone at home and at your office. We noted two items of interest. One, your second in command, Jaime Balart, is, for the time being, doing very well at managing the crisis created by your absence. So your business seems to be in good hands."

"Nice to know, but I've only been away for about ten days."

"Which brings me to my second point. Ilona Rodriguez keeps calling your home number as well as your office daily. She is worried about you. You should invite her to Zurich under the pretext that you are reconsidering your decision about not taking over from Caligula and that you would welcome the opportunity to talk this over with her in the presence of Dr. Hauptmann."

"Why there?"

"I believe Caligula has her under surveillance and will come out of hiding to find out what she's up to."

"Why?"

"She's the real owner of FEG Switzerland, and she will not act without you. As I told you, Caligula No. 2 fears that the two of you, together, will remove him from his job, or at least make changes to how the FEG Group is operated, thereby affecting his control of its activities. Having you and her in

Switzerland together will encourage him either to kidnap or kill both of you simultaneously."

"Charming, but how will that help him?"

"We suspect that Hauptmann was not perfectly transparent about how Caligula No. 1 set up the corporations. We believe that, in the event of the death of Ilona Rodriguez, total control of FEG falls to Caligula No. 2. Even if this info is not true, at the very least, eliminating you and Rodriguez delays the moment when he might be forced to hand over control of FEG operations."

Samos stalled as he was being led out the door. "So, you're tossing me into the deep like chum for shark bait."

Grabowski smiled and slapped Samos hard on his shoulder, as though to stir him out of his dread. "C'mon, old boy! Don't you know, you still have friends who care about you?"

CHAPTER 65

Washington/Zurich

Grabowski's security detail saw Samos to Dulles International and made sure he safely boarded the daily direct Swissair flight to Zurich that left at six in the evening. Nine hours on board had given him ample time to develop a number of scenarios about how to identify, trap, and kill Caligula No. 2.

None of them was simple enough to be foolproof.

To complicate matters, besides having to worry about Caligula No. 2, Samos also had to deal with the problem of Ilona.

Using a special phone that routed through Argentina, he had telephoned her at a time of day when he guessed she was taking her "break" at the Hotel Geneva.

He was lucky. She had answered on the first ring.

Their conversation had been terse and short. "Ilona, I'm in South America and headed for Switzerland. I want to meet you there as soon as possible."

"Thank God you're all right!" She began to cry. "*Querido,* where are you?"

He had cut her off. "Today is Thursday. Set up an appointment for us. I want you to meet me in *Doktor* Hauptmann's office on Monday at 2 p.m. I will call you tomorrow at the same time, same place to find out your flight number."

She had rebelled. "*Querido,* I can't!"

He cut her off again. "You must. Our lives depend on it." He hung up.

Ten minutes before landing at Kloten, Zurich's airport, the steward had asked him to please gather his belongings. A car would be waiting for him at the foot of the exit stairs. "Be ready to disembark ahead of the other passengers," he had said. Inwardly, Samos thanked Grabowski for this small but kind consideration.

Three men were standing, waiting for him at the Merc limo. One uniformed Swissair employee came forward to take his bag and stow it in the trunk while another slipped behind the wheel and the last opened the rear passenger door.

Samos felt, rather than saw, that someone was already sitting there, waiting for him in the backseat. His instincts kicked in and he was already on his back heel, primed to leap free when a familiar voice boomed, "*Willkommen in die Schweiz, mein Schatz!*"

Samos dared to raise his eyes and, wonder of wonders, sitting there, grinning like the Cheshire cat, sat Al McIsaacs, his old Control.

"You old motherfucker!" cried Samos.

They blew past Arrivals and Immigration and, at the employees' parking lot, the two of them transferred to McIsaacs's Mercedes.

"Finally alone," sighed McIsaacs, winking at his old friend.

"Yes, darling," replied Samos, roaring with laughter, taking in the whole scene. "Why are we travelling in a Mercedes made of heavy steel with bullet-proof glass windows?" he asked.

"It's a company car."

"Company with a capital C?"

"Sort of."

Samos understood. McIsaacs hadn't retired. He had just made a sideways *pirouette*.

The American lived in an elegant hillside chalet in *Meilen*, a wealthy village about twenty kilometers south of Zurich. Initially, it had been the home of a large rural family. Now, however, it was a triplex: a spacious four-bedroom apartment on the ground floor overlooked a beautifully manicured garden with a magnificent view of the Lake of Zurich while, above, there were two small, independent, one-bedroom apartments. It turned out that these were inhabited by two couples, employees of a company called Crypto AG, of which, Samos learned later, McIsaacs was the managing director.

"It's a great arrangement," his host told Samos as they tucked into a sumptuous North American-style brunch of mimosas, cream cheese, bagels, and lox. "Adrian is my chauffeur-gardener-handyman; his wife, Heddi, is our joint housekeeper, who shops, cooks, cleans, and irons for us all. Massimo and Alfredo in the other apartment—both trilingual ex-*carabinieri*—are bodyguards who watch over us and help with the maintenance of computers and electronic equipment."

"When did you go to work for Crypto?"

"In 1986."

"Tell me."

"Let's see." McIsaacs refilled both their mimosa glasses. "Crypto was founded in the 1950s by a couple of Swiss engineers who owned it until about 1970. For obvious reasons of personal security, they kept their proprietorship a secret, controlling the ownership of the company through bearer shares. They pretended to be ordinary management employees. No one knew who owned Crypto AG, not even the senior executives. The reputation of the firm grew through their success with first-generation security and intelligence-gathering programs and algorithms and, in 1970 the CIA and NSA offered to buy the business. The deal fell through because, stupidly, at the last minute, the NSA pulled out."

"Why?"

"The NSA was full of people who were technically brilliant, but struggled to grasp Crypto's potential. They impeded efforts to expand its scope and at times put the program's secrecy in jeopardy with sloppy trade-craft. So the

West-German Intelligence Service, BND, stepped in and snapped up half the company."

McIsaacs began to laugh. "The pissing and moaning about the NSA missing this wonderful opportunity continued until a compromise was reached. The CIA and the Germans agreed that I should take over management to protect the NSA's interests. This was in 1986, the year I retired."

Samos was pleased. He raised his glass to his host. "Bravo."

"With headquarters in *Steinhausen,* about fifteen kilos from here as the crow flies, we are a long-established manufacturer of encryption machines and a wide variety of cipher devices. We employ over 200 people and have offices in Abidjan, Abu Dhabi, Buenos Aires, Kuala Lumpur, and Muscat, and do business throughout the world."

McIsaacs emptied his glass. "I was told that you no longer have high-security clearance." McIsaacs winked and continued. "So, you will have to take it on faith when I tell you that we have been criticized for selling back-doored products to certain intelligence services that enabled the American, British, and German Signals Intelligence Agencies to break the codes used to send encrypted messages via certain machines made by us."

"Really? Is that true?"

"Let us just say that, yes, we have been so criticized."

CHAPTER 66

Zurich, April 1990

On Monday, everybody got up early. Heddi served bacon, eggs, buttered toast, jam, and coffee for the troops, then Samos accompanied McIsaacs and Alfredo to the basement. As they got into one of the three Mercedeses garaged there, Samos noted with approval that they were so identical as to be totally indistinguishable, one from the others—even the license plate numbers of the vehicles were the same.

Samos smiled. He remembered the Sunday nights after a restful weekend, Tom Karas would drive back from the beach at Varadero to Havana and watch Fidel Castro's motorcade of three perfectly identical Oldsmobiles come up from behind and then overtake him at high speed. He never stopped admiring the precision with which Castro's three drivers changed the relative positions of the vehicles in the cavalcade, thereby making it impossible for any would-be assassin to pinpoint with certainty the vehicle in which the *Lider Massimo* found himself.

Alfredo was driving and Samos noted his ruddy complexion and copper-red head of hair, odd for an Italian.

"La mia madre icontrato un montanaro scozzese dopo la guerra e finirono in un matrimonio a colpi d'arma da fuoco. Avevano cinque figli . . . tutti rossi!"

"A red-headed, Scots-Italian," murmured Samos, his eyes wide.

"It means I can stuff my haggis with *pasta e fagioli!*"

They got them to the airport half an hour before Ilona's flight was scheduled to land. He knew his way around Kloten and they found themselves in a position to meet the aircraft just as it started to taxi toward the terminal building. By then, they had a Swissair employee in a car with them who met Ilona as she came down the exit stairs. He drove her to the VIP lounge and they followed her in.

They found her dazed and terrified. She thought that she was being kidnapped. When Samos entered the lounge she let out an ear-piercing shriek and threw herself into his arms to his intense embarrassment and McIsaac's great merriment.

Back at the cottage by eight, Samos briefed McIsaacs about the FEG Group in depth while Ilona rested. After a light lunch, they saddled up and set out for *Doktor* Hauptmann's office. Massimo was driving with Ilona in the back, clinging to Samos as if her life depended on it.

The distance between *Meilen* and *Zurich* is only about fifteen kilometers, but it took them half an hour just to reach the suburbs because traffic was heavy. When they passed the

Eden au Lac Hotel on the *Utoquai*, a five-star luxury establishment in which Samos had had the pleasure of staying several times in the past, he began to feel uneasy. There seemed to be no reason for it, but the feeling intensified when they crossed the lake on the *Quaibrücke* and turned right onto the *Bahnhof Strasse*, leaving the *Berkli Platz* behind them. They headed north and the feeling of an unpleasant *déjà vu* became overpowering.

Massimo drew up in front of the Julius Bär building's main entrance on *Sankt Peter Strasse*. There was a police car parked in front of it.

The uncanny feeling overtook Samos: could *Doktor* Hauptmann be dead?

*

As they entered the lobby, Ilona and Samos were intercepted by a woman who turned out to be the secretary of Dr. Freddi Keller, the bank's Vice Chairman. They were escorted to Keller's office where they found two men waiting: Keller and a tall, severe fellow who introduced himself as Chief Detective Inspector Hans Hunniger of the Zurich Metropolitan Police.

"Forgive me," Keller said, "but I find myself in a very difficult position. I know you are clients of our bank and your account manager is *Doktor* Hauptmann. I know that you had an appointment with him this afternoon and that your names are Ilona Rodriguez and Alejandro Samos. Could you help me by telling me what you wished to discuss with *Doktor* Hauptmann?"

Loud alarm bells went off in Samos's head. Something was very wrong. He was particularly concerned about the presence of Hunniger, who was giving him a nakedly appraising eye.

"This is highly irregular," said Samos, the tension coming into his voice even as he fought to control it. He took a breath. "I know that you, Dr. Keller, are an officer of the bank and, therefore, subject to bank secrets regulations, but the inspector is not. Therefore, with all due respect, please explain his presence here before we proceed."

Keller looked uncomfortable and turned to the policeman for guidance.

The man smiled tightly and became unexpectedly forthcoming "You would be right, Señor Samos, if this were a normal situation, but it is not." He sighed. "A crime may have been committed and I am the investigating detective. I have the legal right and obligation to question persons whom I judge to be potential material witnesses."

Ilona was stunned. "What crime has been committed?"

"*Doktor* Hauptmann did not come to work this morning even though he must have confirmed to his secretary, *Fräulein* Studer, that he was expecting your visit today because she had advised the receptionists on Friday evening, that you would be calling on her boss this afternoon at two. Coincidentally, *Fräulein* Studer did not come to work either today. Nobody took much notice of these two absences until another client of *Doktor* Hauptmann's turned up for *his* appointment at eleven this morning and there was no one to receive him."

The uncanny feeling swept over Samos like a wave. He knew what was coming. He had been there before.

The policeman continued. "Reception telephoned both *Doktor* Hauptmann and *Fräulein* Studer at their respective homes and neither answered. They both live alone, so there were no family members to contact. At eleven-thirty, a clerk was dispatched to the Hauptmann flat at the *Stadthaus Quai,* which is not far from here. The clerk reported back that Hauptmann's domestic answered the door and told him that her employer was not there and that it seemed to her that no one had slept in his bed the night before."

"*Fräulein* Studer" Samos, expecting the worst, was getting impatient.

"She lived in *Uitikon,* a suburb where she had an apartment. She came to work daily by train and had never failed to turn up once during her twenty-odd years of service with the bank. Apparently, she loved her work, and was good at it."

"And she was very devoted to *Doktor* Hauptmann," Keller added fretfully.

"Was?" This from Samos.

Hunniger took a sip of the water from the glass he had been holding while he spoke. "The clerk was told to take a taxi from *Doktor* Hauptmann's place to *Uitikon,* but nobody opened the door at *Fräulein* Studer's flat. The clerk had the presence of mind to ring the doorbell of her next-door neighbor, who had a key to her flat. They entered and found *Fräulein* Studer dead in her bed."

Ilona clapped her hand to her mouth. "Oh my God."

"How?" Samos said curtly.

"No idea yet," answered the inspector, then added: "Will you now please answer Dr. Keller's questions?"

*

The four of them were being served tea and scones in Keller's opulent office. Samos shot a look at Ilona, who had taken a seat in the curve of the sofa, one hand pressed to the side of her face, her eyes filled with worry. His mind clicked through the information he felt he could reveal and that which had to be suppressed. He began at a pace a little slower than his usual decisive mode, vamping for time.

"*Señora Rodriguez* and I are co-owners of a company, the FEG Group, which pays your bank over half a million dollars in fees annually, plus unspecified administrative expenses of another $100,000 a year." Samos gave Keller a hard look. "I suppose you did not know who we were because *Doktor* Hauptmann had not mentioned us to you, following the directives that such knowledge be shared only on a need-to-know basis."

Samos noticed that their host's attitude toward him and Ilona changed visibly when Keller realized that he was speaking with a client of some importance. *So*, thought Samos, *we have established that you are a whore for wealth, Keller, and now we know your price.*

However, being Swiss-German and a bit of a pompous ass, and a man who considered himself well above average importance in his community, Keller continued to display a degree of standoffishness that was almost offensive. He surprised Samos by asking for their passports, which he then handed to Hunniger, then waited silently while the policeman examined them with frustrating thoroughness.

This took about five minutes, which felt like five hours to Ilona, who began to fidget. She looked over to her lover, ready to explode, but Samos gently shook his head and she subsided.

"They seem to be in order," the inspector finally said and returned the passports to their owners.

Relieved, Keller turned to Samos. "Now tell me. How can I be of assistance?" He sounded almost friendly. Samos seized the opportunity to gain more time for himself.

"Under the circumstances, Herr Vice-Chairman, it would perhaps be best if we gave you time to read your files about the FEG Group, then appoint a replacement for *Doktor* Hauptmann with whom I could start working on the FEG documents I wish to inspect."

"This sounds unnecessarily complicated."

Samos stood and unwrapped a bit of stick, and sharpish.

"*Doktor* Keller, read the files." Samos's tone was curt. "And you'll see that your *Doktor* Hauptmann was acting chief financial officer of the Group and, ably assisted by the late *Fräulein* Studer, kept close control of the Group's financial activities. Hauptmann has disappeared and *Fräulein* Studer is dead. And you . . ."

Samos turned abruptly to Inspector Hunniger. "Are standing here, wasting time with questions that have no bearing whatsoever on his possible disappearance!"

Hunniger shot to his feet, ready to object, but Samos had already swung his heavily lidded eyes back to Keller.

"The Group consists of a holding company and two very active manufacturing plants that need constant attention. If you want to keep the Group as a client, you'll have to appoint someone in Hauptmann's stead as CFO—the sooner, the better. Do you understand?"

Keller swallowed hard. "When do you want us to meet again?"

"Not later than the day after tomorrow, at ten in the morning. As you bankers always say, 'time is money.' We need to return to our other business obligations as soon as possible."

Hunniger intervened. "Where do you live, if I may ask?"

"Mrs. Rodriguez, the wife of a Mexican ex-cabinet minister and *very* senior diplomat, lives in Mexico City, where she owns an elegant and popular *patisserie*. I live in Panama City, Panama. I am a CPA and own a company that provides management to over a hundred international offshore companies. "

Keller picked up on that. "Where will you be staying while in Zurich, señor?"

"Probably with friends."

Hunniger didn't like the answer. "Could you be more specific?"

Samos wheeled on him and made a show of his impatience, tempered with a desire for cooperation with authorities.

"Certainly. In *Meilen,* with an old friend, Allan McIsaacs."

The policeman swallowed again. "The managing director of Crypto AG?"

"The very same. Why? Do you know him?"

Hunniger turned to Keller. "*Das ist dann doch eine ganz andere Geschichte.*" He nodded toward the two visitors. "*Aufpassen. Die zwei könten sehr einflussreiche Leute sein.*"

"Well said, Hunniger. Very well said," Samos replied, watching the man's face turn red. "You *should* be very careful. We *are* very influential people."

CHAPTER 67

Zurich, early April 1990

After being driven to the *Hotel Eden au Lac* in the bank's limousine, Samos had to help the somewhat distraught Ilona to check in. He then made the mistake of accompanying her to her room, expecting her to feel exhausted. Clearly, she was not. Some people react to emotional stress by curling up in a ball and weeping. Some pull off their clothes. She attacked him as soon as the *lohndiener* left the room, then, sexually satisfied, fell asleep in his arms.

He felt acutely chagrined. Once again, as so often before in his life, he was behaving like a cad. He recalled the mantra he had adopted in 1945 when he was eleven: love no one, trust no one, mourn no one and nothing, except missed opportunities. He felt the old, comforting chill seep into his being as he kept on repeating the words until he had convinced himself again of the illusion of a man with no illusions, that nothing meant anything, except survival.

He carefully disentangled himself from the sleeping woman, snuck out, and took a taxi to *Meilen,* where he spent the evening with McIsaacs catching up.

*

Tuesday was tough. He returned to Ilona's hotel early to breakfast with her, then spent the morning explaining the facts of his current life. He told her how rotten he felt about not being able to be with Maria-Isabel's family to mourn with them because he feared that Caligula No. 2's people would be there, waiting to kill him. He told her in general terms how close he had gotten to getting killed in *Las Peñitas* and how urgent it was to find out the identity of Caligula No. 2.

"And if you do find him?" Ilona asked, her face an open book.

"I'll have to think about a way to neutralize him, perhaps through the Swiss police, before he has a chance to try killing me again. Or you, for that matter."

Ilona's reaction was predictable: wide-eyed fear, building to hysterical terror that could only be calmed by physical contact. He moved closer to her, putting a comforting arm around her shoulder.

"I'm fairly sure of what his plan is. First, he wants me dead and then, with me out of the picture, he'll find a way to force you to do his bidding."

Ilona was having difficulty managing all the bad news and pulled away from Samos. "Who are you, anyway? And who is McIsaacs and his men? Why are you staying with him and not me?"

"Because being with me exposes you to risk."

"Did you really shoot the man who came after you in *Las Peñitas?* Did you kill many people? Are you an assassin?" Ilona was close to tears. She begged him again and again to stay with her and he finally relented.

*

The Wednesday morning meeting was held in Hauptmann's office with six people in attendance: Keller, his senior secretary, *Frau* Sprüngli, Chief Inspector Hunniger, Ilona, Samos, and Johan Langlois, the senior account manager whom Keller had assigned to replace Hauptmann. Langlois was in his late forties, a London School of Business graduate, fluent in German, English, French, and Spanish, quick of mind and with a good memory. Samos found the man very *sympatico*.

Keller was visibly uncomfortable and abrasive. He led off with bad news. "We have not heard from *Doktor* Hauptmann and don't expect to hear from him in the short term. *Fräulein* Studer is dead and, according to the police," he nodded toward Hunniger, "murdered. Suffocated by someone using her own pillow."

Hunniger picked up the story. "As soon as we established that a crime had been committed, we were forced to follow the protocol dictated by a murder case. "

"Meaning?" Samos asked for the record, but knew well what was to come.

"We started to search for motive and suspect, and we believe that we have found both, but we need affirmation of our beliefs before proceeding further."

The policeman glanced at Samos; his look was not friendly.

"I have spoken to Mr. McIsaacs. He told me very little about you, except that you were a man to be taken very seriously. Given what I know about Mr. McIsaacs, I do not need an interpreter to get his meaning. If I understand correctly, you believe that your life and that of Mrs. Rodriguez *may* be under threat from unknown parties, because of your position as part-owner of CH.FEG.GmbH. Yes?"

Samos showed him a face that was inscrutable behind his heavy, imperiously hooded eyes. The inspector returned to his precis.

"If you believe that you are under threat, would you be good enough to explain why, if you can?"

Samos took a deep breath, unfolded his hands, turned away from the inspector, and fixed Keller as if he had a diamond drill between his eyes.

"No."

The inspector looked up, his mouth coming open in surprise. He was unaccustomed to being spoken to in this manner. Keller leapt in like Nijinsky, pirouetting elegantly.

"If I may, I think what my *client* is saying is that, under our own Banking Secrecy Act, he may not be at liberty to reveal information that might cast an unfavorable—indeed, illegal—light on him, from a Swiss point of view."

Hunniger sat back, tapping his pen on his briefcase. "I see."

Tap-dancing madly, Keller offered an olive branch. "But perhaps our friend can provide us with a little illumination, in the abstract, of course, that might assist our chief inspector?"

Suddenly, Samos was all smiles.

"Well, if it will help," replied Samos, turning to Hunniger. "Once upon a time, there was a highly placed government minister in a former Soviet Bloc country. He was an extremely intelligent and resourceful person with contacts all over the world. This person knew that the winds of change were eventually going to topple his regime and decided to plan for the future. He looked around for a country that had a safe and secure banking system, that respected secrecy above all, a country like Lichtenstein or Monaco. . . ."

It took Samos less than an hour to recount a carefully curated and cautious, "abstract" version of the facts, which named no names, gave no hard facts. He finished with the already-known chapter that had led him and Ilona to became involved with the FEG Group, starting with meeting Ilona at a Christmas dinner and finishing with his leaving an unnamed Central American country.

While he talked Frau Sprüngli, took notes in English. A light working lunch was served at one, during which she typed up her notes. Copies were provided to everyone.

The meeting ended shortly before four o'clock, when Frau Sprüngli announced that the FEG documents of interest were kept in a locked, specially armored filing cabinet for which no key could be found. Similarly, Hauptmann and his secretary's desk drawers were also locked and, therefore, the services of a locksmith were required before any relevant documents could be viewed.

"How about *your* vault?" Samos asked. "Couldn't we have a look at what's in there about FEG?"

Keller bristled. "Not before tomorrow morning when the vault's lock timer opens its main door. Besides, our system requires that account managers keep five years' files in their private office areas before rotating them to the vault."

"So, we are done, I suppose." Samos made his disappointment felt. "Could we meet early morning then?"

"Not before 2 p.m., I'm afraid," came the frosty response from Keller. "The locksmith will need time to do his work, as will I. Under the circumstances, I feel I have to consult with our attorneys with regard to how to proceed from here on."

Here we go, said Samos to himself. The Euro-waltzing has begun. He was caught short. Only fifteen days had passed since Maria-Isabel's death.

CHAPTER 68

Zurich

"Don't think we've been idle this morning, Señor Samos."
It was Thursday afternoon, and, once more, they were in
Hauptmann's office. Langlois sounded preoccupied. "At
the crack of dawn, *Doktor* Keller got a locksmith to work
on the file cabinets and desks in Hauptmann and *Fräulein*
Fischer's offices.

Only four people—Langlois, *Frau* Sprüngli, Ilona, and
Samos—were in attendance.

"And what did you find?" queried Samos

"It's what we *didn't* find is the problem."

"Meaning?"

Langlois consulted his Filofax, reading a note in his
crisp script.

"We could not find the minute book, the shareholders' register, or the share certificate stubs of the FEG

Group. Somebody who knew what he was doing, probably Hauptmann himself, carefully removed all files relevant to Caligula No. 2 and his regime. Emails, copies of instructions to the subsidiaries, and material relating to 'persons of influence,' all gone. Not even the file folders remain."

"How about the quarterly lists showing who is to be paid what?"

"Gone. We searched the archives and the most recent lists we could find were five years old, all pre-Caligula No. 2." Langlois did not conceal his discomfort and Samos's radar went hot. "There is more bad news. Keller and I met with our attorneys yesterday evening. They told him they would like to see documentation proving beyond doubt that you two are indeed the owners of the group."

"That should be easy." Samos was relieved. "The share certificates in the company's safety deposit box have our respective names on them. Let's retrieve them."

Langlois sighed and rose to his feet, his hands thrust into his pants pockets as he began to pace.

"Easier said than done. We inspected the boxes at noon and found that the locks had key stubs in them—that is to say, their keys' blades were in the locks, but their heads had been snapped off. The blades have been epoxied into the locks so that the only way we could access the contents of the box would be by cutting it open with an acetylene torch."

"So?"

"Very risky. The torch's flame would surely ignite whatever paper is in the box. Our share certificates are printed on paper that is unusually flammable. It will cost the bank about ten grand and the possibility of finding nothing but ashes in the box."

Samos began to laugh. "Yan—may I call you Yan? You can call me Alex."

"Of course, Alex."

"You are a man after my own heart, a true banker, always maximizing profit while being super cautious." With this, Samos rose to his feet, assuming an aggressive stance. "But you are dragging your heels and you are taking us for fools! I could not give a rat's ass for your ten grand. Get our boxes in *your* vault, in *your* God damn fucking Swiss bank, opened!"

Ilona cut in, trying to diffuse the situation. "Tell me, based on the documents they have seen up to now, who do your attorneys believe the owners of the FEG Group are?"

"Good question." Langlois handed her a sheet of paper." This is the memo, in German, of course, that Hauptmann sent to the files when somebody called Ilona Keszthelyi started the Swiss FEG company. It names Peter Lakatos and Ilona as having been issued one bearer share each, to be kept in a safety deposit box here at the bank. There is also an unsigned copy of a will in which each of Ilona and Peter leave their respective share to the other should either of them die. Assuming that the shares and the will are in the box and assuming that your maiden name is Keszthelyi, we would construe that you would become the owner of the two shares upon the death of Lakatos."

Ilona sensed victory. "So what's the problem?"

Langlois sighed again, taking a seat. "There are many problems." Samos remained standing, his arms tight at his side, his eyes fixed on the banker's face.

"Such as?"

"We need proof that your maiden name is Keszthelyi. Then we need proof that Peter Lakatos is dead. Then we have to somehow retrieve the two bearer shares and the signed will from the box. Then we have to probate the will. Then we have to give the shares to you to make you the owner. Once you are the rightful owner, you can do what you want: change the signing officer of the company's various bank accounts, retain a new general manager to replace Hauptmann, fire Caligula No. 2, and so on."

Langlois took a deep breath. "But you claim that the bearer shares were changed into nominal ones and that one bears your name and the other Alejandro Samos's. Unfortunately, we have found no documentation evidencing this. In fact, we have no record of what transpired during your last meeting with Hauptmann."

Ilona suddenly changed attitude. The timid woman disappeared and the Hungarian freedom-fighter-refugee emerged. She challenged Langlois. "But the bank does acknowledge that there *was* such a meeting, do you?"

"Yes, because our reception log shows that you and Señor Samos had visited *Doktor* Hauptmann during the early days of March."

Ilona produced two folded sheets of paper from her ample bag. "Well, then, what do you make of these?"

Langlois bent over to peer at the documents while Ilona surreptitiously ran her perfectly formed, delicate baker's hand up the back of Samos's thigh and gently nudged his testicles.

The documents were photocopies on bank stationery of two FEG share certificates, one in the name of Alejandro Samos, the other in the name of Ilona Rodriguez, their date of issuance clearly visible: March 5, 1990.

"Well?" challenged Samos.

Langlois removed his reading glasses. "The locksmith will be here in the morning."

*

Assisted by *Frau* Sprüngli, they spent the remainder of the day familiarizing themselves with the few FEG documents that Hauptmann had missed. It soon became evident that the FEG Group required only a small amount of Hauptmann's time, spent mainly looking after the Group's investment portfolio. He had nothing to do with managing the daily problems of the two manufacturing plants, those being the purview of their two respective managers, with guidance from Caligula No. 2.

"It's clear, right? Hauptmann was only active on the FEG files at the end of each quarter when he had to analyze and report on the financial results of the subsidiaries to Caligula no. 2 and to pay the so-called 'persons of influence,'" Samos remarked to Langlois.

"I quite agree and understand what you are driving at," said the younger man, who, after the morning show-down with Samos, had decided to assume a friendly, let-me-tell-you-about-myself, approach. He did not want to be blamed for the bank losing the FEG account.

"I'm originally a computer geek from Basel. We're French, far more laid back than Zurchers."

Langlois looked around, pretending to verify that they were not being overheard. "In the beginning, this set me back in my career at the bank because the powers that be tended to write me off as a lightweight, a Frenchie, an outsider with no Zurich *gravitas*. Then computerization happened in the late sixties and I received a couple of quick promotions because I was ahead of the curve; I was familiar with electronic record keeping."

"How long have you been with Bär?"

"Over fifteen years."

"So you know your way around the place, I suppose."

"I dare say I do. Question is, what do you want to look at next?"

Samos knew exactly what to ask for. "I'd like to look at the originals of as many lists as possible from Caligula No. 1 & No. 2, dealing with 'persons of influence.' Since the most recent ones we can lay our hands on are five years old, it would be nice if you could arrange for someone to comb through the bank's money transfer records and identify as many relevant FEG transactions as possible."

"In other words: recreate the missing lists. That would be one hell of a job." Langlois was shaking his head. "How many years?"

"At least two."

Frau Sprüngli was dispatched and then reappeared thirty minutes later with an armful of papers.

"Here are five years' worth, including the last list prepared by Caligula No. 1. Sixty sheets."

She gave them to Samos who began leafing through the pile. The reports were in date order, with the most recent on top. For each year there were four reports respectively dated January, April, July, and October. Some sheets had handwritten annotations on them, others the odd small slip or two with numbers stapled to them. In other words the ensemble of documents resembled a dog's breakfast.

Seeing Samos's face twist into a grimace of frustration, Langlois intervened. "It's almost six. Let's reconvene tomorrow at ten."

CHAPTER 69

Zurich

"The police have their methods and I have mine and I'm not going to wait around for them to come up empty. It's not in my nature to put my fate in the hands of others."

Langlois, and *Frau* Sprüngli listened to Samos intently as Ilona kept flipping through the FEG documents.

"It is in all our interests to identify, as quickly as possible, the motive for the number of acts of violence, including your *Fräulein* Fischer's murder, that have taken place during the past three weeks. I am convinced that the information hidden in the FEG documents will lead us to the perpetrators and, maybe, show us a way to neutralize them."

The banker and *Frau* Sprüngli exchanged glances. Samos appealed to them, "To succeed, I need your help."

The Swiss dawdled over their morning coffee and cookies in the small conference room they had established as their own.

Samos continued. "I strongly suspect that the perpetrator is Caligula No. 2. He fears that Ilona Rodrigues, or, *Fräulein Keszthelyi*, the presumptive ultimate owner of the FEG Group, will succeed in convincing me to take over running the Group. Hauptmann probably warned him about that. If such a thing happened, he fears that the Group would either be wound up or sold, which would mean that Caligula No. 2 would lose his job and the Group's clients their arms supplier."

Langlois wasn't convinced. "That might explain the attempt on your life, but not Hauptmann's disappearance or Studer's murder."

"I believe that since the death of Peter Lakatos, Hauptmann and Caligula No. 2 have been in cahoots and that *Fräulein* Studer discovered this. Perhaps she caught her boss rifling through the FEG files prior to his taking them home. When she remonstrated, Hauptmann panicked. He knew that we would be visiting him and dreaded the possibility that she'd talk to us about his duplicity. He called Caligula No. 2, who told him to empty the files and to kill his secretary. Or perhaps Caligula No. 2 came to town and it was him who killed her."

Samos shrugged and went on. "I'm also sure that by the time we are through with looking at bank statements and the like, we will find that the sweet old *Doktor* Hauptmann has helped himself to enough money from FEG on the side to retire in style in, let's say Brazil, a country that has no reciprocal agreement with Switzerland covering criminal extradition."

The banker Langlois considered Samos's conjectures, but shook his head absent-mindedly. When he realized he was being observed he smiled shyly. "Sorry, lost in my own thoughts."

Samos leaned forward. "Care to share them with us?"

"Well, I'm not any kind of policeman, Señor Samos, though I'm beginning to think that your CPA is not the limits of your professional experience," he started, his eyebrows raised at the ersatz Panamanian.

Samos demurred, modestly.

"But it occurs to me that such a series of events assumes spontaneity. Hauptmann may turn out to be a lot of things, but not spontaneous." He shook his head with conviction. "I believe that the whole process, starting with Hauptmann informing Ilona Rodriguez of Peter Lakatos's death, was carefully pre-planned. Things went wrong for Caligula No. 2 and Hauptmann when she brought you along with her."

Samos was taken aback. "Are you suggesting that Hauptmann was planning to eliminate Ilona right from the start?"

"Perhaps not at the very beginning, but after Caligula No. 1's death, yes. He wanted her out of the picture one way or another. They both assumed that she was greedy . . . excuse me, madame," he said shyly, casting a glance at Ilona who brushed aside his reticence. "I think their plans assumed she would have gone for the fast buy-out, which would have made her a comfortable millionairess. If she didn't see it their way, and if everything else failed, they could always have her killed later."

Samos processed it all, looking into the kinky corners for fault lines to the banker's hypothesis.

"Then why the hell did Hauptmann inform her that Lakatos had died in the first place? Why ask her to come to Zurich? Would it not have been easier just to let sleeping dogs lie?" Samos asked, puzzled.

"Hardly a dog, my love," murmured Ilona.

"Meaning?"

"Was Hauptmann not in a position to do the transaction without her knowledge?"

Langlois thought for a moment then searched in a file of clippings. He found what he was looking for, a copy of a tiny "filler" from the *London Times* announcing the death of Peter Lakatos, ex-minister of defence and prominent ex-Hungarian politician. He handed it to Samos.

"No one who didn't care would have noticed this," he went on, "But it was in the *London Times* and disseminated worldwide. Caligula No. 2 and Hauptmann could not risk it coming to the attention of *Señora Rodriguez.*"

Langlois caught the nod to herself, lost in memory.

"So you agree with me that the murder and disappearance are linked to Caligula's and/or Hauptmann's fear of forced change in the way FEG was being run now?"

"Think about it," Langlois continued. "During the last discussion you had with Hauptmann, *Señora Rodriguez,* you were trying to convince *Señor* Samos to take over the management of FEG. Do you understand what that would have meant for the scheme? So, yes, I do agree."

Samos sighed and sat down next to Ilona, addressing her directly. "It follows then that we have no choice. If we don't want to be looking over our shoulders for the rest of our days I must find a way to drag Caligula No. 2 into the light and neutralize him. And maybe that rat Hauptmann, as well."

Ilona reached for Samos's hand and squeezed it.

Frau Sprüngli went to look for more biscuits. When she returned she not only had more biscuits, but also a couple of sheets of fax paper in her hand. These she handed to Samos without a word.

Samos glanced at the top sheet of wire transfers to various accounts and something stirred in the recesses of his memory. It was there for the length of a breath, then, gone. He reached into the shadows, imagined himself back in Hauptmann's office, brought back the sights and the sounds and the textures and then it came back. He held his breath, firming up the details in his mind before addressing the woman.

"During your search of the files and desks did you, by any chance, come across a little book titled *Three Men in a Boat?*

The secretary was about to shake her head no, but then caught herself.

"There is a book, in *Doktor* Hauptmann's desk. It's in the central drawer." She left to fetch it.

Samos turned to the puzzled Langlois. "Every tenth day of the first quarter of the year, that is, April tenth, both Caligulas faxed a list of bank accounts belonging to 'persons of influence' so that Hauptmann could pay their commissions, or incentive payments, if you prefer." He waved the two sheets in his hand at the banker. "Today is the tenth of April, and, *voila,* like clockwork, here is the latest list, right on schedule."

To say that the banker was surprised was a gross understatement. "Business as usual? But I don't understand. If Caligula No. 2 is behind the murder and Hauptmann's disappearance, who is he sending this fax to? He must know that Hauptmann is not here."

Samos stopped Langlois.

"Step by step, my friend." Samos took another look at the faxes.

"OK, but we just concluded that . . ."

Samos interrupted. "Did Hauptmann leave any standing orders to the bank to execute these transfers?"

Langlois shook his head rejecting this notion.

"Impossible! This needs Hauptmann's direct authorization. He would have to sign off on these."

Ilona raised her hand, like a schoolgirl asking for leave to speak.

"Maybe Caligula No. 2 does not know what is happening here. He has no idea so to him, it *is* business as usual?"

Samos turned to Ilona shaking his head. "He knows exactly what is going on here. I think he is not only sending the usual list, but also a message."

Samos walked over to where Langlois was sitting and pointed at the fax. "See these lines of numbers? They are a code. Caligula No. 2 knows that we know how to solve it."

"And do we?"

"Give me a few minutes and I'll tell you yes, or no." Samos walked to the other side of the beautiful rosewood table, cleared a space for himself and then, using the well-used copy of *Three Men in a Boat*, began the laborious work of deciphering the text.

Meanwhile *Frau* Sprüngli and Langlois helped Ilona to review FEG Switzerland's first quarter Financial Statement for the year 1990.

*

Samos was fuming. It had taken him thirty minutes to finish decoding and he was shaking his head in disbelief. The women and Langlois formed a semi-circle around him as he read out the message which was in English. "If you'll pardon the language, ladies, Caligula No 2 is a shameless, selfish, and dangerous bastard who believes he has got me by the balls."

Samos took a moment then read out loud:

"To the errant imposters, as long as no change is made in the protocols covering operations of FEG and as long as no efforts are made to change the ownership of the companies and as long as no attempts are made to identify the author of this message, peace will reign. More instructions will come with second quarter list."

*

By five o'clock, tempers were running high and patience was short, especially Ilona's. She wanted out—to go home to her hotel and rest.

Samos felt frustrated, having spent all afternoon leafing through 'persons of influence' bank account lists and getting nowhere. He was convinced that the solution was to 'follow the money' and he knew that there were only two ways he could develop a trail: one was through monthly salary payments to Caligula No. 2 and the other through quarterly payments to 'persons of influence.'

Frau Sprüngli was also getting tired and nervous. She, too, wanted to go home, so Samos surrendered. He picked up the folder containing Caligula No. 1's lists and carried it over to her where she sat at the late *Fräulein* Studer's desk.

Through frustration or exhaustion, Samos stumbled as he reached out to hand over the file, and the lists slid out of the folder, scattering helter-skelter all around the floor, with one sliding far under the desk. He tried to retrieve it with his foot and partially succeeded. One sheet slid out and when he eased out the other he saw a word, highlighted in yellow, written in the top left corner of the second sheet. He hadn't noticed it before because, when folded over, the first sheet hid the corner of the second.

As the others gathered their things to leave the office, Samos carefully pried the staple open and managed to separate the two sheets with minimal damage. The list in his hand was the last that the original Caligula had worked on. Samos squinted, hesitating. The word *Telflu or Telfiu*—he could not quite make it out because the staple had damaged the paper, but it seemed to be beckoning him as it glimmered in its canary yellow brilliance under the bright office lights.

Frau Sprüngli watched Samos anxiously, her eye on the clock above the door. She picked up the desk stapler, waiting for the two sheets so that she could staple them together again, file them and lock the folder into her desk before going home. Ilona, coat over her arm, stepped up beside Samos. He turned to Ilona and showed her the sheet. "What do you make of this?"

"What am I looking at?" she asked.

Samos pointed with his pinkie, "That word."

She was not wearing her reading glasses, and squinting to see better, read out slowly. "*Telfiu.*"

"What do you think it means?"

She shrugged impatiently. "It's sort of Hungarian, short for '*telefonálni fiunak*'—a reminder to call his son."

The hackles rose on Samos's neck. "You mean to tell me that Lakatos had a son?"

Frau Sprüngli cleared her throat as Ilona took a step back, her eyes fixed on Samos who felt himself getting hot under his collar.

"Yes. He did."

*

Back at the Eden au Lac, they had a monumental row that the hotel staff could not ignore. After a supercilious assistant manager showed up, bowing and scraping and pleading for a return to decorum they calmed down to a low simmer.

"I'm going back to Mexico. I've been away too long as it is and we are getting nowhere except on each other's nerves.

You stay, work things out with the bank and send me what-ever documents I need to sign so that you can run FEG."

Samos was incensed, and almost roared, "I'm not your lackey, Ilona! You are in this as much as I and we need to out Caligula or he will smoke us and bury the ashes. Surely you understand?"

Ilona stood wavering for a moment before breaking down, her face twisted in fear and tears. Samos was at her side in a moment, his arm around her shoulder and his mouth close to her ear. He had regained his *sang froid* and laid it out once again.

"The bank considers you the legal, ultimate, sole-owner of FEG and me your lowly consultant," he whispered. "With you gone, I will have no authority to tell Langlois, or anyone else involved, what to do. Being a careful, conservative and selfish banker, he will initiate absolutely no action to jeopardize the bank's position as administrator of the Group. Do you understand?"

Ilona nodded her head, reaching for a tissue and blowing her nose forcefully. Samos fought his frustration with this glistening ball of chestnut cream, but was having difficulty to retain his cool.

"But, he's such a nice man, Alex," she moaned, her eyes still glistening. "He supports you, he's trying to help."

"But, darling, don't you see? Langlois' sole interest in this complicated affair is to do as little as possible for as long as possible for the half-million dollar fee the Group pays the bank every year."

Ilona became adamant. "So what? I don't care. As long as FEG keeps going I will be making money. If and when the two subsidiaries are forced to close for whatever reason, I will take the company's investment portfolio out of the company and adios!"

"And where will you hide?"

"I won't hide. I will travel around the world in style with or without you and live *la dolce vita,* as the Italians say."

Samos couldn't believe her naiveté. "Ilona, look at the facts. *Fräulein* Fischer was found in her own bed, smothered to death. Hauptmann is AWOL. Do you really believe that Caligula No. 2 would allow you to do this?"

Ilona flared, princess-like. "Why not? He is my employee. He doesn't own the company. I do! He has no legal right to tell me anything."

The ersatz Panamanian began to laugh. "You are acting like a spoiled child, Ilona. Upset because I am telling you to do something you don't want to do. Are you going to hold your breath and start stomping your feet?"

Her anger overpowered her and she did.

Samos stepped over to her, enfolded her in his arms, and held her close. She tried to push him away, but he wouldn't let her. With his lips next to her ear again, he whispered, "Calm down and listen. Caligula No. 2 is not just an employee. He is convinced he is the owner of at least half of FEG or perhaps all of it. To him, you are a ridiculous Hungarian-Mexican baker with lovely big boobs that will rot along with the rest of you in the coffin he will put you in. To Caligula, you are a nothing, an irritation he can safely disrespect because he knows that, at heart, you are a high-class whore with whom he can bargain."

Samos sensed rather than felt a front of ice-cold fury come off his lover and something steely and seething underneath. Before he could react, Ilona lashed out at Samos, catching him square on the side of his face, a stinging, insulting blow. He quickly pinned her arms. He had had enough. She struggled for a moment then the chill dissipated, leaving an odd, torn tension between them. Finally, Ilona released her breath, melting just a bit. Samos looked into her eyes and caught a glimmer of something he had never noticed in her face before: shame. He kissed her on her lips.

"Caligula No. 2 is the son of your ex-lover Peter Lakatos and he believes you have stolen at least half of FEG from him."

That finally got her attention.

CHAPTER 70

Zurich

The late spring breeze felt warm and caressing on their faces as Samos and Ilona drank mimosas and grazed lazily over an elegant brunch on the balcony of their hotel suite. Beneath them, Lake Zurich glittered in the warm sunshine, its surface periodically ruffled by the random squall that propelled a small flotilla of white-sailed boats on their way toward their chosen destinations.

Both felt pleasantly exhausted and still languorous after their night of rude and fervent lovemaking, an event that always followed whenever they made up after one of their heated disagreements.

Ilona felt sexually sated, but was still perturbed by Samos's gift of truth. Samos knew that this and the three mimosas she had drunk while demolishing two poached eggs with

Osetra caviar and toast with coffee would make her more amenable to listening to reason.

Still, he waited while the tension of their banal conversation wound her up. Finally, she blinked.

"It was stupid of me not to think about mentioning *Jozsi*," she volunteered. "But, you need to believe me, Alex, it never occurred to me to consider him a player in this game."

She looked up to note the question on Samos's face.

"Peter's illegitimate son."

Samos sat back, reaching for his coffee. He narrowed his hooded eyes and focused.

"Peter was born in Arad. If you are Hungarian, you know that this city represents a lot of bitterness for us. In 1849, thirteen Hungarian generals were executed there by hanging for having participated in the Hungarian Revolution of 1848."

Ilona reached for one of her little cigars and he fired the tip for her. "Arad had belonged to Hungary, but was ceded to Romania in 1920 after the First World War at the shameful Treaty of Trianon."

She shrugged. "Then in 1940, Hitler came along and gave Transylvania and Arad back to Hungary as compensation for having signed up as an ally."

She held out her glass for more champagne and Samos obliged. "Most people know this, but Lakatos is a Roma name—you know, gypsy. There are many Roma in Romania, most of them living in abject poverty." She knocked back her drink. "But not Peter's family."

"How come?"

"His older brother, Gyula, was, and still is, I believe, an absolutely brilliant musician, a renowned concert violinist, virtuoso of classical and Romani music, in great demand on stage and at parties, able to rent out and run three Romani quartets at the same time." Ilona was well on her way to becoming very tipsy. "He made many recordings and kept his entire family in goulash."

Samos filled her glass. "Peter loved Gyula, but, at the same time he was jealous of his success. So when Gyula agreed to finance Peter's education at *Temesvár* University . . ." Ilona burped discreetly. "Peter did two things to spite him: he joined the young Communists' Party, which was a smart move because this got him started on a career as a successful politician."

Ilona stopped talking.

"And? The second thing?"

"What second thing?"

"The second thing he did to spite Gyula, his brother?"

"Oh, that!" Ilona considered the question gravely, the way inebriated people do. "In his second year in college, he became careless, fucked a young, stupid, local girl, and knocked her up."

"And what did Gyula say to that?"

"Went to see the girl, made a deal, and when the boy-child was born, he adopted him. Gyula was not for abortions, no, *señor*." Ilona's eyes were glazed, almost asleep. "*Jozsi* was a talented guitarist as a youngster and played in one of Gyula's quartets regularly. One day, *Manitas de Plata*, the famous Flamenco guitarist, came to Romania on a tour.

Gyula took *Jozsi* to the concert in Arad and *Jozsi* fell in love with Flamenco music. At age fifteen, he escaped the country and ended up in Spain."

Samos helped his lover to stand up and guided her to her bed. "He even played with *Manitas de Plata* before his drug habit destroyed him," she whispered and fell asleep.

*

It was late afternoon.

They were walking along the Lake of Zurich promenade in front of their hotel, Ilona's idea. She felt she needed the fresh air and to stretch her legs after the four-hour, alcohol-induced slumber to which she had succumbed after brunch.

"His real name is *Baliardo*, but everyone knows him as *Manitas de Plata,* everyone who loves the Flamenco guitar. Do you?"

Samos shrugged, shaking his head.

"He has sold millions of records and he has this Roma charisma. He seduced Chaplin and Brigitte Bardot and even Picasso with his music."

She linked arms with Samos, her red hair blowing in the wind. To Samos, she looked beautiful. "They say that *Manitas* never learned how to read or write. I guess *Jozsi* related to this; he hated school."

"So *Jozsi* met him?"

"Yes, once, when he was thirteen years old."

"So, when did you start seeing Peter?"

Ilona stopped to light a cigarette, taking a lot of time to find her lighter.

"Peter?" she said, finally, lighting her fag. "In 1950. A few years after university. We were mad for each other. but he put limits on our relationship. He was very compartmental-ized, if you know what I mean."

"I think most men are."

Ilona laughed, her lush lips framing her fine white teeth. "I was his mistress, his good-time gal."

"For ten years."

Ilona stopped and turned on Samos, green eyes flashing. "Yes, for ten years," she mused, getting all dreamy. "I was practically his slave. I served as his pretty, charming light-ning rod to stop him from doing or saying something that would not be acceptable to the Party."

Her dander was up, her temper flaring. Frustrated, she began to cry. "For two years, we planned how we would escape and what we would do to make a living in the West. And then, when the opportunity presented itself, he sent me ahead. Alone."

"And never followed up."

"That's not true. He did follow up, but too late. I guess he was scared."

"Of what?"

"The AVO, Hungarian KGB, and the GRU. He knew too much and the AVO, knew that he knew too much. That was the Catch-22 of Communism."

Ilona pulled back a little, giving Samos an appraising look over. "You would not know this, but the Party was always desperate for competent people to make things work. Competent people have to learn things in order to do their job, otherwise, they get disappeared. So, they learn things. They learn how things *really* work and that knowledge is dangerous. The Party cannot have such people, with such knowledge, walking around because the Party knows that people with this knowledge know enough to try to escape. So, after a while, the Party eats them, consumes them. Makes them disappear."

"Which is why Lakatos never tried to escape."

"He knew that the AVO or the GRU would find him and kill him wherever he went."

Samos felt he had to keep on playing the *ingénue*. "Who's the GRU?"

Ilona, paused, running her appraising eyes over Samos's face. "The GRU is the main intelligence service of the Soviet army," she answered finally. "Defence Minister Lakatos had to make nice to them all of the time."

They sat down on a nearby bench and watched the sunset for a while in silence.

"What about this *Jozsi?* What happened to him?"

Ilona sighed and reached for another cigarette.

"It is an interesting story and I think it is true. You see, Gyula's side of the family was never in danger from the Party. They were apolitical and Gyula was famous, and a great source of '*valuta.*'"

"What's that?" Samos asked, hiding his fluent Hungarian behind his lidded eyes.

"Foreign exchange. Gyula and his quartets were generating a lot of foreign currency, so when *Jozsi* skipped, nothing happened."

"When did you last hear about him?"

"*Jozsi?*" Ilona stopped to reflect. "In 1967, in Vienna. I was told by someone—I don't remember who—that he was in the south of France and playing guitar with *Manitas de Plata,* as a sideman."

They walked back to the *Eden au Lac* and had an *apero* at the bar. When the drinks arrived, Samos raised his glass. "To the most exciting and temperamental woman I know."

She blew him a kiss. "What else did you expect of a woman with Roma blood in her veins?"

Samos was surprised. "Come on!"

"I'm serious! My father, *Arpad Keszthelyi,* comes from a so-called pure, old Hungarian family. However, my grandparents on my mother's side were Roma people born in *Temesvár.*"

CHAPTER 71

Zurich, Switzerland, late April

McIsaacs was agitated. He paced back and forth on the quay as Samos watched the lake yachts bob and dip on the incoming waves.

"I don't like it," McIsaacs said finally. "You are being led around by your *schvantz* and you know it!"

Samos shrugged, his heavy-lidded eyes invisible behinds his Ray Bans.

"I don't know what else to do, Al. We are at a stalemate with the bank and Ilona has no desire to wait around any longer till things start to move. She's played out her hand and has her eye on the money."

"Smart woman, "McIsaacs nodded. "At least one of you has their priorities right."

Samos approached his old friend with the humble air of a supplicant. "Will you do this for me, Al? Can you do this?"

McIsaacs shook his head and cuffed Samos on his neck gently. "This is going to cost a ton and I can only write off so much as company R&D."

"I've got money."

"Which you will need for your very long and hemorrhoid-bound old age!"

Samos chuckled and stepped closer to McIsaacs. "Will you do it?"

McIsaacs would not meet his eyes and spoke in a very low voice. "We can get you away from here. The total *WHITEWASH*: new name, new legend, new passport. It will come straight from the agency, I still have those connections. You do not have to go head to head with this fuck."

Samos sighed and made a play of considering this sage advice and the over-generous offer.

"He'll find me. No matter where I go. He will find me. He was suckled on spycraft. It's first nature to him. He'll find a way. The weak spot, the incautious moment, a reckless glance, and he'll be there and I'll be nowhere."

McIsaacs stopped the bullshit and nodded gravely in agreement. He raised his eyes to rest with affection, maybe even love, on Samos's face.

"Will you do it, Al?"

BOOK THREE

CHAPTER 72

Biarritz, April 1990

GRU Captain *Jozsi Shlesar Lakatos* was slowly but surely going out of his mind. His world was crumbling around him, dragging him into hell. Chaos reigned and disaster occurred every time he attempted to solve one of his many problems. Even his on-and-off girlfriend was giving him serious grief.

When his father, Peter Lakatos died the previous December, *Jozsi* had tried mightily to resist, but had been unable to duck out of inheriting the Caligula role his father had played so successfully and profitably for two decades. There were reasons: one, he had been guilted into helping his father during the old man's last years and was therefore familiar with the minute details of the FEG operations; and, two, the GRU Directorate in which he was secretly serving had experienced serious shortages of qualified manpower for the two years prior to the dissolution of the Soviet Bloc. There was no one else to play the part.

The Soviet Union was coming apart at the seams, its satellite states bailing one after another—East Germany, Hungary, Czechoslovakia.

Ilona had not lied, exactly. She had just not told the whole truth, but what she did tell was the truth, and nothing but the truth. Captain *Jozsi Shlesar Lakatos* was born in Transylvania, to be precise, in the city of *Arad*, and was therefore not a Russian. He had been recruited into the GRU as a result of a series of extraordinarily, almost unbelievably fortuitous circumstances.

Jozsi was the illegitimate son of Peter Lakatos, the Hungarian minister of national defence in the government that came to power the year after the 1956 Hungarian Revolution. Adopted by his uncle Gyula, a world-famous Romani violin virtuoso, *Jozsi*, by age nine, was discovered to be a musical child prodigy himself, and played guitar in his uncle's quartets. At the age of fifteen, he ran away from home to join *Manitas de Plata*, the famous Flamenco guitarist, and bummed all over Europe with the man's remarkably popular Flamenco ensemble. In the process, by the time he was eighteen, he learned to speak and write fluently in his mother-tongue Hungarian, plus English, French, Spanish, Russian, and a smattering of German.

He came to the GRU's attention during a visit of *Manitas de Plata's* 1986 tour of Russia, where *Jozsi*, to both of their great surprise, was reunited with his estranged biological father, Peter Lakatos, who was vacationing in Odessa as the guest of the Soviet army's high command.

The GRU, always on the lookout for talent, became enthralled with the opportunities *Jozsi* seemed to offer: language skills, travel for which his lifestyle provided a perfect cover, and unquestioned loyalty through family connections. When the recruiting officers managed to arrange an interview, they discovered another facet to this potential gem of a mole. *Jozsi* had recently become the lover of *Dolores Yoya*, a leader of ETA, the terrorist Basque separatist movement.

The Russians approached Peter Lakatos and asked that he try to convince his son to become a GRU asset. The older Lakatos was not thrilled by the idea, but his pure steel mind was already ticking over like a cipher machine, calculating the advantages. For one, recruiting *Jozsi* might solve the problem of who would replace him as Caligula, since his forfeiture of that role was inevitable.

After a brief training period, disguised as a stay in a cozy drug rehabilitation center, *Jozsi* was commissioned as captain and assigned three remits: helping his father in his work as Caligula and managing the secret slush funds; paying and servicing the twelve-person network of GRU informers in southern France and northern Spain; and reporting on the inside structure and activities of ETA, the Spanish terror group that the GRU supported to a significant extent.

Jozsi enjoyed his *sub rosa* job and the regular money he derived from it. As a further incentive, his father split his $40,000 monthly emolument from FEG with him. In a short time, *Jozsi* went from a sweaty knave of a flamenco sideman to a polished, confident young playboy.

All went well for a couple of years and then his father died in December of 1989. Before *Jozsi* took over definitively as Caligula No. 2, there was the obligatory *post mortem* audit of the FEG finances, during which it was discovered that the Swiss banker, Dr. Hauptmann, was stealing from FEG. *Jozsi* admonished him. Hauptmann protested that the detected, unauthorized payments to fictitious 'persons of influence' were the result of a clerical error on the part of his secretary, *Fräulein* Studer

Jozsi realized too late that remonstrating with Hauptmann had been a mistake. The banker had moved immediately to protect his indispensability by contacting FEG's second shareholder, a person whose identity *Jozsi* did not know.

The woman, a buxom Hungarian-Mexican baker, turned up in Zurich, dragging along her hapless boyfriend.

Jozsi took action. After some perfunctory inquiries into the identify of *Alejandro Samos* and a briefing from Hauptmann, *Jozsi* decided he needed the boyfriend out of the way in order to frighten the second shareholder into compliance. *Jozsi's* GRU handler, an old Cold-Warrior by the name of *Botvinik,* arranged for the boyfriend to be killed, but the attempt went wrong, as did a second attempt.

It was then that *Jozsi* found out two things that shook him profoundly: to start with, the second shareholder of FEG was not simply a boisterous, sexually hyperactive, frivolous *női pék,* but rather his own estranged biological mother, and, that the woman's boyfriend was clearly not the harmless

Latin Lothario he appeared to be, at least, not according to GRU intelligence. The very idea of Samos worked its way under the mantel of his consciousness, where it lay there, vexing him, provoking him to end this affliction.

There was no way out.

He desperately needed time to develop a strategy by which he would gain sole ownership of FEG for the GRU so that he could put to right everything that had gotten messed up. And the first step was turning Alexander Samos into a jar of ashes.

CHAPTER 73

Panama City, late April 1990

Samos saw Ilona off at the Zurich airport the next morning. There were no tears, no hot, wet kisses. A very wifely embrace and a promise to meet up as soon as possible in Mexico City. She started for the gate and then stopped as though suddenly remembering something very important. She walked back smartly.

"You will not do anything, will you?"

"About?"

Ilona ran an appraising eye over her lover once more, measuring, assessing. She picked her Hungarian words carefully.

"Hagyjuk abba ezt a kis komédiát. Elbűvölő, és igen titokzatos megjelenést kölcsönzött neked, de ötven méterről érzem a gulyás illatát."

Samos saw that it was pointless to go on pretending, but he did so anyway, out of spite.

"Sorry, my love. You lapsed into Hungarian."

Ilona smiled and sighed, clicking her tongue as an admonishment. She moved closer to Samos, her lips near his.

"I care only for the money. Do you understand? If I can have you and the money then I am very happy. If I can only have the money . . . I am very happy. Do we understand each other?"

"Always."

"So, you will not do anything, will you, my love?"

Samos stepped even closer, his hands now on her arms like a vice. "I won't put on a blindfold for anyone. Certainly not that *pissant little bastard that dribbled out of his dead father's cock. He failed to get me, twice*! And, trust me, the third time's not a charm. And if that costs you, your 'very happiness,' fuck you." Samos kissed her hard on the lips and then pulled away. "My love."

Samos released the sweet-faced baker, pushing her slightly toward the boarding gate. When she turned back to look at him, he saw that his message had been received. Fear was the spur.

*

When he stepped into his apartment in Panama, he was gratified to see that his return orders had been carried out to the letter. His second in command and NSA minder, Jaime Balart, had arranged for him to be met at the airport by a huge side of lean, angry beef named Oswaldo, a discreetly-armed off-duty federal policeman who would be part of a trio working eight-hour shifts as his chauffeurs, body-guards, major-domos.

Now inside his flat, he could see that the place had been cleaned and was spotless. The fridge had been emptied out and restocked with his favorite foods. Balart had updated his home office computer so that he could access the company network and catch up on all the clients.

A small desk and comfortable chair had been set up just inside his door in the spacious foyer. This would be the command center for the security shifts. They had standing instructions to help themselves to whatever they wanted to eat and access to the guest bathroom. This was costing Samos a fortune, but all of the costs had been defrayed. A small amount was being written off as legitimate business security. Another part would eventually be reimbursed by Roberto Mauro, partly out of gratitude for settling his business with Interpol, and partly as a new commission on his ongoing gold exchange business. As long as Maria-Isabel was alive, he didn't feel right taking a commission for introducing the two. Now, things were different and business was business.

The lion's share of his new security costs were being paid directly by the management of the building. Both he and Maria-Isabel's family had launched multi-million-dollar lawsuits against the building owners. The police inquiry, headed up by Samos's good friend, Police Lieutenant Carlos Del Santo, had revealed several severe and inexcusable lapses in the building's security systems. CCTV cameras had been broken and not repaired, security guards had phoned in sick the morning of the bombing, the private garage had been left unattended for several hours before the explosion.

The Rodríguezes were in mourning, but some members were rubbing their hands at the thought of the millions at stake.

Jaime Balart had confirmed that, following the bombing, several long-term residents and companies had left the building and the owners had filed an eviction notice on Samos on both the flat and the office space. *Chutzpah*, thought Samos, smiling.

Samos was divided. Of course he wanted to punish the guilty and negligent but he knew from his training that no amount of security, no number of working CCTV cameras would have stopped Caligula No. 2 from the attempt on his life.

One of his first meetings after his return was with the building's owners. He made things simple for them; doubling down, he took the notice of eviction and tore it up in their faces. He then showed them a sheet of expenses that he demanded they assume, most of it for his security detail and the rent on his commercial space for the next ten years and a substantial lump sum for "loss of affection" caused by the death of Maria-Isabel. When they protested, Samos waved a copy of their own insurance policy under their noses, the pertinent liability clauses highlighted for their convenience. He also reminded them that fully a quarter of the commercial leases in the compound were due to his direct influence and he had a file of commission letters from the building administration to back this up.

"You're covered for my demands and for the Rodríguezes. Pay."

Samos had some hard decisions to make and first among them was how to restructure his business. Balart was a godsend and had held down the fort but, as Grabowski had intimated, his loyalties were divided and, going forward, Samos needed absolute blind loyalty. In any case, Balart could be pulled away by Foggy Bottom with very little "by your leave, sir" and Samos could not have that.

This meant that he had to find a partner and fast, qualified enough to take over from him in case he got even more involved than he already was with the Ilona-FEG situation. Then there was the problem of the venerable and venal Rodríguez family, and last, but not least, he had to deal with the existential threat posed by Caligula No. 2.

The Rodríguezes had always considered him an outsider, a *parvenu*. They tolerated him because he was somewhat influential, but principally because of his relationship with a favorite member of the family. With Maria-Isabel gone, there was only her sister, Elvira, left to proselytize for him. And her voice was feeble because she was involved with yet another outsider, Longhurst, even though the man was the scion of an affluent and prominent family.

Surprisingly and somewhat miraculously, the Rodriguez family, by way of shameless nepotism and through its connections with the Ruling Party, managed to arrange that Elvira succeed Maria-Isabel as commercial director at the mint, which meant that Mauro's business gained a new lease on life. And this was important because Elvira also inherited M-I's share of the jewelry business.

Samos set to work on Longhurst, both of them lonesome widower polecats- in-waiting, for who knows what. The American, whose scheduled betrothal had to be postponed because of Maria-Isabel's death, needed continued support in his quest for Elvira's hand. As for Samos, he was very much in limbo; everything depended on how the Ilona-FEG situation got resolved, but that did not mean that he was idle.

Of course Samos always had ulterior motives. Having an ex-Treasury man like Longhurst in his orbit meant that he was a less attractive and a more forbidding target for Caligula No. 2. As long as he was close to Longhurst, people who might be tempted by a lucrative "contract" would think twice about attempting anything.

After sketching out the general terms with Longhurst, Samos negotiated a deal involving his masters in Washington whereby the American would retire from his career with the Treasury Department, give up his senior security clearance, and sign on as general manager of the consultancy with Samos remaining as CEO and PR person. Longhurst and Balart would be doing the heavy day-to-day lifting. Longhurst liked the idea for a number of reasons. He was fed up with playing international policeman in a bureaucracy that did not fully appreciate his talents and where his earning potential was limited. Furthermore, the constant travelling his job demanded was getting him down. It made him feel even lonelier than he already was.

Which meant that he happily accepted Samos's offer and was looking forward to making his home in Panama with Elvira, away from the corrosive influence that he feared the Rodríguezes might try to exert over his married life. It wasn't all wine and roses. To everyone's great regret and true to her reputation in the family as the "second-rate sister," Elvira whined and bitched about her onerous responsibilities at the mint until, after only a few months, she gave up her sinecure. On the advice from Samos, she ceded her shares in the jewelry business to Mauro, who became sole owner.

It had taken Samos nine months of negotiations on all fronts to get some measure of security and stability back into his life and he relished it. When everything finally came together, those involved were so pleased that they jointly arranged for a splendid gift: one of Mauro's remaining gold bars.

Meanwhile, Samos had to survive the Ilona-FEG situation, and to restructure his own finances, as well. He was wealthy, but far from rich, a situation that his successful play against the owners of his building had improved, but much of that success would be eaten up by the cost of the brief he had handed McIsaacs upon leaving Zurich. So, one step forward, two steps back, the old routine.

The Panama business paid him a handsome annual dividend, ample to live well on as a fashionable widower. Of course, he would have to reduce that for the time being while Longhurst found his footing and started producing enough new business to cover *his* salary. But with Longhurst as a junior partner, the business would be worth more than its present value, which Samos estimated to be close to two million bucks. Then there was his luxurious apartment and the premises his office occupied in the same building, choice real estate valued at about a million and a half, should he ever decide to sell out.

'Add to this, young man,' he silently egged himself on to keep his chin up, 'about three million dollars' worth of gold, plus one and three-quarter million dollars in market-able securities accumulated during the last decade or two, for a total *tangible* net worth of between $6 million and $6.5 million'.

But he had started off with $5 million, he reminded himself. He realized with a gut-churning shock that all he had achieved financially during the last two decades was to live high off the hog and convert the money he had initially received from the Veterans Affairs charity—part of the pro-ceeds of his life insurance policy—into gold, real estate, and stocks and bonds, give or take a million dollars or so.

Not a stellar performance by any means, he mused as he faced turning fifty-seven this year. He berated himself mer-cilessly. Where is the big score? The pay-off, for a life . . . no—two lives, Karas and Samos, lived almost constantly on the edge of disaster!

In the year that followed, as Longhurst found his business footing and Samos withdrew considerably from public life, he had plenty of time for such introspection, a novel way for him to pass the time as he waited for the results of McIsaacs's research. A year, twelve months that had profoundly changed his circumstances, again. A year of change and stock-taking, of profound, uncomfortable brutal self-examination, healing, and renewal. So much had changed in his two lives. What had not changed was the hurt and shame he still felt about the wrongdoings and missed opportunities of his past. That pain was like a wicked vintage that only grew more bitter, sour, and astringent with every passing moment.

He thought about Disda, taking that path once again into the past, retracing the steps that led to their separation and painfully regretting the harm he had caused her.

He thought of all the women he had known and had kept at a distance, betraying their love and affection, sinning the great sin of refusal and denial.

And he was haunted, almost every night, by the shameful memory of the way he had ceased to love and respect his parents. This new awareness ached in a way he had never known before. He was humbled and humiliated.

He had often thought about this loss of affection. Was it his fault or theirs? They had seldom spoken about their ancestors; his father was especially reluctant to talk about his predecessors. There was no reason to wonder. They had kept the fact that they were converted Jews a secret from young Samos. He was almost ten years old when he finally discovered why his father had never appeared naked in front of him. He was circumcised while his son was not. A silly secret, unworthy of the family. A kitsch parody of a Greek tragedy, and so unnecessary.

Neither of his parents had siblings, nor did his grandparents, so there existed no model of family togetherness to imitate. A reversed, fun-house mirror image of the

Rodriguezes and their cloying attachment to family, blood, and honor. The sad truth was that his parents had little knowledge of parenting and Samos was not mature enough to understand this. In any case, as a child, he seldom saw his parents, the governesses looked after the daily child-caring chores during the first decade of his life.

There were seldom hugs from his mother and almost none from his father, just that constant, hollow admonition: "always first at everything."

Perhaps, if his parents had been more forthcoming about his ancestry after the war and he had been more inquisitive about his family roots, things would have been different, but more likely, it was too late. But by then, traumatized as he was, he had no interest in anything other than physical and mental self-survival at all cost.

And now there was the new hurt, a hurt he kept trying to ignore, but that hounded him during his sleeping hours, how he had cheated on Maria-Isabel and how, though unintentionally, he had been the cause of her death. At least, he did something about keeping her and her family's reputations free of blemish, he reflected, recalling the Longhurst-Mauro near scandal.

Twelve months of auditing the personal and the professional man, and arriving at no answers to the question of who was Alejandro Samos? A year of never getting close to something he could resolve and lay to rest. His journey had been a pilgrimage through a land of temptation and upheaval, followed by *entr'actes* of dissipation and Epicurean indulgence. What was the answer?

In the long term, it would not be Samos who decided whether or not the journey has been worth the shoe leather. In the short term, the answer lay entirely on how he resolved the Ilona-FEG dossier. Double or nothing, Samos. And all he had to do to see how this tragic comedy played out, was to stay alive.

CHAPTER 74

Meilen, late April 1991

It moved Samos deeply how good it felt to see his old friend McIsaacs again. No wonder. The man was the only remaining link he had to his Tom Karas past.

"So what did the brilliant Panamanian authorities do about finding the people who had wanted to blow you up?" McIsaacs asked, all business. Time was short and they had a lot of catching up to do.

"My old buddy and client Police Lieutenant Carlos Del Santo made a good show of calling me in and spent a whole day asking leading questions like, Why did I run away? Did I have any known enemies? Did I think the situation had political overtones? You know, the standard stuff to placate the press."

"And what did you say?"

Samos laughed and took a pull of his beer, a blond *Unser Bier* the Swiss favor. "I told them what they wanted to hear. That the attempt on my life was the work of an anti-US local group that wanted to protest American dependence by attacking soft targets that were pro-US."

"And?"

"As Del Santo predicted, they bought it. In fact, they trumpeted about it in the press and then put it to bed forever."

"What about the rest of your woes?"

"Well, Del Santo arranged for my round-the-clock security so, at least, I breathed a little easier. Maria-Isabel's simple-minded sister, Elvira, married Longhurst last June."

"We heard about that," interrupted McIsaacs. "Foggy Bottom was practically abuzz! A straight man like Longhurst up to his neck in Mexican family compact."

Samos smiled and shrugged. "Apparently, Longhurst never knew one could have sex with the lights on."

McIsaacs laughed, almost spitting his beer up through his nose. "Timed that one perfectly, you bastard!"

Samos smiled again and then got a little quiet. "We buried Maria-Isabel in the family crypt. The Rodríguezes ostracized me ostentatiously. Petty, vulgar shits."

McIsaacs nodded, commiserating. "And the fabulous Ilona Keszthelyi?"

"Caught between a rock and a hard thing. Dear old Uncle Octavio is a problem. He certainly does not like me and especially not Ilona's frequent trips to Panama 'on business.'"

*

Heddi brought them roast beef sandwiches and more beer. It felt good to be spoiled in a family-like atmosphere and Samos luxuriated in the calm and safety McIsaacs's home provided.

McIsaacs waited until his guest finished eating then brought up a touchy subject. "You know you'll always be welcome in my house, my friend, but I have to ask you again: who will pay for the expenses Crypto has been incurring on your behalf for the research my employees have spent on the FEG dossier?"

"I told you, Al, I will," Samos said without hesitation.

"It's going to be a chunk of change, old pal. Industrial level. And who will pay *you*, if you don't mind my asking?"

"I guess Ilona will, in the end, though I must admit that our fee arrangement is rather unorthodox."

"Oh, yeah?"

"Once all the legal chain-of-title bullshit is over, I can trigger a shotgun clause we agreed to. And, once the fun and games with Caligula No. 2 are resolved, I'll exercise it and Ilona will buy my share in FEG for $1 million, plus expenses."

"Resolved," McIsaacs repeated, wincing. "You do know that trusting her is risky, don't you?"

"Acceptable risk."

McIsaacs winced again and then stood, moving away from the table. He turned back to Samos, who was still seated. "Who do you think Caligula No. 2 is?"

"From my point of view, either Peter Lakatos's bastard son *Jozsi* or the good *Doktor* Hauptmann."

McIsaacs pondered Samos's answer for a long time, then nodded. "You may be right. Peter Lakatos*'s* bastard son. And *Jozsi's* mother?"

"No idea. Ilona said she's a woman Lakatos knocked up at *Temesvár* University when both of them were very young."

The American looked at his erstwhile *protégé* with great sympathy. When he spoke again his voice was barely a whisper. "That's true," he said. He then asked softly, "Do you know where Ilona Keszthelyi went to school?"

It took maybe a micro second longer than it should have, but as the fog cleared, Samos was rendered speechless. How could he have been so stupid as to miss seeing the forest for the trees? Of course Ilona was *Jozsi's* mother. If that was the case, she must have known where he was, how to contact him. If he was Caligula No. 2, why did she not simply contact him and invite him over to Zurich following Lakatos's death? Why this charade? Why involve him in the FEG dossier in the first place? Why the two attempts to kill him? He shook his head, trying to get rid of the cobwebs that were affecting his brain.

"So that means *Jozsi* is not Caligula No. 2 and, therefore, it must be Hauptmann."

McIsaacs remained silent, staring at his old recruit. He seemed not to be in agreement and Samos grew impatient. "For Christ's sake, Al, say something!"

McIsaacs held up his hand, a signature gesture, to stop him from continuing, then got up and left the room. Samos fretted, but remained seated, waiting. McIsaacs returned within minutes with a thick file in his hand, which he placed on the table and opened with a flourish.

"You were partially right when you said that *Jozsi* was not Caligula No. 2, but wrong when you concluded that, therefore, it must be Hauptmann. It's far more complicated than that. Neither of them is the real Caligula No. 2—they have merely acted as if they were."

Samos was totally lost. "What the bloody hell does that mean?"

"Simply this. When you asked me a year ago to start following the money, I did. You also mentioned an insignificant detail that I thought was a little oblique, but, out of my respect for your instincts, I considered it, as well. Do you remember?"

Samos thought out loud and then seized on it. "The $5,000?"

"The bloody $10,000. It was in your notes on your meetings with Hauptmann. He spilled it. The origin of the $5,000 Lakatos used in 1985 to start FEG. The $5,000 Ilona *Keszthelyi*, Lakatos's good-time girl, carried in her underwear, next to her fragrant minge, across the border right up to Hauptmann's *Julius Bär Bank*."

McIsaacs drew out several Soviet-era accounting ledger sheets from the file folder and lay them down in front of Samos with a flourish.

"Well, it came from the GRU. Lakatos, in addition to being Hungarian minister of defence, was a GRU asset who created and ran FEG as instructed by the Glavnoje Razvedyvatel'noje Upravlenije."

McIsaacs sat down facing Samos and referred to the documents compiled in the Crypto folder.

"Lakatos asked his lover, Ilona, to organize FEG Switzerland, which she did, following his instructions to the letter. The story about the two original bearer shares was a fiction intended to put the *Julius Bär Bank* to sleep. Lakatos never intended to keep Ilona involved in the FEG business. Because of his genius and connections, the operation became a resounding success from every point of view: safety, security, money generation, 'legal' arms manufacturing, and further illegal market penetration of the international arms industry."

McIsaacs drew out a CIA report on GRU activity in Western Europe marked "Internal: Top Secret." "It also was a safe and efficient setup to self-finance and pay a network of GRU informers in Western Europe."

Samos scrutinized the report as McIsaacs continued his presentation. "All went as planned until 1986, when Lakatos got sick and had to find a reliable and disciplined Caligula No. 2. He and the GRU had two problems. One was to keep the bank, including Hauptmann, in the dark about FEG's true owners, and the other—how to transmit the GRU's orders to the two subsidiaries and Hauptmann without showing its hand."

"We speculate that Lakatos somehow managed to persuade the GRU to accept his son, *Jozsi*, as a substitute Caligula. Such an arrangement would of course require that Caligula No. 2's identity be kept absolutely secret."

"And they went for it?"

"They did. Remember we're talking late 1988. Soviet security infrastructure was unraveling. The GRU didn't have many other options."

"They could have sold up and pocketed a few million," ventured Samos.

McIsaacs shook his head. "You're not remembering the time, Alex. The world was coming down around their ears. Everyone in the Party was looking for a bolt-hole and a sinecure. FEG was the golden goose that just kept laying. It could finance the lives of a hundred *apparatchiks* and their families."

Samos nodded, seeing the logic. "So, they fingered *Jozsi* as successor."

"Problem was that *Jozsi* was young, successful in his own right, and very busy. He had his musical career to worry about in addition to having to help his father out. With the help of his dying father, Jozsi eventually came around and was tasked with implementing a general audit of the FEG files kept at the bank. That's when he discovered that, after Lakatos died in December 1989, Hauptmann had begun stealing."

"I knew that Swiss kraut was bent!"

"The audit uncovered three or four extra inexplicable 'persons of influence' on the books. *Jozsi* confronted Hauptmann who claimed that these were mistakes made by his secretary, *Fräulein* Hunter, and he hoped that his new client, Caligula No. 2 might let it pass. Hauptmann, of course had no idea who Caligula No. 2 really was or about the GRU connection."

McIsaacs extracted another sheet from his file and handed it to Samos. It was a copy of an article, a sort of obituary that had appeared in the German news magazine *Der Spiegel* about the passing of Peter Lakatos. The writer speculates that Lakatos had been able to remain Hungarian minister of defence in Kadar's governments for such a long time because he was "well-regarded" by Moscow.

"That article was the first inkling that Hauptmann had that Caligula's torch had been passed on, but he had no idea to whom. Scared the crap out of the man. He cast about for a way to protect himself and he remembered Ilona and got in touch with her, asking her to come visit. Soon enough, she turns up in Zurich accompanied by you. Doing your due diligence, as a friend of the family, you insist that the bearer shares be converted immediately into nominal ones. Ilona, in a spirit of blind confidence, insists that one of them be made out in your name. Hauptmann sees an opportunity to protect himself and enthusiastically supports your suggestion and promptly acts on it. He is not responsible, having followed the will of the original Caligula to the letter."

Samos was working hard to digest all this new information and quickly reacted to it. "So, with the stroke of a pen, the GRU loses legal control of FEG Switzerland, the holding company."

"Correct."

"They must have been in one hell of a panic. But what could they do?"

"Initially, not much. You should know in this context that, in fact, the 'persons of influence' consist of three groups:

GRU informants who are being paid through FEG; real 'persons of influence' who are driving business to FEG; and, finally, totally fictitious 'persons' created by Hauptmann so he can use *their* bank accounts to enrich himself."

Samos's head was spinning. "So why didn't they just kill Hauptmann and be done with the problem and take over running the show directly by themselves?"

McIsaacs reached for a bottle of Jameson and two heavy glass tumblers. He poured them a couple of fingers each.

"The entire scheme depended on a compliant bank. Any legitimate bank required documentation, corporate filings, articles of incorporation, books, ledgers of transactions, ownership titles. If Lakatos made one error, it was including Ilona in the mix, which allowed Hauptmann to change the status of those bearer shares. As soon as they were changed into nominal shares, the game changed. That one decisive move, instigated by you, triggered what was to follow."

Samos was astonished and shook his head at the irony. "Too clever by half, isn't that what you used to say about me? Me and my smart mouth."

"Once the bearer shares were registered in your names, they had to keep Hauptmann around to deal with Ilona. They couldn't find a substitute for him in time—say, another corruptible senior manager at the bank—without betraying the members of the informants' network they had so carefully built and nurtured all these years."

"I really fucked them up, didn't I? And Ilona?"

"We are reasonably sure that her involvement in FEG was limited to acting as the incorporator of the FEG Group. She was what we call the 'beard,' the front, used by the GRU to put everyone to sleep at *Bank Julius Bär."*

"So, not political. Not a true believer."

"Hard to say. It's likely she pretended to be a Communist fellow traveller to be allowed to keep company with Lakatos. My guess is that she started life with two strikes against her from the get-go and had to fight hard to survive."

Samos opened his lidded eyes a bit wider. "What did you find out?"

"Poor and ostracized, probably because of her Roma origins, she somehow climbs out of her shit only to fall back in when impregnated by a fellow unfortunate. She gives birth, like so many of her ilk, to an illegitimate child. She does her old lover a favor by setting up FEG. In return, he gets her out of the country with a little cash to start fresh."

"That's the 'legend' she spun for me."

"Once in the West, the survival skills she developed under the regime made her a winner. She worked hard, followed her ambitions and her instincts and ended up in Ottawa, Canada. She opened a small but exclusive bake shop and attracted the attention of the foreign service set. She allowed herself to be seduced by an aging Mexican diplomat and sealed the deal with blowjobs. She changed countries for the last time, married the Mexican, and settled down to a comfortable, high bourgeois life. Then Lakatos dies. Hauptmann panics and moves to secure his future and contacts her. She gets re-involved in a problem the solution of which she is not equipped to find alone. So she turns to you for help, knowing absolutely nothing about your background."

The ersatz Panamanian looked at his American host with awe. He had always known that the man was capable of deep insight into other peoples' souls, but this was a performance worthy of the Great Wallenda, without a net! But then, Samos mused, McIsaacs was the epitome of motivators—and that *did* require insight.

Samos became aware that McIsaacs was watching him and he lowered his lids, almost closed his eyes. "Read my mind."

McIsaacs chuckled. "The eyes are the windows of the soul."

"Here, I'll give you a hint," said Samos as he made a show of opening his eyelids a little wider. "Blood or mud?"

"Blood is blood," sighed McIsaacs. "She gave birth to him. He may know it, he may not. She may have contacted him, you said she was crazy about *Manitas.*"

"Knew all about him," Samos confirmed.

"Can't rule out that play, can we?"

Samos gave in. "Who wrote the playbook for the performance we are now to participate in? Grabowski?"

McIsaacs grimaced and then broke a crooked smile. He shrugged, his palms open.

"When I saw the amplitude of what was in play and who was behind it all, I had no choice, Alex. Too big, too important. And, yes, Grabowski, with a serious edit from me."

"Narrate the end game for me."

"You neutralize Ilona. We will help you hunt down her son and Hauptmann and then you take over ownership of the FEG Group."

"Are you out of your mind? That's a one-way Hail Mary! Why would I do that? What's in it for me?"

"Peace of mind and the FEG investment portfolio, which we estimate is worth about $15 million, presently."

"And the two manufacturing plants?"

"They become the property of the United States of America. Officially and above board. The remnant elements of the GRU will be blue with anger, but they won't be able to do anything."

"What about Ilona and her son? What happens to them?"

"Nothing. She's a Mexican citizen and an ex-Soviet sympathizer who has committed no provable crime in Hungary or Austria or Switzerland or even Panama, as a matter of fact, except making her aged husband a cuckold with a certain ersatz Panamanian who shall remain nameless." McIsaacs stopped talking and began to laugh. "Last time I looked, that's not a crime."

"What about her son, *Jozsi*?"

"He is a Hungarian citizen living in Spain or France earning his daily bread by playing guitar and acting as a very well-paid, part-time consultant to a Swiss conglomerate. What is wrong with that?"

"So the fall-guy is Hauptmann."

"Bingo!"

*

Heddi reappeared and brought even more beer. She was shaking her head and laughing. Samos, thankful, drank deeply then asked: "What's the joke?"

"Your beard. I can't get used to it. For me, it makes you look not like you. It makes you look old. Shave it off."

Samos protested. "No way, It took me a full year to grow it." He turned to McIsaacs. "Al, I am blown away. Really. How the devil did you unearth all that intel?"

McIsaacs's grin reached from ear to ear, He was grateful for his ex-agent's praise because he knew full well that Samos was 'in the know,' aware of how difficult it must have been to uncover the type of information he had just finished relating.

"It wasn't a walk in the park, and I would not have succeeded without help from the Crypto team. After the two of you went home last year, we laid low for six months, as you suggested, and allowed the Swiss police to work on the Studer murder case without interference. As you predicted, their efforts were in vain. No leads, no motive, no explanation. They gave up in June and posted Hauptmann with Interpol as a missing and wanted person, a suspected murderer." McIsaacs was reading from the top sheet in the file in front of him. "Meanwhile, the bank people managed to get FEG's safety deposit box open."

"And what was in it?" Samos asked, for the record. He knew the answer.

"Nothing. No share certificates, no minutes of meetings, no will, no documents whatsoever."

"So the bank accepts the *status quo*."

McIsaacs was quick to answer. "Yes. As far as the bank is concerned, FEG's only legally recognizable shareholder is Ilona *Rodriguez-Keszthelyi*." Then he added. "For the time being, that is, or at least until another person turns up with a valid share certificate."

This last remark worried Samos. It reinforced the feeling he had been harboring for some time, that the situation was loaded in favor of Ilona if ever she disputed his right for the million-dollar buyout. And given the circumstances, this, of course, was surely going to happen. He made a mental note to attend to the matter without delay.

McIsaacs turned the page. "By mid-July, we had two new quarterly reports to work with, as did you." The American looked at Samos. "This allowed us to swing into analytical mode and to apply the 'follow-the-money' principle. We started with examining how Caligula No. 2 was being paid his monthly salary. It was quite ingenious."

"How?"

"By credit card. *Jozsi* is a musician who travels widely and frequently. As such, he has ATMs at his disposal all over Western Europe. FEG deposited his salary in an account at *Bär* against which he could then draw at his leisure by using a 'no limit,' 'no name' credit card frequently issued to very good customers of Swiss banks. We plotted the withdrawals geographically and determined they were more or less consistent with *Manitas de Plata's* travelling schedule."

"A perfect cover."

"Two specific regions emerged as the most frequented— one is the Northern Spain-Southern France corridor along the Atlantic from San Sebastian to the south and Biarritz in the north. The other was the Camargues-Marseille-French Riviera along the Mediterranean coast. These confirmed that *Jozsi* was our man."

"What about the fax machine used to send Hauptmann his quarterly instruction? I assumed it was in one of the factories, probably in Spain?"

McIsaacs's eyes crinkled with pleasure as he shook his head.

"You won't believe it when I tell you."

"Dazzle me."

"The Soviet Consulate in Biarritz! *Jozsi* has an apartment there. That's where he lives." McIsaacs laughed as Samos stared, his usually heavy-lidded eyes now opened wide.

"His is a sweet setup. The property was called *Villa La Roseraie* before it was bought by the Russian government. The consulate is in the chateau and Jozsi lives in the coach house. Plenty of room to play the guitar every day without disturbing anyone and discreetly communicating with the FEG managers or Hauptmann. Using Crypto techniques, we 'backdoored' the machine and started reading Caligula No. 2's messages to make sure we were not pissing up the wrong pole."

"Where is *Jozsi* now?"

"Either at home or playing guitar somewhere."

CHAPTER 75

Meilen, late April 1991

Samos's plan of action required cooperation from Langlois the banker, from the team headed by McIsaacs and, of course, Ilona herself.

He headed for his room just before midnight and, using one of McIsaacs's high-security lines, placed a call to Ilona who, he knew, was anxiously awaiting news in Mexico City. She sounded like a nervous wreck. No wonder. She was running her pastry shop, trying to keep an eye on Langlois and FEG, placate a jealous husband, manage her relationship with Samos without antagonizing him, and remember all the falsehoods she had told him.

After assuring her that things were under control, Samos steered the conversation to the subject of *Jozsi*.

"Do you have any idea where he might be?" He made himself sound pensive and tired.

"Probably on the Riviera playing guitar with *Manitas*," came the answer.

"Do you realize that he is Caligula No. 2?"

There was a long, overly pregnant pause and Samos could hear Ilona's breathing stop and then start again. When she spoke, it was in the small, submissive voice she used to not arouse his anger.

"Do we have proof?"

"Yes, we do. It is circumstantial, but very convincing."

Another, shorter pause and a return to her firm, decisive voice.

"Well, then, let's fire him and have done with it and get on with our lives."

What naiveté, what absence of imagination, thought Samos to himself. He silently congratulated Ilona on her ability to see everything in black and white, dismissing the inconvenient but vital details complicating the situation facing them.

"*Querida,* I wish the solution were as simple as you imagine it to be." He had practiced this next little bomb so that he could tell her the whole truth without embellishment. "*Jozsi* is working for the GRU." He paused, waiting for her reaction.

Nothing.

"They're probably holding Dr. Hauptmann and the pile of FEG documents he has stolen as prisoner somewhere. McIsaacs determined that the $5,000 you smuggled into Switzerland for Lakatos to start the FEG Group emanated from elements in the former GRU. Whoever they are, they seem to feel that the FEG Group belongs to them. Formally,

Caligula No. 2 can only be properly removed by FEG's share-holders, and, as you know, the identity of those shareholders is presently in serious doubt."

Ilona interrupted. "The banker told us that *Bär* recognizes me as the sole shareholder."

"Yes, for the time being, and because doing so is convenient for them under the present circumstances. But, I assure you, as soon as a legal attack is mounted against this decision, and there will be, the bank will heed the plaintiff's plea and freeze the *status quo* because that is advantageous for the bank. As for *Jozsi* and the GRU, they won't give a damn about what the bank thinks."

That Ilona expressed no agitation at the mention of the GRU did not surprise Samos, considering his back-and-forth with McIsaacs. He now had to confront the probability that his luscious Magyar baker with the clever hands suspected from the very start where the FEG start-up money had come from and had decided to ignore the consequences. Her powers to compartmentalize were positively masculine. She had washed her hands of the entire affair by conveniently "forgetting" about FEG's existence, for her, the only way out.

Or had she known all along what FEG was about and been ordered to keep it secret? And by whom? And from whom? And what about *Jozsi*? Why had she lied to her lover about her own son?

Samos knew that Ilona was no fool. He was sure she realized that the moment of reckoning was at hand. "I have done what I could alone here." His voice was sharp. "I need you at my side for my meeting with Langlois on Monday at noon so promise to take the Saturday flight to Zurich. I want you rested by the time we see him together. Much depends on how he'll react when I outline to him the whole picture."

"You mean about the GRU?"

Samos could not stop himself from giving her an unkind shot. "That, and other things," he said and hung up.

"I'll be there," she whispered and rung off.

On balance, Samos thought to himself, in such a case, the only person operating in blissful ignorance of the underlying essentials had been Hauptmann, who had only done what any self-respecting Swiss banker would do: steal from the client. A lot for his employer and a little for himself.

CHAPTER 76

Zurich, late April 1991 (1)

The drive from Kloten airport to the hotel had been difficult.
Samos and Ilona were sitting side by side in the back of one
of the Crypto Mercedeses and Alfredo was driving. Ilona was
trying to snuggle up to him, but Samos kept disentangling
himself, gently but firmly. He kept nodding toward the
driver and murmuring "Later, later . . ."

In their suite at the *Baur-au-Lac,* he had arranged for a
bottle of Cristal champagne to be in the room when they
checked in. He hoped to get her a little buzzed to soften
the inevitable dust-up he knew was coming. He popped the
cork, but she declined, saying she had had plenty to drink
on board.

Ilona had sensed that she was in trouble. After unpacking
her nightgown and toiletries, she sat down opposite Samos
in the living room and, to his great amazement, said simply:

"I have been lying to you, you already know that. But you need to believe me, I did not do it to hurt you. I had no idea that I was exposing you to any danger until Maria-Isabel was murdered."

Samos was taken aback. "So why did you?"

"Because I had nobody else to turn to." Her lips were trembling. She looked close to tears. Was she acting or was she sincere? He elected to push her without mercy. Let her make or break.

"What did you lie to me about?" An open-ended test question.

"I knew that Peter was in with the GRU. They were all fabulous drinking buddies. They had their fingers to the wind. They knew what was coming. I knew that the $5,000 he had given me when I left Hungary was probably from them. He warned me not to talk about it. He also said that, once I had spoken with the Swiss bank and had arranged for the formation of FEG, I should forget about the whole thing."

"And you did."

"I did," she repeated, her lovely face almost dreamy as her thoughts wandered. "And, believe me, there were many times when I was down on my luck, I wished that I could have accessed some of the FEG money, but I was afraid to call Dr. Hauptmann."

"Why?"

"Because the GRU would have found out about it and come after me." A reasonable fear, thought Samos.

"What else did you lie about?" he asked.

"I should have told you about *Jozsi,* but, frankly, I did not think he had anything to do with FEG. He was too light-headed, unreliable, a drug addict. Not someone the GRU would have wanted anything to do with."

"How did you know about the drugs?"

Ilona's face turned red. "Somebody, I don't remember who, must have told me before I left Hungary. *Jozsi* started doing drugs when he was quite young, you know, with his uncle's musicians. So I wasn't surprised." *A cover-up answer,* said Samos to himself.

"So who was *Jozsi* to you anyway?"

Ilona flinched ever so slightly.

"Nothing. The illegitimate son of my lover whom I hardly saw. That's all."

Blood or mud? A little of both? Samos was getting a fresh image of his lover.

He unfolded the piece of paper in his hand and gave it to Ilona. "You read Hungarian, don't you?" he asked quietly. "Could you read it and tell me what it is and what it says?"

Ilona's hand trembled as she took the document from Samos, but it was clear from her reaction that she knew what it was even before looking at it.

"It's a certified copy of an adoption document which states that *Gyula Lakatos,* a resident of Arad, is adopting a baby boy, yet unnamed."

"And who signed the document?"

"The applicant is *Gyula,* and the mother is . . . me." Ilona was crying silently. She raised her face to Samos, defiant, almost spiteful. When she spoke he could hear her practised recitation, cold and mechanical.

"Yes, *querido, Jozsi* is my son, but I never lied to you about him. I said he was Peter Lakatos's illegitimate son and so he is. I said the mother was a young Roma girl that is true too and I also told you that he was adopted by Peter's older brother, *Gyula.*"

"You only omitted a little detail." Samos was incredibly bitter and let it show. This confirmation made him feel profoundly betrayed.

"I was afraid that if I told you I would lose you, and I didn't want that."

"Why?"

"Because I fell in love with you. Please, please forgive me. I have nobody to turn to, I have nobody to love, I have no one who wants to look after me."

"You sleep every night with Uncle Octavio, your husband!"

Ilona shook her head as though to scramble the image Samos presented.

"He's old and getting senile. His family hates me and treats me with contempt. He was my way out, but I never loved him."

Samos interrupted. "But he was useful and you shamelessly exploited him. Like me."

"No *querido*, no. In the beginning it was all business, I needed a banker to help me with Dr. Hauptmann. You know that it's true. I never expected to find that FEG was as big and as complicated as it is. I thought Dr. Hauptmann wanted to see me because Peter had left me some money, a little inheritance, and he wanted to give it to me. I was as surprised as you when I heard that FEG was a multi-million-dollar arms manufacturing group.

Samos rose to his feet, towering over the woman.

"Do you really expect me to believe this horseshit?" Samos was getting angrier by the minute. "And you want me to forgive and forget that your son is responsible for the death of Maria-Isabel and for two attempts on my life!"

There was no way for Ilona to answer.

CHAPTER 77

Zurich, late April 1991 (2)

That night Samos left Ilona to her own devices, ignoring her pleas for him to stay. This carefully thought-out move was part of the plan to find out which way she would jump. "Leave her to stew for a while, say from Saturday night to Monday morning," McIsaacs had counselled. "I'll arrange to have her phone tapped, as well as surveillance to see with whom she meets. Come back to *Meilen* and let me help you figure out what our next move should be."

As arranged, Samos met Ilona at eight sharp for breakfast on Monday morning in her hotel's terrace cafeteria. She looked a mess. Puffy eyes, presumably from weeping through the night, trembling hands from frayed nerves and a look of confusion on her face, most likely from having had more than one nightcap before falling asleep.

Samos was all business. "If you want to save whatever little there remains of our relationship I am willing to give you a second chance, provided you accept the following conditions. And they are non-negotiable."

Ilona made a show of listening attentively.

"For the next foreseeable future you will, one; do whatever I ask you to do until this situation is resolved, two; you will not lie to me, three; you will not keep secrets from me, four; you will not contact *Langlois* or *Jozsi* without my permission, and five; you will meet with them only in my presence."

He waved to a waiter and ordered an American breakfast, then asked him to take Ilona's order, coffee and toast.

Ilona began to whimper and then cry again.

"Ilona, stop crying and don't make a spectacle of yourself." The *Baur-au-Lac* was not a hotel in which one made a scene. In spite of himself, Samos took pity on the weeping woman in front of him.

"Take your time eating. After breakfast, we'll go over to *Bank Vontobel*. We have an appointment at nine with *Herr Joachim Joscht*, a friend of McIsaacs's. The bank is eight blocks straight down from here on *Gotthardt Strasse*. A taxi will get us there in five minutes."

"Why are we going there?" She was munching on a piece of toast and trying to dab at her eyes with her serviette at the same time. Samos had never seen her so uncoordinated, so lost. She was showing every one of her sixty years.

"Before I tell you, I must have your formal promise that you accept my conditions. Do you?"

"I do," she said, sighing and rolling her eyes.

"Do you swear on your life?"

"I do." She popped a piece of toast in her mouth and crossed her heart. Her relief was palpable. Her hands stopped trembling, her posture relaxed, and she stopped crying.

Samos watched her as she dug into her breakfast plate and his at the same time, her appetite clearly returning. He could not stop looking at her. This woman had worked her way under his skin against all his better judgment. What was this alchemy? Does she really intend to keep her word or is she just putting on a superb performance for my benefit?, Samos kept asking himself.

He was sure he'd never trust her with anything important ever again. And, since he had expected that she would deceive him sooner or later, the current feeling of betrayal stung, but was not deep enough to make him want to break with her.

Trust no one. Love no one.

He knew all about betrayal, having gotten used to it during the long years of his lonely and bitter life. He was now clear in his mind about how he would protect himself against it.

He turned his heavily lidded eyes to hers. "Remember, you swore on your *life*. Remember what you have learned about me, what happens to people who try to hurt me."

She nodded, the fear he once inspired in her eyes was now surrender.

"Very well, then. We're going to open a joint bank account," he said. "I or my nominee will have the right to sign on it alone. You will also have the right to sign, but only jointly with me or my nominee."

"And what is it for?"

"You are to transfer the entire investment portfolio of FEG to *Vontobel*." Samos watched her, his eyes outwardly indolent.

She flinched. "And why would I do that?"

Samos smiled. "Because if we do not come to terms, my dear one, I will leave you hanging in the wind for the GRU to find and pick your bones as clean as your lies."

Ilona blanched and laughed nervously, trying to judge whether or not Samos was serious, but his face was Sphinx-like, immutable.

"So you want me to be your slave."

"Yes, but only for three years."

"What does that mean?"

"We will withdraw, in advance and for three years, an annual emolument of $300,000, starting mid-April this year. Each of us will, of course, be permitted to do whatever we want with this money."

Ilona was quick. "That's next Friday."

"Correct."

"Three hundred thousand dollars." Her face revealed her innate avarice.

"That's right." *Got you, you greedy bitch*, thought Samos.

"And after three years?"

"We split whatever is in the account and go our own way."

"If we want."

Samos held out his hand. "If we want."

They shook hands and Ilona started crying again, but, this time, with relief and not from fear. And she did not let go of his hand for a long time.

CHAPTER 78

Nice, France, Early May 1991 (1)

The last time Samos had visited Nice had been in 1949. He was at boarding school in England and had come over to stay with his parents for a couple of weeks. They had rented a villa for the summer just west of the port on *Avenue de la Mer* near *Rocque Plage*.

He could never forget those two weeks. He was fifteen and in top physical shape after recovering from the war-time deprivations. English public schools emphasized physical fitness—soccer, athletics, rugby, cricket—and he took to it as a natural. In Nice, he ran in the early morning, picked up *Le Figaro* and some *croissants* for breakfast, then lazed around talking to his parents, a rare event at that time. A walk to the market or the beach followed—no structure, no pressure.

In the evenings after dinner, the three of them would wander along *La Promenade des Anglais,* absorbing the wonderful *ambiance*: the breeze from the sea, the smell of suntan lotion on young bodies, the multitude of great eateries. There were the nightly concerts at the casino's bandshell featuring famous names such as Harry James, Django Reinhard, and the Hot Club de France and big band music by France's own Ray Ventura and his Orchestra.

For the French Riviera, it was *l'Epoque de la Folie*. Picasso, Rita Hayward and Ali Khan, the recently abdicated Egyptian King Farouk, and Matisse, living in nearby Grasse; Roger Vadim, Brigitte Bardot, Sophia Loren, Carry Grant, Jean Cocteau, Elizabeth Taylor, Yves Montand, Gina Lollobrigida, Marlon Brando and Grace Kelly, they were all there, in Cannes, Nice, and the Antibes.

*

Manitas de Plata, "The Rage of the Riviera," and his band were scheduled to play at the Nice Casino's bandshell on May fourth and fifth. The casino, on the ground floor of the *Palais de la Mediterranée*, a luxury hotel, had been substantially renovated the year before. *Manitas* and his people were featured as the openers for *La Saison* and, as such, were comped two adjoining suites on the third floor for four nights. McIsaacs's people had checked on their reservations. In addition to *Manitas*, whose real family name was *Baliardo*, there were four sidemen, all guitarists, three *Baliardos*. The fourth sideman was one *Jose Vargas*, a Spanish citizen.

Samos and Ilona, registered as *Señor* and *Señora Sanchez-Obregon*, from Puerto Rico, occupied one of the ocean-facing suites on the eighth floor. Their reservations were for six nights. McIsaacs's Crypto men, Massimo and Alfredo, scored a deluxe room, also on the eighth floor, opposite Samos's suite.

McIsaacs's room was on the third floor near the *Manitas* suites. He had left a message for Samos to meet him in his room alone. When he entered, he found McIsaacs arranging a selection of six eyeglasses on his commode, all thick-framed, dark colored, with standard thick lens corrections, not the super-light, frame-less spectacles Samos favored.

"Pick one. They are all in your prescription."

Samos took one look, and scowled, "Wouldn't be caught dead."

"That's what we're trying to avoid, putz."

"What, they shoot out lasers or something?"

McIsaacs gently removed Samos's glasses and turned him around by the shoulders to face a wall mirror.

"Your peepers. It's the one thing about you everyone remembers. The beard will get you most of the way there, but if Caligula No. 2 marks those eyes, it could be game over before we start."

It was a persuasive point. Samos picked up the least stylistically objectionable and put them on. The prescription was perfect but the weight of the thick dark frames was annoying. He checked himself in the mirror.

"I look like a Puerto Rican gynecologist."

"Perfect," said McIsaacs.

*

Samos was having an after-late-lunch espresso on the hotel's terrace enjoying the view consisting mainly of bikini-clad, almost naked young women, when a silver Lamborghini Spyder drew up in front of the main entrance. The doorman and two bellboys rushed to meet the driver as he extricated himself from his machine. Tossing the keys to a valet, he headed to a table near where Samos was sitting and a waiter with a drink on a tray that looked like lemonade appeared almost immediately. The man lifted the glass from the tray, caught sight of Samos, and paused. His dark, handsome face revealed nothing. He then raised his glass toward Samos and downed his drink in one huge draught.

Then he got up and went inside.

Samos had immediately recognized him from the picture McIsaacs had shown him:: *Jose (Jozsi) Vargas*, alias *Jozsi Lakatos*, guitarist and captain in the GRU. Caligula No. 2.

CHAPTER 79

Nice, France, early May 1991 (2)

Samos sauntered into the large Gaming Room of the Casino and noted with satisfaction that *Manitas* and his crew were already at it, a scant hour after they had finished their show to thunderous applause and three encores.

Samos knew they would be there. McIsaacs's research on the man and his entourage had been thorough and accurate. *Manitas* was a creature of habit who loved gambling. "Little Silver Hands" and his band would invariable end up at the gaming tables to smoke cigars, drink espresso and *Calvados,* and tempt Lady Luck before retiring for the night.

Manitas was playing roulette rather haphazardly, betting large sums on random numbers. His son, *Tonino,* standing next to him, was doing the same while his younger brother, *Hippolyte,* was working hard at trying to restrain both from losing yet another fortune.

Jozsi, on the other hand, was reported to be a cautious gambler, except when he played poker, which was not happening on that particular night. He was at the slots, playing modestly, but for long stretches at a time. McIsaacs had explained to Samos that *Jozsi* needed to show *Manitas* that he was one of the boys, a gambler like his boss. *Jozsi* was not blood and he had to work extra hard to be accepted into *Manitas*'s inner circle, which was composed of trusted family members, his band, and a few ardent admirers. These were the people *Manitas* liked to have around him whenever he went out in public.

There was another reason, too, a practical one. GRU spies and moles under *Jozsi's* control knew that if they needed to contact him, they needed only to cruise the slot machines in any casino in Europe where a *Manitas* concert was being staged.

In his early forties, slim and tan, with a full head of jet-black hair, *Jozsi* emulated the Spanish-Roma look of the rest of the band. He wore a beautifully embroidered, long-sleeved, loose silk shirt, tight-fitting pants, Cuban heeled boots, gold chains around his neck, but no jewelry on his wrists and hands except for a gold ring around the fourth finger of his right hand signifying that he was spoken for.

Samos watched him for a while and noticed how the guitarist moved from machine to machine, always choosing a machine next to one that was unoccupied. Easy and discreet access for anyone who wanted contact.

And that suited the ersatz Panamanian perfectly.

When *Jozsi* got up to move again, so did Samos, and he managed to plop down on the seat on his target's right. After four pulls on the handle of his machine, Samos turned to *Jozsi* and gave him one of his *I-am-your-best-friend* smiles.

"I loved your solos tonight," he oozed in Puerto-Rican-accented Spanish. "You may not be as fast as *Manitas*, but you are more classically disciplined than he with your *compás*."

Jozsi stopped pulling and smiled back. He was cautious. "I'm flattered you noticed. Did you ever play flamenco guitar yourself?"

"Trying, but not doing well."

The musician laughed—a friendly, open laugh. "Aren't we all."

Samos noticed that the man's tanned and chiseled face, obviously Roma, bore a remarkable resemblance to Ilona's. The guitarist swivelled in his seat to face Samos. "Do I know you from somewhere? You look very familiar."

Samos was ready for the question. He knew that the beard he had grown during the past year disguised his looks somewhat, but not completely.

"You saw me on the terrace when you pulled up in your Lamborghini. You waved to me, lemonade in hand."

"That was a *Pastis,* but that was not my car. *Manitas* lent it to me for the trip. He also has a Rolls-Royce and a Mercedes-Benz. As you have probably heard, his passions are music, women, and expensive cars."

"Lucky you."

"Lucky he." *Jozsi* relaxed. "So where are you from and how do you know enough about *compás* to hear when they are not being played in their proper sequence?"

Samos mentally congratulated McIsaacs for the detailed brief about this particular aspect of Vargas's playing.

"I'm from Puerto Rico, here on vacation with my wife. She doesn't like gambling and is waiting for me at the bar. Come, let's have a drink with her. She is the true *aficionada* of flamenco music in the family and absolutely mad for *Manitas*. She would be thrilled to meet you and would never forgive me if I didn't insist!"

Samos took out his handkerchief and blew his nose, the signal for McIsaacs to fetch Ilona, who was waiting for them in the lobby.

Jozsi was a touch slow to accept, but not doing so would have been ungraciously rude to a fan, a serious "no-no" for members of the band. "All right, but just for one drink. We have another show to prepare for tomorrow." He got off his stool and allowed Samos to lead him to the bar.

CHAPTER 80

The Casino Bar, Nice, early May 1991

Jozsi was intrigued by the Puerto Rican who spoke Spanish with a vaguely foreign inflection. Rarely, if ever, had he met an amateur musician who could recognize the difference in approach of the way he and *Manitas* played flamenco music.

Other than the speed.

While they waited for the wife to show up, they discussed the art of flamenco.

"*Manitas* plays definitely faster, and he's capable of greater sustained bursts of speed than I am, but our techniques are almost identical. But that's no mystery. *Manitas* has polished my technique since I was an adolescent."

"How old were you when you started with him?" Samos kept his eye on the entrance to the bar.

"I left Hungary when I was fifteen after hearing *Manitas* in concert. Perhaps, the real difference between us is that I'm a Hungarian gypsy and I let my head lead me, while *Manitas* is a Franco-Spanish Roma and plays with his heart."

Samos could not let that one go. "Excuse me, young man, but I saw true passion coming from you on stage tonight."

"*Muchas graçias.* But, if you saw passion, it was from both of us. We have both survived great misery, but *Manitas* has been blessed with family love. You can see it when he is with his brothers and cousins, all the *Baliardos. Manitas* was raised by his father and mother. I was given up for adoption at birth."

A waiter brought two tulip glasses filled with Calvados and, with a discreet sign from Samos, left the bottle.

"Running away at age fifteen was the only solution for me. I could not survive the hurt and the constant heartache, the shame." *Jozsi* raised his glass. "But you know what they say—bitter grapes can make the sweetest wine."

The two men toasted each other as Samos wondered why this stranger was opening up to him.

"Music has always been there for me. A way to block the pain. And one day, who knows? Maybe I will get the chance to heal all that pain."

The door had been opened and Fate was beckoning him on. Samos was unable to resist, nor did he want to.

"And your father?"

Jozsi grimaced as he swallowed his drink. Samos filled his glass.

"My father," the younger man almost snorted. "I only really got to know him a few years before he died. We were working toward a *rapprochement* but there was not enough time. I tried to be a good son to him. Too late, really."

Samos found himself feeling emotions that he thought were buried decades ago on that cemetery hill in Montreal. "Fathers," he sighed.

"Fathers," *Jozsi* repeated, raising his glass again. "Let's hear it for absent fathers who had no clue."

The two men clinked their tulip-shaped glasses as *Jozsi* took a much closer and harder look at his host. When he had locked eyes on the man on the terrace something had stirred in his memory. That was why he had tipped his glass in his direction. And now here they were, brought together by serendipity, discussing his father in a casino where destiny and charmed bodies aligned.

When Peter Lakatos died, *Jozsi* thought his appointment with destiny had finally arrived. The day of revenge. But *Doktor* Hauptmann's greed had intervened. And then that fucking Panamanian, his mother's lover. The GRU said the man had no past, was a foundling discovered by a priest on the steps of his church.

Motherless, like him.

Jozsi noticed that the Puerto Rican had listened attentively to his story, with true empathy. He could tell when people where play acting. This was real. For some reason, he reminded *Jozsi* of the Panamanian. He had never met the thorn in his side. The picture he had seen, taken some time ago, had shown a clean-shaven male in his late forties with thinning hair and wearing glasses. A bit of a pampered menial, not at all like the virile, bearded musician sitting opposite him and drinking up a storm of double Calvadoses.

And his eyes are not . . . too late! Those hooded eyes were no longer on the younger man, but were trained on the bar entrance.

Jozsi looked up toward the entrance and saw a woman enter, then stop. She surveyed the room as if looking for someone and *Jozsi* shook his head. He thought that his mind was playing tricks with him. The woman looked very much like his mother, but older than she had looked when he had seen her last, decades ago.

The woman came to their table and the Puerto Rican stood and pulled out a chair for her. She was stone-faced.

The shock of recognition was too much. *Jozsi* leapt to his feet and lost control. All the pent-up bitterness, the years of yearning, of suffering, of self-denial burst from his lips in Hungarian.

"*Miért árultál el engemet ma te büdös kurva?*" "Why did you betray me today, you stinking whore?"

Samos rose up and back-handed the younger man so hard it lifted him off his feet, the sound echoing off the walls

"*Mert meg akartam menteni az életedet!*" "Because I wanted to save your life!"

Jozsi was staggered by the blow, but turned to launch himself at Samos.

"*Nem!*" cried Ilona.

Jozsi stopped, and looked around. McIsaacs was standing behind him. One of his bodyguards, Massimo, to his left and the other, red-headed Alfredo, to his right. The

Puerto Rican was on his feet facing him. His mother was sobbing uncontrollably.

Samos spoke first. "Please calm down, everybody. We're not here to hurt anyone, *Jozsi*. I just want to clear the air between you and me and then try to find solutions to our mutual problems."

Jozsi rubbed the side of his face that bore the reddening imprint of Samos's back-hander.

"And who the fuck are you?"

"Your mother's financial consultant."

"Ah, Samos, the mystery man. The Panamanian foundling and puppet of Uncle Sam."

"Yes, Captain *Shlesak Lakatos,* puppet of the GRU, that's me, Alejandro Samos, at your service."

*

It was half past one in the morning and they were in the sitting room of Samos's hotel suite. Ilona was pouring coffee from the carafe the room-service waiter had left them and trying hard to hide her nervousness. She was close to tearing up again.

Massimo and Alfredo were discreetly cooling their heels in the bedroom, but could be seen through the open door.

"Let's get down to business, captain, by agreeing, for starters, that you and I are more or less in the same situation."

"Meaning?"

"Neither of us is a principal in the present operation. We're both just agents representing our clients. You're representing the GRU's interests and I'm representing your mother's. These two principals both claim that they own the FEG Group and each can marshal arguments in defence of his claim."

"Not true!" *Jozsi* was still seething. "You're treating the situation as if it were just a run-of-the-mill business transaction. There is more to it than that."

"Like what?"

"Fraud, murder, and outright theft."

"I beg to differ. Let me outline how I see the way the present situation has come about." Samos took a sip of his coffee. "May I?"

"Go ahead." *Jozsi* was wary. He was confused by the man's civil behavior. He assumed that Samos knew the role he played in the attempted assassinations. But while McIsaacs's men were just a whistle away, there was little he could do but play along.

Samos sensed that he had the moral high ground. "Any judge, presiding over a court in a country such as Switzerland, with its strict banking laws, would be called upon to opine about the following facts: a woman visits a senior officer of a bank known for handling numbered accounts with great discretion. She gives the bank officer $5,000 and instructs him to form a limited liability company that can issue bearer shares. She tells the banker to issue two bearer shares. The owners would be herself and a man called Caligula, who would turn up to sign the required paperwork within the year. The paperwork includes a document that states that, should either the woman or Caligula die, the survivor would automatically inherit the deceased's bearer share. How am I doing so far?"

"Go on."

"Sure enough, within the year, Caligula turns up, identifies himself as being the Hungarian defence minister, and puts more money—$5,000—into the company's bank account. He tells the banker that the company will receive regular transfers of money from around the world and asks him to build an investment portfolio with the money as it comes in."

Jozsi was now listening with a certain unconcealed interest, which Samos noted.

"The banker obliges. For him, such arrangements are a dime a dozen. Because of the initial investment by the shareholders being such a paltry sum, less than $10,000, the banker does not consider it necessary to investigate the money's origin. He assumes that the two shareholders had somehow saved up the moneys over the years. In any case, it's not his concern."

"Exactly. Why would it be?" *Jozsi* confirmed.

"For whatever reason, which we do not know, the banker assumes that the funds flowing into the company's coffers from the four corners of the world, which are becoming considerable, are bribes, payments for favors granted to people by the defence minister.

"With the impending implosion of the Soviet union, cadres are scrambling to set up such schemes. Swiss banks are avidly courting them."

Samos continued. ". So, remember, at this point in time the owners of the company are deemed to be the person or persons that have possession, physical or constructive, of the two bearer shares. Since the bank has physical possession of the shares, which it holds in a safety deposit box on its premises, in a fiduciary capacity for the benefit of the designated founding shareholders, the law dictates that the owners of the company are constructively the two founding shareholders."

Samos stepped closer to *Jozsi*. "Do you agree?"

Jozsi nodded.

"Thus far, no Swiss laws have been broken. Do you agree?"

Jozsi nodded again.

Samos bent low into the younger man's face. "Do you acknowledge that when your father, Peter Lakatos, died, ownership changed because your mother had inherited his share as per the signed and deposited agreement, thereby becoming sole owner of the company, to keep or dispose of at her pleasure?"

Jozsi lowered his head and nodded for the third time. Samos straightened up.

"Well then, on March fifth of this year, your mother and I met with *Doktor* Hauptmann at his office and your mother instructed him to cancel the original two shares and to issue one new share in her name and another in mine."

Jozsi began to chuckle, surprising Samos. This was not the sound of a defeated man. On the contrary, to Samos, it sounded more like a subtle declaration of victory. *Jozsi* pointed at Ilona, his face taut with emotion.

"That's what you and your client claim, Señor Samos, but you cannot prove it. Photocopies of share certificates are not proof. Produce the originals if you can."

Obviously, *Jozsi* was well informed. Samos suspected that Ilona had had a hand in that.

"You know damned well that we can't. Your treacherous stooge, the murdering thief, *Doktor* Hauptmann, must have them." Samos swung into attack mode. "But I believe we have enough circumstantial evidence to convince a judge that our cause is just."

That's when *Jozsi*, the talented poker player, showed his last, but lethal, card. "*Doktor* Hauptmann is not our stooge, Señor Samos. He is our enemy. He stole a lot of money from the company, millions, misappropriated the shares you referred to, stripped away the documentation relevant to their existence, and then disappeared after murdering his secretary to cover his tracks."

"Are you telling me that you don't know where he is?" Samos did not bother to hide his incredulity.

"That's precisely what I'm telling you. We have been looking for him all over the world, but so far, have not been able to find him." *Jozsi* shrugged and held up his hands in frustration." If anyone in the world is the owner of the FEG Group, it is *Doktor* Alfred Hauptmann. He has the two original bearer shares in his physical possession."

"Hold on." Samos was grasping. "I saw him prepare the share certificates in my and Ilona's names and we have photocopies of them. Surely, they supersede the validity of the original ones because they are more recent."

"But did you see him destroy the original ones?"

Samos could not remember.

Jozsi moved in for the kill. "What Hauptmann has in his possession then, is a set of two bearer shares properly issued sometime in 1968 and another set, issued on March 5, 1991, of which one is in your name and the other in Ilona's. All he needs to assure ownership of FEG for himself is to destroy the shares dated March fifth, as well as the documentation relating to their issuance."

Jozsi stood up to leave. "In my opinion, he has already done that and all he is doing now is searching for a buyer for the original two."

"You mean a buyer who can prove that he bought them without knowledge of their stolen origins." Samos turned to Ilona, shrugging. "I have to admit, your son makes sense."

Jozsi countered. "Or a buyer, such as the original owners of the shares, like the GRU, ready to buy back something that they already owned."

Jozsi and Samos burst out laughing simultaneously, but the younger man stopped first, casting an appraising eye on the older.

"You are very good, Samos, but, you are not perfect."

CHAPTER 81

Nice, May 1991 (4)

It was almost noon the next day when Samos and Ilona finally got out of bed.

They were both exhausted—she, from having been on a three-day ride on an emotional roller coaster, he from the effort to organize and conduct the meeting with *Jozsi* in a civilized manner without revealing how virulently wrathful he was feeling toward Ilona and her son, especially the son, the sonofabitch whose life was stained with the innocent blood of Maria-Isabel.

Ilona emerged from the bathroom, drying her hair. She confronted Samos. "I always suspected that you understood Hungarian, now I have proof!" she said, sounding victorious.

Samos laughed dismissively. "How so?"

"Last night, when *Jozsi* called me names in Hungarian, you understood and hit him."

Samos thought quickly. "You're mistaken again," he smiled deprecatingly and added, "Some of my clients are Slavic speakers. They taught me the handy little word '*kurva*,' prostitute. When *Jozsi* called you a 'kurva,' I lost my temper."

She sat down to the table and Samos joined her. She picked up the glass of freshly squeezed orange juice and Samos cut into a croissant. "There is a saying that holds that you can't suck and blow at the same time," he mused, winking wryly at the woman sitting opposite him. "Well, you might be the exception that tests the rule."

"What do you mean?" a very much subdued Ilona asked.

"It's simple. You have to choose: either you want to make sure that you remain the owner of the FEG Group or you want to win back your son, *Jozsi*. You cannot do both."

"Why not?"

"Ilona, we are in a race with the GRU and the winner will be he who finds *Doktor* Hauptmann first. At present, we have the advantage; your knowledge of your ex-lover Lakatos's shenanigans before you left Hungary. If you tell your son all you know, you will destroy our advantage. He will tell his bosses what you tell him, thereby enabling the GRU to get to Hauptmann first. We don't want that. He knows where the two bearer-shares are. Remember? And so?"

Ilona interrupted. "Goodbye, money."

"Precisely. So make up your mind. Either choose your words carefully when you talk to *Jozsi*, or even better, don't talk with him at all, or kiss your newfound money, *and me*, goodbye."

She grew pensive. "What do you mean by '*and me*?'"

"I don't undertake dangerous assignments without at least a fair chance of success." He gave Ilona a hard look as her eyes began to shine. "And don't start crying, it won't work with me!"

She took a deep breath, but, surprisingly, did not become argumentative as usual. "What do you want me to do?" she asked instead. "How can I be of help?"

He relented. "I would like to spend the next day or two talking about Peter Lakatos with you. I want to know everything that you know about him, about his friends, about his education, his job or jobs, where and how and when you met him, everything, but especially about how he knew about *Doktor* Hauptmann."

"Fine. Where?"

"What's wrong with staying here and going for long walks when we get tired of the same subject?"

"Sounds good to me." She smiled and came over to embrace him. "Please, please, don't be cross with me," she whispered into his ear. "I'd be lost without you; I couldn't manage alone anymore."

He disentangled himself from her while wondering how she was able to arouse him so effectively, even through his wrath. "Then make sure you don't talk with *Jozsi*. I assure you that if I find out that you are communicating with him I will not hesitate to leave you."

*

The next day they walked from their hotel to the Nice marina for lunch. Getting nicely tipsy from the excellent Chablis she drank with the *filet de doré à l'amandine*, Ilona stopped and gazed over the port as though searching for something. She finally turned to Samos, a crooked smile creasing her shaded face.

"I remember. I had forgotten but, it is there."

They sat on a bench as the beautiful Niçoises paraded back and forth. Samos could just catch the occasional glimpse of Massimo, loitering at a comfortable distance, blowing kisses at the lovely women. Alfredo was invisible.

"Peter never wanted to be minister of defence, you know, because he knew how dangerous that position was."

"Why dangerous?"

"Because the regime ate clever people like Peter. They needed them to run things but, inevitably, they destroyed them out of fear. You had to watch out for criticism and outright attacks from not only the AVO, but also from conniving and jealous colleagues in the Communist Party, as well as from the Russians."

"You mean the KGB?"

"Yes, and the Army GRU."

"The poor bastard. He must have been a nervous wreck from the stress."

"That he was."

"So how did he manage?"

"His patron, Kadar, the premier, allowed him four weeks' vacation out of the country each year, to be taken two weeks in the spring or summer and two in fall or winter. Generally speaking, we went on these vacations together, except for the first week of the Fall break, which he stretched into three weeks by combining it with the annual meeting of Soviet Satellite Defence Ministers, traditionally held either in Odessa or Cyprus in October of each year."

"Satellite?"

Ilona laughed. "Not like Sputnik, dummy! As in members of the countries under Soviet rule." She was relaxed and happy to be in the sunshine and looking at the expensive boats anchored in the marina. "In 1964, the meeting was held in Cyprus. That's where he met Hauptmann. It was no accident. Hauptmann was there trolling for black money. He, too, had his finger in the wind."

"Black money?"

"You know, illegal money belonging to members of the Soviet *Nomenklatura*. Peter told me that they would park it in Cyprus on its way to investment in Switzerland."

All the bells in Samos's mind began to ring in unison and stirred his sense of rectitude profoundly. They chimed, "Go back to Zurich and check on how many times Hauptmann holidayed on Cyprus."

CHAPTER 82

Meilen, mid-May 1991

They were in McIsaacs's office at his home in Meilen, sitting in front of Crypto's secure teleconferencing camera, with the visibly annoyed Assistant Deputy Director of the NSA Richard Grabowski at the other end of the wire. The Assistant Deputy Director was deeply underwhelmed. He was getting irritated with his ex-asset Samos/Karas, or whatever he was calling himself now; as far as Grabowski was concerned, the man's name was Tom. He resented turning Samos loose and being bothered repeatedly about the persistently irritating problems of a stupid little Swiss company called FEG.

He had other fish to fry, far bigger and more urgent.

"For the last time, Tom, the NSA is not the police. We do not interfere in people's private quarrels and, I'm sure you remember, I told you that we can *assist* you in only a very limited way and strictly on an informal basis." He let his uncharacteristic irritation seep into the tone in his voice.

Samos persevered stubbornly. "Director, the reason we arranged this teleconference was to save you time, not waste it. If we cannot resolve the problem for you now, you'll soon see that you will just have to spend more time on it down the road. By then, the situation will have deteriorated considerably."

McIsaacs, who was in the room, looked over to Samos. The paper Panamanian was on the verge of apoplexy. The American shook his head and held up his hand to restrain Samos from saying something fatally stupid.

Grabowski grunted and gave in. "You have ten minutes."

Samos calmed himself, organizing his arguments. "The FEG Group, a Swiss company, owns two arms manufacturing facilities fabricating principally Kalashnikovs and related weapons, one in Nicaragua, a country within the sphere of US influence but presently run by the Sandinistas, who have no love for Uncle Sam; the other in Northern Spain, an area presently destabilized by the presence of Basque terrorists. Ownership of the Group is presently in dispute. One claimant is a Mexican-Hungarian immigrant for whom I act as financial consultant, the other is the Soviet GRU."

Samos took a deep breath and plunged on. "Ownership is evidenced by two bearer shares, which we believe are presently physically held by a fugitive from justice who is wanted for murder, fraud, and theft by Interpol pursuant to a request by the Swiss police. The warrant for him has been outstanding for over eighteen months and the GRU has been searching for him all that time, too."

Grabowski lost patience. "Tom, for shit's sake, I know all that! So what new information have you got?"

"I believed until recently that *Doktor* Alfred Hauptmann, the fugitive, and my client's ex-Swiss banker, was in bed with the GRU. I have now determined that the GRU has no idea where Hauptmann is. In fact, it is also actively searching for him, as are Interpol and the Swiss police."

"So?"

"I have now obtained reliable information that Hauptmann may be in Cyprus."

"Does the GRU know that?"

"About Cyprus? I believe not."

Grabowski stared into Samos's soul from 6,000 kilometers away, but the effect was as though he was giving his ex-asset a lap dance. When he spoke, it was in a tone that indicated a slight waver.

"Al?"

McIsaacs came up behind Samos. "I'm with Tom."

Another long pause and then Grabowski rose from his desk and left the screen, but his voice rang clear.

"Fax me the file and I'll see what I can do."

The screen went black.

McIsaacs raised his eyebrows, but otherwise revealed nothing.

A very discouraged Samos dragged himself to the nearest fax machine to send the salient information in the Hauptmann file to Grabowski in Fort Mead.

CHAPTER 83

Cyprus, mid-summer 1991

Captain William (Bill) Baktis had graduated from the *College Militaire St Jean* in the Province of Quebec, Canada, at the age of twenty-two as a second lieutenant and requested initial posting to the Canadian Army's Military Intelligence Unit. He figured that, with his language skills, he would be assured quick promotion.

He was not wrong

A born linguist, by age eighteen, he was fluent in English and French, the two official languages of his native province, Turkish (his mother being from Istanbul), Greek, Hebrew, Yiddish (his father born a Jew in Thessaloniki, who spent ten years in Israel after the war), and Serbo-Croatian, learned from his favorite grandmother, who hailed from Sarajevo.

His family life was a remarkable example of how members of communities traditionally hostile to each other by culture and tradition could live together in peace. Turks didn't like Greeks and vice-versa, and neither liked Serbs or Jews, yet members of the Baktis family respected each other and, in fact, were proud of their mixed ethnicity and cultural backgrounds. The Canadian winters had something to do with this—too cold to hate anyone when your car needed to be pushed out of a snowbank.

Baktis was not only an excellent intelligence officer, but an *intelligent* officer, as well. His pleasant disposition, empathy, and willingness to give just a bit more than was required of him made him popular with both subordinates and superiors. Given his particular set of language skills and his outstanding performance in the Canadian Army as an IO during repeated deployments with the UN Peacekeeping Force, he was now, at age thirty-two, promoted to major and seconded for an indefinite term as head of intelligence of UNFICYP, the United Nations' peacekeeping force in Cyprus

It was toward the end of his second rotation in Cyprus that the letter from Grabowski's office reached him. Addressed to him personally, marked Strictly Confidential and Urgent, it had been delivered by military courier and signed by Grabowski's chief of staff on NSA letterhead. In part, it read: *The enclosed Interpol warrant has now been outstanding over eighteen months. We have recently been informed that the subject of the warrant, the Swiss national, Doktor Alfred Hauptmann, is living in Cyprus. ADDNSA Grabowski has tasked me to find a way, official or informal, by which the search for the subject could be intensified.*

Baktis was no fool. He realized that the author of the letter had identified his name, rank, and position through the FIVE EYES network, an intelligence alliance comprising Australia, Canada, New Zealand, the United Kingdom, and the United States, and was appealing to him for help as a brother Greek. He read the signature again carefully—Captain Nicholas Dragonis, Chief of Staff of Assistant Deputy Director, Richard Grabowski, National Security Agency.

Looks like finding this bugger Hauptmann, Baktis thought to himself, is my ticket to make lieutenant-colonel within a year.

CHAPTER 84

Panama City, Panama, May 1991

The call came a few minutes after six in the morning. Cursing, Samos got off his treadmill and picked up the phone on his night-table. Ilona had gone back to Mexico City the day before and was, therefore, not around.

"Sorry to wake you up, Señor Samos," said a male voice that Samos did not recognize, "but our window of opportunity is short. What is the time in your neck of the woods, anyway?"

"Six a.m. Who are you?"

"Sorry, sir, my name is Nicholas Dragonis and I'm Director Grabowski's chief of staff. It seems that the Canadian Army might have located Dr. Hauptmann for you. He's in Cyprus. "

"You mean the Peacekeepers, the Blue Helmets?"

"Ah, then, you are awake, Señor Samos. I must tell the Director that, contrary to what he thought, you are an early-rising man of action."

The man laughed, a full-bellied, friendly laugh. "This is your lucky day. There's a military plane leaving Howard Airport at ten-hundred, headed for Antalya in Turkey, just a short jump from Cyprus. If you are not too busy today, you might consider catching it." Another laugh.

Samos liked what he was hearing from Dragonis. "Why are you torturing me? Why don't you tell me more?"

"Director Grabowski told me not to." Dragonis was having fun. "Two more things. Use one of your fancy diplomatic passports because the flight is NATO. When you get to Nicosia, locate the UNFICYP headquarters, it's at the airport there, and ask for Major Baktis. He'll be waiting for you with bated breath.|"

"What's the second thing?"

"Buy an expensive bottle of brandy somewhere. May I suggest Metaxa 12 Stars? And tell Major Baktis that it's from the Director."

*

The Boeing 747's lower deck was configured for cargo, a turn-off for Samos when he entered the aircraft. However, when he climbed upstairs, his faith in his good luck was restored: the sheer comfort of the arrangements reassured him that the over fifteen hours in the air that he had decided to endure to reach his goal quickly were justified. He found himself in a first-class cabin with twelve luxurious seats, six on each side, that turned into comfortable beds. As he passed through, he noticed that, forward, there was a spacious lounge that allowed passengers to stretch their legs and mingle.

He was shown to his seat by a female flight attendant wearing an army uniform with a name tag that said "Stella," and told that the row, the last one, would be entirely his own. Being the senior diplomat on board, he was entitled to maximum privacy.

Just as well, he said to himself. He needed the space, the time, and the solitude to face the problems that were slowly but steadily driving him into depression.

Once again in his life, he felt lost because he no longer had a moral compass and he had begun to wonder if he had ever had one.

The first decade of his life was spent in survival mode, the second in adaptation. During the third phase, the crucial one, he had succumbed to his thirst for revenge and the need for respectability. The action taken had led to achievements in two directions which he had to follow simultaneously: excellence in business and exemplary skills in the arts of intelligence.

And did I follow any moral compass? he asked himself silently. His reverie was interrupted by the attendant, who poured some red wine to accompany the steak and mashed potatoes he was being served for lunch.

Of course the answer was an unambiguous "no." The things he had been asked to do were certainly not *moral* most of the time, but he did them out of loyalty to his masters and *The Cause*, even though he knew that everyone, like himself, had their own agenda. But no one gets out of such a life clean. One way or another, you pay. And the price? Devastating. Ruinous.

He lost his identity, his face, his parents, and the love of his life.

But you climbed out of the shit into which life had pushed you, he argued with himself. No small achievement. Better than ending up as smokestack ash floating in a stagnant pool in some Eastern European forest.

After he had taken a sip of the cognac that Stella had brought him with his coffee he was suddenly seized by a fit of giddiness so overwhelming that he laughed out loud, and then looked around to see whether anyone other than her had heard him.

It wasn't me, but my *alter ego,* Samos reminded himself and added with a vicious twist of his jaw, but the fleeing Jew, Tom Karas, He, for sure, had broken his moral compass a lifetime ago on the blood-stained cobblestones in front of the "*csillagos ház,*" the house with the Star of David on its front door.

Sleep was beginning to overcome him and he pressed the button to deploy his seat-bed. Must remember to buy a bottle of Metaxa for the major, he remembered and allowed himself to fall victim to Morpheus.

The announcement that they were about to land in Tenerife to refuel woke him up three hours later.

CHAPTER 85

Cyprus, May 1991

They landed at Tenerife a few minutes before midnight local time. While the aircraft was being refueled, he visited the duty-free area and, wonder of wonders, scored a bottle of Metaxa *Angel's Treasure* in the liquor section. The manager, getting ready to close up, agreed to sell him what he called his store's showpiece for a paltry $200.

Samos knew that he was being soaked, but, what the hell, he wanted his luck to hold, and he owed Grabowski big time.

It took another five hours of flying to reach Antalia from Tenerife. Sadly, his attempt to communicate with his travelling companions failed miserably because they were all Turks with halting English, members of their national tourist organization's board of directors, who had been rewarded by NATO as a friendly gesture to a new member. So he gave up and went back to mentally flagellating himself for a couple of hours longer before coming to the sad conclusion that the only moral anchor in his life had been Disda, an extraordinarily brave and outstanding human being of principle and faith who paid dearly for both.

Another discovery he made during his tortured hours of self-analysis was that he needed to revise his perception of the various modes in which he had operated during the almost six decades of his life. The modes were not different, they were all the same; they were all *survival modes*!

CHAPTER 86

Cyprus, late May 1991 (1)

Major Baktis was as Canadian as they come—young, handsome, attentive, and very respectful.

He met Samos at the foot of the stairs leading to the tarmac at *Larnaca* Airport. Samos was curious. "How the hell did you know which flight from Antalia I would take?

The major was amused. "As head of intelligence I have access to all flight manifests into and out of Cyprus, so I told my 2IC to watch for you."

They were sitting in the back of a white UN SUV. The major's orderly was driving.

"Are you carrying?" asked the major in a voice that demanded a truthful answer.

Samos hesitated for a moment then gently patted his jacket under his left arm. Major Baktis nodded, looking in Samos's eyes, considering.

"Better keep that under wraps, "he replied finally. "Is this your first visit here?"

Samos nodded.

"Let me give you the Reader's Digest version then," the officer said. "The Greeks hate the Turks. The Turks hate the Greeks. The UN intervened in 1967 and a peacekeeping force was established to keep the two factions from annihilating each other. Canada was asked to provide the policing manpower and we have been here ever since."

"How many of you are here?"

"A full division, about 1,000 soldiers, both men and women."

"And how do you keep the peace?"

"We've established a buffer zone between the Turkish part to the north and the Greek part to the south along what we call the Green Line and we patrol it regularly. We have created observation posts in the zone itself and crossing points that we man jointly with Turkish and Greek authorities. The zone runs for more than 180 kilometers from east to west and has an area of 340-odd square kilometers. Its widest portion measures over seven *kilometers*, its narrowest, twenty-one *meters*.

"Sounds kind of complicated."

"It is, but it works. We've been at this for over twenty years, you know."

Samos was impressed. "And you? How long have *you* been here?"

"This is my third two-year rotation, so just about six years. They're keeping me here because I speak Turkish and Greek."

"Really?"

"Family. My mother is Turkish, my father Greek." The major looked out of the window. "We're heading to *Pyla*, one of the four communities on the island in which Turks and Greeks live in peace side by side. I want you to meet someone there."

*

Samos was impressed by *Pyla*, a small town with a church on one square and a mosque near another. He glanced at a sign on the wall announcing a doctor's office as they walked by. It was in three languages: English, Turkish, and Greek.

Peace and quiet. Pedestrian traffic very light.

Baktis stopped at a door and rang the bell. They were admitted by a very attractive, fortyish woman to an entrance hall and corridor that led into a spacious courtyard garden with a small fountain at its center.

"Meet Sofia Argerakis," Baktis said to Samos by way of introduction.

"*Kali mera, Kyrios* Samos" replied the woman. "Good day to you, Mr. Samos."

"Ah, you know my name." Samos was pleased.

They sat down in the garden and a young girl brought them lemonade.

"I hope you had a good trip and that you are not too tired." Sofia was charmingly polite.

Samos took a gulp of the drink before him. "Tell the truth, I am exhausted," he confessed. "It was a very long trip."

"Let us then get down to the matters at hand without delay so that you can go and rest." The woman's British-inflected English was very good. "Has Major Baktis told you who I am?"

"I'm afraid not."

Their hostess smiled, which made her even more attractive than at first glance. "Here we go." She launched into a tale that Samos found remarkable.

Sofia had met Major, then Captain, Baktis at her husband's funeral two-and-a-half years previously. Her man had been killed when an unexploded piece of ordinance blew up at the construction site of the hotel being built in nearby *Paralimni*.

As a widow and woman alone, Sofia said, she would not have been able to complete the bureaucratic procedures involved in obtaining compensation from the Turkish, Greek, and UN authorities without Baktis's help. He had patiently guided her through the Byzantine corridors of officialdom and, as a result, she had been able to secure financial help with which to buy the house in which she and her widowed mother were now living.

"The major also helped me to get a job at the hotel that was built on the scene of the accident and where I am still working as the front desk manager."

"Well done," said Samos politely while wondering about what all this reminiscing had to do with him and Hauptmann.

Sofia smiled tightly as she read his mind. "I'm telling you all this because I want you to understand in detail why I have presumed to ask you, *Kyrios* Samos, to see me."

The ersatz Panamanian leaned forward in his chair and poured some more lemonade from the carafe on the table. Sofia continued. "When Major Baktis showed me the Interpol wanted notice, I initially ignored it. It was one of many. Cyprus has become a magnet for bad people after the hostilities and it was routine stuff. But the major insisted. He said it would be a feather in his cap if he could find the *Herr Doktor* because some very important military people were looking for him. If it were him who helped find this man, he would get promoted." Sofia flashed a motherly smile at Baktis, who almost blushed. Samos felt his heart miss a beat. The woman had a sweetness about her that he found extraordinarily endearing.

"Without help from Major Baktis, I would have been lost after my husband's death, so I felt I owed him at least one try."

She looked at Samos. Her eyes, black and deep like a darkest of lakes, mesmerized him. "Then, for some unexplainable reason, when I looked at Hauptmann's picture again, I thought about the Austrian." She laughed and Samos was sure she saw right through him.

"What Austrian?"

"Let me explain. During the busy season, our staff, including our manager, is seriously overworked. To give him a break, the owners provided the first -ver manager and his family with a nice apartment above the mini shopping center, which they also own, a block and a half from the hotel. However, the *current* manager has no family and lives in the hotel, so he rented out his apartment to this Austrian person for a year."

Suddenly, Samos was all ears. "When was this?"

"About a year and a half ago, and it worked out pretty well for both the Austrian and Nico, our manager."

"Did it."

"Nico, who works almost twenty-four-seven, gets a little extra money, and the Austrian gets access to the swimming pools, one of which is heated, and to the gym."

"And to free breakfast," Major Baktis added. "He also gets the benefit of not having to register as a hotel guest or apply for a permit for temporary residence or show a passport, which is required from everyone who wants to stay on Cyprus longer than six months."

"Yes, that, too. I stand corrected," confirmed Sofia.

"What's this man's name?" Samos asked.

"The name on his international driving license and on his American Express card—both of which, by the way, I saw—is Gerhardt Arnold."

"Do we have a picture of him?"

Sofia handed Samos a copy of the colored picture on the badge issued to the hotel's guests to allow access to its facilities.

Samos tried hard not to reveal his emotions, but it was proving difficult. His hand shook just a little—a twitch, really. He peered at the photo. It showed a clean-shaven, sun-tanned, well-built, bald-headed man with brown eyes, no sign of Hauptmann's pale face, thick beard, full head of dark hair, and blue eyes behind thick glasses. The man in the picture looked to be in his mid-fifties, at least ten years younger than the murderous banker.

Samos was painfully disappointed.

Sofia sensed how upset her visitor was and attempted to salvage the situation. "You may well ask what possessed me to think that Arnold was Hauptmann. The simple answer is: instinct."

She turned to Baktis. "Major, tell our guest what I did next."

"Sofia got the number of the driver's license from the file and asked me to have it checked out. Then she took a picture of Arnold's photo on his hotel pass and went to work on it. She grew him a beard, gave him a full head of hair, and lightened the color of his eyes."

Baktis handed the doctored photo to Samos, who nodded, but was unconvinced by the amateur sleuthing, however well-intentioned. "Yes, that looks very much like Hauptmann. But I'm afraid it's not clear enough for me to say that the man really *is* Hauptmann."

Sofia wouldn't give up. "Consider this. The man arrives here more or less at the same time Hauptmann disappears from Switzerland. He must have been here previously because he somehow knows everything about Cyprus: the new hotel being built, the registration procedure, the residency requirements, and, most importantly, the existence of the manager's apartment being up for rent, something that would allow him to circumvent the need to show a passport."

She drank some tea then continued. Samos noticed that her hands were trembling. "Most of these bad people are caught because they do not know how to stay under the radar. The Austrian does. He hasn't shown a passport, he has not registered in a hotel, but uses the facilities of one every day. He never invites people to visit him, as far as I know. He goes on early morning walks so as to avoid meeting people, he eats at modest restaurants at night in the company of women whom he imports from off-island for a week or two at a time and pays to stay with him in his luxurious apartment shielded from the curious crowd. Don't you see?"

The woman clenched her handsome jaw with determination as she addressed Baktis. "Let's face it, he has succeeded in making fools of everybody, including me. He is sought by Interpol for murder, he manages to live openly in great comfort for eighteen months right under the noses of the Greek and UN authorities without them knowing anything about him, in fact, without *anyone* knowing anything about him. *Kyrios Samos*, why would someone do that?"

Samos felt sorry for her. "I'm sorry, madame."

He made motions as though to leave, but then turned to Baktis.

"Why have you made me come all this way if you knew that you didn't have enough evidence against the man to prosecute him?" he said accusingly. "And why did *you* encourage her by signalling to us?"

Like a true son of the Great White North, Baktis remained cool and unoffended. He remained civil, unlike Samos, who, he would later admit, had lost it.

"Because, after they took their sweet time about answering, we finally got word from the International Automobile

Association. According to their records, the license number we sent them belonged to a batch of license blanks that had been lost or stolen in Ireland and which meant, therefore, that the license in question had never been officially issued."

"What the hell does that mean?" Samos was almost at the end of his tether.

"It means we had to fall back on the only other piece of documentation we had with respect to our Austrian friend, which was . . ."

Samos interrupted curtly: "The American Express credit card issued to very good clients of certain Swiss banks, the identity of whose owners is protected and is never revealed without a court order."

"And this would take months to obtain," Baktis added, a slight coy smile on his lips.

"By which time, our Austrian friend will have disappeared." Samos was furious. "Of course, we could ask him for his passport," he mused. "But that would spook him and he'd take off."

"Quite so," said the major. "And that's why we asked you to come. Sofia has worked out a way in which to trap him, but for this we need your help."

"And it has to be tomorrow morning," said the woman with a tight, disciplined smile.

CHAPTER 87

Cyprus, late May 1991 (2)

The phone rang on his night-table and Samos picked it up. "Time to get ready for the show," a female voice said. It took him a few seconds to recognize Sofia.

"Where are you?"

"Downstairs, where else? I have just started my shift."

"What time is it?"

"Six a.m. and the Austrian will show within the hour. He'll be coming from left to right, from northwest to southeast, and may be wearing sunglasses, depending on the sunshine."

Still exhausted in spite of six hours of deep sleep, Samos pulled himself together. He staggered into the bathroom to marshal his thoughts while brushing his teeth. When he returned to his room, his memory was sharply jolted into the present by the sight of a tripod-and-binocular combination strategically placed a couple of steps behind the doors leading to the balcony and aimed at the seaboard walkway below.

The equipment had been brought to his room by the major's orderly the previous evening after they had driven him to his hotel from Sofia's house. It was military grade: a Steiner 20x80 glass, mounted on a solid Vintage tripod. Obviously, the Canadian Army knew its business.

Well, so did Samos. The material had reminded him of his Karas days.

"Get some rest. Tomorrow might turn out to be a tough day," Baktis had said when he bid Samos good night.

"What about you? When will I see you again?" Samos had wanted to know.

"I haven't seen my wife for days, so I'm going home to have a midnight snack and a drink with her. We live in Nicosia in the married officers' quarters. Tomorrow is Saturday and I plan to sleep in. Sofia will look after you during the day. I'll come back tomorrow evening and we'll decide what to do. Everything depends on what you find tomorrow morning."

Samos adjusted the height of the tripod so that he could look through the binoculars while standing erect. He opened the curtains and began calibrating the glasses. The optics were fantastic; they produced twenty-time magnification.

The street below was empty, save for a couple of skinny Cypriot cats. Samos focused on them for a moment and then was suddenly conscious of a figure coming into his field of view. The Austrian appeared a few minutes before seven. He wore white sockettes in his Nike running shoes, green shorts, a white T-shirt, a Nike baseball cap, but no sunglasses. They were not needed; it was cloudy out.

The man walked fast and remarkably smoothly, certainly not with the stiff, shuffling gait of Ilona's banker. Samos concentrated first on his face. There was definitely a resemblance to Hauptmann, but the brown eyes were strikingly different from the light blue that Samos remembered.

It took the Austrian about three minutes to get past the center of Samos's arc of vision. Once he turned his back, the powerful binoculars clearly showed the man's calves and Samos distinctly saw the traces of the varicose veins about which Hauptmann had complained repeatedly.

Was all this enough to conclude without a reasonable doubt that he was indeed looking at the good *doktor*? Samos was still not quite convinced. He needed a gotcha moment to be certain, so he got dressed and went in search of Sofia to firm up arrangements for implementing their Plan B.

*

For the last few weeks, Sofia had noticed that the Austrian had started becoming more friendly toward her. Each morning, Sofia had arranged to be at the front desk when the Austrian left the dining area after breakfast. Spotting her, he would invariably stop and chat for a while about mostly banal quotidian affairs. That morning was no exception and it gave her the opportunity to form a Plan B.

"Good morning! How was your breakfast, *Herr Arnold?* I heard that Chef was preparing your Budwig."

The Austrian's eyes crinkled with pleasure at the opportunity to pass a few moments in conversation with this fascinating and attractive woman.

"Jah, jah, but, I'm afraid she hasn't got it right still."

Sofia displayed professional concern. "But we gave her your instructions and told her to follow them to the letter!"

The Austrian waved Sofia's concern aside with a gesture of his hand. "No, no, you mustn't be concerned. It is just my habits, you know."

"Yes, but tell me so that I can correct it, *Herr Arnold.*"

The Austrian was trying hard to keep his profile low and lowered his voice, causing Sofia to bend closer. "She has to not grind the flax seeds until I arrive at the table, jah? As soon as she grinds the flax seeds, they begin to oxidize and the power of the flax seed oil diminishes."

Sofia took both of *Herr Arnold's* hands in her own. "But that is totally my fault. I didn't tell her this."

Arnold slipped his hands out of her grasp, but remembered the comforting warmth long after the conversation ended.

"No damage. Really, no one's fault—certainly not yours, Miss Sofia."

The woman assumed the manner of a person taking responsibility and making amends. "No, I do recall you mentioned this to me and I totally forgot to tell Chef. You must allow me to make it up to you."

The Austrian squirmed a bit, turning his head to see if they were being observed, but they were alone in the lobby. "Really, there is absolutely no need."

"I'm having a cocktail party tonight at my house, starting at seven. I want to invite you for dinner after."

"Oh, thank you, Miss Sofia, but, you know I am not much for crowds."

Arnold tried again to slip away, but Sofia caught his hand again and held it firmly.

"Don't be silly, *Herr Arnold*. No crowd, just people you already know: my mother and Dina, the other receptionist, Nico, and Major Baktis, the Canadian Blue Helmet and his adjutant, Captain Beaulieu."

Again, the Austrian tried to demur, but Sofia held his hand in such a charming, familiar way, he began to relent.

"There would be seven of us," she cooed to him. "Hardly a crowd."

Herr Arnold felt flattered by Sofia's attention and accepted.

*

Sofia had a knack for waking Samos up. Exhausted by the last few days' activity, Samos was trying to pay off the debt of sleep he was carrying around and had gone back to sleep after his inconclusive binocular rendezvous with the Austrian. The phone rang around 08h00.

"Yes?

"We're on. I had to push him a little, but he accepted. He'll be there tonight at 07h00."

"Thank you, Sofia." There was a pause on the other end.

"I have done what I can. The rest is up to you, *Kyrios* Samos."

Samos rang off and found himself still muddle-headed, sitting on the edge of the bed, trying to organize his thoughts.

Once again, he found himself in a situation where he was being forced to react to forces outside his control, and he didn't like it. How could he have let a slimy, greedy, unprincipled banker like Hauptmann rule his life? What kind of creature was he? What kind of absurd agent of destruction and anarchy was this spare, thin-lipped Aryan prick?

Hauptmann did not wake up one morning and say to himself, "Today, I will be responsible for the death of Maria-Isabel Echeverria. I will rob Alejandro Samos of his love and life partner. I will attempt to take his life, as well. And I will steal millions of dollars from Ilona Rodrigues." And yet, in his reckless desire for other people's money, that is what Hauptmann had done.

The center of Samos's life was not holding, but was gyrating eccentrically, worming itself out of orbit, smashing everything in its wake.

No, thought Samos. If the Austrian is Hauptmann, then the anarchy stops tonight. He felt under his pillow for the familiar shape of his Glock. He dropped the mag and then slid back the slide, locking it with his thumb, checking to make sure that there was no bullet in the chamber. He carefully removed the slide, the spring, and the barrel and found the little innocuous-looking cleaning kit in his travel bag. He oiled and cleaned all the parts and assembled the gun, checking the mechanism, comforting himself with the sound of metal on metal. He picked up the mag, dropped all the bullets, and then reloaded it.

Hauptmann did not wake up one morning and decide to kill Maria-Isabel, but Samos could not say the same about his intentions toward the errant banker.

*

They had choreographed it in advance and in great detail, but "Man proposes, God disposes," as the saying goes.

Samos had spent the rest of the day agonizing over how to confront the Austrian in a way to make the man give himself away, assuming, of course, that he really *was* Hauptmann. This meant that he could not get to the party before the Austrian got there, so he arranged with Baktis to have the orderly stay with Samos around the corner in his Jeep, walkie-talkie in hand, to await word from the major indicating that the "guest of honor" had arrived.

The ersatz Panamanian hoped that his sudden appearance on the scene would shake the Austrian enough to do something stupid, like resist arrest, an action that would ultimately end in his having to admit that, yes, he was, indeed, Hauptmann.

In any event, it was clear to Samos that, whatever the confrontation, it would surely develop into a situation of do or die. He had been told that neither Captain Beaulieu nor Baktis could risk arriving armed. Therefore, confronting a possibly armed Austrian would have to be Samos and none other.

Was he up for it?

He realized that the matter was not a question of bravery, but willingness on his part to take yet another life, possibly an innocent one.

All went well at the start. Driven by Baktis's orderly, the major and the captain arrived dead on time. Dina was already there, helping to lay out the snacks the hotel had provided. The Austrian showed up a quarter of an hour later and, with his back to the door, began chatting with the captain.

Bouzouki music was playing and the conversation was quite loud when Samos entered the room followed by Baktis's orderly. The Austrian did not notice him arrive.

Samos moved two steps toward him, took a breath and primed his voice.

"Hauptmann!" he shouted.

The fake Austrian started, then spun around on his heel, his arms coming up as though to fend off a blow. The entire room fell silent, the musicians froze. The only sound was of the fans spinning on the ceiling. With everyone's eyes on him, Hauptmann lowered his arms and pulled back his lips, revealing his greying dentures. His eyes narrowed, settling on Samos.

"Samos, *du Scheisskerl*! Bastard!" he hissed and charged, catching Samos on the back foot and knocking him aside as he aimed toward the door. Captain Beaulieu stepped into the exit.

Hauptmann skidded, his eyes turning toward the rear door and finding Baktis already there. The Swiss reached down and flipped open the kidney pouch on his hip, extracting a mini-frag, V40 hand-grenade. Before anyone could tackle him, he pulled out its pin and held the grenade high for all to see.

"*Halt!* Stop!" he shouted as the stunned people backed away. He turned again toward Samos and spoke in his typical calm voice. "You think you have me, don't you?" he asked in English. "Well, you don't."

He turned to Baktis. "Major, as the ranking military officer, I am holding you responsible for what may happen if I accidentally drop this."

"You don't want to do that," replied the Canadian.

"No, that is correct. But, I am an old man and I don't mind dying, but some of you might." He pointed his chin at Baktis and Beaulieu "You, inside, away from the door!"

As his allies backed away, Samos bargained for time.

"*Warum?*" asked Samos.

The desperate banker turned on Samos.

"Why? Why what?" snarled Hauptmann, edging closer to the exit.

"*Warum diese wahnsinnig grosse Dieberei?*"

"Why steal? Because, you fool, I knew how," said Hauptmann, as he walked out the door.

Samos pulled his Glock from its holster under his arm and raced after Hauptmann, followed by Captain Beaulieu, who was unarmed. The banker was running awkwardly toward his Vespa, parked in sight about fifty meters ahead. Samos could see by the way he was running that he was fiddling with the grenade as he ran, trying to reinsert the pin.

Hauptmann checked over his shoulder, saw Samos gaining on him, and didn't stop at the Vespa. He had worked himself into a corner: stop to insert the pin and risk capture or drop the armed grenade and try to get away. With Samos almost on top of him, stopping would mean certain capture.

No choice. He had to keep running, and faster.

He accelerated, trying to pull away from Samos, who suddenly stopped, dropped to one knee, raised his gun, drew a breath, held it, and fired. The Glock barked and even in the evening gloom Samos could see that he had hit the man. Hauptmann fell. The banker rolled over, propped himself up on one arm, and drew back the other.

"He's going for it, get down!" cried Beaulieu, hugging the curb.

Samos did not wince, but took careful aim and popped two rounds into Hauptmann's arm, catching the wrist where it joined the throwing hand. Shocked, Hauptmann didn't cry and could only stare incredulously as the grenade rolled down what was left of his forearm to nestle in his lap. The last act of his life was to raise his eyes to Samos, who remained poised like a wraith on one knee, before he found himself dragged down to the macadam by Beaulieu, who threw his muscled arm over Samos's head.

The explosion was spectacular. A blinding white flash, followed by a sharp, percussive *BANG* and a literally deafening shockwave that shattered windows in the square and blew Hauptmann to pieces. The Vespa skidded violently sideways and crashed into the wall of the nearby house.

The air stank with explosive primer and the metallic scent of charred blood and viscera. The pseudo-Panamanian was slightly deafened, but otherwise unhurt. Beaulieu's forehead had been gashed by a small piece of shrapnel that was quickly staunched by Baktis. Sofia shooed her guests out of the house and into the night and then she, herself, disappeared. They could hear the distant sound of the Cypriot Police sirens as Major Baktis issued fluent orders in three languages over his Jeep radio.

Samos felt rather than heard Beaulieu and Sofia running to help him to his feet. Fronting an air of nonchalance, he managed to take three steps before collapsing from shock.

EPILOGUE

$\mathcal{WHITEW\mathcal{A}SH}$

The sudden and violent demise of one *Herr Doktor* Alfred Hauptmann, corrupt Swiss citizen and murderous banker, created a mountain of legal problems that would never have been solved had it not been for the surprisingly cooperative attitude of all those involved in the case.

Money talks, or, rather, whispers, and bullshit walks, except that lots of money whispers loudly indeed, thereby reaching a wider, more obedient audience. Selfishness, coupled with greed, is a great mediator.

The Cypriot Police inquiry, aided by the unquestioned eyewitness, Major Baktis, confronted the big questions on behalf of INTERPOL: was the man's demise an accident or suicide? He had obviously lost control of the grenade, but why did he not just throw it away to save himself? Did the three shots fired from the illegal Glock of the Panamanian citizen Alejandro Samos actually hit Hauptmann or did he stumble by himself?

Then there was the question of jurisdictional rights over the case. Hauptmann died in *Pyla*, situated in the middle of Cyprus's Green Zone, which is controlled by the Canadian Blue Helmets representing the UN. Did the Cypriot authorities and INTERPOL for that matter, have any dominion?

After letting the interested parties flail around bureaucratically for a day or so, Major Baktis took charge, claiming that the banker's actions amounted to attempted manslaughter, a criminal offence in a military zone, and took possession of the deceased's assets in Cyprus, all in Hauptmann's apartment.

That's when the waltzing started.

With a wink and a nod to the powers involved, Ilona and Samos sued to freeze the FEG shares, presumably located physically somewhere in Cyprus. They also tried to seize Hauptmann's assets worldwide on the basis that the money the banker had stolen had belonged to FEG. The GRU did the same through a Turkish law firm engaged and directed by *Jozsi*.

When the flurry of short-term legal toing-and-froing abated, Major Baktis arranged for the inspection and cataloguing of the assets in Hauptmann's apartment. Samos represented himself and Ilona, *Jozsi* the GRU.

It took two days for Samos, Jozsi, and two police inspectors, one Turkish and the other Greek, working under the supervision of Major Baktis and assisted by two Canadian soldiers to do the lifting, to examine and list all the furniture, fixtures, memorabilia, pictures, books, clothes, and records in the large, comfortable apartment in which the defunct Swiss banker had spent the last nineteen months of his life.

The purpose of this exercise was, of course, to find the documents—principally the FEG bearer shares so lusted after by all—that Hauptmann had stolen, so that they could be redeemed by whomever successfully claimed to be their rightful owners.

The effort had been a waste of time. Nothing of any significance was found: no shares, no passport, no jewels, no gold, no credit cards, no will and, surprisingly, no cash, except for a couple of hundred dollars in one of the night table drawers.

After taking advice, Baktis waited for six months and then auctioned off the apartment's contents, giving the money he raised to Nico, the apartment owner, for back rent.

Meanwhile, faced with the irreversible facts, Samos and *Jozsi* were persuaded by Ilona to negotiate an agreement whereby FEG Switzerland would be wound up and its assets distributed. The Spanish factory would be turned over to the GRU, the one in Nicaragua to the NSA, so McIsaacs and Grabowski were, at least, half-happy. No one contested the transfer of the FEG investment portfolio to *Vontobel* Bank, which was approved *post hoc*.

The last time Samos and Ilona saw *Jozsi* was at *Julius Bäer*—a cold, clinical affair in the major boardroom where the miles of documents to be signed were laid out next to the bank's bespoke Montblanc fountain pens. McIsaacs had insisted on being present and brought along Alfredo as driver and *garde de corps*.

Despite Samos's gentle warning, Ilona did make one "last stand" effort to connect with her son, but the man was elsewhere in his mind and spirit. He smiled warmly, he indulged her *angst* that she might never see him again, and then, he told her "anytime," for the price of a ticket at any *Manitas* concert. Ilona's face twitched at the glacial coldness of the remark and left the room, allowing Samos to complete the paperwork.

Jozsi watched impatiently as the banker, Langlois, collated, compiled, counter-signed, and applied the notarial seals to each copy of the documents, winding up FEG's affairs. As *Jozsi* accepted his copy, Samos stopped him and drew up close.

"Who planted the bomb in my car? Who fingered me in Nicaragua?"

Jozsi stared down at Samos for far longer than anyone else in the room thought was harmless. Quietly, McIsaacs and Massimo moved closer to the two men, the Italian's hand already into his waist band holster.

"Must have been bitter, fucking up so badly, losing a man," needled Samos.

Jozsi took a step back and finally cracked a tight, grim smile. "It might have been, had I been responsible. But I wasn't."

"Oh?"

Jozsi shook his head ruefully "I only wish I had. Then this whole affair," he continued, waving his elegant, musical prodigy hand in front of Samos as though wishing him to disappear, "Would never have happened." The flamenco guitarist simply stepped around Samos and headed for the door, but then stopped, turned back, and pulled up the sleeve of his Lacoste sweater.

"If you care to visit the Faroe Island of *Vágar,* you might look up an old Russian shepherd who goes by the name of *Botvinik.* He has a GRU tattoo on his left forearm, just like this one. You can ask him your questions yourself."

Samos grunted, but was not satisfied, "Who fingered me?"

Jozsi smiled with a tinge of pity creeping in. He shook his head again. "Does the name '*Leticia*' mean anything to you?"

After *Jozsi* left, Samos had to sit down, his forehead in his hand as he took in the perfidy, the cold, transactional betrayal. McIsaacs walked up behind him, placing a comforting hand on his shoulder.

"Managua. Santiago's secretary," he muttered, the bile rising in his throat. "I asked her about FEG."

McIsaacs listened then squeezed Samos hard on his shoulder. He motioned to Massimo, who had been listening attentively. The Italian nodded, confirming.

The account at *Banque Julius Bäer* was then closed.

*

A few months later, Ilona divorced an acutely senile Uncle Octavio and married Samos thereafter. On a whim, they returned to Cyprus for their honeymoon and stayed at the same hotel where Samos had spent a morning watching Hauptmann through Major Baktis's binoculars walking up and down the road, taking his early morning exercise.

During their stay, a very odd thing happened.

While chatting with Dina, the Romanian senior receptionist, and reminiscing about the Hauptmann incident, she said out of the blue: "You know, my sister Annabella manages the store under the apartment where the Austrian stayed. She is very often there until midnight to lock up. She liked the man and misses him. He used to come down to chat with her for a while in the evenings, which was nice, because it broke up the boredom. They'd talk mainly about wine. She even ordered some for him."

"Yes, he was very fond of good wine," Samos had said absentmindedly, to be polite.

Dina had continued. "They are very expensive wines though, and there isn't much of a market for them in a convenience store. She still has a few bottles of his collection as a souvenir."

Samos had gone tense. "You know, expensive wine should be stored at the right temperature, humidity."

"Yes, yes, he insisted on it. She keeps them in a small wine cooler at the back of the store. Hauptmann ordered it and let them use it to store the local wine they sold."

Ilona was eager for her post-lunch nap so Samos left her and walked over to the grocery store underneath the late *Doktor* Hauptmann's apartment. Annabella was behind the cash and Samos bought the remaining bottles of Hauptmann's Italian *Chianti Riserva Ducale*. While Annabella was packing them for travel, Samos examined the cooler—a small, square, glass-fronted, counter-height model one might find in a hotel room or on a boat.

He soon found the two release buttons—at the top rear inside corners in the cooler that had to be pressed simultaneously to release the thin, spring-driven drawer under the cooling coils at the bottom, the evaporation tray. The tray revealed a packet formed by two sealed commercial-grade plastic freezer bags.

Samos carefully opened the bags and found inside the two original FEG bearer shares, Hauptmann's Swiss passport, and, in the passport, a "no-name" Visa card with a 1996 expiration date, issued by the Cayman-based *Alta-Jir* bank. There was also another bearer share issued by a numbered Caymanian limited liability company that was being hosted by the same bank.

Samos slipped all the documents into the inside pocket of his seersucker jacket, picked up his bag of wine, paid and bid Annabella adieu.

Back in the hotel room, Ilona had left a note indicting that she was at the beach. In her absence, Samos carefully examined Hauptmann's passport. Between the last page and the cover, right next to the 'spine' of the document, someone had glued a small, twelve millimeters by four millimeters, sliver of paper with HA386514 printed on it.

To the untrained eye it looked like part of the document, just another identification number for the bureaucrats in Switzerland who had issued the passport.

Samos's eyes may have been sleepy, but were everything but untrained.

*

In early 1994, Longhurst who was doing remarkably well as a financial advisor, bought out Samos's share in his Panamanian service company. For tax purposes they decided to close the deal in Grand Cayman. The occasion gave Samos a valid excuse to visit the island and he decided to make a voyage out of it for himself and Ilona.

Roberto Mauro's Interpol warrant had kept him trapped and under cover in Nicaragua for years. Despite the Longhurst memo certifying that Robert Mauro was not Greg DiMauro, the sluggish European bureaucracy still had him on the international wanted list. Finally, prompted by Samos, Longhurst convinced the overworked Europeans that they did not have the right guy, the fingerprints did not match. Mauro soon learned that he was no longer a "person of interest" and, as a present, offered to personally sail Samos and Ilona to the Caymans on his beautiful yacht.

Once they checked in at the hotel, Ilona went off to bask in the sun while Samos visited the *Alta-Jir* Bank, giddy with the anxiety of a wallflower at the prom. He showed the executive who received him Hauptmann's passport and drew his attention to the number on the little sliver of paper. He also exhibited the bearer share he had found in Cyprus and the Visa credit card. The executive then asked him whether Hauptmann was dead, whereupon Samos produced a death certificate prepared by UNFICYP, the United Nations Peacekeeping Force in Cyprus and signed by Major William Baktis. The executive pursed his lips and looked over all the documents carefully, spreading them out on his desk, calling in some of the bank staff to validate the paperwork.

After a tense, murmured confab, Samos was then handed a file containing a great number of bank statements, the most recent of which showed a credit balance of seventeen million Swiss Francs. He was also informed that, as the owner of the bearer share, and in light of Hauptmann's death and having found no standing orders to enforce in light thereof, the Cayman numbered company and its account were now his to do with whatever he wanted.

It came late, but better late than dead.

*

While Samos was settling accounts in the Caymans, in sunny Managua, Minister Santiago noticed Leticia touching up her make-up at her desk in preparation for a date she had been talking about. An Italian this time, someone she had met in a bar the previous evening when she had been out with friends. Leticia was thrilled because the man exuded an air of danger. He was a real gentleman—patient, cautious and tall, in great shape and handsome, with a head of thick copper-red hair.

*

The Faroese villagers on *Vágar* had grown accustomed to the somewhat strange Russian who had bought the defunct Poulsen farm about ten years ago. He was rarely there and left his forty-odd head of sheep at the Mikkelsen's whenever he was away. Paid well for it, too, so, no complaints. When he was in residence, he was always busy improving the farm. He'd paid a small fortune to a mainland company to drill down and install a geothermic plant for his cottage and barn. He had installed a helical windmill and the latest solar panel array to generate electricity so efficiently, he fed back into the island grid. He had one of the island's only greenhouses, hydroponic. In the pub one night, as the Russian bought his round of aquavit, someone joked that he was getting ready for Putin's apocalypse, but he didn't laugh.

He had been warned about gathering puffin eggs by himself. The islanders had caught sight of him, dangling in a bosun's chair, tethered to a cable attached to the front winch of his Range Rover. The Russian had a remote control to lower and raise himself. It was dangerous work that was normally done by younger men, tied to ropes and held by a group of strong, older men. So, people were saddened to hear of the accident, of the faulty remote control that played out all the cable so that it slipped the winch, allowing *Botvinik* to plunge to his death. There were no inquiries. No one claimed the body. A rumor drifted out of the mortician's office that the man was actually much younger than he appeared to be and was covered with Russian military tattoos. Mikkelsen kept the forty head of sheep.

*

While still in the Caymans, Mauro stuck close to Samos, but the Panamanian could tell that he was itching to go off on his own. Weighing anchor, Mauro took his boat from the marina at Lime Tree Bay to Rum Point. Leaving the boat and crew docked at the hotel's jetty, Mauro set out on a rented scooter, following the directions Samos had slipped into his shirt pocket as he bid him farewell. He found the unmarked road he was looking for intersecting Rum Point Drive and turned off.

He spotted his cousin from a distance. Neither years nor illness nor misadventure could hide that gait and noble profile. Mauro parked the scooter and pulled off his helmet, watching as the broken, sunburnt, withered figure of Mike DeAngelis sauntered over, muttering and gesturing toward the blue sea beyond. "Goin' out? Wanna go out? "

*

When Ilona discovered that Panama and Hungary did not exchange full diplomatic ambassadors, she set to work. After a couple of years of vigorous lobbying and sufficient *backsheesh* to those who required it, Samos was named Panamanian ambassador to Hungary. Ilona wanted desperately to return to her newly democratic home in a blaze of glory and she succeeded even beyond her own fantasies.

For years after presenting his credentials to the Hungarian president, members of Budapest's *in crowd* keep wondering how the new Panamanian ambassador had managed to become fluent in Hungarian in just eighteen months. They ascribed this miracle to his wife Ilona's extraordinary talents as a teacher and to Samos's innate linguistic talents that had allowed him to master German, English, French, Italian, Spanish, and now, Hungarian.

Jozsi Lakatos did not wonder, because he suspected that the ambassador spoke Hungarian even before coming to Hungary. He also suspected, due to what he had heard from his superiors at the GRU, that the ambassador was not the person he was pretending to be, certainly not a Panamanian foundling.

Useful knowledge for a captain in the GRU.

ACKNOWLEDGEMENT

Writing an authentic-sounding story about imagined happenings that span over half a century a long time ago takes a great deal of time and effort. This daunting task would have been impossible without support.

I had the good fortune to meet the very talented Jacob Potashnik who agreed to edit the final manuscript. Collaborating with Jacob was a peak experience, both personally and professionally. Our complementary skills melded and created a superior product. I am greatly indebted to him.

Erika Fabian spent countless hours providing invaluable feedback, for which I am very grateful.

And, of course, there is the team at FriesenPress, led by the highly efficient Renzel, who put all the bits and pieces that go into the makings of a book together.

The cover design is the creation of the remarkable Ivan Smith, talented actor, singer, painter and teacher.

Thank you all.

Robert Landori, Montreal, August 2021

ABOUT THE AUTHOR

Born in Hungary, Robert Landori (whose full name is Robert Landori-Hoffmann) was, for most of his professional life, a senior Public Accountant, Mergers & Acquisitions specialist, and a Trustee in Bankruptcy in the Cayman Islands.

But behind the facade of the quiet man of numbers lay a life of intrigue and mystery. He traveled widely throughout South America and the Caribbean where he came into contact with international financiers, notorious con men, well-known artists and entertainers... and members of several countries' intelligence communities.

Robert Landori also developed a highly charged and double-edged relationship with Castro's Cuba, and was, at one time, held in solitary confinement for over two months on false accusations of espionage.

He was eventually freed, and is now a writer of international intrigue and espionage thrillers.

WHITEWASH is Robert Landori's ninth book.

Robert Landori lives in Canada where, when he is not writing full-time, he consults as a Business Development Strategist.